Praise for the novels of
New York Times bestselling author Megan Hart

"Hart's beautiful use of language and discerning eye
toward human experience elevate the book to a poignant reflection
on the deepest yearnings of the human heart
and the seductive temptation of passion in its many forms."
—*Kirkus Reviews* on *Tear You Apart*

"A fantastic story that will stick with readers."
—*RT Book Reviews* on *Tear You Apart*

"A tense look at dark secrets and the redemptive power of truth."
—*Kirkus Reviews* on *The Favor*

"Heartfelt…the detailed physicality involved in caring for
an elderly loved one is portrayed vividly and compassionately."
—*Publishers Weekly* on *The Favor*

"This is a quiet book, but it packed a major punch for me…
[Hart]'s a stunning writer, and this is a stunning book."
—*Super Librarian* on *The Space Between Us*

"[A] haunting, devastating, heart-wrenching tale…
this story will stay with you long after you reach the last page."
—*RT Book Reviews* on *Precious and Fragile Things*

"*Deeper* is absolutely, positively, the best book that I have read
in ages…the story line brought tears to my eyes more than once.…
Beautiful, poignant and bittersweet…Megan Hart never disappoints."
—*Romance Reader at Heart*, Top Pick

"Well-developed secondary characters and a compelling plot
add depth to this absorbing and enticing novel."
—*Library Journal* on *Broken*

MEGAN HART

lovely wild

HARLEQUIN® MIRA®

Recycling programs
for this product may
not exist in your area.

ISBN-13: 978-0-7783-1675-6

LOVELY WILD

For questions and comments about the quality of this book, please contact us at CustomerService@Harlequin.com.

Printed in U.S.A.

First printing: December 2014
10 9 8 7 6 5 4 3 2 1

To the wild at heart
who walk in grass with bare feet and catch the fireflies

To my children, my greatest achievement—
I love you more than anything else

And to Emily Ohanjanians
for helping to turn that book into this one, here's to many more!

lovely
wild

ONE

IN HER DREAMS, SHE IS STILL WILD.

But she's not dreaming now. At the moment, Mari Calder stands at her kitchen sink rinsing out a pot in which macaroni and cheese is still stubbornly clinging. She takes the sponge, rough on one side but not so much that it will scratch the expensive, shiny pot, and she scrubs. Macaroni softens under the stream of hot water that turns her fingers red. White suds cover her hands, and noodles stripped of their cheesy orange coating swirl into the drain where they catch and swell.

They look like maggots.

Tenderly, Mari scoops them into her palm. She leaves the water running, the rush and roar of it nothing like the sound of a waterfall. She dumps the sodden, bloated macaroni into a trash pail overflowing with the similar dregs of meals left unfinished. She stands over the trash for some long moments, staring at the waste.

She's never hungry anymore, at least not the way she used to be. Here in this house she has a pantry full of cans, jars, bottles and boxes. Waxy containers of chicken broth snuggle next to bags of exotic rice in multiple colors and boxes of instant mashed potatoes. Cookies, crackers and potato chips in crumpled bags shut tight against the air with plastic clips, or sometimes dumped without ceremony into tight-lidded plastic containers. Clear, so she can see what's inside. So she can run her fingertips over the contents without actually touching them.

And always, always, snack cakes. They come wrapped in plastic, two to a package, in flimsy cardboard boxes. She likes the chocolate kind best, though she'll eat any flavor, really. Her very favorites are the special ones that come out for holidays. Spongy cakes shaped like Christmas trees or hearts or pumpkins, covered in stiff icing she can peel away with her teeth. Mari buys them a box at a time, casually, like they don't matter to her at all, but she never puts them in the pantry or in the special drawer where all the other snacks go. She hides them. She hoards them.

She doesn't have to. Her fridge is always full. The freezers, too, both of them, the small one in the refrigerator here in the kitchen and the full-sized chest freezer in the garage. Sometimes, mostly at night when everyone else is asleep, Mari likes to stand in front of the freezer and peer inside at all the wealth she has collected.

Ryan never seems to notice or care how much food there is in the house. He comes home from work and expects—and finds—dinner waiting for him. No matter what kind of effort Mari has to make to provide it, she makes sure there's always a full meal. Takeout or homemade, there's always a meat, a vegetable, salad, a grain, a bread. Fresh bread. She can't get enough. Mari usually makes it herself. She uses a bread machine to help her, but she's still the one who fills the pan with carefully measured amounts of water, flour, sugar, salt, yeast. Every morning she bakes a fresh loaf, and every night they eat it.

Sometimes, Ethan helps her with the preparation. Kendra used to, but now she's too busy with her cell phone or iPad, texting and tweeting and whatever it is teenage girls do. But

Ethan is still young enough to like cracking the eggs and measuring the flour.

At eight, Ethan is still young enough for Mari to relate to. Oh, she loves Kendra, her firstborn, her daughter. They do girly things like shop for shoes, paint their nails, hit the chick flicks in the theater while Ryan and Ethan stay home. Mari loves her daughter, sometimes with a fierceness that takes her breath away...but she doesn't really understand her.

It's not that Kendra is unknowable. Even at fifteen, she still talks to her mom. Unlike her friends, whom Kendra has revealed barely speak to their parents unless it's to complain. Sure, there have been some bumps along the way. Temper tantrums, pouty faces, arguments about curfews or grades. Mari supposes this is normal and is grateful it's never been worse.

Kendra is knowable, she hasn't grown away from them, hasn't taken to painting her nails and lips and eyelids black or disappearing into her room to burn incense and listen to music with bad lyrics. It's Mari who cannot quite seem to bridge the distance between the toddler with curly white-blond hair who liked to serve tea in plastic cups while wearing only a half-shredded pink tutu, and this tall, lanky and gangly teenager with iron-straightened hair the color of sand. Kendra might still sleep with an array of stuffed animals at the foot of her bed, but she's already talking about college and moving to California to live on her own, about getting her driver's license and access to a credit card. About growing up and growing away.

But Ethan, the boy who favors her. Him, Mari still understands. Because he's only eight, not yet nine, though that birthday will sneak up on her before she knows it, and then he, too, will start to grow away from her. But for now she understands him because Ethan, like all children under the age of ten, is still mostly wild.

At the sink, Mari uses the sprayer to rinse the stainless steel

clean. She turns off the water. Dries her hands. She looks out
the window, over the tips of basil, rosemary and thyme she's
growing in her container garden on the sill. Out into the
grass, which for the first time in as long as she can remember
is getting too long. Ryan usually trims the grass so tight to
the ground nothing living could ever possibly hide in it. In
the spring, summer and fall he rides his mower every weekend, beer in hand. He might not be able to find the laundry
basket, but the yard is somehow tied up in his manly pride.
It's not like him to leave the yard untended, but over the past
few months he's been working long hours. Coming home
late. The weather has been rainy for the past three weekends,
leaving him to sit inside on the couch watching a series of
whatever random programs he finds when he taps the keys
of the remote.

Now the grass would tickle her shins if she were to walk
outside into it. So she does. Barefooted, step-stepping carefully
from the wide wooden deck onto the slate patio and finally, at
last, into spring-soft grass that bends beneath her toes and does,
indeed, tickle her shins. Mari sighs. She closes her eyes. She
tips her face to the late-afternoon light and breathes in deep.

She listens.

A bird chirps softly. A dog barks, far off. She hears the murmur of voices, a television or radio, from the neighbor's house
on the other side of the yard. A passing car. The squeak of bi-
cycle wheels. There is sometimes the rustle of squirrels in the
trees or rabbits hopping into the brush, but most of the wild-
life in this neighborhood has been eradicated by family pets,
loud children or exterminators.

These are the sounds of her life. She misses the sound of
running water that had been the constant backdrop of her
childhood. Two houses down, the Smithsons have a plastic
waterfall set up in their backyard, but it's too far away for her
to hear. Mari used to have a container fountain on her deck,

just big enough to grow a single water lily, but last winter she forgot to bring it in before the first freeze and the pump burned out. Ryan tossed the entire thing in the trash, and she hasn't yet replaced it.

Her feet swish in the grass as she steps forward again. A twig crackles and snaps. Mari pauses. She breathes in deeply again, lashes fluttering on her cheeks, but none of this is the same as what she's missing. This is not what she's hoping to feel.

That she only gets in dreams.

She opens her eyes and looks at her yard. Ryan mows the lawn but won't bother with weeding. They have a service for that. Mari hates to pull up what the Home Owner's Association calls weeds and she calls wildflowers. She despises pulling up plants only to put down the chopped-up bits of dead trees. Mulching seems like the utmost waste to her. Ridiculous and expensive. She and Ryan fought about it when they moved into this neighborhood, but the HOA had rules about "curb appeal." She notes the carefully pruned beds that should be beautiful and yet leave her cold, still wanting. Still suddenly desperate for something lovely. Something wild.

The only beauty Mari sees is in the far back corner of the yard, the one that butts up to the tree line and beyond that, the last farmer's field that will be another subdivision by the end of the year. Tall oaks, weather-worn, defend her emerald-green and perfectly manicured lawn from the tangled, reckless patches of clover that edge the soybean field. Here's where the gardening crew tosses the cuttings, the scrap, the leftovers. It's where Ryan dumps the grass from his mower bag. It's a shady place, a haven for small, running creatures. It's hardly overgrown, but it's the closest she can get to the forest. There's a word to describe it that she once read in a book. *Verdant.* That's what this place is.

There's a fairy ring of mushrooms here, too, in the small, chilly bit of shade. They're edible, though Mari knows better than to pluck them, rinse them and sauté them in butter. Her children won't eat mushrooms no matter how they're prepared, and Ryan will only eat the kind that comes in a can if they're on top of pizza. Besides, nobody she knows eats mushrooms they find in their yard. As with many of her long-standing habits, it would be considered…strange. Mari touches the velvety cap of one and leaves it to survive in its small patch of soil.

This is where Ryan finds her, sitting on an old lawn chair he's tried three or four times to toss into the trash. The plastic woven strips are frayed and sagging, molded to her butt, and the metal legs have rusted. Mari keeps it because it doesn't seem like such a sin to sit on a chair like this one in this forgotten bit of backyard, while taking one of the newer, fancier deck chairs would. Ryan says nothing about the chair now. In fact, he says nothing at all.

Mari stands. "What's wrong?"

She's alarmed when Ryan's mouth works but no words come out. Ryan is never without words. It's one of the better reasons she fell so hard in love with him, his ability to always find a way to communicate with speech what she could only say with silence. She's more alarmed when he gets on his knees to bury his face in her lap. Her hands come down to stroke the short, clipped ends of his pale hair. When she ruffles it, glints of silver shine in the gold. Ryan sighs, shoulders rising and falling, and his face is hot against her bare thigh.

"What's wrong?" she asks again, neither of them moving until Ryan lifts his head to look at her.

"I have bad news," her husband tells her, and not for the first time, her entire life changes.

TWO

BESIDE HIM, MARI SLEPT. THE PEACEFUL IN-OUT of her breathing normally soothed Ryan into sleep himself, but tonight he lay wide-eyed and wakeful. Unable to relax enough for dreams.

He could wake her. A kiss or two would do it. He turned his head to look at her. She lay facing away from him, the smooth slope of her shoulders and hips clearly outlined because she slept, as she almost always did, with only a sheet to cover her. She went to bed naked even in the winter. Hell, Mari would be naked all the time if she could get away with it.

He could push up behind her. Inside her. They'd move together the way they always did, and it would be good for both of them with hardly any effort on his part. It was one of the things he loved so much about her, her easy and effortless response. He knew it had nothing to do with his skill or his prowess, but that it was something innately sensual inside her. He was the only man she'd ever been with—Ryan knew this. But would she respond that way to any man? Or was he somehow special? Thinking of this depressed him so that he couldn't even feel the twitch of an erection, couldn't even lose himself in that small and simple distraction.

Too bad his dick hadn't felt that way a year ago, when Annette Somers had strutted her way into his office with half the DSM-IV listed in her file as diagnoses. All the classic symptoms, traits and characteristics of at least three different mental illnesses, along with hints of half a dozen others. Knowing she knew how to play the game hadn't kept him from being played.

It was too much of a cliché, but here he found himself in the awkward, not to mention financially disruptive situation of having been placed on probation at reduced salary by his practice. Worse was the very real possibility that not only could he lose his license, but Annette's husband, Gerry, had been making noise about malpractice.

Even if eventually it all worked out and he didn't lose his job, money was going to be tight for a while, no question. They'd have to cut back. Way back. The kids wouldn't be happy, especially Kendra, but they'd just have to understand that this summer there couldn't be a pool membership or that expensive sleepaway camp. No horseback riding lessons. They could cancel their cable TV if they had to, he thought. Cut back on dinners out. It could work. It would have to work.

In the dark, Ryan swallowed against a surge of sourness. For a moment he thought about shaking Mari awake to see if she'd bring him an antacid, but he stopped himself with the barest brush of his fingers along her shoulder. She would get up, if he asked her to, but it wasn't going to make him feel better.

Maybe he could get a teaching position. Maybe he could go back to school for a new career, something like software engineering or website design. Maybe he could run away to Europe and become a heroin addict.

Maybe he could finally write that book he'd been thinking of writing for years.

The idea wiggled, a worm on a hook, in his brain. He had his dad's notes. All the files, the hours of film and video. Just because the old man had never taken advantage of the gold mine didn't mean Ryan couldn't. Or shouldn't. In fact, wouldn't it be something his dad would want Ryan to do? And who better to put it all together, to make something out of his dad's life's work, than Ryan? After all, the only man who knew Mari's story better than his father was, of course, Ryan himself.

Eased a little, he sat back in the dark, scarcely realizing he'd sat up in the first place. Yeah. The book. Even if all the rest of this turned out okay, if he got reinstated, kept his license, dodged the malpractice suit…even if all of that worked itself out, now still might be the time to write the book. What had his father always said about a door closing while a window opened?

Beside him, Mari stirred and murmured in her sleep. Ryan was used to her sleep talking, usually half-formed sentences and mumbled phrases that made little sense. Sometimes, more rarely, she moved her hands in those fluttering motions that he knew were language but which he'd never been able to interpret. Remnants of her childhood slipping out in unconsciousness. If he woke her too roughly, she'd come awake instantly. No rubbing of eyes, no yawns. Instant clarity. She'd probably be halfway across the room, too, hands up to protect herself but eyes wide. And silent, even those silly, muttered phrases gone. She wouldn't remember what she'd been dreaming. She never did. Well, she said she never did, and Ryan had no reason to believe she'd lie. Nor did he have any real interest in prodding those memories. He wasn't a Freudian psychiatrist; dreams were of little use to him.

He listened now, though, trying to make out what she was saying. Her low chuckle quirked his own smile. Mari had an infectious laugh as easy and free as the rest of her impulses. He loved that about her. Envied it, too.

His smile slipped away. What would she do when she found out everything, the whole truth? She hadn't questioned him when he'd said he was being threatened with a malpractice suit. That had happened before, more than once. It was part of being a doctor. Probation meant he'd still go to the office every day, so he'd downplayed that part of it. She wouldn't notice anything different about his schedule. But the rest of it, the part about Annette, what would she do about that? She wouldn't leave him. How could she? He was all she'd ever known. The second most important man in her life, and once his dad had died, the most and only. She wouldn't leave him. She couldn't.

Could she? Oh. God. Could she really?

His hands fisted in the covers, a blanket and quilt for him because even with the summer-weight flannel pajama bottoms and T-shirt, he was still too cold to sleep without blankets.

All he'd told her was that there was some trouble with a patient at work, and she hadn't pressed him for answers. She never did. That was something else he loved about her.

If Ryan said the sky was green, Mari could be counted on to give it a curious glance and a shrug, a smile. To go along with it. Not that she couldn't be stubborn, because she could hold tighter to an idea or a desire than anyone he'd ever known. When Mari wanted something, she sewed herself up tight inside it, so whatever it was she'd set her sights on became a part of her. Inextricable. It was just that she so rarely wanted something hard enough to hold on to it that way.

So, she wouldn't press him for answers about what had happened. What was still happening. He could give her any number of explanations, and she'd accept them the way she'd always done because he'd never given her reason to doubt him. She trusted him.

Sometimes, Mari's trust in him was a weight Ryan wasn't sure he could carry. Sure, he'd always liked it that way, pitying his buddies whose wives controlled the bank accounts, their sex lives, hell, what their husbands wore. What cars they drove. But that trust was a huge responsibility, too.

Lying in the dark beside her and hearing the soft whistle of her breath, that low chuckle that told him she was dreaming again, inside that place he could never go, Ryan wanted to wake his wife and tell her everything. Confess. Spill it out, no matter what might happen. He wanted to turn to her, take her in his arms, kiss her until her eyes opened and she focused on him.

But then somehow the alarm was going off. He'd slept without knowing it. Daylight filtered through the windows, brighter than he expected, and in the sunshine the truth suddenly didn't seem as appealing as it had in the dark.

THREE

THE BOY IN FRONT OF HER LOOKS VERY SERI-
ously at the glass measuring bowl, ducking so he can see directly into it. From this angle, his face is distorted through
the glass. All big eyes and twisted mouth. He's concentrating
fiercely, pouring exactly the right amount of oil.

"Is this enough, Mama?"

Mari eyes the red line on the glass bowl. Shimmering
golden oil inside it. And her boy, looking up at her now as
though the answer to this question is very, very important.
She supposes to him, it is.

"Looks good to me, honey."

"Now the eggs?"

"Now the eggs."

Ethan carefully takes one egg. Then another. He cracks the
eggs into the small glass cup the way Mari taught him and
checks each yolk carefully before dumping it into the oil. As
far as she knows, her son has never cracked open an egg and
found a half-formed fetus inside, but Mari has. The eggs she
ate in childhood weren't like the kind you get in stores, all of
them candled to make sure they're okay before they're shipped
off to market. Chickens penned with roosters often had eggs

with babies waiting inside. Mari always cracks them first into a separate container.

"Three eggs. A third of a cup of oil." Ethan reads this from the cookbook, one finger pressed to the stained pages. A massive volume, over five hundred pages, it's the only cookbook Mari's ever owned. It had been a gift from her adopted father, who'd considered cuisine as much a part of her curriculum as reading or writing. An important life skill, he'd said, to be able to make more than boxed macaroni and cheese. Being able to cook a decent meal was part of being an adult. "Quarter cup of water. We forgot the water."

"Go ahead and add it." Mari doesn't hand it to him, knowing he wants to do it himself.

Ethan adds the water. "It says we should mix it."

"Yep. Put it in the bowl and turn it on. Low," Mari emphasizes, because Ethan's been known to flip the speed to high and spatter the kitchen with batter.

He giggles. Her heart swells with love for her boy who reminds her so much of herself. Yet who all too soon will become entirely more foreign to her than that mixer.

Already his legs and arms are growing longer. His fingers and feet bigger. If she were to press her hands to his, palm-to-palm, his would be nearly the same size. Sooner than she knows it, he will be a teenager like his sister. After that, a man.

And what will she do then? When she can no longer hold him on her lap. When she is not the one he comes to for fixing boo-boos and putting together toy trains that have fallen apart. What will Mari do when her boy turns into something else?

She doesn't understand men. Never has. Probably never will. Sometimes she will stare at the damp towel tossed on the bathroom floor instead of hung neatly on the hook and wonder how Ryan, who was raised by a woman for whom there was no such thing as being too neat, can stand being such a slob. How he can blow his nose so raucously in the shower like he's the only one to use it, or leave his dirty socks in a pile by his favorite recliner until at last, frowning, he comes to her wanting to know why the sock drawer is empty. It's because he never had to pick up after himself, of course. His mother never made him. Nobody had done that for her; she'd learned early on how to take of herself. Clutter and mess disturb her, remind her of bad days long past. Mari can't stand to live in filth.

If Ryan's asked to clear away a dish or return a gallon of milk to the fridge after drinking from it, he gives Mari a blank look as though she's asked him to perform an unexpected brain operation. Asked to fold towels, he leaves them rumpled and in leaning stacks, not neat piles. She has learned over the years to simply move behind him, tidying, a silent force he doesn't even notice but would surely miss if it were gone. Her job, she supposes. To keep the house together, her husband and children organized and on track. Her job, Mari thinks while watching her son, to make sure her children are capable and responsible human beings who can cook and clean and take care of themselves.

Ethan, lower lip pulled between his teeth in concentration, lifts the measuring bowl and prepares to pour the contents into the metal one he needs to use with the mixer. Slick fingers, a hard tile floor. All at once there is glass and oil and eggs all over, and a small boy's cry echoes in the kitchen.

"Mama, I'm sorry!" Ethan moves toward her with one hand out before Mari can stop him.

"No, Ethan—"

Too late. One bare foot comes down on shattered glass. He cries out again, this time in pain. There is blood.

Blood, and the low, harsh panting of a dog's breath. Four punctures in the back of her hand, but pain all over her. The dog growled, lunging again, and Mari didn't take a second to think about it. She kicked, hitting it in the jaw. The side. The dog yelped and fled, but she stood with her wounded hand cradled against her and watched the blood spatter on the floor until everything tipped and turned and she ended up on the ground, her burning face pressed to the cool, smooth surface....

"Mama!"

Mari is no longer frozen. That long-ago time, those long-ago sounds and smells, don't fade away. They simply vanish. Pushed aside as she leaps across glass to lift her boy.

She settles him on the kitchen island and plucks the shard from the sole of his foot. She twists to drop it in the sink, careful to avoid the glass on the floor with her own feet. Mari grabs a clean dishcloth from the drawer, folds it into thirds and presses it to the wound.

"It hurts," Ethan says.

"Let me take a look." Mari lifts the white cloth, stained now with red. The wound is oozing too much blood for her to get a good look, but it appears that the glass has sliced a long section of Ethan's foot, and the skin is flapping across the cut.

"Shh," she murmurs. Presses the cloth against the wound. "This might need stitches."

She could do it herself, of course, but Ryan would frown on that. Taking Ethan to the hospital will take time and expense, and ultimately, nobody can do a better job at tending her child's hurts than she can—but nevertheless, it's not what's done. Just like picking mushrooms from your yard, sewing up your son on the kitchen table is bound to lead to whispers and looks of the sort Mari should be used to, the way she's accustomed to blood, but would like to avoid, anyway.

"Nooo!" Ethan wails, and she hushes him as the back door opens.

"Gross!" Kendra, incredibly, stops midtext to stand in the

doorway and stare at the bloody, oily, eggy puddle on the floor.

"I cut myself," Ethan offers through tears.

"I have to take him to the place where they fix people when it's an urgency." Mari says this matter-of-factly, but Kendra's already blanching, turning her face. More like her dad than her mom, that's for sure.

"Emergency," Kendra corrects. "I think I'm gonna puke!"

"Text your dad, please," Mari says. "Tell him I've taken Ethan to the hospital."

"Do I have to go, too?"

Mari thinks, knowing she's always been able to trust her daughter who might have a flair for drama but who's still a good kid. "No. But nobody's allowed to come over. Don't answer the phone unless it's me or Daddy. Don't answer the door. Don't use the stove."

It's a little overkill, but Mari's not thinking quite straight. The smell of the blood is teasing her head into spinning again, and she blinks away the past. *Focus. Focus. This is now,* she thinks. *I am here.*

Kendra's already tapping her dad's number into her iPhone, a much-coveted birthday gift that never leaves her side. "Got it."

"Mama? Will it hurt bad? The stitches?"

"Yes. But they'll give you something so it doesn't hurt so much."

"A shot?" Ethan's lower lip trembles; a bubble of clear snot forms in one nostril.

"Yes. A shot, probably."

"Nooo!"

"You can have the shot, which will help the pain," Mari says, "or you can choose to not have the shot and take the pain when they stitch you. Up to you, buddy."

Other mothers coo and coddle. She knows this because

she's seen it on playgrounds with scraped knees and during playdates when her children played with other children and she was left to make conversation with their mothers. Other mothers tell "little white lies" to ease their children's fears. Maybe those are better mothers than she is, Mari's never sure. All she knows is that lying rarely ever serves any good purpose, and she'd personally rather know if there is going to be pain than be told not to expect it when it is surely coming.

Ethan is much like his mother. "Okay. I'll take the shot."

She hands him a tissue for his nose and calls out to Kendra, "Honey, don't come in here until I get back, okay?"

"No worries! Gross!"

Mari laughs, shaking her head, and gives Ethan a wink. He smiles back. Mari finds her purse, her keys, her wallet with the insurance card inside. Ethan helps her wrap some masking tape around the dishcloth to keep it on his foot. Then she lifts her boy, his arms around her neck. She presses her face briefly to the sweet boy scent of his hair, closing her eyes. For now, he's still hers.

FOUR

ALONE IN THE HOUSE.

Kendra couldn't remember the last time she'd been here without someone else. The first thing she did was lock the doors. Kendra's friends bragged about their parents leaving them alone and the sorts of things they got up to when they did. Most of it was bullshit. If the kids in her class did half as much drinking and messing around as they said they did, they'd all be in rehab or pregnant.

Some of it was true, though. Last week there'd been a party at Jordan Delano's house, and three girls got so drunk they ended up posting naked selfies on ZendPix. So stupid and gross. But that was the sort of thing kids did when they were left alone. It seemed as if almost all the kids in her class had parents who both worked, or moms who, if they didn't have jobs, spent a lot of time at the gym or getting massages and mani-pedis. Kendra had been in an accelerated private kindergarten, and was almost a year younger than the rest of her classmates. Most of them had already passed their driver's tests. Lots of them drove brand-new cars, sixteenth birthday gifts meant to make up for the fact they were left to themselves so much, she thought.

Her dad would never buy her a car. He'd say she didn't

need one, not when she had her mom to take her where she needed to go. Kendra's mom was almost always home. She'd never had a job. She didn't volunteer for charity or politics. She didn't spend hours on yard work or doing crafts, either. She cleaned a lot. And she cooked. She was always there when Kendra needed her, and when she didn't, too.

Her mom didn't get on her case about boys or clothes or even grades like Sammy's mom did, always wanting to have "a talk" with Sammy, like she ever really listened. Kendra's mom was always there for her, though, ready to listen. No matter what Kendra needed to say. She'd always liked that.

Other mothers wore designer clothes, or at least outfits that matched. Shirt, shoes, belt, purse. Kendra's mom wore tank tops and sheer, flowing skirts, and the only time she wore shoes was if she had to. Her purse didn't bulge with makeup or a hairbrush or coupons or anything like her friends' mothers kept in their bags. Mari didn't even wear makeup. She was smaller than other mothers. Kendra had grown taller than her in sixth grade. And Mom didn't care about a lot of stuff other moms did, like working out at the gym or going to church.

She was still more beautiful than any other mother, so much so that it was kind of embarrassing. Hard to live up to, too. There were times Kendra looked in the mirror at the mess of her face and wondered why she'd had to end up looking like her dad instead of her mother.

Her phone buzzed from her pocket. "Dad."

"What happened?"

"Ethan cut his foot on some glass. Mom took him to the hospital."

Dad sighed, and Kendra imagined him pinching the bridge of his nose with his eyes closed. "Shit. Is he okay?"

"There was blood everywhere." Kendra made a face.

"Did she say she wanted me to meet her there?"

"I don't know, Dad." God, he could be so annoying. "Why don't you call her and ask her?"

"I did. She didn't pick up."

"She's probably okay," Kendra said. Mom often forgot her phone or turned off the ringer. But her mom could handle just about anything, while it was another family truth left unspoken that her dad mostly...couldn't. Or maybe just didn't.

"Yeah. Well, if she calls, tell her I have some stuff I need to handle here and I'll be home a little later."

The call disconnected, and Kendra put her phone back in her pocket. *Alone in the house,* she thought, wishing for a second she was the sort of girl who'd invite everyone over for a party. Tear everything up, get wasted, make out with whoever she wanted. That's what her dad might've done, she thought suddenly, when he was young. But not her mom. Her mom would've been good and done what was expected of her. And that's what Kendra did, too.

FIVE

"MARI? MARI CALDER, RIGHT? ETHAN'S MOM."

Mari turns with a half smile she was taught long ago was considered polite. "Yes?"

The woman in front of her looks as though she stepped out of one of the magazines Mari reads every month but rarely enjoys. Perfect hair, perfect outfit. Perfect smile that makes Mari cover her own mouth with her hand in reaction, though her teeth are no longer gray and broken and jagged.

"I'm Lorna. Davis?" The woman pauses. "Bev's mom."

Bev. Beverly. Beverly Davis... Mari vaguely recalls a girl with curly red hair and a set of sprouting buckteeth. She is in Ethan's class.

"Oh. Yes. Bev." Mari nods, wondering how it is that Lorna Davis knows who she is.

"Bev told me Ethan had an accident. Is he okay?"

"He'll be fine."

"Good. Kids," Lorna says with a laugh and shake of her head. "It's amazing any of us survive childhood, am I right?"

Mari has mastered the social smile, but laughing at something she doesn't find funny is a skill that still escapes her. "Children are capable of surviving a lot."

It wasn't quite the right answer. She sees that in Lorna's blink, her raised brow. The woman recovers quickly.

"Right. Yes. And thank goodness it was just a cut, not something worse, am I right?"

"You're right," Mari says.

Lorna nods. They stare at each other there in the bandage aisle of the pharmacy. Mari has a package of gauze pads and antiseptic wipes in her hand. Lorna's small basket contains mascara, feminine deodorant spray, skin lotion, a beauty magazine.

"You know, you should think about coming to one of our Mommy's Day Out meetings," Lorna says suddenly.

It's Mari's turn to blink. "Umm…"

"You don't work, am I right?"

"I take care of my kids," Mari says.

Lorna laughs. "Oh, yeah, which is a full-time job, I know that. I feel you. I just started back to work last year, part-time. Gets me out of the house, but leaves plenty of 'me' time."

There's a silence that goes on too long, until Mari says, "What's Mommy's Day Out?"

Lorna's eyes gleam. "Oh, we get together once a month at someplace really delish for lunch. Then sometimes a spa treatment, manicure, something like that. We have a great place we go to that does this amazing chi rejuvenation or a sugar scrub or hot stone massage, really everything they do there is fantastic. It's a chance for us to get together away from the husbands and kids, you know what I mean? If I didn't have my 'Mommy's' days, I'd lose my mind."

Mari shudders involuntarily at the thought of suffering a massage, of being touched so intimately by a stranger. "I like spending time with my kids."

"Oh…of course. Me, too. I love my kids. Of course." Lorna puts a friendly hand on Mari's arm. "Just, you know, they can drive you crazy. You know what I mean?"

The touch makes Mari's skin crawl, but she doesn't back away. Mari puts on that same polite half smile she's practiced for so many years. She will never be a social hugger, but she's learned to tolerate a lot.

"Of course. Well, I'll think about it." Mari holds up her packages. "I should get home."

"Oh, right." Lorna pauses, expectant.

Mari has no idea what she's waiting for and the silence stretches on until she nods and smiles and ducks away from Lorna, who stares after her.

In the car, she thinks about what she will say if Lorna actually does invite her to a Mommy's Day Out. It might be nice, she tells herself as she lines up with the other mothers in the school parking lot, each car inching forward slowly, though the kids haven't been dismissed yet. To do something with other women. Have some…friends.

Except it wouldn't be nice. It would be strange and awkward. For them, not so much for her. Mari gets along with most anyone. It's other people who usually don't know how to react to her.

"You're too honest," Ryan told her once, long ago, in the very beginning when things between them were fresh and new and still strange. He'd tangled his fingers in a strand of her dark hair, pulling it along his much lighter skin to show the contrast between them.

"You'd like me to lie?"

"I don't think you know how to lie," had been his answer, and he'd kissed her.

It isn't that she doesn't know how. It's that she doesn't see the point. Lies are secrets, and there's no use for them, either.

"Hey, honey," she says when Ethan at last limps to the car and slides into the backseat. "How was school?"

"It was okay." He shrugs, clicking his seat belt. "Can we get cheesesteaks from Pat's for dinner?"

Pat's, King of Steaks, isn't on the way home. In traffic, it will take them an hour or so to get there and back. Still, Mari looks at her son's hopeful face and doesn't have the heart to say no. His grin and shout of laughter when she nods is enough to make her laugh, too.

Small things, she thinks as she pulls away from the school. *That's what matters. Small but beautiful things.*

SIX

THE NUMBERS DIDN'T ADD UP. RYAN HAD FIG-
ured them four or five times, and every time, no matter how
he worked them, they still turned red. He'd gone online to
check balances and shift some money, but there was only so
often he could do that. The checks coming in were too small,
and eventually might stop coming at all. He'd have to do
something, and soon.

He could tap into the money his dad had left Mari. The
funds had been meant for her to go to college, if she could, or
at least to live on her own in case she wasn't able to support
herself. She hadn't done either of those things. She'd married
Ryan as soon as she'd turned eighteen, and he'd taken care of
her ever since. Ryan checked the balance in the account now,
as always with a somewhat sour taste in the back of his throat
at the amount that had accumulated.

It wouldn't be hard to get her to agree to use it. He'd pulled
from it before. The down payment on this house, for example. And he hadn't felt bad about that, because providing Mari
with a home of her own had been exactly what his father had
meant the money to do. And once, they'd taken the kids to
Disney World, a trip that in Ryan's opinion had been six grand
tossed away. Ryan didn't like sweating and dealing with hordes

of sticky, screaming kids, so the trip had been something of a nightmare for him. Mari and the kids had loved it, though. That was something, and giving her that experience, something she'd been lacking in her childhood, had been a perfect use of the money, too.

Even after dipping into the account twice for two big expenses, there was still plenty left. There'd been donations, fund-raisers and grants in addition to what Dad himself had set aside. Dad hadn't known, of course, that Ryan would be able to provide her with anything Mari ever wanted or needed. He'd wanted to make sure Mari would never have to worry about money because he knew how little the concept of it meant to her. Some people who grew up poor became misers, others spendthrifts. Mari simply didn't understand money. She just saw it as numbers.

It was Ryan who'd suggested the Disney trip. Who'd bought her the fancy iPhone that, as far as he knew, she barely used. Ryan wanted HD cable television with all the premium channels, the fastest internet. The fancy car that came with the fancy payment, too. All numbers, when you broke it down.

And now, the numbers didn't add up.

Technically, her account was separate from the one they kept jointly, but of course, Ryan knew Mari's passwords and PINs. Just like he knew she never checked the balances. He looked again at the balance in Mari's account. The numbers stared at him smugly. He only needed a thousand or so to cover the credit card bill for this month.

He should ask her, first. It was her money. But he knew she'd just give him one of those quizzical looks and a smile. She'd never deny him. He'd just do it and tell her a little later. Or better yet, he'd just replace the money when he started getting his full paychecks again. She'd never know. It wouldn't matter. It wasn't as if they were going bankrupt or anything.

A quick tap-tap of the keys and it was done. A thousand

dollars shifted from Mari's account to the joint one. It nicely covered the upcoming bills, with a little left over in case he needed to hit the ATM for some cash. It all worked out just fine.

Ryan had just closed the browser when his wife came in. He swiveled in his office chair to find her holding up two glasses of red wine. She smiled as she closed his door.

She kissed him before she gave him the wine. She smelled good. She tasted good. Rich and earthy, like wine but so much better. She settled herself on his lap, straddling him, careful not to spill.

"Hey," she said.

"Hey." Ryan took a glass and sipped it. "That's good."

"I read about it in that magazine you subscribed to. It got a great rating. I saw it at the liquor store and figured I'd pick up a bottle."

The wine cost, by his best guess, about forty bucks a bottle. Ryan winced. "It's really good. Thanks."

"You like it?" She sipped and swallowed. "I do."

He did like it; that was the problem. Probably more because he knew the price tag. Behind him, the computer monitor cast an accusatory glow around them. Ryan ignored it.

"I like it a lot." He inched her closer. "Where are the kids?"

"Ethan's asleep. Kendra's video chatting with someone."

"Who?"

Mari shrugged. "Different person every time I go into her room."

"Boy or girl?"

She gave him that look. That tender, amused look. "Both?"

Ryan frowned. "Not that Logan kid. The one with the pierced lip?"

"Honey, I don't know. Anyway, what difference does it make? She can't get pregnant from a video chat, thank goodness. She's going to talk to boys, Ryan. It's part of being a pretty fifteen-year-old girl. If she didn't have boys wanting to talk to her, you'd worry about that."

He didn't want to admit that was true. "I don't like that kid."

"Because he has long hair and paints his fingernails?" Mari laughed. "You're such a prepper."

She meant preppy, but he didn't correct her. "She should be in bed. It's almost eleven. Doesn't she have to get up for school tomorrow?"

"Yes. But she knows that it's on her if she's tired in the morning. She's not a dummy. Besides, they have three half days this week, and then they're done for the summer. You know they won't be doing anything in class, anyway. And don't you have to get up early for work tomorrow? Isn't it your early day?"

Twice a month for the past ten years, Ryan had been volunteering his time at the Sexual Abuse Resource Center, offering free counseling. He went in two hours before work to see patients. But with the investigation going on about Annette Somers, he'd thought it would be best to step down from that volunteer position.

He hadn't told Mari and now faced with the chance, found himself unable to.

"Yeah. I guess so."

"Don't hit the snooze button three times," she warned him. "I might have to poke you. Hard."

Ryan put his glass on the edge of the desk and used both hands to anchor her on his lap. He tipped his face to look up at her. "Poking permission granted."

His wife sipped more wine and set down her glass, too. "I can't believe it's almost summer. I'm not sure I'm ready for it. I still haven't figured out about camp. I'd like them both to go at the same time, but the one Ethan likes is shifted a week earlier this year. Oh, and Kendra's riding instructor called to say they were changing lesson times. Ethan says he wants to learn to play the guitar, so I don't know when we'll fit that in. What's the name of that place where your friend's son took lessons?"

"Yeah…about that…" Ryan's mouth, still thick with the flavor of red wine, dried. His tongue stuck in place. He swallowed heavily. "Maybe the kids need a break from some of that stuff this year. I mean, studies are showing that kids are so overscheduled these days."

Some of the wives of Ryan's friends never stopped moving. Multitasking queens, never still. Some of them were pluckers, forever picking at imaginary bits of lint on their husbands' shirts. Others were texters, chatting briskly even as they held a series of entirely different conversations with their fingers. Bustlers.

Mari had a stillness that was more than quiet. She could go perfectly motionless and silent. She could almost disappear. Ryan almost always found this calming. She did it now, looking him over, and this time it didn't soothe him.

"I thought you liked it when the kids were kept busy."

"You could get a break, too. Why should you spend your summer playing chauffeur?" He spun his chair with her still on his lap to gesture at the computer. "Sign them up for the library reading program. And hey, they have that free bowling program at the Cinebowl."

"We do those things every summer. But the kids look forward to those other things, they're not chores." Her head tilted slightly, her brow furrowing. "Kendra loves the riding lessons, and Ethan is already talking about the guitar thing. They both like camp, too, because they see their friends from other years there. And I don't mind driving. I mean…it's what I do. I'm their mother. It's my job. Would you rather I spend all my time getting massages at the spa?"

The brittle tone in her voice set him back for a second.

"No." Definitely the opposite with the financial situation they were in.

"My kids don't make me crazy," Mari said quietly. "I like doing things with them. And for them."

"I know. But you shouldn't have to spend all your time driving them around from activity to activity. It's summer. We should be focused on simpler things. And with you running around all the time, we get too much takeout."

Her lips quirked in amusement. "I thought you liked Pat's cheesesteaks."

"I do." He did, that was true. But a simple dinner for four had added up to almost forty bucks. "It's better when you make dinner, that's all."

"So…your idea of my having the summer off includes me keeping the kids entertained and cooking even more dinners? Great." She tilted her head to give him a curious look. "That sounds really relaxing."

"No. No, that's not what I mean." He took her hand and brushed the knuckles across his lips. "I just think it might be better to cut back on some things. That's all."

"Is it money?"

Ryan wondered if the reason Mari hardly ever questioned him about anything was because somehow, some way, she just…knew.

She pursed her lips. "How much less are you getting?"

Damn it, she cut to the heart of things when she noticed them. Ryan put on a neutral face and lied. "I'm at 85 percent of my salary, that's all. Just during this investigative period."

"That's not so bad, is it?" She looked over his shoulder at the computer screen, but all she'd see was his aquarium screensaver. She looked back at him, serious eyes, serious mouth. "But if you want me to cut back on expenses, I can do that."

He knew she could. Hell, Mari had survived the entire first eight years of her life living at a level so far below poverty he wasn't sure it could even be registered. Mari could trim the fat of their lives so close to the bone there'd be hardly anything left.

"No, babe. We don't have to do that. It'll be okay." He said it with more confidence then he felt; a moment later he forced himself to believe it. To forget about the money he'd just transferred. "This'll pass. No problem."

Mari ran her fingers through his hair, then cupped his chin in her palm, forcing him to look into her eyes. What she saw there, Ryan could not have said, but whatever it was seemed to satisfy her because she nodded and kissed him. She held him in her arms, the warmth of her familiar and arousing.

"It's only for a little while, anyway. Couple of weeks. A month, tops. Just until we get this stupid investigation out of the way," Ryan said.

Mari nodded. She believed him, and why not? She always did. She always would.

SEVEN

MARI STANDS IN THE PANTRY. THE SHELVES groan with the weight of cans and bags and boxes. She runs her fingertips over them, mouthing the names of all the good things but not speaking aloud. Beans, rice, pasta. She can make a hundred meals from these ingredients. Enough to last for months even if she didn't go to the grocery store for that long.

This comforts her, the sight of this wealth. The cool wood and shadows soothe her, too, even if she has to take only two steps to get back into the brightly lit kitchen. She closes her eyes, breathing in the scent of spices. She can smell the brown paper bags stacked carefully in the rack, ready to be reused. The biting stink of ammonia in the bottle toward the back, and also of vinegar closer to the front. A bottle of floor cleaner is supposed to smell "flower-fresh" but doesn't.

"Moooom!"

Mari sticks her head out of the pantry. "What?"

Kendra jumps, startled, at the kitchen table. "What are you doing in there?"

"Thinking about what to make for dinner. What do you want?"

Kendra must want something from her mother, but she

doesn't say what it is. The idea of dinner distracts her. "Can we order pizza?"

"No." Mari thinks of Ryan's words from a few nights before when she'd brought home the cheesesteaks. "I can make some."

Kendra makes a face. "Forget it. I'm going over to Sammy's house, then."

Samantha Evans has been Kendra's best friend since first grade. She lives a few houses down the street. Her parents have been on the edge of divorce for years, and neither are probably home now. They both work. They both stay out of the house a lot so they don't have to see each other. Mari would prefer it if the girls came to spend time in her house where she can keep an eye on them, where she can do her meager best to give Sammy some semblance of normal family life—but she understands that two teen girls want to spend their time in independence, such as it is.

Besides, Sammy's parents usually seem to leave her money for pizza.

"Just you and Sammy?"

Kendra looks faintly scornful. "Of course. Who else would come over?"

"I don't know. Maybe that boy…what's his name? Logan?"

Kendra bites her lip gently. But then she shakes her head, her hand going unconsciously to the pocket of her jeans where her phone buzzes. Ah, Mari thinks. She *does* like him. But something has gone wrong.

"Sammy's parents don't let her have anyone over when they're gone. Just me."

"I know what they allow and don't allow, Kendra. But I also know they're not home and it can be tempting…." Mari trails off before she can spout more daytime drama admonitions. Aware more than ever that Kendra is living a life com-

pletely different than Mari's teenage years. "I just want you
to be safe. That's all."

"Mom. C'mon. We're going to watch TV and stuff. Her
mom said when she got home from work she'd take us to the
mall and see a movie. I can sleep over. Is that okay?"

"What time is her mom supposed to be home?"

A shrug. "Dunno. Seven?"

It's a Friday night. School's out for the summer. Sammy lives
just down the street. Mari thinks she ought to protest more,
but without the allure of pizza, a trip to the mall and a movie,
what does she have to hold her daughter here? Ryan has already said he'd be home late again. It'll just be her and Ethan.

"Call me when you get back to Sammy's house tonight."

Kendra's grin lights up her face. Mari sees herself in that
grin and is relieved to feel that connection. For a moment,
she remembers the weight of a sleeping infant in her arms,
the sweet smell of Kendra's fuzzy baby head. Time is passing
too fast. But isn't that what time does?

Mari makes pizza, anyway. She and Ethan eat it on the back
deck. The cut on his foot left a scar, but he's healed fast enough
that he barely limps. She watches him build with Lego blocks
as she flips through a parenting magazine she bought from
the school fund-raising campaign. Nothing in it seems rel-
evant to her, but she tries hard to pay attention to it, anyway.
She pages past glossy photos of mothers and children posed
around platters of decorated cupcakes, modeling hand-printed
T-shirts. She skims the articles, skipping the words and phrases
that give her trouble. She can read competently enough. It's
the lack of context that confuses her.

When the fireflies come out to dot their tiny yellow bright-
ness against the backdrop of night, Mari calls Ethan away from
his toys and hands him an empty canning jar. Together they
stalk the lightning bugs and capture them until the jar is full.

"Hold it up," she tells him. "Aren't they lovely?"

"We can't keep them," Ethan says solemnly. "Wild things deserve to be free. Don't they, Mama?"

"They do. But we can hold them for just a little while, right?"

He laughs and holds up the jar. "Yep. Then we'll let them go."

"Let's have some ice cream."

"Hooray!" Ethan dances, forgetting that lovely wild things also don't like to be shaken around in their glass houses. The bugs swirl and dip, falling off the jar's slick insides.

Mari takes it from him as he runs ahead of her into the house. She sets the jar on the deck railing as she goes inside to scoop large bowls of ice cream for them both. Whipped cream. Fudge sauce. She loves sweets, even if her teeth ache in memory of past indulgences. She should limit herself and, she supposes, Ethan, too, to one scoop. But she can't help it. Even with the memory of thousands of dollars and dozens of hours of dental work to repair the damage done to her teeth through childhood neglect, Mari can't resist.

Ryan comes home as she and Ethan have settled into chairs on the deck. The sweep of headlights illuminate the backyard for a second as he pulls into the drive, then it's all dark again except for the jar of tiny living lights. A square of light appears as he opens the door from the garage into the laundry room.

"Hello?"

"Out here!" Mari turns in her chair to greet him with a smile. "Want some ice cream?"

"No, thanks." He kisses her briefly and ruffles Ethan's hair.

"Dad, look at the fireflies."

"I see. Where's Kiki?"

"She went to Sammy's. Her mom's taking them to a movie. Then she's sleeping over."

This is a normal conversation. Mother, father, son. Ice cream on a new summer night, fireflies in a jar. It could've come right out of the pages of a magazine. It's everything she was taught to believe and want, right there in front of her. And she deserves this, doesn't she? This normal life?

"She'll never be right, Leon. She'll never be normal. You have to realize that. I know you want to keep working with her, but—" The woman in the sorrow suit shook her head.

No, not sorrow. The color of her suit was called navy, and the skirt Mari wore was the same. She didn't like this skirt. Too tight at the knees. It meant she couldn't run. Couldn't jump. Couldn't crawl. Had to sit up straight like a good girl, a nice girl.

Normal girl.

"Is it time for us to let them go, Mama?" Ethan, mouth smeared with chocolate, hair standing on end, holds up the jar.

Inside it, fireflies wiggle and flash. They're so pretty, all gathered there. Mari looks out to the yard, then beyond that to the fields just past the tree line. There, in the knee-high crop are thousands—no, millions, if it's possible, of fireflies blinking out their mating signals.

She stands. "Oh, look at how many there are."

Ryan's already gone inside the house, turning on the lights. Ruining the view. Ethan oohs and aahs with her, though. Together she and her son run through the grass toward the trees, hand-in-hand.

"Let them go now," Mari says.

Ethan unscrews the lid. He shakes the jar until the bugs inside realize their freedom and drift upward. Out of the glass, into the night. Into the field, where they blend in with the others, until at last the jar in her son's hand is empty. His hand slips back into hers as they stare out at the field.

This, she thinks, is her real life. Her normal life. Short

minutes tick-tocking out in the darkness, watching fireflies.
These moments of small beauty, shared with her boy. This is
where she was always meant to be.

EIGHT

IT WAS A FARCE, AND RYAN KNEW IT. AS SOON as Annette Somers's husband brought the case against him, every doctor in the practice knew it would probably ruin him. They'd pretended they were behind him, of course. Putting him on leave from seeing patients, giving him the shit work to do, dictating notes and culling files. They couldn't outright fire him, not without proof he'd done what Gerry Somers said he'd done. Most of them had faced malpractice suits in their careers, it seemed to be the way medicine was going, everyone entitled to believe they deserved something they didn't, that doctors weren't allowed to make mistakes, not ever. But this was different. This was a matter of ethics, and while his partners might cluck and shake their heads, Ryan knew not a one of them was going to risk being pulled down along with him.

Not that he blamed them. If it had been one of them, he'd feel the same way. It still royally sucked, though. Walking into the office with a smile for the secretary, even though he had no patients to see. Holing up in his office to stare at the walls or sift through old case files. Taking calls from his lawyer who assured him this would all be resolved without too much hassle.

Mari had packed him a lunch this morning. Sandwich,

chips, a pear, a juice box, for god's sake. One of those snack cakes she loved so much. That stopped him for just a second. She hoarded those snack cakes as if they were gold. The fact she'd put one in his lunch—the fact she'd made him a lunch at all, when she knew he always ate lunch out—told him a lot about what she'd noticed about the situation he'd so carefully tried to keep from describing in full detail.

It was too much to sit in this office any longer, doing make-work while he waited for the ax to fall. Ryan took the lunch bag and slipped on his sunglasses. He passed a hand over his hair and straightened his tie. He didn't bother telling Ceci the secretary where he was going or to hold his calls.

Rittenhouse Square Park, only a few blocks from Ryan's office, was a popular place at lunchtime. Joggers, moms pushing strollers, men in suits just like his staking out primo spots on the benches. Ryan snagged a bench and opened the lunch bag to stare inside without interest. Really, he'd have preferred a greasy cheesesteak from Pat's, "wit" onions and Cheez Whiz. Then a hard workout later to keep it from settling on his gut. Instead, he had a turkey sandwich on whole wheat with fat-free mayo, tomato and lettuce, a piece of fruit, a snack cake and a damned juice box.

He'd asked her to cut back, but facing the results of his wife's efforts, Ryan wanted to punch something. Or run for a long, long time, until everything about him ached and he wore holes in his socks and left bleeding blisters on his feet. Instead, he put the bag next to him on the bench and tipped his face to the late-spring sunshine.

His father would've been ashamed of him.

Oh, it wasn't like they'd ever been close. Ryan had been his mother's son, her pride and joy. Her best work, she liked to say, which was sort of a laugh since she hadn't ever had a job. It had just been the two of them for a lot of years while his father spent hours at work. In the lab, with patients. His re-

search. He'd left his wife and son to their own devices, showing up late for dinner or not at all, completely clueless and
unaware of the silence in the house that grew over congealing
meatloaf and cold mashed potatoes. When he did show up, he
talked about himself, his discoveries, his breakthroughs and
his studies. Always himself.

Eventually, Ryan's mother had simply stopped setting a
place for her husband. More than once, Ryan had come into
the kitchen at night for a bedtime snack to find his father
standing at the sink, a plate of leftovers in one hand and a
beer in the other.

They'd never been close, but it hadn't been a terrible relationship. When Ryan decided to go into psychiatry, Dad had
been there to support and advise him, steering him away from
the world of academia and into a more practical path.

"It's where the money is," Dad had told him over glasses of
decent Scotch that Ryan was too young to drink, one night
late after Mom had gone to bed. "You're going off to college, then med school, that's great. But don't end up like me,
begging for scraps to keep working. Don't be a researcher."

It was the first time Ryan had tasted liquor. The taste of it
would always bring back the memory of that night, the first
time his dad had talked to him man-to-man. His father's hand
clapped to his shoulder. Dad's bleary gaze. The feeling the entire world was opening up to him, just turned eighteen and
ready to conquer.

And now look at him. What the hell had happened? What
had he done?

He'd messed up. Big-time.

But…the book.

His father had spent years on research. Compiling data,
theories, proving them right. Or wrong. He'd scrabbled for
money to fund his work and in the end had made almost nothing from it. But he had left behind a legacy.

Ryan sat back again, thinking hard. Excitement stirred inside him, tender shooting sprouts that promised to grow into something more. A book about his father's work was a sure thing. Guaranteed to be a bestseller, he knew it.

Beside him on the bench, the paper bag rustled. With a frown, Ryan poked it. He had the right to share his father's work with the world, no question of that. But did he have the right to share the story of his dad's greatest success?

It wasn't Ryan's story to tell. It was Mari's. If he asked her, he thought, picking up the crumpled paper lunch sack, she would certainly say yes.

But if he didn't ask her, she couldn't say no.

The man who shuffled up to him then looked homeless. Wild hair, scruffy beard on pale cheeks. Cargo pants loose on his hips and hanging low, no belt, mismatched shirt. Ryan flinched automatically, expecting a wave of stink, but this guy didn't reek of booze or piss. That was something to be thankful for, anyway. The guy looked hungry, though.

Ryan wasn't in the habit of giving handouts, especially cash. Let them buy their booze and drugs on someone else's dime. He held up the lunch bag, though, thinking he could do a good deed and then have an excuse to grab some lunch that suited him better.

"Hey, buddy. My wife packed this for me, but you can have it."

"My wife used to pack *me* lunch." The man's gravelly voice rasped on Ryan's ears. "What do you think of that?"

Ryan's fingers crumpled the brown paper lunch bag. Shit. Why'd he always manage to attract the confrontational ones? "I don't—"

The man laughed, tossing back his head for only a couple seconds before fixing Ryan with a fierce glare. "You don't have a clue who I am. Do you?"

Uncomfortably Ryan looked from side to side, but if anyone in the park was bearing witness to this drama they had the good sense to pretend otherwise. Also, he noticed uneasily that the man looked unkempt, but not necessarily unhinged. "Should I?"

"You should, since you screwed my wife and then killed her."

Shit. Shit and damn and double damn. Ryan stood, lunch bag forgotten. He towered over Gerry Somers, but the other man didn't even back up enough to give Ryan room to take a step. Trapped between his former patient's husband and the bench, Ryan had the sick feeling he was going to have to get physical.

"I didn't kill your wife."

"You might as well have. What the hell kind of doctor are you, anyway?" Gerry spat to the side before fixing Ryan with another long, hard stare. "You knew all about her. Knew her problems. And you screwed her, anyway. What did you think would happen?"

Ryan flashed back to a memory of Annette, naked, breasts pendulous and swaying as he watched her in the mirror. Taking her from behind. Then with her on top. She'd gripped him with her insides, riding him frantically, shouting when she climaxed. A slow trickle of sweat slid down his spine.

"Your wife had a lot of problems. I wasn't her first doctor. She came to me with a lot of issues, and I'm sorry I couldn't help her with them." Ryan swallowed and looked into the man's eyes. "But it's not my fault she killed herself. She was no longer in my care at the time and hadn't been for six months."

Gerry blinked rapidly without moving away. Ryan pushed gently past him to put distance between them. The man turned to follow him, grabbed at Ryan's sleeve to stop him.

"She said she was going to leave me for you. Did you know that?"

Ryan had not. He swallowed again, thick saliva against an

uprush of bile painting the back of his tongue. "She was delusional. She had transference issues. She'd had them before. You know she did. If you know anything about her at all…"

"I knew everything about her! I knew when she came home stinking of you!" Gerry leaned to sniff dramatically at Ryan's neck. "Fancy-ass cologne. How much you pay for that?"

"I'm really sorry about your wife, but I can't talk to you any more about this. My lawyer—"

"Oh, right. Your lawyer. Well, let me tell you something, Dr. Calder. Your lawyer isn't going to be able to do shit for you. I'm going to take everything you have. I'm going to ruin you."

"Don't threaten me," Ryan said without much heat.

Gerry laughed and backed up, finally. His eyes gleamed. He scrubbed at his mouth with the back of his hand. "No threat. The truth. You're going to pay for what you did. I'm going to see to it."

Gerry took another few steps back, then turned on his heel and stalked away, leaving Ryan to stare after him. The sun beat down, suddenly too much. His stomach lurched again. He tossed the uneaten lunch into the trash and headed back to his office.

In the waiting room, neutral beige and hung with paintings of seascapes, Ryan found out just how determined Gerry Somers was. Normally after lunch there were at least three or four patients waiting their turn in the sea-foam green and mauve chairs. Not today. Today Ceci was sobbing quietly behind the glass window while Ryan's partner Jack Kastabian patted her shoulder. Two cops with notepads turned when Ryan opened the door.

Someone, and it wasn't hard to figure out who, had spray painted *Dr. Ryan Calder Is A* in red, dripping letters on the waiting room wall. Across one of the bland seascapes, he'd scrawled *Wife Fucker.*

Ryan felt his knees wanting to go weak, but he locked them to keep from sinking into one of the chairs. The world went a little gray around the edges of his vision. He heard the roaring of surf that had nothing to do with the ocean.

"Ryan," said his other partner, Saul Goldman. "We need to talk."

NINE

"HE'S TOTALLY INTO YOU." SAMMY SAID THIS SO confidently that Kendra had to roll her eyes.

"Sure he is. That's why he spent the whole study hall talking with Bethany." Kendra shrugged, swiping the screen of her phone to check for notifications from ZendPix. Sammy had sort of bullied her into sending Logan a selfie, but that had been more than an hour ago. He'd opened it, but hadn't replied. "That's why he's ignoring my ZendPix. Shit, Sammy."

Kendra wanted to cry. It was bad enough that Logan knew she liked him, but now he knew she knew that he knew… So now it was this big freaking mess. So embarrassing. It had been better when they were just friends. At least then he'd paid attention to her. Ever since Sammy'd told Logan's best friend, Rob, that Kendra wanted to get with him, he'd been acting weird.

"He likes you. Rob told me he did." Sammy leaned to grab a handful of pretzels from the bowl on the floor, then tossed one in her mouth. She crunched, still talking, which grossed Kendra out. "And besides, it's totally obvious."

"It's not obvious to me." Kendra groaned and rolled onto her back to stare at the stick-on plastic stars attached to Sammy's ceiling. The fan blades whirring around made them seem to pulse and vibrate, which made her head hurt. She closed her eyes.

"My mom said we could order pizza. You want pepperoni and mushroom?" Sammy poked Kendra with her toe.

"I think I'm gonna go home."

"What? Dude, no!" Sammy frowned and sat up. "Why? Are you mad? Don't be mad, Kendra, God!"

She wasn't mad. Well, a little. Still mostly embarrassed. "I'm not. I just don't feel like having pizza for dinner. My mom's making chicken parm."

For a second, Sammy's face fell, and Kendra felt like shit for rubbing her friend's nose in the fact that her parents had left her alone again. But then Sammy tossed her hair with a shrug, so they both could pretend she didn't care, and it was cool between them even though Sammy had kind of ruined Kendra's life for now.

"He does like you," she said again in a lower voice when Kendra was leaving. "I'm sorry he's being a jerk about it."

"That's what boys do, right? Be jerks?" Kendra said, like she had tons of experience, when they both knew Sammy'd almost lost her virginity last summer and Kendra, so far, hadn't even been French-kissed.

Sammy looked wistful. "Yeah. I guess so." She brightened. "Hey, I have an idea. Let's invite them over!"

"Who?"

"Rob and Logan!" Sammy was already whipping out her phone and scrolling to dial.

Kendra tried to grab it from her hand. "No way!"

She wasn't fast enough. Squealing, Sammy rolled over the bed to bounce upward, phone triumphantly in hand. "Yes, way!"

"Your mom and dad said—"

Sammy's face twisted. It was the wrong thing to say. Kendra had lost this battle, for sure.

"Eff them," Sammy said coldly. "They're both out screwing other people right now. They think I don't know. Shit, they each think the other one doesn't know. So as far as I'm concerned, I can have a few friends over."

Kendra didn't know what to say. She knew things with Sammy's parents were bad, but not like that. Other people? She didn't even want to think about her parents doing it with each other, much less anyone else.

So that was how she found herself in a dark room, lit only by a few candles, sitting across from Sammy with a Ouija board between them. Rob sat on one side, Logan on the other. The boys had found the liquor cabinet and helped themselves to peach schnapps with dust on the bottle, mixed with some orange juice. Kendra refused it, the smell turning her stomach.

Sammy'd had a whole glass already. Her eyes gleamed. She was acting weird, all jerky and hectic, like she was hopped up on something. It was because of the boys, Kendra thought, watching her. She was showing off.

"Spirit, is there someone in this room right now you have a message for?" Sammy intoned before breaking into a giggle.

YES

"What's the message," Logan said.

SAMY, spelled the board. LOVES

Sammy took her hands off the planchette so fast the plastic piece spun around and almost scooted off the edge of the board balanced on their knees. "Not funny, Kendra."

"I didn't do anything." Kendra looked at Rob and Logan. "I didn't!"

Rob nudged Sammy. "Sammy loves...who?"

Under Kendra's fingers, the planchette jerked toward the letter *L*. She took her fingers off it immediately. Sammy stared at her. Rob, teasing, snatched up the planchette and settled it back into the center of the board.

"C'mon, let's ask it something really freaky," he said. When nobody answered him, he looked up. "What? C'mon!"

"I'm going to go home." Kendra stood. The room spun a little, which wasn't fair since she hadn't even had a sip of booze. She stared down at Sammy, her best friend.

Sammy was slowly turning green. She got unsteadily to her feet and headed for the small powder room off the rec room. "I'm going to puke."

"Can't handle her alcohol," Rob said with a shake of his head. "Lightweight."

Kendra looked at Logan. They'd been friends since fourth grade, when Miss Beatrice had made them work together on the project about El Salvador. In sixth grade he'd been with her when her sled went out of control in the park and she hit a tree. Logan had been the one to walk her home. In eighth grade, they'd gone to their first formal together, as friends, but he'd bought her a corsage and she'd bought him a boutonniere, and his mother had taken pictures. Hers had forgotten the camera. Kendra still had one of the pictures in her top drawer, under her socks. She'd been looking at it a lot more, lately.

"I'm going home," she said and didn't wait another second for anyone to try to stop her.

Not that any of them did. Sammy was busy yakking, Rob was raiding the liquor cabinet again. And Logan...Logan didn't like her in that way.

Her phone buzzed from her pocket as soon as she got out the front door. It was Sammy. Kendra swiped to read it, though she wanted to ignore it.

Don't be mad

Kendra typed as she walked. When?

Last year. When you were at camp. But he really likes you. I
swear to God!

So Logan was the guy Sammy had almost gone all the way
with, not some stranger she'd met at the beach like she'd said.
It made sense. Kendra could hardly be mad, in a way, since
it wasn't as if she and Logan had a thing going on. She understood why Sammy would've wanted to get with him, and
why she hadn't told Kendra about it.

But she didn't understand why Sammy would've lied about
Logan liking Kendra.

She didn't answer the text, her stomach sick and churning,
her throat tight and hot. Her face felt stretched. Like if she
blinked too hard it would crack and fall off. A mask.

"Hey, Kiki. I thought you were staying over at Sammy's."
Mom appeared in the kitchen doorway as Kendra put her foot
to the stairs. "What's wrong?"

"Nothing," Kendra started to say, but the words got lost in
a sudden uprush of tears.

Her mom's hand squeezed her shoulder, guiding Kendra to
the dining room table. "Sit."

Kendra sat. Mom sat next to her, saying nothing. Waiting
while Kendra sobbed, handing her a napkin when the snot
ran too freely. When Ethan wandered in, Mom murmured for
him to go away and leave them alone, though he did pause to
give Kendra a bewildered look first. When the tears tapered
off, Kendra blew her nose and waited for her mom to ask her
what had happened.

Instead, her mom got up and disappeared for a moment,
returning with a crinkling package she opened. She handed
Kendra a pack of chocolate snack cakes from her secret stash
without a word. Kendra stared at it for a moment, then took
a bite. It wasn't very good, but she ate it, anyway.

Her mom at last said quietly, "Do you want to talk about it?"

That was the last thing Kendra wanted to do, yet she opened her mouth and spilled out her guts, anyway. "...And I know she says he likes me, Mom, but he doesn't. Not like that. He must like Sammy."

"Why? Because he fooled around with her?"

"Well. Yeah." Kendra swiped at her face.

Mom laughed softly. "Kiki...I know you don't need me to tell you that boys will take chances when they get them. It doesn't mean they love the girl they take them with. Or even like her all that much, sometimes. And even if he did, it doesn't mean he doesn't also like you."

"She's my friend," Kendra said miserably.

"He's your friend, too. Both of them have been for a long time."

Kendra looked at her mother. "Is that supposed to make it better?"

"I don't know. Does it make it worse?"

"No." Kendra took a deep breath, considering what her mom had said. "Not worse. But not better."

"Maybe it won't get better," her mom said, "for a while."

They sat in silence for a minute or so. Kendra's mom took her hand, squeezing the fingers. Kendra squeezed back.

"Did you ever like a boy who didn't like you back?" Kendra asked.

Her mom coughed a little. "Umm...no."

"Because you were pretty," Kendra said sourly, looking at her mom's thick dark hair and vivid blue eyes. In her wedding picture, she looked like a movie star. Kendra's own hair had been blond and curly as a kid, but now it was just straight and plain and sort of brown.

Her mother looked surprised, eyes wide, mouth dropping. "Pretty, me? No. Oh, Kiki."

"Ugh, Mom, you were so pretty." Kendra scowled.

"Not when I was younger."

"When you married Daddy you were pretty," Kendra said.

Her mom nodded after a moment. "I guess so. He thought so, anyway. And your dad's the only boyfriend I ever had."

Kendra wasn't surprised. She'd known this, even though knowing it and really believing it weren't the same thing. "Really?"

Her mom looked uncomfortable, which made Kendra wish she hadn't asked. "Yes. Really."

"Wow," Kendra said when the silence between them grew too big. "That's…"

"It's what it is," her mom said firmly and stood, clapping her hands together. "Dinner is almost ready. Let's set the table. And after dinner, I need to run to the mall. We can look at those sneakers you wanted."

It felt a little bit like bribery, but if so, Kendra didn't mind. It was what some parents did when their kids felt bad about something. Bought them stuff. It was what some of them did to distract their kids from asking questions, too. Whatever her mom's reasons, a new pair of shoes couldn't take away the sting of realizing Sammy and Logan had been together.

But it helped.

TEN

THE FIRST DAYS OF SUMMER VACATION ARE THE best. The kids haven't had time to get bored, they still have their annual trip to the beach to look forward to and sleeping in is still a luxury and not yet a habit that will need to be broken when school starts again. It's only been a week, though, and they haven't yet settled into any routine. Now Mari's not sure they will.

Because this year, Ryan's home.

This is bad for several reasons. One is because Ryan isn't used to the way things are in the house when he's not there. He snaps at the kids for watching too much television and manufactures chores for them to do in the name of "helping" her, though Mari has the house utterly under control. She neither needs nor wants her children scrubbing toilets and changing sheets, no matter how little she cares for the tasks herself. She's told him this before, when Ryan says the kids need more responsibility and she says, let them be kids. Teaching them to take care of themselves and turning them into their personal maid service isn't the same thing. He's either forgotten their previous conversations or doesn't care. Or maybe, she thinks, listening to the muffled sound of Ryan lecturing Kendra on something Mari knows their daughter will ignore, Ryan simply believes himself to be the better parent.

On another day, another time, this thought would slip away from her with no more than a blink and wink of effort. Today, with her husband still home after a week and a half, Mari's patience is worn to transparency. They rarely argue. The house and the kids have always been her domain. Now without the respite of Ryan leaving for work, Mari finds herself chafing under his constant suggestions and advice. Never mind that he's never cleaned a toilet, scrubbed a floor or folded a basket of laundry in his life, now he knows just how it should be done. She hasn't quite snapped at him. Not yet. It will surprise him if she does, and she'd rather not.

There's another reason it's bad that Ryan is constantly home. It means something has changed in their lives. It's been a long time since she felt this way—uncertain of what is coming next or how to handle it.

There is a way to relieve the sting of this anxiety. Mari stretches high, fingertips searching the back of the cabinet, behind the special Thanksgiving table decorations she usually forgets to use on the table. There. She snags a package of snack cakes, chocolate, shaped like hearts. The wrapping is gone in seconds, the sweet creamy cake clutched in her fist.

They gave her hot, wet mess in a bowl, she dug her fingers into it, it burned, she tossed it down. They came with yelling hands and faces, open mouths. When she told them what happened, they took her hands and held them tight so she could not speak. They gave her a spoon, instead.

They made her normal.

Mari stops herself from shoving the cake into her mouth. Her jaw aches. Her throat closes, making it hard to swallow.

She finally manages to throw the cake into the trash, then has to drink from the faucet to wash away the taste of her own desperation.

She's never without her secret stock of snack cakes, but it's the first time in a long, long time that she's wanted to eat one that way. Gobbling and desperate. Mari closes her eyes for a moment, then shakes off the desperation.

Rough time, she thinks fleetingly before focusing on the cupboards in front of her. Tea, coffee, spices. Containers of candy sprinkles and cake decorations from Kendra's fascination a year or so ago with making fancy cupcakes. Luxuries, not necessities, and at seeing this, the excess, calm should wash over her, but it doesn't. Nobody should be able to survive very long on rainbow jimmies and silver marzipan buttons. But it's surprising what people can survive on.

Kendra stomps into the kitchen, scowling. "Mom. Can't you talk to Dad? God!"

Mari turns from her silent contemplation of the bounty in her cabinets. Kendra sees this and sighs. Her arms fold across breasts larger than her mother's (the result of better childhood nutrition or genetics, who knows?). For a second, Mari sees a woman in front of her instead of a girl and she's more ashamed by how threatened she feels by this than the fact Kendra's embarrassed by her kitchen quirks.

"Mom! Hello!"

If Mari has her way, Kendra will never know what it feels like to want for anything, much less a meal. She doesn't explain herself, though. She and Ryan have never talked to the kids about the way Mari grew up. Ryan, she thinks, is happy not to be reminded, and Mari is certain she wouldn't be able to package her life into a shape her children could possibly understand.

"What do you want me to talk to him about?"

"He's just… Gah!" Kendra throws her arms wide, infuriated in the way only teen girls can manage. "He's all over me about my room. And being on the phone! He said I had to get off my computer, too. That I had to find something to do. Well, Mom, being on my computer *is* doing something."

Mari looks to the ceiling. Silence from upstairs. "Your dad's under some stress right now, Kiki."

Kendra bites her lower lip. "His job."

"Yeah. His job. So let's try to give your dad a break, huh?"

"What happened?"

Ryan is experienced at parental white lies; Mari doesn't know how. "He's been put on probation."

"What did he do?" Kendra says flatly.

"There was some trouble with a patient."

The girl sags, head drooping. "Sammy says she heard that Dad got in trouble. She heard her mom talking about it."

Sammy's father is also a doctor. Family medicine, not psychiatry, but Mari supposes the medical community, even in Philadelphia, might be small enough that rumors spread. From what she knows of doctors, they like to talk. So do doctors' wives. And daughters, apparently.

Ryan *is* in trouble, and with something more than a frivolous malpractice suit. Mari isn't sure just how much, or what kind, or what for, though she knows it has something to do with a patient who died. Suicide comes along with the job, Ryan told her long ago, the first time one of his patients killed himself. Doctors have to be prepared for it. He'd cried back then, horrified and ashamed of what he must've felt to be a huge personal failure. He hadn't wept this time.

"Sammy says her dad said one of dad's patients is the woman who jumped in front of the SEPTA train."

"You heard about that?" Mari is startled and shouldn't be. Kendra's plugged in to things Mari's always hearing long after the fact.

"Yeah. Everyone at school was talking about it. Logan—"

Kendra's voice cracks for a second before she clears her throat and continues "—said his older sister was on the train when it happened. They made everyone stay on until they could get her out. She was squished."

Mari wrinkles her nose. "Kiki."

"That's what Logan said." Kendra doesn't seem to take any glee in this morbid news, but she's not terribly disturbed, either.

The parenting magazines would say Mari should be concerned at her daughter's lack of compassion, but since she's well acquainted with how easy it is to find distance from tragedy, she can't be. "So you and Logan are talking again?"

Kendra skips that question. "Squished right between the train and the platform. She made everyone late."

Mari shakes her head, at last finding reproach. "She died. Be kind."

"Sorry. But was she? Dad's patient?"

"Daddy's patient got squished by a train?" Ethan has appeared from the basement where he's been playing video games with the sound turned low and the lights off to escape Ryan's attention. The strategy had worked so well Mari had forgotten he was there. "What?"

"It's going to be okay," Mari says. "We're going to be all right."

Both of her children turn to look at her with nearly identical expressions. She might expect a hint of doubt from Kendra, who's growing up too fast and has naturally begun doubting all adults, but not from Ethan. Still, both of them have turned to stare with half-open mouths and raised brows.

"What?" Mari says.

"You…" Ethan starts to tear up. At eight he thinks he's too old to cry but hasn't yet mastered the ability to hold back tears.

"Lame," Kendra mutters and crosses her arms again. "Really lame, Mom."

Mari repeats herself. "What?"

She tries to think of what reason they have for such shock. Her voice echoes back at her. What she said moments ago. The tone of her voice. Then, she understands.

Ryan's always been the one to tell the kids about the Tooth Fairy, Santa, the Easter Bunny. Myths of childhood Mari never learned from experience and therefore couldn't share. This is the first time she's ever consoled them with a statement she's not sure is true.

"Oh, God!" Kendra bursts into sobs. "It's bad! It's really bad, isn't it? Is he going to jail? Did he do something that bad?"

Mari wasn't terribly put off by Kendra's bland description of the dead woman's demise, but she is disturbed by how easily her daughter assumes her father could be guilty of something worthy of jail time. "Kiki. No. Daddy's not going to jail."

"But it's bad, isn't it?" Kendra's sobs taper off, and she swipes at her eyes, smearing her mascara.

Ethan's crying silently, silver tears slipping down his cheeks. Mari gestures and he moves close enough for her to hug. She reaches to snag Kendra's wrist, even though the girl's not much for hugs anymore, and pulls her close, too. The three of them hug tight. Mari's arms are still long enough to go around them both. She holds them as hard as she can.

Her children have never really known anything terrible, and she will do whatever's necessary to make sure they never do. "It's going to be fine. I promise."

They both sniffle against her. They both pull away before she's ready to let them go. Ethan rubs his nose with a sleeve while Kendra has the sense to use a tissue. Mari looks again at the ceiling. Somewhere above is her husband, the father of her children.

"I'll be back," she says. "You two take some change from the jar near the phone and walk down to the Wawa for some slushies."

She doesn't need to tell them twice. It's a privilege their dad would squawk about; even though he wants them to "get out of the house and do something," walking a few blocks to the convenience store isn't one of them. The world's a dangerous place, Ryan says. Mari knows he has no real idea of what that means.

He's locked himself in his office, where she hears the shuffle and thump of him pulling open drawers. When she peeks inside she sees he's pulled out half a dozen file boxes from his closet. The papers are spread out all around him and he's bent over them, studying them so fiercely, he doesn't even notice she's opened the door until she raps lightly with her knuckles.

"Ryan?"

"Yeah, babe." He pushes his hair back from his forehead.

The sight of him looking so rumpled when Ryan is always so put together lifts another current of unease inside her. "What are you doing?"

He gives her a smile so broad, so bright, so full of even, white teeth, there is no way she ought to be afraid. "I'm doing it. I'm going to do it."

"Do what?"

"I'm finally going to write a book."

Mari isn't sure she ever knew Ryan wanted to write a book. Frankly, she can't recall ever seeing him *read* a book. Magazines, yes. Medical journals and *Sports Illustrated* and *Consumer Reports* when he's on the hunt for some new toy. But books? Never.

"What kind of book?"

His gaze shifts just a little, cutting from hers to look over the piles of folders and papers. "A case study."

"So, not fiction." That made more sense to her.

"No." Again, that shifting gaze, the cut of it from hers. "But that's not the best part, babe. This is even better."

He holds up a folder. The front of it says Dimitri Management Rental Properties. She doesn't know what that means, but something about it doesn't sit well. "What?"

"C'mere." Ryan gestures, and Mari goes.

He settles her onto his lap and nuzzles against her, hiding his face for a moment before lifting it. His eyes are shiny bright, his smile, too. He looks so much like his father that her breath catches. Ryan doesn't notice.

"You know I love you, right?"

"I hope so," Mari says. "You married me."

He laughs a little too loud for the space and for being so close to her. "And you know I'll always do my best to take care of you, right?"

Something twists deep inside her. "I know that."

His hand tightens on her while the other puts the folder on the desk. "And you trust me, don't you?"

"Of course I do."

"We're going to move."

Alarmed, Mari shifts on Ryan's lap to look into his eyes. "What? Where? Why?"

"Just for the summer," he says quickly. "Someplace that'll be great for the kids. For us, too. A place that'll be perfect for me to write and for you all to just get away from the city."

She doesn't point out that they don't exactly live *in* the city. "Ryan. What aren't you telling me?"

"I don't want you to worry," her husband says. "Let me take care of this."

"What about our house?"

"I've arranged to rent it to a psych fellow."

"And where are we going?" He's taken care of everything, made all the arrangements, but she still has to ask.

Ryan draws in a deep breath. "Pine Grove. Babe, I'm going to take you home."

ELEVEN

MARI HAD MADE DINNER. NOTHING SPECIAL. Pasta with sauce and some salad from the cold box…no, the refrigerator, she reminded herself. She'd set the table. Two plates, one. Two. She stopped herself from counting them out on her fingers. When she caught herself singing under her breath, she stopped herself from that, too. Leon didn't like it when she sang. He said it distracted him.

He enjoyed the food, though. "You're becoming quite the little cook."

His praise, as always, warmed her. She wanted to stretch herself like a barn cat, rub herself beneath his hand. But Leon never touched her. Not since she was small.

He asked her about her studies. What lessons she'd completed. Had she practiced her handwriting? She must get better at cursive. Had she read the book he'd left for her on the desk?

"I tried." Mari pushed pasta around on her plate, her belly full but appetite not sated. Sometimes, she felt like as long as there was food in front of her, she would eat it until it made her sick.

"What do you mean, you tried?" Leon's fork spattered red sauce on his white shirt, which Mari will put in the laundry later to soak so that it doesn't stain. "I expect more from you than trying. You can do better than that. It's not too difficult for you. You're a smart girl."

She has explained in the past, or tried to, that it wasn't that the books he chose for her were too difficult. She could read the words. She could understand the meanings. She simply couldn't understand what they were about.

"*Anne of Green Gables* is a classic," Leon continued. "All girls your age should read it."

Anne of Green Gables was about a girl with red hair who is adopted by a family who really wanted a boy. Mari supposed Leon thought she might be able to identify with the concept of being adopted, and in a way she did. But the rest of it, the talk of clothes and school and friends and love…that, Mari did not comprehend.

She said nothing. She ate her dinner and packed away the leftovers carefully, letting her fingertips dance over the plastic containers stacked in the refrigerator when Leon couldn't see and tell her to keep her hands still. She washed the dishes and put them away, and she remembered not to sing under her breath.

"My son," Leon said from the kitchen doorway. "Ryan. He'll be here in about an hour."

Leon had spoken many times of his son. He'd shown her pictures and video movies of Ryan as a child. Leon had even given her some of Ryan's old things, not like they were hand-me-downs but as though they were precious gifts she should be honored to claim.

In fact, a few of the things he gave her *were* precious to Mari. Not the cast-off football jersey that didn't fit and still smelled slightly of sweat. And not the boxes of plastic bricks she'd never really learned to put together to make something bigger. But the stuffed bunny, fur worn off on the ears and the tail entirely lost—that she loved. That she still slept with next to her at night though at fifteen she had abandoned all her other dolls and stuffed toys. Leon, who hadn't asked her to call him father but encouraged the use of his first name, had given Mari that toy when she was much younger and had nothing left of her life before. Later, there were fancy toys and brand-new dresses, brought by well-meaning people who had no idea of what she held as valuable. But the bunny that once belonged to Ryan was something Mari would forever hold precious and dear.

In the year and a half since she'd been living here, she'd never even known Ryan to call the house. There'd been some trouble with Leon's wife when he decided to give Mari a permanent home. Mari didn't know the whole story, had only caught bits and pieces overheard in shouting conversations on the phone late at night when he thought she was asleep. She knew the doctor's wife didn't want to become a mother to some random, cast-off girl nobody else wanted, and she couldn't say she blamed the former Mrs. Doctor Calder. After all, Mari's own mother hadn't wanted her, either.

It might've been the trouble with Ryan's mother that kept him away, or something simpler. He'd been in college, then med school. He was a grown-up. With a girlfriend, Leon said with a small curl of his lip that told Mari exactly what he thought of *that*. And though Leon had kept many of Ryan's things and felt free enough with them to give them away, he'd also been honest about the fact he wasn't very close with his son.

Mari, Leon often said, was a second chance.

Since Leon Calder was the only father Mari had ever known, he was her only chance.

But now Mari stood in the kitchen, in shadow, watching Ryan come in from the outside. He stamped his feet to get the snow off his boots. Brushed it off his shoulders. It was melting in his blond hair, leaving rivulets of water trickling down his temples and making puddles from the hems of his pants on the floor.

He didn't see her, and she didn't want him to. Mari went quiet; she went still. She was silence. Not a breath, not a sigh, not a blink. And Ryan passed by her little corner of shadow and headed for the living room, calling out for his dad.

She had time to run upstairs and hastily comb through her hair. Put on clean clothes. She didn't have many pretty things. Leon preferred her to dress in something like a uniform. Appropriate clothes, he said, because he wanted nobody to say there was anything inappropriate going on. People already had enough reason to whisper, he said, though he'd never explained exactly what that meant. Mari didn't like the plaid skirt, the white blouse, the saddle shoes and knee socks. She'd rather have the sorts of clothes she'd seen the kids on TV wearing. Jeans and sneakers. Now, though, she wished she had something pretty. Flowy. Something soft, like a princess would wear.

For the first time, she understood why Anne cared about what dress she wore to impress Gilbert Blythe.

When she crept down the stairs again, her heart pounding, Mari saw Ryan in the living room with his dad. They were drinking from glasses filled with Scotch. Ryan didn't look very much like his father, but they both turned at the same time and she saw there was something very much the same in their smiles.

"Ryan," said Leon, "this…is Mari."

"Hey, little sister," Ryan said. "What have you done?"

"Nothing," Mari answered and was confused when Ryan choked with laughter. "What?"

"She doesn't know Billy Idol, Ryan."

"Oh. Right." Ryan nodded like he understood, but the quirk of his smile said he didn't. Not really.

He was the most beautiful man she'd ever seen. He was her

brother, Leon said, but there was nothing brotherly about the way he looked at her.

Mari wanted him like some girls wanted rock stars or movie stars or TV celebrities.

Later, when Leon had gone to bed and Mari was still in the kitchen scrubbing the floor because of the mess Ryan's shoes had made, he found her. "Hey. What are you doing?"

She looked up at him. "Cleaning. I don't like it to be dirty."

"My dad makes you clean like that? Doesn't he have a housekeeper?"

"I don't mind." It had never occurred to her that it was something to be ashamed of, taking care of Leon. After all, he'd taken care of her.

"Pretty girl like you shouldn't be up late scrubbing the floor. You should be out having fun." Ryan's gaze had cut away from her before sneaking back like a dog looking to steal from the table.

The next time he came home with a pink T-shirt with a unicorn covered in sparkles on the front of it. It wasn't a princess dress, but Mari would eventually wear it to shreds. He took her to the movies, which she hated, too dark, too loud, the chemical scent of the popcorn butter distasteful. He took her to a restaurant, and she liked that much better, especially when she got a giant sundae for dessert. Three days he spent at home, three days he spent teasing her into laughter and making her shine.

"You take care, kid," he told her on the day he left and chucked her under the chin.

She watched him walk to the car, her hand raised in a half wave that was the best she could muster, considering the thought of him leaving her so soon was enough to make her want to curl in a ball beneath the blankets and cry.

A day later, he called the house to talk to her. Not to his father, who handed her the phone with a raised eyebrow, but no comment. Mari took the phone curiously, uncertain, but the moment she heard Ryan's voice, everything that had seemed dark became light.

For two years, Ryan was there when she needed someone to talk to, though in truth she often did more listening than speaking. He taught her how to drive. Ryan was there when Leon didn't understand what a young girl needed—pretty clothes, not dowdy uniforms. Trips to the park and the zoo and the mall instead of being kept at home and out of sight. Ryan was the one who told his father that Mari needed to be allowed to wear mascara, get her ears pierced, if she wanted to. To look and act like other girls her age, even if she'd grow up to be a different sort of woman. He was her champion, her advocate.

He was her prince.

And then, Leon died.

She was not surprised when it happened, though it was sudden. One moment he was sitting in front of the meatloaf she'd cooked for dinner, asking her about her studies—she was a month from finishing the homeschooling courses that would give her a GED—and the next he was facedown in the mashed potatoes. A few hours after that, the man who'd given her a life had lost his.

Death was nothing new to her. She'd seen it on the farm with chicks and puppies and kittens, and her grandmother, too. Some part of her had been waiting for Leon to abandon her since the day he'd taken her home. She wept, of course, at the loss. Leon had saved her…but he'd never been her savior, had he? Not really.

She had a prince for that.

The night before Leon's funeral, Ryan came home late. Mari was waiting for him in the living room in front of the fireplace. She didn't know about seduction, but it turned out she didn't have to. She wanted him and now she had him.

Eight months later, they were married.

Beside her sleeping husband, Mari thinks of all this now. How some choices were made for her and some she's made for herself, but that the whole of her life has led her to this man, this house, this space. This life. And it's a good life, full of love and so much more than she'd ever have guessed she could have.

If Ryan says they need to go back, he must have a good reason. And if she trusts him, as she's always done, then she also has to trust that everything will be all right. When he tells her he's taking her home, he has no real idea of what that means to her and never has. She doesn't want him to know. But she trusts Ryan as much as she loves him, and that means Mari will follow him wherever he thinks he needs to go.

Ryan is not the first man to rescue her, but Mari has always believed he would be the last.

TWELVE

IT WOULD'VE BEEN A TOTAL CLICHÉ FOR KEN-
dra to hate her parents for this. They'd taken her away from
her friends, the pool, all the stuff she'd been looking forward
to this summer. Her riding lessons. She'd been planning to
do the adult summer reading program for the first time, and
it was a better one, because the little kids get stuff like coupons for Rita's Italian Water Ice and Subway, but when you
did the grown-up program you got entered for gift certifi-
cates to Amazon.com and places like that. She'd already put
together her reading list, and though her dad had promised
there'd be a library where they were going, Kendra knew it
wouldn't be the same.

She totally should've hated them. Her dad, because it had
been his stupid idea. Her mom for going along with it the way
she always did, not even asking any questions. Not even complaining. It would've been too easy to blame her parents for
ruining her life when all it really meant was she had to spend
a few months in some country town while her parents got
their act together. That wasn't life. That was just the summer.

It could've been worse.

Or maybe not, she thought as her mom at last pulled up
in front of a peeling, white-painted farmhouse with a sag-

ging front porch and windows like dead eyes. This looked
pretty gross. They got out of the car at the same time as her
dad and Ethan got out of his. Dad gave her and Mom a gigantic, toothy grin.

"Well? What do you think?"

"I think it stinks." Ethan put a hand to his nose. "Pee-yew."

"It's a skunk," Mom said in a quiet voice. "That's what
they smell like."

"Smell that, kids? That's a skunk!"

"Dad," Kendra said, "you don't have to sound so excited."

Her dad grabbed her mom's hand. Then he kissed her. Kendra turned away.

Still couldn't hate them.

Across the raggedy field that could hardly be called a yard,
in the woods, something moved. The leaves, mostly green,
turned pale sides up like the wind had ruffled them, but the
weeds and grass were barely moving.

The inside of the car had been cold enough for her to need
a sweatshirt, but out here within seconds her armpits started
sweating. The sun was bright enough that she had to put up
a hand to shield her eyes—monkeybrat had totally wrecked
her favorite sunglasses and she hadn't gotten to the mall to
replace them before Dad packed them up to bring them here.
Kendra blinked against tears she blamed on the sun, even
though maybe it was really because of something else. Her
vision blurred, and she blinked hard to clear it, trying to see
what had caught her eye.

Ethan made a face. "I don't like it here."

"Shut up, monkeybrat."

Ethan sighed heavily and kicked at the dirt under the toe
of his sneakers. "I don't have to."

Kendra looked over her shoulder. Her mom and dad were
still next to the car, their heads bent in conversation. Neither
of them looking this way. "I saw something in the woods."

"Like what?" Ethan looked up. "Dad said we could get a dog."

"You don't want a dog, not really. You'll have to clean up its poop and stuff." Kendra took a few steps away from the car toward the field and the woods beyond it, not really paying attention to her brother.

"Not out here, I won't. He can poop in the yard or in the field. I want to call him Zipper."

At this, she looked at him. "Zipper? Why would you want to name the dog that?"

Ethan shrugged. "I just like it. And you'd like a dog, Kiki. I bet you would, anyway."

Kendra looked again at the car, where her parents were leaning toward each other, faces serious. Her father's mouth moved while her mom stayed as silent as she had for the entire trip. Her dad's hand went out to caress her mom's hair.

It felt sort of creepy to watch them like that, like maybe they might start to make out again or something, so Kendra looked once more at the house. It sat at the end of a really long lane, the trees so close on either side that it had been like driving through a tunnel. Only one other house on the lane, and it had been much closer to the main road. To the side of the driveway was a crumbling sort of garage or barn off to the right, and beyond that the field of tall grass and wildflowers. The trees came right up to the edge of the field, and beyond that, a mountainside littered with scrubby pines.

"I don't like this place," Ethan muttered again, scuffing at the driveway and sending up a small cloud of dust.

"It's only for the summer. Dad said."

He snorted. "Yeah, right. I bet we have to live here forever."

A shiver tickled down her spine at that. Being the new girl in a new school was the sort of thing they made movies about, but something about this place told Kendra she wasn't going to meet some super hot jock who'd totally fall in love with her even though she didn't fit in with the rest of the cool kids. The problem was, at her own school she already was one of the cool kids. At least cool enough. She really didn't want to start over. Not out here in the middle of nowhere.

Nothing moved in the field or in the trees beyond but a couple of birds that took off into the sky. Kendra shaded her eyes again to follow them. Her dad came up behind her to squeeze her shoulders until she pulled away.

"Isn't this great?"

"Mom, are you okay?"

Her mom was also looking toward the woods, and when Kendra spoke to her, it took her a few seconds to turn. "Fine."

She moved closer to Kendra and put an arm around her shoulders. Together they looked across the field, into the trees. Lots of shadows there. Whatever she'd seen moving could still be in there, just hidden.

Something shivered inside her.

THIRTEEN

HERE IS THE HOUSE WHERE EVERYTHING HAP-pened.

This is what Mari thinks as she glides on bare feet over floors that have been covered in unfamiliar carpet, tile, even laminate wood. She seeks out the places she knew best.

The closet beneath the stairs is painted brightly now and not hung with veils of tattered cobwebs. Inside is a bucket, mop, broom, vacuum cleaner. Cleaning supplies hang neatly on pegs and wire shelving.

The space beneath the sink is impossibly tiny. She could fit one leg inside it, maybe. Certainly not her whole body the way she used to. She traces the glimmer of curving silver pipes with her fingertip. This, like the gleaming stainless steel sink above, is new. At least to her.

So much is new. Looking at it is like seeing two photos, one transparent and laid atop the other so that both can be seen but neither clearly. She blinks and blinks again, shaking her head against this feeling. She clutches the sink, her head bent, eyes closed. She listens for the sound of chair legs scraping on worn linoleum and the mutter of voices speaking above and around but never to her. The clatter of the dogs' nails and their soft woofing, begging for scraps or fighting over what fell from the table.

She turns to see the table, also new. She can crouch beneath this one, though it's round with a pedestal center and has no knitted afghan thrown on top of it. It's not a cave, and the cool tile floors hurt her butt and knees when she crawls beneath. Still, Mari draws her knees to her chest and presses her forehead to the bare flesh. She listens.

And this, she knows. She remembers. The creak of an old house settling doesn't change, even if you paint the walls and replace the flooring. Even if you clean it, the memory of all the dirt still remains.

Under the table, Mari draws in breath after breath. No longer small, she's been made tiny again by this place. A little wild.

"Mama?"

"Yeah, honey." She looks up to give her boy a smile.

Ethan crawls under the table with her. "Whatcha doing?"

"When I was a little girl in this house, I used to hide under the kitchen table. I was just remembering it, that's all."

"Oh." Ethan is silent for a moment, his pose mimicking hers. Small knees drawn up to small chest, small chin digging into the tops of them. "Why did you hide?"

Mari opens her mouth to answer, but Kendra has entered the kitchen. She doesn't see them immediately the way Ethan spotted his mother. Together, Mari and Ethan watch Kendra's feet turn in a half circle. She's wearing battered Converse sneakers just like the ones Mari had always wanted but had been denied as a teen, and something tight and tense unwinds a bit in Mari's chest at the sight.

"Mom?"

Ethan clamps a hand over his mouth against a flurry of giggles. Mari knows Kendra will be angry if she looks under the table and sees them. She'll think they're hiding from her. But Mari can't help laughing, either.

"What—" Kendra bends to look under the table. "Oh, God. What are you guys doing? Weirdos!"

"Come in, Kiki, there's room." Mari holds out a hand.

And maybe because it's late and they're in a new place or because Kendra's in a good mood or for some reason Mari can't figure, her daughter takes her hand and crawls beneath the table. There's not enough room under there for all of them, but they scootch in close enough to make it work. Their knees bump. They grip each other's hands and make a circle.

"Mama used to hide under the table when she was a little girl," Ethan explains.

Kendra's eyes are wide and blue. Her father's eyes, though, not Mari's. But they look at Mari with an awareness Ryan hasn't had in a while, if ever. "How come?"

"Oh…" Mari shrugs. "My grandmother had a long old wooden table. A trestle table, I think they call it. With benches along the sides instead of chairs. Instead of tablecloths, she always had it covered with a few afghans she'd knitted herself. Orange, green, yellow."

She can remember the stripes, the zigzag pattern of holes in the yarn that let in the light. If there's one thing she could've taken with her from this house, it might have been one of those blankets.

"Like a fort," Ethan offers.

"Yes. Something like that."

Kendra looks upward, then around this table's center leg at her mother. "But why did you hide?"

There is so much to be said, if only Mari could find the words, but they don't come easily. They never have for her, and here in this house they seem to be slipping from her brain even faster. She doesn't lie to her kids, but they've spent a lifetime not knowing everything there is to know about her.

How can that be changed in a few minutes beneath a kitchen table in the house of her childhood, especially when she's so uncertain of what really happened here, herself?

"Sometimes, people came," Mari manages to say without fumbling. She breathes, remembering how Leon taught her to think the sounds of the words before saying them, so they wouldn't stick in her throat. "My grandmother thought they'd take me away from her if they knew I was there. So, I hid."

Kendra's brow furrows. There are days she looks far older than her age, but now is not one of those times. "Would they have? Taken you from her?"

"Yes."

Before anyone can ask her another question, a heavier tread sounds in the hall outside. They all look and go silent together. Ryan's feet appear in the kitchen. His are bare, his ankles covered by the hems of his favorite pajama bottoms. His feet move toward the fridge, which opens.

Nobody laughs.

They listen as husband and father pulls something from the fridge, a can of cola or maybe a beer by the sound of the crack and hiss. They'd brought only a few supplies with them, but he'd made sure to include a couple six packs of his favorites. Ryan drinks, the sound of his gulping very loud.

Only when he leaves the kitchen do the children let themselves dissolve into giggles. Mari wishes she could join them, but this act of hiding is no longer a comfort and certainly not funny. It is too uncomfortably close to those old days. There's a lot that's gone fuzzy with time, but some memories can never fade. She unfolds herself, legs already stiff and reminding her she is no longer a child.

"C'mon, guys. It's late. You should go to bed." It's a motherly and normal thing to say, even in the summer when there should be no such thing as bedtime.

They don't protest, though. Her darlings. They hug and

kiss her good-night and climb the stairs to the rooms they managed to pick out without squabbling earlier.

After they've gone, Mari looks at the kitchen and tries to see it with new eyes. She blinks and blinks, but beneath the clean and shiny cupboards, the new appliances, the new table, she can see the ghosts of what it was before.

Mari goes upstairs. All of this is new to her. The narrow hall with the bathroom at one end, a doorway with stairs to the attic next to it. Doors line the hall. Three bedrooms and a hall bath with a claw-foot tub and old-fashioned shower. There used to be four bedrooms, but someone, sometime, turned what must've been an excruciatingly small bedroom into a master bath she knows she'll appreciate.

It's all strange to her not just because of that change, but because she never came up here as a child. The door at the bottom of the back stairs into the kitchen had always been locked with a simple hook-and-eye fixture set up way too high for little fingers to reach. And as for the front stairs, the ones leading from the living room with its fireplace and heavy wooden mantel, well...she hadn't been allowed in the living room.

The kitchen had been her place, and the woods outside. The stream and the mountain beyond. But never the front room. Hell, today was only the second time in her life she'd been through the front door and the first had been when she left this house through it.

She pauses in Kendra's doorway. A curved iron bedstead, painted white, has been made up with Kendra's sheets and comforter from home. The dresser, also painted white, is already laden with combs, jewelry, the miscellaneous detritus of a teenage girl's life. Kendra's phone's plugged in to the charger, and Kendra is curled up on the bed with her iPad on her lap. Under much protest and with the assurance that password-protecting it would keep "her stuff" safe, she'd left her desktop computer at home.

"Mom, when will we get the internet?" she says without looking up. Her fingers glide across the touch screen faster than Mari can type on a regular keyboard.

"I don't know. You'll have to ask your dad. He was supposed to take care of all that stuff."

Kendra groans. "Ugh. That means never."

"Kiki." Mari shakes her head, but she can't exactly deny that what her daughter says is probably true.

"And no signal on my phone!"

Mari can't help it. She laughs. "You won't die, Kendra!"

Kendra scowls and sets the tablet aside. "What am I supposed to do without the internet, without my phone?"

"We'll head into town tomorrow, okay? Find the library. Maybe there's a mall."

Kendra gives her a look of such scorn that Mari wishes she'd said nothing.

"Probably not a mall," she amends. "But something. And I'll see if we can't get your dad to work on the internet. Okay? It's going to be fine. Really."

"You really grew up in this house?" Kendra sits up, crossing her legs and plucking absently at the soft fabric of her summer pajamas. When she was a little girl, it had been almost impossible to keep her in clothes. Much the way it had been for Mari herself.

Mari stops herself from crossing to her daughter, hugging and kissing her, holding on to her so tight both of them would lose their breath. "Yes."

Kendra looks around. "Was this your room?"

"No." Mari's tongue sticks and unhinges on a truth that is a lot like a lie. "My room's not here. They changed a lot about this house."

Kendra accepts this without question and settles back against her pillow. "Why did dad bring us here? It's going to suck."

"It's going to be all right. Think of it as..." Mari fights to think of the word she means. "What people do when they have something exciting and different, sometimes they go someplace…"

"An adventure?"

"An adventure," she says, relieved, curling her fingers tight against her palms because they'd been trying to speak for her.

Kendra shakes her head. "Yeah. Right. Here in the middle of nowhere."

"You never know," Mary says and again wants to hold her daughter close.

She settles for a murmured good-night and pulls Kendra's door closed, but her daughter stops her.

"No. Can you…leave it open, just a little?"

Kendra has never been afraid of the dark, not even as a little girl. Ethan's the one who insists on the night-light in the hall, his cracked-open closet door. But now Mari nods and leaves the door open just enough for the hall light to peek inside.

"Thanks, Mom. Love you."

"I love you, too, honey." A small taste of bitterness forces Mari to leave the room without embarrassing her daughter with too much affection.

Ethan, on the other hand, is ready for snuggles and cuddles. He's grown again. His ankles stick out a full two inches below the hem of his pajamas, and his bare feet look impossibly huge. Man-sized, almost, though she knows that's impossible. He's reading when she comes in, but puts the book aside to give her a solemn look.

"Daddy says there are chickens."

"Are there?" Mari's surprised. Ryan hadn't mentioned them, though of course, there were always chickens. A peacock or two. A few goats. A least six dogs and countless mewling, sidling cats.

"He says the lady from down the road will come to take care of them, but I can help. And we can eat the eggs."

Mari doesn't stop herself from reaching to brush away the hair on Ethan's forehead. "That'll be fun. You'll like it. Chickens are fun."

"Did you…" Ethan hesitates. "Did you have chickens when you were a kid?"

"Yes."

"How many?"

"Oh…" She tries to think, but the words for numbers escape her, replaced by the vague idea of "many." More than the fingers on one hand, that was many. "A lot."

"Did you eat the eggs?"

"Yes. The chickens, too, sometimes."

Ethan's eyes go wide. "You did?"

"Sure." She smiles. "Fried chicken. You love it."

"But…your own chickens? How did you do that, Mama?"

Mari settles onto the bed beside him. This room is painted with dark blue walls and a wallpaper border of "folksy" Americana stars and stripes. More white-painted furniture. It's not Ethan's style, but it was the less girly room. She puts her arm around him and he turns toward her to rest his head on her shoulder.

"They weren't pets," Mari says. "And we were hungry."

"I don't want to eat these chickens," Ethan says firmly.

"You won't have to. I promise. Just the eggs, and only if you want to."

He yawns. Their legs are stretched out along each other's, and she notices with another pang that his feet reach to just past her knees. She remembers when his tiny toes barely reached her thighs.

"It's going to be okay here. Right, Mama?"

"Yes, honey."

"Daddy's writing a book, huh?"

"Yes. That's what he says."

Ethan is silent for the span of one breath in, one breath out. "It's not a storybook."

"No."

He looks up at her, that sweet face so much like her own that Mari has to blink and blink again. "But…you're okay?"

"Oh, yes. Don't worry. I'm okay. Your daddy just thought it would be good to get away from the city for a while. Give him some space and quiet to write the book. He thought maybe it would be good for you kids to live in the country for a little while."

"What about you?"

"What about me?"

"Do you think it'll be good for us to live in the country?"

She smiles, able to answer honestly. "Sure. Why not? It'll be different for you, but it should be fun. And it's not forever, remember. It's like a vacation, that's all."

This seems to satisfy him. He yawns again. He doesn't protest when she kisses his forehead or holds him close. His arms go around her, holding her back.

"Night, Mama."

"Night-night, baby. In the morning we'll check out the chickens, okay?"

"Okay." He nods and snuggles down into the nest of his blankets he's made since he didn't really make the bed but simply tossed the sheets and comforter on top.

Tomorrow, she'll help him strip this down to the mattress and fix it, but for now it's late. They're tired. She kisses her boy again, holds him close for a minute or so. Then she says good-night, leaving the door open without being asked.

In the bedroom she and Ryan will share, she finds him already in bed. Surprisingly, Ryan has a notepad and pen, his reading glasses slipped to the end of his nose. He's scribbling furiously, but he looks up when she comes in and sets it aside.

"I'm beat," he says. "How about you?"

"Yes. Pretty tired. Lots to do tomorrow."

He nods, though she knows of course he has no idea what she means or intentions of helping her do any of it. "But this place. Great, huh?"

She sees so clearly in his eyes that he wants her to say yes, but how can she, when she's not sure it would be the truth? "Ryan…"

Before she can continue, her husband says, "Mari…listen."

She listens, silent and still.

He runs his fingers over the hair falling over her shoulder, tangling his fingers in it. "I know this isn't what you would have ever expected. I know this isn't what you dreamed of."

He's wrong about that. Mari has dreamed about coming home. A lot.

"But I want you to know, this is going to be great. I promise. It's going to be all right. I know it must feel strange—"

"No. Not really."

It should be weird to be back here after all this time. After how she's grown and changed. Yet nothing about this house feels strange, and that's somehow both a comfort and a strain. She can't explain it to him, not Ryan, who's lacked for nothing in his life. He thinks deprivation and hardship is being forced to watch the commercials instead of forwarding through them. He would never understand how she feels. She's not even sure how she feels, herself, just that there is something so familiar about coming back here that it's almost as though she never left…and she definitely doesn't want to tell him that.

Ryan looks so relieved, almost like he might cry. "I want you to know how much I love you. You know that, right?"

"I know. I love you, too." She means it, of course. She has loved Ryan from the first time she saw him. A prince, come to rescue her.

"This is going to be good for us, Mari. I promise you."

Ryan has broken promises to her before. Mari nods and

kisses him. Long and slow. She can feel him reacting, though in truth she's not sure if she intends to make love to him or if she's simply seeking the comfort of his mouth.

They make love.

After, Ryan turns out the lights. Beside him, eyes wide-open to the dark, Mari listens to the sound of his slow breathing. "Ryan."

He mutters something that he probably thinks is a full reply.

"How did you find this place? How did you arrange for this?"

He snuffles. She thinks he might be too fast asleep to answer her, but he's only taking his time. "What do you mean?"

"This house," she says. "How did you find it? How did you arrange to rent it for the summer? What happened to the people who were living here before?"

"Oh. That. That was easy, babe, don't you know?" He chuckles sleepily. "No, I guess maybe you didn't think about it. I had the management company take it off the rental sites. The house came furnished. Not the greatest, but it's only for a few months."

"You gave the…?" Mari sits. "I don't understand."

"Babe, this house," her husband says and interrupts himself with half a snore. "My dad was renting it out and when he died, I just kept up the agreement with the listing agency. It's yours. It still belongs to you."

The bed shifts and rocks as he turns on his side. Silence. He's asleep.

Mari blinks. Blinks. Blinks. The sudden, raw and unusual sting of tears forces her to get out of bed and stumble to the bathroom, where she splashes her face with water over and over until she fears she'll either drown or get washed away down the drain. She stares at her face in the mirror until she recognizes it. It takes a long time.

"Would they have taken you away?" Kendra had asked, and Mari had answered yes.

Yes, someone had come and taken her away. Someone had found her hiding beneath the kitchen table and pulled her out, kicking and screaming and clawing, desperate to get away. Someone had stolen and rescued her at the same time.

And now Ryan's brought her back.

FOURTEEN

KENDRA COULDN'T SLEEP.

At home, her dad made them all close their windows in the summer to keep the air-conditioning inside. This house didn't have air-conditioning, which meant open windows. Which meant she was like, sweltering. Even kicking off the blankets didn't help.

She turned on her side to stare at the two windows overlooking the backyard. The night was too dark out here. No street lamps, nothing. She knew the mountain rose behind the house and all she'd see was trees even if there was light, but trees would be better than the huge, blank void outside the glass.

She just wasn't used to this, that was all. Everything was too dark and too quiet. It was all too new, and not in the exciting way like the night before Christmas or a vacation or the first day of school. She yawned, eyes heavy, but sleep just kicked her in the teeth and ran away.

She heard something outside.

Something like a crunch, crunch, crunch. The shuffling noise of feet in leaves or grass. The snap of a twig.

Kendra sat up straight in bed, heart pounding, ears straining toward the open window. Instead of being too hot, now she was too cold. The sweat trickling down her back was like ice.

This room was so small that her bed was within reach of the windows, but she totally didn't want to get any closer. Not even to see. Kendra put her fingertips on the windowsill and pushed her face under the wooden frame, anyway, not quite close enough to press her nose against the screen. She blinked and could see nothing but darkness. But then…there. No, higher. A flash of light. Two flashes. Not like lightning. More like what it looked like when you shone a flashlight in a cat's eyes in a dark room, there and gone so fast she thought she might've imagined it.

The shadows moved. The shuffling sound grew louder. Kendra held her breath, listening and staring, but if something detached itself from the trees and moved across the yard toward the house, she couldn't see what it was. She could hear it, though.

Across the room from her, the wink of light from her dresser mirror caught her attention. She bit back the urge to say *Bloody Mary* three times, calling forth the spectral girl from that slumber party game they'd all played in elementary school. There was nothing there, Kendra told herself. Nothing.

Something screamed.

Kendra stumbled back from the window, hit her bed with the backs of her knees and fell onto it. She clapped her hands over her mouth to hold back her own scream. She wanted to yell for her mom and dad, but all she could do was listen for more screams. What was out there?

The noise didn't come again, not for a long ten minutes or so. Kendra relaxed. There was nothing out there in the night screaming. Whatever she'd heard wasn't a monster or anything like that. Monsters didn't exist. If she went and told her parents she was scared of something she'd heard outside, they'd just laugh and tell her she'd been dreaming. Or maybe they'd go out to see what it was and end up getting killed and eaten by some backwoods freakazoid hillbilly monster that had flashing eyes and screamed like a woman.

Kendra put her head under the pillow, but it took her a really long time to fall asleep.

FIFTEEN

IN THE MORNING, THERE WAS BREAKFAST. COF-
fee, brewed just right. Toast and eggs that Ethan was excited
to tell Ryan came from the chickens scratching in the yard
behind the barn. Scrambled, mixed with cheese and bacon,
the way Ryan always liked them. His dad had liked them that
way, too.

"This is great." He filled his mug with sugar and cream,
sipping it.

She looked at him over the rim of her mug. She sipped,
watching him. "What are you up to today?"

Ryan cracked his knuckles and rubbed his palms together.
"Unpacking the boxes of files. Setting up my office. Shouldn't
take long."

He'd taken the small den off the kitchen. It had been a
screened porch a long time ago. Now the screens had been replaced with glass, turning it into a three-season room. It would
be too cold to work out there in the winter, but on the shady
side of the house with a ceiling fan going, it would be fine
even in the summer heat. In pictures of the time when Mari
lived there, towering cardboard boxes had overflowed with
magazines and newspapers. New stacks of boxes now filled it,
but he'd be unpacking them later today and organizing all of

it. Anticipation made him a little giddy as he grinned across the table at his wife.

Impulsively, he leaned to kiss her. "Thank you."

"For what?"

"Being you."

Mari smiled. "I don't have much choice, do I? I am me."

"No. But you're awesome, you know it?" Screw his psychiatric career, Mari was going to help Ryan exceed anything he'd done in the past.

Hell, anything his old man had done, too.

"Am I?" She tilted her head in that curious way she had.

"Yes. You are." Ryan got up, leaving his plate on the table but taking his mug to refill it from the coffeemaker on the counter. He leaned on the counter to look at her as he drank with an appreciative smacking of lips. "You make kick-ass coffee, you know that?"

"Learned from the best, I guess."

She meant his dad. "Do you ever miss him?"

Mari looked faintly surprised. "Don't you?"

Ryan didn't, really, in anything other than the vaguest of ways. He'd loved his dad. Idolized him, to a certain extent. But they hadn't been close. He shrugged.

"Sure, sometimes I think about how I'd like him to see what I'm doing with my life. See the kids. That sort of thing."

"People die," Mari said quietly with a shrug. "Everything dies."

She had such a way of putting it all into perspective. Ryan kissed her temple. "Yeah. I know. Listen, I'm going to get to work. Lots of paperwork to sort through. What are you going to do?"

"Unpack, I guess. Run some laundry. I can hang it up on the line," she added, sounding pleased. "The smell of sunshine on sheets."

"Great, great." Ryan was already far away, looking through

the kitchen into the screened porch. "Hey, babe, is the 'net hooked up?"

"I thought you were going to take care of it. Kendra said last night it wasn't working."

"Right." Ryan frowned, then shook it off. "You know what? Let's go off the grid this summer." He grinned, excited at the thought, and kissed her again. "It'll be good for us. Get disconnected. Really just get back to nature."

"Are you sure? The kids—"

"They'll survive." Ryan squeezed her. "I'm gonna get to work."

There was a door he could lock between the kitchen and the den, and one from the den into the backyard, which meant at any point during the day that he needed a break he could slip out onto the soft grass and the hammock strung between two trees. But not now. Right now, Ryan was going to get busy.

Putting his mug down on the long, battered wooden table set up beneath the row of windows, he found his laptop case. He pulled out the computer and settled it into place. The wireless mouse, next. He'd brought his computer chair from home, so he'd be sure to have a comfortable place to sit, and for a moment, that was all he did.

From the kitchen, muffled through the closed door, he heard the murmur of his wife talking to someone. Probably Ethan. Ryan closed his eyes and imagined what it had been like all those years ago, when Mari had been in this house, not speaking at all.

What had it been like for her?

He was going to find out. For a moment, listening to the lilt of her voice, the soft, low chuckle he always admired, Ryan thought about packing them all up and taking them back home. Abandoning this project before it had begun. Before it could change things, he thought, opening his eyes and watching his wife's shadow move under the crack at the bottom of the door.

But things had already changed, hadn't they? And they would keep changing, because that was the way the world worked, and if he didn't change with them, he was going to let his family down.

Ryan looked around the room at the stacks of file boxes, each neatly labeled in his dad's hand. *Files. Recordings. Research Materials. Video.* In one corner, an ancient and gigantic television sat on a spindly legged table that didn't seem strong enough to hold it. Also, a VCR and DVD player, along with a tangle of cords and cables. That's where he'd start, but for the moment Ryan just sipped his coffee and looked around at the mess that was going to make his future.

He wasn't going to let anyone down.

SIXTEEN

NOT EVERYTHING IN THIS KITCHEN IS NEW. THE cupboards under the counter are still lined with paper covered in orange-and-green flowers. They're faded and dirty, in some places scraped by the pressure of pots and pans. The house included kitchenware. Mari's not sure what sorts of meals she'll prepare in these unfamiliar pots and pans and serve on strange dishes, but she's sure they'll be better than half-warmed franks 'n' beans or boxed macaroni and cheese made with water, not milk and butter. Much, much better than dog biscuits. But not, she thinks with half a smile, better than a chocolate snack cake.

She bought a box this morning and wants to find a place to hide it…just in case. Not up high where she'll have to stretch for it. Someplace low. Tucked away. A place where nobody would think to look for it.

Not that any of them would. She bought plenty of snacks. Fruit and crackers and cheese sticks for Kendra, gummy dinosaurs for Ethan and a package of Snickers bars for Ryan to keep in the freezer. She didn't even really buy the snack cakes for her to eat.

Just to have.

Bending, she pushes aside some cookware to shove the box

back into the shadows of the cupboard. Her fingers brush against something; she recoils by instinct, but it's nothing nasty like a spider or even a dead mouse or rat—she's seen plenty of them in her time. Mari pulls out a crinkling package. Yellow cake inside. Her mouth squirts saliva at the memory of the taste of spongy cake and thick, sweet cream made without a hint of anything dairy.

She rocks on her heels, the package in her hands. It's been in that cupboard for a long, long time, undisturbed. No sign of mold or rot, though the cake itself has shrunk. Dehydrated. If she opened the plastic, maybe it would crumble into dust right there. She bets eating it would make her vomit...but it would still be sweet.

The normal thing to do would be to toss this remnant in the garbage and forget she ever saw it just as she'd forgotten hiding it there in the first place. It's no good to her now. She doesn't have to eat it and couldn't if she wanted to.

"Here. Eat this. It's good. It's called a treat." He pressed it into her hand.

Mari sniffed it. Took a lick. Then a bite. Then shoved it into her mouth, three bites, it was gone. It was good. She made a pattern in the air with her fingers.

More?

"One's enough." His hand stroked the tangles of her hair. "More will make you sick. Where's the comb?"

Her hair was soft and smooth when he finished, and Mari couldn't stop touching it. With clean, soft hair, she felt...

Pretty.

"Yes," he said, watching her hands move. "Very pretty."

More?

He laughed and shook his head. "It's called a treat because it's special. If you have one all the time, it won't be so good."

From inside the house came the sound of Gran's mumbletalk shouting. He looked at Mari. "Don't tell her."

Mad, Mari said.

"She won't be mad. But she'll want them for herself." He tucked the box away into his backpack and stood. He ran a hand over her hair. "Be good, Mariposa."

Be good.

"Babe?"

Startled, shamed, Mari shoves the box of new snack cakes and the old one back into place in the far, far back corner of the cupboard. She gets to her feet, brushing off her hands. "Ryan. What's up?"

"What are you doing?"

"Putting away some things. Thinking about what to make for lunch." Mari clears her throat and crosses the floor—tile now, not worn linoleum. It feels cool and slick on her feet, though beneath it she still senses the slope of the boards. She kisses him. "How about some chicken and biscuits?"

"You're gonna make me fat." He grins and snuggles against her.

"Hush," she murmurs. "You're not going to be fat. You care too much to get fat."

That came out strange, but Ryan doesn't seem to notice. He's too busy dancing with her in the kitchen. Twirling her out, then back. Dipping her. Mari can't help laughing at this—Ryan's not the best dancer, not that she is. It doesn't matter. Dancing with her husband is fun. She links her arms behind his neck as the dance slows. They move in a small circle, their toes touching.

"I love you," she says. It's important to say it. For him to hear it.

Here in this kitchen, Mari needs to be this woman. A wife and mother. Someone loved and who loves in return.

"Love you, too, babe." Ryan kisses her, his attention already being pulled back to the boxes of papers he's got stacked so high in that den. "What time's lunch?"

"Soon."

He grins and twirls her again. Another dip. Another kiss. Then he's back in the den, and she can hear the sound of his whistling. Of her husband being happy.

Well, Mari can be happy, too. She can be more than that. She can be good.

SEVENTEEN

"DON'T CHASE THEM, IDIOT." KENDRA TAPPED the keys of her phone to send a text to Sammy as she watched Ethan run after a squawking chicken. "God."

Sammy hadn't answered the last couple texts Kendra had sent, but since Kendra was only getting two or sometimes three bars of signal, that wasn't a surprise. Dad said that they didn't need the internet, that they should use this time to do other things and to not be distracted, which was totally unfair since it wasn't Kendra's fault he couldn't be self-disciplined enough not to go online when he was supposed to be working.

He was writing a book, he said, and that didn't make any sense. Her dad was a doctor, not a writer. When Kendra was in seventh grade and had the worst English teacher ever, she'd tried to get help from him, but he'd totally messed her up. Her mom had been the one to figure out how to diagram a sentence, working hard with Kendra at the kitchen table, going back and forth from the textbook to the paper, struggling until finally, she'd cried out, "I get it!" And had been able to show Kendra how to do it. Now her dad was writing a book?

"What a joke," she muttered.

"I'm not joking. Or chasing them!" Ethan made a face at her. "I just want to pet one."

"They're not pets, monkeybrat."

"That's what Mama said," he mumbled.

Kendra looked at her phone again, hoping for an answer from at least one of her friends. Nothing. She shoved it into her pocket.

The barn was run-down but pretty cool. It was mostly empty inside. Part of it had been converted into a garage. Part into a chicken house with a small doorway for the chickens to get in and out. The other stalls were too small for horses or cows. Goats, maybe. Around the back was a tall box of small cages stacked on top of each other, also empty. It looked as though it had once had pigeons or something in it. Outside behind the barn, closer to the field, was a high, round cage made of wire like something you'd see in a zoo. Inside was a doghouse, but it didn't look like the sort of cage you'd use for a dog. A monkey, maybe.

Or a person.

The chickens were cool, too. Red ones, white ones, a few speckled ones with fluffy feet and heads. That was the sort Ethan was trying to catch, and Kendra had to admit, they did look soft and fun to pet. But they were all wild, running around and dodging his grasp. It was funny to watch.

"Ain't the way to catch 'em."

Kendra and Ethan both turned at the sound of an unfamiliar voice as an old woman shuffled around the edge of the barn. She wore a brightly colored muumuu, rubber boots and a baseball cap with a picture of a tractor on it. She waved at Ethan, who moved at once to Kendra's side. Kendra put her arm around him, knowing it was stupid to be afraid of an old woman, even if she did show up all of a sudden out of nowhere.

"I'm Rosie, from down the lane. Heard we was getting some new folks." She had a funny accent. "Dawn the lane," it sounded like. She grinned, showing straight teeth way too white and big for her face. White hair floated from under the ball cap, some of it tied behind her but most of it loose. She jerked a thumb toward the driveway. "I look after the chickens. Used to take care of the squabs, too, and the peafowl, but they're long gone now."

"Is that what was in that big cage?" Kendra pointed.

Rosie nodded. "Yep, yep. A hen and a cock. Victor and Victoria was their names."

Ethan giggled when the old lady said cock, though Kendra was pretty sure he wasn't supposed to even know that was a dirty word. "Peacocks!"

"Yep, yep." Rosie shuffled forward.

"What happened to them?" Ethan asked.

"Oh…they runned off. Victor and Victoria are probably dead by now. But I think they had some chicks or something. At any rate, I find their feathers sometimes, so…" Rosie shrugged.

"So they are around?" Ethan bounced. "Can we see them? That would be really cool!"

"Maybe they're out there in the woods, though if they can live on their own out there without getting et up by a fox or coyote or somethin' they can surely hide from you."

"Coyotes?" Kendra's lip curled. "I didn't know there were coyotes in Pennsylvania."

"Yep, yep, sure there are." Rosie laughed. "But don't you worry 'bout that. These chickens here, now, they'll squawk and kick up a ruckus if so much as a possum comes rustling around, and coyotes mostly keep to themselves up on the mountain. They come down once in a while to get into your garbage, but so will a bear if you don't keep it locked up. Raccoons, too. All kinds of things have a mind to get into your trash."

"Bears?" Ethan looked up at Kendra. "Kiki, for real?"

Surely the old lady had to be exaggerating, but she didn't look like she was. Kendra shrugged. "I dunno, kid."

Rosie studied him. "Tell you what, little man. Why don't you help me feed these chickens, and I bet we can catch ourselves one of those pretty ones for you to pet, if you want. And I'll show you how to collect the eggs. How about that?"

Ethan looked up at Kendra, already one step away from her but his expression questioning. Something panged inside her. She remembered the monkeybrat being born, how it had been to hold him as a baby. Sure, he was a booger and did all kinds of boy stuff she didn't like, and sometimes she wished he'd been a sister and other times she was glad he was a boy so that she could still have her mom to herself for girl things, even if she did believe her mother preferred Ethan to her. But mostly, she liked her little brother, and when he looked at her like that, she was reminded how responsible it felt to be the older sister. To make sure he was okay.

"That sounds like fun, Ethan. But maybe we should ask Mom first." Kendra nodded encouragement with a quick glance over her shoulder toward the house. They'd had it drilled into their heads too many times—never, ever go with a stranger. Not a policeman, not a fireman, not someone who said they were a teacher or who said they'd come to pick you up from school because your parents had been in an accident.

Their mom was coming out the front door, anyway. She was wiping her hands on a dish towel and had pulled her hair up into a messy bun on top of her head. She must've been cleaning. Or maybe putting away the fifty zillion bags of groceries she'd bought that morning. At home, Kendra was often a little embarrassed by her mom's pack-rat habits but somehow knowing that hadn't changed despite the move made living here a little more...familiar.

"Hi, can I help you?"

"She's Rosie, from down the lane," Ethan said. "She's here to take care of the chickens."

"And youse, if you need it," Rosie added. "I do the cleaning and whatnot for you short-term folks. Though you're scheduled to be here for more than a week or so, ain't?"

Mom blinked, giving Rosie one of those blank looks that so often embarrassed Kendra. "Yes. For the summer. But we don't need someone to clean for us."

Rosie's eyebrows rose. "No? It's included. I come in weekly, replace the linens, give the place a scrubbing."

"My husband didn't say anything about it." Mom wiped her hands on the dishcloth, giving a quick glance at the house over her shoulder. "We can handle it, I think. Thank you, though."

Kendra wouldn't have minded someone coming in to clean, if it meant she wouldn't have to do it. Lots of her friends had cleaning ladies, but her mom never had.

"If you change your mind, I guess you'll know how to find me," Rosie said with a sniff that said Mom had insulted her. Her teeth jutted out of her mouth before she sucked them back in. "Been taking care of these chickens for all the renters for a long time. Told your boy here he could help me out. Seems he's taken a liking to the chickens."

Ethan gave Kendra a wide-eyed stare and pressed his lips together against a laugh. Kendra wrinkled her nose and nudged him with her hip. Their mom moved toward Rosie.

"I'd like to help with the chickens. C'mon, honey." Mom held out her hand to Ethan, then looked at Kendra. "Kiki, love? Coming?"

Kendra rolled her eyes. "Um. How about, no?"

Mom laughed. "Okay for you. What are you going to do?"

Kendra slipped her phone from her pocket. No new messages. She waved it. "I thought I'd go for a walk, if that's okay. Try to find a better signal, maybe."

Rosie clucked again. "Oh, girlie. Be careful in those woods."

"Should I be worried about bears and coyotes?" Kendra asked, just to see what her mom would say.

Rosie got a strange look on her face and stared toward the woods. "Maybe. Maybe something else."

Kendra thought about whatever she'd seen moving in the woods yesterday. About the scream she'd heard the night they moved in. It hadn't been a coyote. Not a bear, either. "Like what?"

"Yes," Mom said. "Like what?"

"Oh…nothing." Rosie shook her head and laughed. "Nothing. Just stories."

"Scary stories?" Ethan asked.

"If they are," Mom said, "we don't need to hear them."

"No, no, I guess not." Rosie looked again toward the woods, then shrugged. "How about them chickens, huh? C'mon, fella. Let's go catch us one."

Ethan set off after the woman, but her mother snagged Kendra's wrist. "Kiki. Be careful in the woods. Don't go far. In fact—"

"Mom. I'll be fine. Seriously." Even if she was a little worried, a little anxious, it was the very last thing in the world Kendra would admit to.

Her mom looked back and forth to Ethan, then Kendra, and just as Kendra expected, her mom picked Ethan. "Fine. But be back before lunch. I don't want to have to come look for you."

"Got it." Kendra was two steps away before her mom stopped her by snagging the hem of her shirt. "What?"

"Be careful, Kiki. Promise."

"I promise, Mom. God."

This time, she danced out of her mother's grasp before she could grab her again. Kendra crossed the yard toward the back of the house, passing the porch. She waved at her dad through

the glass, but he was busy sorting through boxes and didn't
see her. The grass back here was long and tickled her shins.
Grasshoppers hummed and hopped, freaking her out a little
bit until she stopped to look at one on a long blade of grass
just at the edge of the yard. She took it on her finger, where
it promptly spit on her and she let out a low cry of disgust before flicking it away, then quickly looked around to be sure
nobody saw her.

Not that there was anyone to see her, she reminded herself.
This place was what Sammy liked to call B.F.E.—BumFuck,
Egypt. It always made Kendra laugh when Sammy said that.
It didn't feel so funny, now.

Here, the woods nudged up against the yard instead of having the length of the empty field between them and the barn.
Kendra paused to look over her shoulder at the house, at her
dad through the windows. He was only a shadow. The trees
reached tickling fingers toward her as she pushed through
them and into the woods.

She moved deeper into the trees where it was instantly
cooler and somehow quieter, something she wouldn't have
thought possible considering how everything here was so
much quieter than at home. She heard the soft tweet of birds
and the crunch of her flip-flops on the thick carpet of brown
pine needles and dead leaves, but that was it.

A small stream lined with soft grass edged its way through
the trees. There were enough rounded rocks sticking out that
it wouldn't be hard at all for her to hop across them, but Kendra carefully tucked her phone into her pocket and slipped
off her flip-flops to dip her toes into the water. It was cold,
the bottom thick with mud that made her curl her lip. Ethan
would love this. He'd probably fall in and get soaked, though.

Kendra stopped to sit on one of the bigger rocks and dan-
gle her feet in the water. The trees were thin here, and the

sun shone through, making it hot so the cold water felt extra nice on her feet. Her phone was a lump in her pocket, but she was just lazy enough right then not to bother to check it. She tipped her face up to the sky, closing her eyes against the glare and seeing only red.

It was easier today than it had been yesterday to be annoyed with her parents for bringing her here, wasting her summer. Still, she couldn't quite hate them. If what Sammy had said was true, whatever her dad had done was pretty bad. Stuff like that got around.

A twig snapped.

Kendra opened her eyes, heart pounding, already getting to her feet and almost falling into the water the way she'd thought Ethan would fall, given half a chance. Though she'd had her eyes closed, all she could see now was still the red haze spattered with gold from staring up at the sky. She blinked rapidly, hands out to catch her balance as her feet slipped on the now-wet rock.

Visions of bears and coyotes made her see a large, looming shadow on the other side of the stream before her vision cleared enough for her to see it as nothing but the wind pushing the trees. She drew in a breath, heart pounding.

"Stupid."

Something glinted through the trees on the creek's other side. Then again. Like the gleam of sun on a mirror, flash, flash. Kendra looked again, but saw nothing.

"Hello?"

She was halfway there before she thought about Rosie's sideways mention of a scary story, something that wasn't a bear or a coyote. Of the flash of light she'd seen from her window. Whatever it was, it wasn't an animal. Something was there in the woods just beyond.

In her pocket, her phone vibrated. She pulled it out of her shorts. Two bars. Crap. Still, it was an answer from Logan.

:)

Kendra frowned. Like things weren't weird enough since she'd found out about him and Sammy? Not that she'd said anything to him about it, but she figured Sammy had. They'd barely talked until she told him she'd be gone all summer, and then he'd made her promise to keep in touch. Since they got here, she'd sent him at least three texts talking about this new house, how much it sucked that she was going to miss the whole summer at the pool and stuff. And that was what he replied? What an ass.

She kicked at the leaves before realizing that wasn't the smartest thing to do in flip-flops. As she thought about whether to tap out a reply or ignore him, the signal bars went from two to three.

"Yes!"

Kendra took two steps forward. Three bars. Then another two, and briefly, four bars showed up before slipping back to three. There was no path here in the woods, but the trees were far enough apart that it wasn't hard to pick a way through them. Kendra followed the idea that somehow, someway, she'd get full signal strength for her phone, maybe enough to even make a freaking call instead of relying on texts to get in touch with her friends. If any of them bothered to answer when she called.

Whatever it was, it was farther away than it looked. Or else it was moving. Because every time she got close to where she was sure she'd last seen it, there was nothing but trees and leaves, swishing in the breeze. Until at last she'd gone much farther than she knew her mother would've wanted, up the mountain and deeper into the woods.

Flip-flops weren't the best shoes for this climb, but she was at least rewarded with a five-bar signal on her phone and a flurry of trills and vibrations from all the texts that came flooding in. Even the chime letting her know she had a couple voice mails.

But that wasn't really the most exciting thing.

She'd found a peacock feather. Bedraggled, but still brilliant. Kendra plucked it from where it had snagged in a low, scrubby bush. Something screeched just as her phone vibrated and rang in her pocket.

Kendra screamed in a breathless, wheezy gasp, and pulled the phone from her pocket. She dropped it into the dirt and let out a string of muttered curses as she jumped to snatch it up, the feather still clutched in her other hand. "Hello?"

"Kiki, where are you?"

"Mom." Kendra laughed and swiped at her forehead. It was hot here in the clearing, because even though the trees moved in a breeze, she couldn't feel it. She listened hard for that strange screeching again, turning in a nervous circle as she tried to keep everything in sight all at the same time.

"It's going to rain. Where are you? It's almost lunchtime."

"Sh…oot," Kendra amended, though her mom really didn't care if she swore. Her dad did, though. "I guess I lost track of time. Sorry."

"Where are you?" her mom repeated. Now she sounded angry, or at least upset.

Not good. "I hiked up the mountain a ways. I'm okay." Kendra opened her mouth to tell her mom about the screaming, but when she looked at the phone and saw five bars, full strength, something stopped her. If this was the only place where she could get full strength, she wasn't going to give it up.

"Come home. Now."

"Okay, okay, jeez." Kendra clamped the phone to her ear

and started picking her way through the rocks in the clearing, pausing to look at the bush where she'd found the feather.

"Kiki, I mean it. Come home!"

"I'm coming, Mom, God!" Even just a few feet away in the trees, her signal was down to four bars. Three. "I'm coming home right now. But my phone's going to lose the signal."

"Kiki —"

But Kendra had already disconnected the call. She'd just say she lost the signal if her mom complained. She left the clearing, busy tapping at the keys of her phone to get in as many text replies as she could before the signal died, and by the time she looked up, she was back at the stream.

EIGHTEEN

THE PICTURE ON THE TV WAS GRAINY. NOT OUT of focus, just aged and filmed on equipment that had been the most up-to-date for its time but couldn't compare to current HD technology or even the clarity of film transferred to DVD. Ryan remembered his father's video camera as a huge thing, held on one shoulder much like the cameras used by television news teams. There had been a hanging mic, separate from the camera, to capture additional sound. Add to that the fact the videotapes had been sitting in unprotected storage for years, and no wonder the colors were faded and fuzzy, the sound a little muted.

The only noise on the video now was the click of wood on wood. The small girl in the video had been set to the task of putting wooden shapes—circle, square, rectangle—into appropriately matched holes in a board. Painted in bright, primary colors, the puzzle was probably fit for a child of eighteen months. This girl was the size of a five-year-old, but Ryan knew her real age was eight years, four months. Though eventually she'd developed normally, extreme malnutrition and deprivation had caused her to suffer from Kaspar Hauser syndrome, or psychosocial dwarfism.

The little girl in the video was his wife as a child.

He'd set up his laptop so he could tap away at notes as he watched, but he also held a notepad and his favorite Montblanc pen on his lap so he could scribble down his thoughts. Both the computer and the paper were ignored. He'd been through three of these videotapes so far and had only been able to watch, stunned, without taking any notes at all.

By the time Ryan's father had adopted Mariposa Pfautz and brought her home, Ryan had already been out of the house for several years. Off to med school. Deciding if he wanted to follow in his dad's footsteps or maybe do something different. Internal medicine, maybe. Or even pediatrics.

Ryan had known, of course, about his dad's work. In those pre-internet days, Dr. Leon Calder's success with the "Pine Grove Pixie" had been written up in medical journals and used in textbooks. His dad had taken these countless hours of notes and filmed all of this video. He'd spent a great portion of his life studying the girl he'd later adopted as his own daughter. It had destroyed his marriage and hadn't been too good for his relationship with his son, either.

And all along, Ryan had thought he'd known everything about what had happened simply because he'd overheard bits and pieces or had read a few of his dad's articles.

Watching her in these ancient videotapes, there was no mistaking who she was. Ryan saw echoes of Kendra and Ethan in that little girl. The tilt of her head was purely Mari, but the sound of her giggle when she fit a piece into the right place was so much like his daughter's as a small child that Ryan's heart twisted. The young Mari's furrowed brow of concentration was the same as Ethan's when he was working on a Lego model.

Ryan, as it turned out, had known nothing.

On the video, young Mari managed to get the pieces into the puzzle after a few false tries. She looked beyond the camera to whoever was watching—was it his dad? She rubbed her stomach, then touched her mouth. Then again. A third time, looking stubborn and angry.

"Are you hungry, Mariposa?"

That set of motions again.

Ryan paused the video and reached for one of the files with the earliest dates. He flipped through the pages, some browned with age at the edges. "Patient appears to understand language, though vocabulary is extremely limited. With no physical reason for her inability to speak, it's nevertheless clear the patient has adapted a series of signs to indicate simple communication. Hunger, cold, fear and, most surprisingly, compassionate responses are all indicated by hand motions occasionally accompanied by grunts, growls and even barks. It's unlikely, based on initial observations, that the patient will ever be able to communicate normally."

Ryan rubbed at his face, letting his hand cover his eyes for a minute or so. Elsewhere in the house, he heard the faint sound of raised voices as his wife called to their children. No hand motions and grunts there. She *had* learned to speak.

"Jesus," he muttered. "Jesus Christ."

How had he not understood this? How had he thought that his wife's story was in any way similar to those he'd read in med school or during his psychiatric residency? How could he have thought she'd survived something as simple as poverty, abuse and neglect?

He unpaused the video.

"Mariposa? Are you hungry?"

Young Mari made the same motions, a moue of frustration on her small mouth. She added what sounded suspiciously like a growl. Through the TV's small and inadequate speakers came the sound of rustling paper and the murmur of voices. Mari pounded her hand on the table, making the puzzle pieces jump.

Ryan's dad came into the frame. God, he looked so young Ryan had to pause the video again. His dad had died too soon, no question. When this video had been made, he'd been just about the same age as Ryan was now. It was creepy, not just watching the juxtaposition of his children over his wife's childish face, but seeing a reflection of himself in the image of his dad.

His finger pressed the remote again. His dad moved toward Mari, who erupted into a whirlwind of screams and grunts. She pushed away, dumping her chair and scattering the puzzle pieces. She dove beneath the table.

His dad looked at the camera and whoever was in the room with him. He made a "hold on" gesture with his hand, then squatted beside the table. The camera moved, though whoever had set up the tripod hadn't meant for the angle to accommodate a view of under the table. His dad was still in focus, but only a small piece of Mari's dress stuck out.

"Mariposa, it's all right. We're not going to hurt you. It's me, Dr. Calder. Remember? I gave you the soft dolly you like to take to bed with you at night. And I have something for you today, too." He pulled something from the pocket of his sweater. "Look what I have for Mari."

A small hand reached from under the table, but Ryan's dad inched it back. "Ah, ah. If you want it, you have to come out from under the table."

And so it went, like teasing a scared dog from its den. Ryan watched his dad tempt out the small girl from her hiding place with the promise of a treat. His dad looked at the camera, triumphant, when Mari stood in front of him, tearing open the plastic on a chocolate snack cake. She flinched and muttered when he put a hand on her shoulder, but she didn't immediately run away. It must have been some kind of triumph, Ryan thought, watching his father. He couldn't even imagine.

"Ryan?"

Quickly, he clicked off the TV and swiveled in his desk chair toward the doorway. He'd have to make sure to keep the door locked. Now that he knew the contents of those tapes, he couldn't risk Mari or the kids stumbling in on him while he was watching. It would be worse than catching him watching porn.

"Yeah, babe?"

"I'm taking the kids to the library. Want to come?"

"I'm working."

His wife looked over the room, then settled her gaze on him. "You could take a break."

Even if he could, why would he want to? He wasn't here for a vacation. He was here to work.

But he didn't let any annoyance filter into his voice. "I wish I could. But you guys go. Have a good time."

"Okay." Mari in the doorway was nothing like the little girl in the video. She spoke in words, not gestures. Mari now, not Mari then. "We'll be back in a few hours."

"Have fun."

She nodded and turned, then glanced at him over her shoulder. "How's the work going?"

"Great." The enthusiasm burst out of him, unfeigned. A wide and somehow hot grin spread his mouth wide. "Really great."

Mari blinked. He watched her, noting the tilt of her head. The way she stood still, then moved. Damn it, the work...this was work, here. This was history unfolding in front of him.

"Okay," she said. "Good. See you later."

Sweat burst into his armpits, along his lip, in the small of his back. Heat that had nothing to do with the sun shining through the glass or the fan lazily circulating sun-warmed air in this small room weighted him like a quilt. Ryan grinned hard at his wife's back as she left him, then turned again to face the TV. He looked at the computer, at his empty notepad.

There was so much more to this than he'd even thought. A book about his father's work had seemed like a natural place to start. Focusing on his dad's most famously successful case of young Mariposa Pfautz, a no-brainer. Bringing them back here had seemed financially wise, not to mention that, yes, of course he'd hoped that by returning her to the place where she'd grown up, his wife could shed some necessary light onto what had happened to her. Flesh out his book with current reactions, fill in the blanks of what it had been like.

But this…seeing what he'd seen, putting it together with what he knew of her now…

Forget his career, forget going back to the drudgery of dealing with bored, rich anorexics with Electra complexes and dull, neurotic accountants suffering from midlife crises. This book, this story was going to make him rich. Better than that. It was going to make him famous.

Ryan started typing.

NINETEEN

MARI DANCED. SHE WORE A PINK DRESS AND A paper crown. She was small, her feet bare. Her hair felt heavy down her back. She spun and spun in green, green grass, arms out, head tipped back to catch sight of the sky above.

She didn't want to go inside the house. Gran was hollering and kicking out at the dogs, who barked and bit and howled. She was throwing things, breaking them. She would grab Mari. Maybe kick her, too.

Mari liked to be outside in the grass. In the trees and the stream, where she dipped her fingers to drink and looked for crayfish. She climbed the mountain to find the clearing at the top where the sun beat down on her head and made the sparkles in her dress glitter and shine.

"I am here! I'm here!"

She looked at her dress and all her happy flew away. There were no sparkles. No pink. Her dress was ugly brown, ragged. It wasn't even a dress. Just an old T-shirt with a rope tie around the waist to keep it from dragging on the ground. No crown. Her hair, tangled, dirty, a mess.

She was alone but didn't want to be. She was waiting for someone to come. Not a Them with loud voices, the ones

Gran shouted at and threatened with her knife. The ones who sometimes came and always left.

Her hands made pictures in the air.

She was waiting for her prince to come, the one who told her all about princesses in sparkly dresses and who would save her from all of this. The one who loved her, kept her safe, made sure she had food and clothes.

She's not small now. Her feet not bare. Her dress has become a pair of plaid pajama bottoms she recognizes as her husband's.

That's how she knows she's dreaming, when she understands what she's wearing.

Of course, she thinks as her fingers twist and turn, telling stories. The forest prince. Of course that's who she's waiting for. And in the dream, Mari opens her mouth to say his name but says it aloud for real, instead.

She wakes with a gasp that stirs Ryan beside her but doesn't wake him. She puts her fingers over her lips, remembering the feeling of sunshine on her face. Just a dream. She's had plenty. She dreams of this house more often than she thinks about it when awake.

She'd been terrified when they took her away. Gran and the forest prince had always warned her what would happen if she didn't hide. If she didn't stay quiet and silent. They would come and steal her, and that was just what had happened.

Mari had been a secret. Something to be ashamed of. When she was small this had seemed to make sense; it was all she'd known, at any rate. Only later, when she had her own children, did she no longer understand how her mother could not have cherished her.

She can lie back down and sleep beside her husband, the man who brought her back here after all these years of normal life. She can even roll toward him and make love to him—he'll complain if she wakes him just to hold her, but if she slides up naked next to him and rouses his dick, he'll be more than happy to comply.

Instead, she swings her feet over the edge of the bed, feeling for the floor that is still too many inches away to feel familiar. Her toes tap hardwood and the nubbled edges of a braided rag rug. She gets out of bed. Now that the children are older, they've become somehow traumatized by the sight of her sleeping nude even though she's done it their entire lives, but she doesn't reach for the robe she always keeps handy.

Naked, Mari pads across the wood floor of this unfamiliar room. Down the unfamiliar hall. The stairs. Only when she's in the kitchen at last does she stop to take her hand from the wall to guide her. Only then she closes her eyes and breathes in deep.

This place she knows.

The table is different, and the appliances, but nothing about the layout has changed. She can find her way blindfolded, or in the pitch dark, or with her eyes closed. Mari glides across the slick tile floor that had once been buckled linoleum, toward the porch Ryan's taken over as his office.

She gives only a cursory glance at the piles of folders, the file boxes. The computer. This is her husband's lair. The reason he brought them here and uprooted them.

"I love my husband, and he loves me," Mari says on a whisper that nevertheless sounds very loud.

There is nothing between her and the night except glass and wood, but that barrier is still too much. She twists the lock on the door to the yard. It opens easily enough with the quietest of snicks. She pushes it open. She goes into the grass.

She breathes.

Oh, how she breathes.

Mari holds out her arms at her sides and lets her head fall back, eyes to the sky. She can see stars, and it's not at all like it is at home, where there's so much light pollution they're lucky if they can make out any of the constellations. And forget about wandering outside at night without clothes, or even in just a nightgown. All the neighbors would know.

A breeze ruffles the grass. The trees murmur with it. She looks toward the woods. Unlike the upstairs floors of the house behind her, she does know the forest. She ran there and searched for food and gathered wood. She played her lonely games there, making up a prince to save her. A family to love her when her own so clearly did not.

She drinks in the night air better than any wine or drug. Free, she turns in a slow circle, the night-wet grass cold on her shins. In her dreams, she is still wild.

In this place, she feels like she could be wild again.

Her gut twists with knowing this, not because it's been some vast secret she could never admit, but because of knowing that no matter how she might want to, she never can. Some poet had once said you can't go home again, and Mari knows that's not true. Because here she is, home again, back in the place that made her.

But what is true is that even if you go home, nothing is the same.

Time has passed and changed her, and no matter what she might have been had she stayed here, she is not that person now. She has a family of her own. A husband. Children she adores and is proud to acknowledge.

She is not the silent, feral girl who fought with dogs for scraps and slept with them for warmth in the snowtime…in the winter, Mari reminds herself. Using the words she learned so painstakingly. She is not that girl. Not anymore.

She's turning to go back in the house when something fluttering in the tree line catches her eye. She crosses the yard and plucks the dancing bit of paper and ribbon from the tree limb that has snared it. She studies it, her eyes wide to take in the darkness. She traces the edges of it with a finger.

It's a butterfly.

A folded paper butterfly, hung up with ribbon. It's been here for a long time, if the way it shreds so easily under her touch is any indication. The paper disintegrates and becomes confetti. The ribbon remains, its edges frayed. Mari smoothes it between her fingers. She can't tell the color.

She looks into the trees, where it's too dark to see. She listens. She breathes again, but smells nothing except night air, wet grass, the warmth of her own body and scent of her soap.

Then she turns and leaves the woods behind.

TWENTY

KENDRA HADN'T HEARD FROM SAMMY OR Logan in a whole week. Yeah, her phone got a crappy signal, but she'd had texts and messages manage to get through from some of her other friends, so it wasn't as if she wasn't getting anything. Just nothing from the two people who were supposed to be her best friends.

"Eff them," she said aloud to the trees and summer sun that was going to burn her face because she'd been dumb and forgotten sunscreen.

She flipped a double bird to the sky. It didn't make her feel better. She scuffed her toes along some gravel. At least this time she'd worn sneakers.

It was hard to be angry when she felt a little sick from the sun. And honestly, she wasn't mad, just disappointed and sad and embarrassed that Logan knew how much she liked him and was still getting with Sammy and ignoring her. That thought burned her more than the sun ever could.

She checked her phone once more, but found nothing. Wishing she'd thought to bring some water, Kendra went back into the coolness of the trees, picking her way down the steep slope. She realized she was a little lost only when some pebbles skidded out from under her feet and she fell on her ass, then looked to see that the path she'd been on was no longer there.

"Shit." Her phone had maps on it, along with location services, but that didn't do her any good when she couldn't get service. She pulled it out, anyway, thumbing the screen to see if she could put in the address of the house. Nothing came up, and Kendra scrubbed at her face. "Shit, shit."

Calm down, she thought. *You're not lost. You're just not sure where you are.*

By the time she reached the edge of the woods and the field, she had a better sense of her bearings. Instead of coming out behind her house, though, Kendra found herself faced with a stereotypical white picket fence surrounding a pristinely kept yard belonging to a house that was in somewhat less repair. She stopped, not certain about going beyond the fencing, though she recognized the house. This was the place at the other end of the lane, the one that shared the long, winding stone driveway leading to the rural road beyond. Rosie's house.

Kendra checked her phone, but the service had disappeared again. With a sigh, she started easing her way around the fence, heading for the driveway. The house's front door opened as she reached the gravel.

"Hey, you! Hey, girl! What are you doing?"

Kendra turned. "Hi, it's me. Kendra Calder. I'm staying—"

"Oh, you." The old woman, Rosie, frowned. "What are you doing lurking around? If your mother wants me to come do cleaning for her, she'll have to wait. My fibromyalgia's acting up."

Kendra shook her head. "No, sorry, I just got a little turned around when I was hiking. I ended up here, I didn't mean to. Sorry."

"Hiking around? What were you doing hiking around? Didn't I tell you to stay out of the woods?"

Another apology rose to Kendra's lips, but she bit it back.

Her parents had taught her to be respectful to strangers and older people. But her mom had also taught her to stand up for herself, especially when she wasn't doing anything wrong.

"I didn't see anything dangerous," Kendra said and took a few backward steps, trying to escape.

Rosie came onto her front porch, moving pretty fast for a woman who was supposed to be suffering. "It's what you don't see that's the most dangerous, girlie. Don't you know that?"

Tightness squeezed Kendra's throat. "I'm just gonna get out of here, okay? I'm sorry I bothered you. I didn't mean to come in your yard and stuff. Sorry."

Rosie stopped, breathing heavily, leaning on her porch railing. "You see anything up there? In the woods, on the top of the mountain?"

"No."

Rosie snorted. "Didn't your mama teach you better? City girl like you should be more careful. People can hurt you."

"I thought you said I had to worry about bears and coyotes," Kendra said smartly.

"Them, too. But they're not the only dangers in the woods."

"Well," Kendra said, feeling bold. "What is?"

From behind her, the crunch of tires on the gravel turned both of their attention to the car. Her mother behind the wheel, Ethan in the backseat. Mom looked surprised.

"Kiki?"

"Mom!" Kendra hurried toward the car. "Where are you going?"

"I'm going to the library and the grocery store."

Kendra got in. "Can I come along?"

"Hi, Rosie," Mom called, but Rosie had already gone back inside the house. She looked over at Kendra, brows raised. "What's that all about?"

"Nothing."

Mom gave her a long, silent look that cut right through her, but Kendra didn't say anything, and finally, her mother started to drive.

TWENTY-ONE

RYAN HAD MEANT TO GET UP EARLY, START working on the book, but hell. He'd been getting up early every day for years. Out here in the fresh country air, with no alarm to wake him or commute to make, Ryan had slept in to the glorious hour of...ten o'clock.

He stretched and rolled in the bed, feeling without opening his eyes but already knowing Mari was up. She was always up. Sometimes he liked to joke to her that she went to bed when it got dark and got up when it got light. Like a pioneer woman. Old habits, he guessed.

He heard the rattle of plates from the kitchen downstairs. Voices. Ethan and Mari, singing one of their silly songs. Ryan stretched again and scrubbed at his face, then swung his legs over the side of the bed.

He padded down the hall past Kendra's half-closed door, then down the creaking wooden stairs to the kitchen. The door at the bottom of the stairs had been propped open, and he paused in the doorway to look at his wife, who was up to her wrists in soapy water and staring out the window over the sink.

He opened his mouth to say good morning, but stopped. Covered in a thin sheen of soapsuds, her hand lifted. Pointed.

Then the other. Both hands went up in front of her face, palms upward, pinkies touching. Then, twisting at the wrists, she pushed outward, toward the glass. His stomach twisted.

"Babe?"

Mari startled and turned so fast she splashed water all over herself and the floor. She didn't scream, but instead gave a low, hissing gasp he didn't have to try too hard to interpret as terror. She blinked rapidly, her gaze unfocused, not seeing him, until she swiped a soapy hand across her forehead and burst into laughter.

"You scared me."

"Sorry." He hopped down the last two steps that stuck out beyond the enclosed staircase and into the kitchen. "What were you doing?"

"Hmm? Washing dishes."

He poured a cup of coffee and turned with it cupped in two hands to lean against the counter. "What were you doing before, though. With your hands?"

She tilted her head for a moment. "Hmm?"

Ryan put the mug on the counter to demonstrate. He said casually, so casually, "Tai Chi?"

His wife only stared, then shrugged. She turned back to the sink and fumbled with the water. In the next moment, the drain gurgled. She ran water from the faucet to rinse her hands and then the sink. She stared outside again, through the glass.

"Are you going to write today?"

"Yeah. Gonna get right to it."

From outside, someone screamed.

At their house in Philly, Ryan was used to the sound of kids outside. The whole damned neighborhood in the summer was full of hollering and shouting. It was easy enough to differentiate the cries of children at play and the sounds of distress.

He'd never heard anything that sounded like this.

Mari was already out of the kitchen, through the screened

porch and out the back door before Ryan could even put down his mug of coffee. He was after her in a minute or two, but it was Mari who got to Ethan first.

He'd been messing around in the creek or something. Up to his knees in wet. Ryan's first and horrifying thought was that something had bitten his son, a snake, oh shit, were there poisonous snakes in Pennsylvania? But then the scream came again. Farther away this time, and definitely not from Ethan's mouth.

"Mom! What is that?"

"Jesus," Ryan muttered. Running out to make sure his kid was safe, he hadn't noticed his bare feet and pajama bottoms, but now he couldn't ignore the fact he was squelching the swampy mud at the edge of the yard and that both his feet and pj's were filthy.

The scream rose again, coming from the woods. It sounded like a kid screaming before the cry guttered away into a series of weird clucking noises. It didn't sound so creepy now.

"Mama?"

Mari shook her head, but her hands moved as she spoke. The fingers of her left hand fanned out and touched the fist she made of her right. "It sounds like a bird. Just a bird, I think."

Ethan brightened. "Could it be a peacock? Is that how they sound, Mama?"

Mari had taken a few steps in the squelching ground, toward the trees, but now she looked down at their son. "Oh, Ethan. What did I tell you about getting wet?"

"I fell in."

"I see that."

"Will they scream again? Hey, Mama, can we go see if we can find them?" Ethan danced in excitement, but Ryan had had enough.

"I'm going back in the house. I need to get started on

work." Ryan turned to head back to the house. What he saw stopped him in his tracks.

The entire side of the house had been splashed with mud. Fist-sized splotches.

"Ethan!" Ryan turned, furious. His kid wasn't an angel, Ryan knew that for sure, but this kind of shit just wasn't acceptable. "Did you do this?"

"No, Dad."

"Don't lie to me."

Ethan gave his mom a pleading look, which only infuriated Ryan all the more. The kid was always looking to his mother to protect him. Hell, both kids were always playing him against his wife. It was like they had their own damned club, and he wasn't allowed in.

"Ryan."

"No, Mari, don't give me that look." He pointed at the house, then at their son. "If you didn't do this, who did?"

He crossed to the boy and grabbed his hand—a guilty hand, Ryan thought, covered as it was in mud and dirt from the stream. Ethan didn't yank it away, just shrugged and looked at the house, too. Mari took a few steps toward them, one hand out.

"Ryan, don't. Look at the house. Look at the mud. It's dry."

"Yeah? So?"

"So, your son is soaking wet and dripping."

"He could've thrown the mud at the house an hour ago." Ryan scowled.

"An hour ago, he was inside with me making pancakes. Ethan, did you do this?"

"No, Mom. I didn't even know it was there. I didn't pay attention when I came out."

Ryan let go of Ethan's hand with a grimace of disgust at the filth on his own fingers and turned to look at the house again. "It wasn't like that yesterday."

"Wasn't it? Did you come back around here and check? I didn't." Mari shrugged. "Ethan. Go rinse off all that mud. I told you not to play in the stream and get wet, didn't I?"

"Sorry, Mama."

She turned back to Ryan. "Ethan doesn't lie."

"Just like his mother?" The words shot from Ryan's mouth before he could stop them. Not that he would've. He was pissed off at the mess, pissed off he was missing precious work time to deal with this shit, when she was the one who was supposed to keep the kids in line.

Her eyes narrowed just slightly. "I'm not a liar. Would you like me to be, Ryan? Would you like me not to tell you the truth?"

"No." He made a shoving gesture at her with his hands, refusing to remember that he was the one who lied. "Forget it. Just…Christ, call the management company and have them recommend someone to take care of that. I have to get to work."

"We can do it with the hose. Ethan will like that, anyway. And he's already soaking. If it doesn't come off, I'll call."

Ryan was already stalking toward the house. "Fine. Whatever. I'm taking a shower, then I'm getting to work, and I'd appreciate it—" he turned to give her a significant look "—if you all could give me a little peace and quiet without interruption. Okay?"

"I'm sure we can manage."

He'd turned toward the house again, but now looked at her. Was that…sarcasm in her tone? Mari never spoke to him that way. "What's that supposed to mean?"

"It means," she said evenly, "that you should get to work. I'll take care of things out here. Go."

He couldn't argue with her. He wanted to. All of a sudden, Ryan wanted to get into it with her, force her to admit she was being shitty to him, have the chance to tell her off, put her in her place. The thought turned his guts. Even if he yelled at her, she'd just look at him with that dumb stare and answer him calmly without raising her voice, or worse, ignore him, which always left him feeling like an ass.

"Screw it," Ryan muttered and stamped through the wet grass back into the house.

TWENTY-TWO

THERE IS A LOVE AFFAIR THAT MOTHERS HAVE with their sons that is not duplicated with daughters.

Mari loves her daughter. When Kendra was born, Mari labored for a day and a half at home, walking off the pains and taking long, hot showers to ease the ache in her back. She'd have given birth at home, too, if Ryan hadn't insisted she go to the hospital. But she held off as long as she could. The nurses who helped her said they'd never seen a first-time mother labor in such silence, or be so relaxed. They wondered aloud, as though Mari couldn't hear them speaking, if her tolerance for pain was just so much higher than normal, or if she was just so committed to her breathing.

They didn't know the pain was excruciating, or that Mari truly thought she might die from it. They didn't know she didn't scream not because it didn't hurt, but because it did. So much.

Holding her daughter for the first time, Mari was over-whelmed with the scent of birth—blood and shit and fluids. Her body felt emptied and loose, her uterus still contracting though the proof of her efforts was resting, wet and warm and squalling on her naked chest. She held her baby close to her and wondered as she had every single day since learning she was pregnant if she would be able to mother this child.

By the time Ethan came along, Mari had begun to believe she could not only be a mother, but a good one. Kendra was seven when Ethan was born. There'd been a long number of years that Kendra had had her mother to herself, when it had been just the two of them. By the time Ethan was born, Kendra hadn't needed Mari so much and still didn't, not in the ways her younger brother did.

Sometimes, Mari wonders if she feels differently about her children because she didn't know her own mother's love. If somehow being unable to completely relate to Kendra is not her fault, then should she feel so… The word she wants escapes her.

Badfeeling.

No. There are more words than one to describe emotions. Mari puts her fingertips to her forehead, between her eyes.

Flashcards with faces showing emotions in front of her. If she got them right, she got a treat. A prize. Candy from Leon's pocket, or extra time outside on the swings. She loved the swings. She loved candy, though not the brushing, brushing with the thick mint paste after.

Angry.

Sad.

Happy.

Anxious.

"Very good, Mariposa. Very good job." Leon gave her a tiny hard candy wrapped in paper.

"Guilty," Mari murmurs aloud.

But she doesn't feel guilty. She understands the meaning of the word. She's seen it in the faces of others. Leon's, when he spoke of his ex-wife. Her children, caught with sticky fingers and lies about what they'd been sneaking to eat. And her husband, of course, when he spoke to her about his trouble at work.

Mari knew the sight of guilt, but not the feeling. Yet was that what she ought to feel, knowing that in her secret heart of hearts, she didn't love one child over the other, but she did prefer one? Understood one better? Should she feel guilty that Kendra has never been the same to her as Ethan, or is it beyond her control?

The desire for a snack cake rises inside her. Not a hunger in her belly, but something else entirely. Mari swallows hard to shove away the craving.

Ryan has gone to bed early, despite all of his forceful fury about needing time to work. He'd turned on the TV after dinner and watched a couple hours of inane shows while drinking too many beers, then asked her if she was ready to come to bed with a leer she recognized and didn't have the willpower to resist. Mari has loved Ryan since she was fifteen years old. Her husband may have infuriated her earlier in the day, but that doesn't mean she can't get lost in his touch.

Now, though, she's left him snoring and creeps down the hall to peek in at Kendra, who's fallen asleep watching a movie on her iPad. Down another door to Ethan, who sighs in his sleep and murmurs whatever secrets small boys tell themselves during dreams.

She doesn't want to wake him. She leaves him to his dreams, and on bare feet Mari creeps down the hall and down the back stairs to the kitchen.

To home.

No pantry in this house like she has in her own kitchen in Philadelphia, but there are plenty of cupboards. Fully stocked. The fridge, too. She runs her fingers over the boxes, jars, packages. She opens the carton of orange juice and sniffs, saliva pooling in her mouth until she swallows so compulsively it's almost a gag.

She's not hungry now, but she used to be hungry all the time.

She has to bend way down to reach the box she pushed behind the pots and pans. She slips out a plastic-wrapped treat, her fingers fumbling so that it flies from her grip and lands on the floor. She's on her hands and knees before she knows it. Hands and knees, naked on the floor in the dark, grabbing at chocolate not because she's hungry or she needs it, but because it is there and the next time she wants it, it might not be. Even though she knows there will always be snack cakes and cookies now, because she buys them for herself and hides them from her children and husband.

Again, she stops herself from tearing open the plastic and shoving the cake into her mouth.

Mari keeps her cupboards full because she never wants her children to have to squabble over food or steal it from a dog's bowl or eat it from the floor where it was dropped by someone who didn't notice. Just as she will never lock them in a kennel for making too much noise or ignore them when they speak to her. Just as she never beat them for making a mess or having a toilet accident.

Crouched on the floor, she presses the heels of her hands to her eyes. Remembering. Not weeping, not making a sound. Keeping it twisted and tight inside her, not because it doesn't hurt, but because it all hurts too much.

TWENTY-THREE

KENDRA WOULD NEVER ADMIT IT, BUT SHE loved the chickens, probably more than Ethan did. She loved to go into the barn and listen to their sleepy, soft cluck-clucking as they sat on their nests, and to slip a careful hand beneath them to pull out the eggs without disturbing them. She'd always hated to eat eggs, actually, and even more so since she'd started taking care of the chickens.

"So, eat oatmeal," her mom said. "Or some cereal. Or a piece of fruit."

Her dad stabbed a sausage with his fork. "You need some protein if you're going to be a vegetarian, Kendra."

"I'm not a vegetarian, Dad." She rolled her eyes. He never listened. "I just don't like eggs."

"Sausage, then."

"Gross," Kendra said. "Sausage is made from asses and snouts."

"Kiki," her mom said gently.

Ethan stopped with a forkful of sausage halfway to his mouth. "What?"

"Don't listen to her. Eat your breakfast. Some people are starving." Her dad shoveled more food into his mouth and washed it down with a mouthful of coffee. He was starting to get fat, just the faint line of a double chin and some extra jelly in the belly.

"You're certainly not," Mom said.

Dad had been reaching to scrape some more eggs onto his plate, but now he looked up. "What?"

"You don't know what starving is." Mom sipped from her own mug. "You wouldn't, and you never will, if you're lucky."

"What's that supposed to mean?"

"It's not supposed to mean anything. It's a fact." Mom shrugged and got up from the table to put her dishes in the sink.

Dad stabbed at the eggs and chewed. Swallowed. "You're full of facts, all of a sudden?"

Other parents fought. Some more than others, but they all did. Sammy's parents practically killed each other over who'd forgotten to take out the trash. But Kendra's parents never fought, not ever.

"C'mon, Ethan," she murmured. She yanked him by the wrist when he sat there like an asshat, staring with a wide-open, sausage-stuffed mouth. "Let's go."

"You sit right there and finish your breakfast." Her dad scowled and dumped eggs on her plate, three times as many as she'd ever eat even if she liked eggs.

"But I don't—"

"Don't back talk me!" Dad shouted.

Mom turned from the sink, her hands clenched. "Don't you yell at her!"

Shit, shit, shit, Kendra thought, miserable, wishing she could fall through the floor. She scooped up some eggs on her fork, opening her mouth and trying to breathe through her nose so she wouldn't puke if she ate them.

Her mom slapped the fork from her hands.

Eggs splattered onto the tabletop. The fork clattered to the floor and went spinning under the table. Ethan let out a small cry, but all Kendra could do was stare.

"You don't have to eat anything you don't want to." Mom's voice shook, but she kept her gaze on Dad's. "Ever. Do you understand?"

Sudden silence made Kendra's stomach hurt. Ethan started to cry, a bubble of snot in one nostril. Under the table, she grabbed his hand and squeezed it.

"My children," Mom said in a low, rasping voice nothing like her own, "will never be forced to eat something just because it's there. Do you understand that, Ryan? Never."

Dad nodded slowly. He still had that angry look on his face, but there was something else in his eyes, too. Something that scared Kendra more than his anger.

Her dad looked scared, too.

Mom looked at all of them, her expression fierce but fading immediately into the same calm look she almost always had. She cleared her throat and visibly relaxed her posture. Normally she'd have comforted Ethan, but now she only looked at him swipe at his eyes. Then at Kendra.

"Go outside," Mom told them both. "Find something to do."

Kendra took Ethan by the hand and away from the table. She had no idea what they were going to do outside, just that they had to get out of the kitchen. By the time they got into the front yard, her stomach had stopped cramping, but Ethan was still sniffling.

"I'll watch you at the creek, if you want," she said.

Since the day there'd been mud all over the house, Ethan had been banned from playing in the water without someone to watch him. In fifteen minutes they were settled by the water, Kendra in a soft patch of grass with her back propped against a rock and far enough from the water that she wasn't going to get muddy or even wet. Ethan on the other hand, jumped right in, both feet.

She bent to her book while her brother happily began gathering sticks and small rocks to block off one of the creek's small side streams. She'd picked something sort of at random from one of the library's back shelves in the fiction section. Soon she'd lost herself in the story, not paying too much attention to Ethan's chatter. Every so often he'd say "look, Kiki," and she'd mumble a response, so it wasn't until she'd made it through two whole chapters without hearing from him that she looked up.

"Ethan?" Kendra put the book aside and got to her feet. "Where'd you go?"

She heard a faint answer from beyond the two biggest rocks, where the creek took a bend. Following it meant splashing through the small pond Ethan's dam had made. Mud squelched around her flip-flops, but the water felt good. Even here in the trees, the summer heat had started to press down on her.

"Ethan!"

"I'm here." Covered in mud and wearing a huge grin, Ethan turned to show her a double fistful of some kind of water grass.

"What the…" Kendra sighed. "Why are you doing that?"

Ethan shrugged and looked surprised that she'd even asked. "Because?"

"You're going to get in trouble for being messy. You'd better wash all that off," she warned, then stretched and looked up at the sky. The trees were thinner here. She could see clouds and sun. "It looks like it's going to rain."

"I don't want to go home," Ethan said at once. "Kiki, do you think Mama and Daddy are still fighting?"

"I don't know. I don't think so. I hope not," she added. "But if they are, we'll just ignore them, okay?"

Something caught her attention as she pulled him upward

from the creek. Indentations in the mud, too big to be from Ethan. Bare footprints.

From far away, thunder rumbled. Kendra looked to the sky but could see little of it through the trees. What she did see looked dark. She looked again at the ground, but Ethan had stepped all over the place, blurring the lines.

"I thought I saw something," she said. "Like footprints."

Ethan shrugged, looking down at the mud. "Oh, yeah. I saw those the other day."

"And you didn't tell anyone?"

He shrugged. Typical. Kendra pushed him to the side to look more closely at the mud, but all she could see were the marks left by Ethan's feet.

Something rustled in the trees behind them.

Kendra turned, but could see nothing beyond the shrubbery. "C'mon. Let's go home."

"I don't want to," Ethan protested, but the sudden, closer rumbling of thunder stopped him.

"C'mon, brat." With barely a backward glance, Kendra stalked back to the rock where she'd been sitting just as the trees began to rustle with first drops of rain.

"But, Kiki, I saw—"

"I don't care!" she shouted. "It's starting to rain, let's go! Or else I'm not playing any games with you, nothing."

That at last got him moving. They made it back to the house just as lightning split the now-dark sky. The rain came a few minutes later. The house inside was dark, no lights on except at the back where their Dad had locked himself away inside his office, complete with the door he'd hung back up so nobody would bother him.

"Where's Mama?"

"Upstairs? I don't know." Kendra, annoyed and wet, didn't really care.

It wasn't until later that night that she realized she'd forgotten her library book. And shit, it would be ruined out there in the storm still raging. Kendra went to the window to look out at the backyard. Her mom would scold her gently, which was worse than if her dad yelled about having to replace it, but there wasn't anything she could do about it now.

The storm lashed the trees, though the lightning and thunder had moved away so there was only an occasional faint flash in the sky. She watched it for a while, wanting to kick herself for forgetting all about the book. But then, she thought, brow furrowed and concentrating, she hadn't even seen it.

That was right. Kendra hopped back into bed, and pulled the covers over her bare legs. She'd gone back to the rock where she'd been sitting, but there was no book there. She remembered putting it down in the grass beside her, but when she'd gone back, there was nothing. She hadn't forgotten the book.

It had simply disappeared.

TWENTY-FOUR

THE SMALL GIRL WITH TANGLED DARK HAIR crouched in a wooden chair sized for her. A woman in a navy blue pantsuit stood behind her, while Leon sat in the in the tiny chair opposite, looking comically oversize.

"Are you getting this, Lois?" Leon Calder leaned toward the child.

Little Mari. Seeing his wife as a child had become easier the longer Ryan watched. Maybe it was being able to see his children in her, or maybe it was being able to see the woman she was now that helped to make the scenes of her in tattered clothes, biting and kicking and fighting to get free, less uncomfortable. It was okay to see her that way, because he knew what she'd been able to become.

She would always be petite, but not freakishly so. If anything, he knew other women envied her ability to say slim without much effort. Her teeth had required a lot of work over the years, but she'd developed an almost obsessive dental hygiene habit, so though she wore caps to cover the damage of years of neglect, nobody would ever know by looking at her.

In the video, she gestured, the same patterns over and over. Lois scribbled notes while Leon watched quietly, occasionally attempting to repeat them. Whatever he was doing didn't resonate with the little girl, who shook her head furiously.

"Mariposa. Are you hungry?" Leon tapped one hand against his mouth, then looked at Lois. "You see that?"

"It's not sign language. Not American Sign Language, anyway."

Ryan remembered Lois. She'd smelled of oranges and had had several cats. Her husband had died young. She'd worked with his dad for years.

"No. Mariposa. Are you hungry?" Leon gestured again.

Ryan watched his wife as a child make the same gesture, adding a flick of her fingers and a low, chuffing growl that sent shivers through him, raising the hairs on the back of his neck. He swallowed uncomfortably, looking at the notes in the folder in front of him. The same notes Lois had taken, was taking in that video. The time-travel, topsy-turvy aspect of all this kind of twisted his stomach, but so did the anticipation of what he was going to make this into.

Ryan paused the video to tap a few sentences into his open document. So far he was only fleshing out some notes and putting things in chronological order. He had a vague idea that he was going to tell this story anecdotally. To appeal to the mass audience, not academia. So far, it wasn't going that well. Writing was a lot harder than he'd expected.

He played some more of the videotape, watching as his father and Lois worked with Mari, marking down her gestures as they tried to interpret them into something they could translate. The notes in front of him listed seven signs they'd been able to figure out at that point in working with her.

Hungry, a rub of the stomach and tap to the mouth with two fingers.

Tired, a rub of the eyes, very subtle.

Dog, fingers hooked to each side of the head to make ears, and a low bark, eerily accurate.

Quiet, a finger to the lips in the standard "shh" gesture.

Run, two fingers "running" against the other palm.

Hide, palms over the eyes, usually accompanied by her actual attempt to hide.

Scared, wide eyes and open mouth with fingers made into claws.

Watching the video tape now, with the bulk of his dad's notes to work from, Ryan could easily see that there were more than those seven signs showing in Mari's communication, right from the start. That was all they'd seen, the obvious ones.

He was jumping ahead, but Ryan plucked out another videotape and slipped it into the creaking VCR just to compare. In this one, Mari's hair and clothes were tidy, her face clean. She sat straight and spoke in clear tones, her vocabulary limited but precise. Most markedly, she barely used her hands to speak. When she'd learned to talk with her mouth, she'd stopped signing.

Except…she remembered it, didn't she? Ryan thought of the flutter of his wife's fingers when she dreamed. The way she sometimes hesitated before replying to something she wasn't sure how to say, and how her hands twisted or turned for the barest second before she found the words. He thought of her at the sink the other day, gesturing in the air in front of her. Just as his father and Lois hadn't noticed Mari's full repertoire of hand signs in the beginning, so had Ryan not noticed any of them all these years. At least not enough to understand what they were.

A chill sweat trickled down his spine, despite the rising heat that threatened to turn the porch into a sauna before the end of the day. He swallowed the final sips of his now-warm beer, the taste of it sour. From the kitchen came the clatter of pots and pans, Mari making lunch. Then the soft shuffle of feet and the rap of knuckles.

He switched off the video and closed the folder, not that she'd ask him any questions or try to see what he was doing. Thank God for the door, he thought, stuttering like a kid caught with his hand in his pants when he told her to come in.

"Do you want another beer?" she asked as though the fight they'd had this morning had never happened.

He thought of the way they'd made up while the kids were out. His wife, naked and warm beneath him, her body moving. Her fingers digging into his back. This was the woman he knew. And yet...

"Sure, babe. Thanks." And then, before he could stop himself, Ryan tapped his mouth with two fingers of his left hand.

"Lunch will be ready soon," Mari replied without missing a beat. "I can bring you a snack if you're really that hungry."

"No. I can wait."

She tilted her head. "You sure?"

"Yeah." He wasn't actually very hungry at all. "Come here."

She came and let him kiss her. He held her close, stroking her hair while she perched sort of awkwardly on his lap. She didn't protest or say anything, but when she pulled away, she looked bemused.

"What?" she said, touching his face for a moment.

Ryan gathered her close, burying his face against her breasts. Breathing in the scent of her. He'd known who she was when he met her, but he hadn't known anything about her. Nothing.

"I love you," he said helplessly, voice muffled against her.

Mari cupped the back of his neck for a moment. "I believe you."

TWENTY-FIVE

"SHAVING CREAM, BE NICE AND CLEAN!" ETHAN sang as he marched. He had a long stick he'd found early in the hike, and he used it to stab at the ground. "Shave every day and you'll always be clean!"

"Mom. Make him stop." Kendra rolled her eyes, though she didn't really mind. "He keeps singing the same verse over and over."

"So make up one of your own," her mom suggested.

Her mom had tied her hair back under a flowered bandanna. She also carried a walking stick and a backpack stuffed with food for the picnic. Kendra had the water jug. Ethan, the little monkeybrat, didn't have to carry anything because Mom and Kendra both knew he'd just drop it, anyway.

"Oh, right," Kendra said. "Like I'm gonna do that."

They'd started from behind the barn, then crossed the field and into the woods, angling upward on the mountain. There was no path there any more than there'd been one behind the house, but Mom seemed to know where she was going. She said there was something up there in the woods the kids would like.

"It'll be fun," Mom said.

"You do it, then."

Ethan dug his stick into the ground and turned over a rock. Bugs wriggled out, along with a really icky centipede. "Look, Kiki! Look!"

"Yuck."

"When I was out hiking with Kiki," Mom sang, "she looked for a good place to sit. But instead of a picnic blanket, she sat in a big pile of sh—"

"Shaving cream!" Ethan hollered.

Kendra had to laugh at that. "Gross, Mom! Gross!"

Her mom laughed. "I told you, you should've made one."

"Which way, Mama? Which way?" Ethan pointed with his walking stick and ran ahead of them.

"Go to this side...that way." Mom gestured to the left and tilted her head back, shading her eyes to look up at the sun. "We're almost there."

It wasn't like the mountain was huge or anything. The path Kendra had taken by herself the other day had actually been steeper, more overgrown and harder to climb. Still, she was glad she'd worn sneakers this time. She wished for a bandanna like her mom had.

"I can give you one of mine," her mom said when Kendra told her that. "I didn't think you'd like it."

"I do. I mean, it's okay. It's good, I guess. For out here."

"In the middle of nowhere, you mean?"

Ahead of them, Ethan was yelping and turning over rocks, so it was almost like she and her mom were alone. Kendra nodded. "Yeah. Out here in B.F.E."

Her mom's brows rose. "Do I want to ask what that means?"

"No. I guess not." Kendra shrugged and also wished she'd grabbed a long stick like her mom and Ethan had. She might not need it for hiking, but at least it would've given her something to do while they walked. She could've swatted at the underbrush or something.

They walked mostly in silence for a few more minutes

with Ethan making boy noises up ahead. Her mom asked for the water jug and drank, then handed it back to Kendra. She drank, too.

"Do you know where we're going, Mom?"

"Hmm? Well…" Her mom looked thoughtful. "Not really. Just ahead, up here. There's something you'll like. I think."

It was totally weird to think about how her mom had lived here as a kid. That this place might've once been as familiar to her as Kendra's neighborhood was to her, except instead of the Wawa and the park, the playground, the swimming pool, her mom had grown up with chickens and forests and mountains and hillbillies. Kendra shot her mom a sideways glance. Maybe she'd *been* a hillbilly!

"What was it like here when you were a kid?"

Her mom stopped, breathing just a little hard, leaning a bit on her walking staff. She looked at Kendra, then up to where the monkeybrat was pretending to fight something off with his stick. "Oh, Kiki."

Her mom never talked much about her childhood. Bits and pieces had snuck out over the years, of course. Like the fact she'd been raised by her grandmother. That she'd been adopted by Grandpa Calder and had then married his son, Kendra's dad. That had made Grandma Calder really mad. They never talked about that part of it, but Kendra had figured it out on her own. It hadn't seemed too weird when Kendra was younger, though now that she was older and if she thought about it too hard, it did. It wasn't like Mom had been raised with Daddy as her brother or anything. That would've been like Kendra marrying Ethan.

Yuck.

Watching her mom's face now, Kendra wondered if the reason she never talked about her childhood was because Kendra had never asked—or if it had been bad. Really bad.

"Mom?" She reached for her mom's hand, something she

hadn't done in a long, long time. "You don't have to talk about it if you don't want to."

"No. It's okay. I just haven't thought about it for a while." She paused and scanned the woods ahead for Ethan. He was still there. Her mom looked down at their hands, fingers linked. "No. That's not true. I think about it all the time."

"So...?" Kendra hadn't walked this way with her mom in forever. She flashed back to a memory of her little self, running after a balloon the wind had taken. She'd almost darted into traffic, but her mom had grabbed her hand. Held her tight. Kept her from getting squished by an oncoming car. "What about it?"

"It's not...easy to talk about."

Kendra had always known her mom wasn't like the other moms. All at once, though, she wished for her mom to be the sort to wear khaki shorts and polo shirts, with a blunt bobbed haircut and matching jewelry. A mom like everyone else's, and not because it would've made it easier for Kendra to fit in, but because it would've been easier for her mom.

"Sammy's granddad is a drunk," Kendra blurted.

Ahead of them, Ethan was swatting at something in the grass. Probably a skunk, it would be just their luck. He was doing karate chops, too. Little moron, she thought, but not in a mean way.

"Is he?"

Kendra nodded. "Yeah. She says it's why her mom never talks about him, but sometimes he calls the house and Sammy talks to him. He sends her cards with lots of money in them. Never on her birthday, though. Just random times. Her mom knows about it, but they don't talk about it."

"It must've been hard for Sammy's mother to have a drunk for a father."

Another sort of mother would've said "an alcoholic" or

maybe even "a dad with problems." But Kendra's mom never shaded things over.

"I guess so. Was your mom…a drunk?"

"I don't know, Kiki. She could've been anything. I didn't know her." Her mom looked up ahead, gaze far away. "My grandmother never talked about her, that I can remember, and she's the one who raised me. If you could call it that. Oh, look. Here we are."

The trees had thinned out directly in front of them, like a giant fist had come down from the sky and punched a hole in the forest. One second they were thick in the woods, the next they stood in a field of boulders. Smooth and gray, tumbled together like in the bottom of a dry riverbed. Ahead of them, the trees closed inward again, and behind that, the mountain rose sharply. It was a space maybe as big as their backyard at home, but totally out of place here in the trees.

Her mom turned to look at her with a broad grin. "This is it."

"What is it? A pile of rocks?"

"Woo!" Ethan hollered, running and jumping on the rocks.

"C'mon." Grinning, Kendra's mom hopped onto the first rock. "Let's go into the middle."

It was hot in the middle of the field, the sun beating down. The rocks were hot, too, and slippery. Kendra's sneakers didn't have deep treads, and she almost wiped out a couple times before she caught up to her mom and Ethan. Her mom shrugged off the backpack and fussed with the zippers.

"Are we eating here? Can't we find a place in the shade, with some grass or something?"

"We're not eating here." Her mom pulled out two hammers Kendra hadn't even known she'd packed. "Here. One for you, one for Ethan. Ethan! Come get this."

Ethan turned, whacking his stick on the rocks as he leaped them like a goat instead of a monkeybrat. "What's this?"

"Hit the rocks."

Kendra and Ethan looked at each other. Their mom had them do some weird things sometimes, no doubt, but this... She laughed and waved her hands at them. Ethan did, tentatively. The rock thumped under his hammer, nothing special.

"You go, Kiki. Hit that one."

Kendra did. The rock...rang. A hollow, metallic sound totally unlike the one Ethan's had just made. A delighted laugh burst from her, and she gave her mom an incredulous look.

"They're special," Mom said. "Go ahead. See which ones you can make sing."

They spent a few minutes pounding away at all the rocks. Most of them made dull thumps when hit with the hammer, but enough of them made that metallic sound to become a challenge. And some of them were higher, some lower, so she and Ethan could almost play a tune.

"Want to try, Mama?" Ethan held out his hammer.

"No, baby, you go ahead."

"Did you use to do this when you were a kid?" Kendra tapped a rock near her mom's foot.

"I did. Sometimes. I came here with..." Her mom trailed off with that faraway look in her eyes again. She shook her head like she could shake out a memory. "Someone. My grandma, I guess. Before she got sick."

"What happened to her?" Ethan balanced on a rock, one arm and one leg out.

"Oh...I believe she had a series of strokes," Mom said. "Eventually, she died."

Ethan jumped across the rocks to hug her, and Kendra wished it were still that easy and casual for her. She envied her brother a lot because he seemed to take up most of her mom's attention, but she had to admit the kid did earn it sometimes.

"I'm sorry, Mama."

Their mom hugged him, patting his back. "It's okay, honey. It was a long time ago."

"Are you still sad about it?" Kendra asked.

Mom looked at her with a small frown and the crease between her eyes that meant she was thinking hard. "I don't think so, honey. I don't think I was ever...sad."

Her mom looked at Kendra, mouth open to say more, but then Ethan screamed. Not the way he'd been hollering before, this was a scream of pain.

"What's wrong? Ethan!"

He pulled his hand away from his face. Blood. Oh, God. There was blood. The world wavered and Kendra's sneakers slipped on the rocks. Her stomach lurched.

"What happened?"

"Something hit me," Ethan said. He wasn't crying, but his lower lip trembled and he wiped the blood onto his shirt.

"Hush," Mom said. "Let me see. Kiki, bring the water."

Kendra had dropped the water jug, but it hadn't spilled. She brought it, head turned so she didn't need to look at the blood. "Here. Is he okay?"

Her mom dug in the backpack for a roll of paper towels she wet from the jug, then pressed against Ethan's head. "Oh, that's not bad."

"What was it?" He sounded like he still might cry.

Kendra couldn't blame him.

"Were you hitting the rocks too hard? Maybe a piece broke off and shot up," Mom said.

But in the next minute, a rock flew from the mountain side of the clearing and spanged the boulder they were sitting on. It left a white mark and made a dull thump. Ethan cried out and Kendra jerked away, searching the edges of the clearing and seeing nothing. No...seeing something, but so far away and so much in shadow she couldn't make it out.

Mom stood.

Another rock, this one smaller but sharper, flew from a slightly different place in the woods. It hit Kendra in the leg. It didn't break the skin, but the pain was instant and terrifying. She clutched at her leg and let out a wail, scooting backward on the boulder and slipping down the opposite side to get wedged between it and the one beside it.

"Kiki, don't move! Ethan, get behind me. Who's there?" Mom's voice carried across the field of rocks, but didn't move the trees.

Nothing moved, not even a breeze. The heat pounded down on them. Kendra's leg hurt, and so did her back from where it pressed the rocks. It was burning from the heat of the sun. Something hissed, sliding in between the spaces in the rocks two feet from her head, and she screamed at the top of her lungs.

"Snaaaake!"

"Get up," Mom said, not yelling, voice firm and calm.

Kendra wasn't calm. She launched to her feet, one sneaker catching in the space she'd been lying in. Stuck. She screamed again, panicked. Snake, snake, oh, shit, where had it gone?

Another rock flew from the trees. Then again. One hit Mom in the stomach, then her side. A third hit Ethan again, this time in the arm.

Kendra screamed, cowering. A rock hit her in the back of the head hard enough to send stars shooting through her vision. She put her hand there, knowing, oh God, oh shit, there would be blood. Blood!

"Stop it!" Mom screamed out into the woods. It was the first time Kendra had ever heard her mother's voice that loud. "What are you doing? Stop!"

The flurry of rocks ceased. The snake had disappeared.

Mom put her arm around Kendra, the other around Ethan, holding them close to her. Protecting them as best she could.

"I think," Mom said in a low voice, "we'd better get out of here."

TWENTY-SIX

THIS MAN KNOWS NOTHING.

The police officer, Barrett is his name, has come in his white SUV and his blue uniform to take their statements, but though he's written everything down in his neat little pad with his cheap little pen, this man cannot or will not help them. Mari sees it in his eyes. He doesn't care.

"Probably was kids," Barrett says and closes the pad to slide it into his front shirt pocket.

"Kids?" Ryan is angry and pacing. He's run his hand through his hair so much it's standing on end. "What sort of asshole kids throw rocks?"

Their own children are sitting, quiet and white-faced except for the bruises, on the couch. Uncharacteristically, Kendra's arm is around Ethan's shoulders, and though Mari hates the reason for it, she's touched to see the sibling love. She has bruises herself, and a wound on her temple that Ryan declared could have used a stitch but instead patched up with a butterfly bandage at her insistence.

"Hillbilly kids," Kendra says.

Mari has raised her kids to be respectful to adults, but she's proud of the look her daughter gives the cop. She knows what kind of kids he means, she thinks. "He means local kids who don't like outsiders."

"The hell is this, *Deliverance?*" Ryan, raised in suburbia his whole life, already has a prejudiced view of rural life, and this isn't helping. "We're in Pennsylvania, for god's sake. We're two hours from a major U.S. city."

The cop stands. "I can file a report, but the best advice I can give you is stay off other people's property."

"Kids don't defend their property with rocks." Ryan sneers. "And even if they did, or hell, even if it's some crazy mountain man up there with a boner about people gettin' on his land—"

Something in the cop's eyes shifts. Ryan sees it. He stops. Studies the guy.

"You're shitting me."

"I'll file a report. Are you sure none of you needs medical attention?"

"I'm a goddamned doctor," Ryan says. "And just hold on a minute. Are you really saying there's some…mountain man… out there throwing rocks at people?"

"Sir, I'm going to have to ask you to watch your language."

"Ryan," Mari says in a low voice. Her husband tosses up his hands and stalks away into the kitchen, where she hears him rattling the glasses in the cupboard and cursing. "Officer Barrett, thanks for coming out. I didn't know the clearing was private property."

Now the man hesitates, gaze going shielded. His mouth works. "Technically, it's state game lands. This whole area back here backs up to state game lands."

"We could have been seriously hurt. My kids," Mari says carefully, making sure he's looking her in the face, "could've been very badly hurt. Killed, even. Rocks can kill people, you know."

"This is the Pfautz place. It's been a rental for years and

years. Anybody who stays here…" Again, he trails off, looking almost embarrassed. "Well, nobody stays long."

"Is that because someone throws rocks at them?"

The officer squares his shoulders. "I'll file the report. That's really all I can do. And maybe…just stay out of the woods."

He's already heading out the front door before Mari can say anything, but there's no way she's going to let him leave like that. Not without a better explanation. She catches up to him as he's sliding into the driver's seat of his patrol car.

"Officer Barrett."

"Look, Mrs. Calder, I understand your concern. I have kids, too."

"What would you do if someone threw rocks at your children?" She touches her temple, the sore spot beneath. "Would you just tell them to stay out of the woods?"

His mouth narrows and thins. "Yes. I would. And I'm telling you the same thing. Just stay out of the woods up there, and you'll be fine."

"If you know someone is out there," Mari says, "isn't it your job to tell me so I can protect my family? Or better yet, how about you arrest the person?"

"I can't arrest anyone without a reason. If you didn't see someone, there's nobody to arrest, now, is there?" Officer Barrett looks personally affronted, like she accused him of letting a pedophile babysit his kids.

He's not going to tell her anything else. She can see that in the way his face has shut down. His shoulders hunch. He won't look at her. She can read him the way she's been able to read so many people over the years. A gift, some have called it, that perception, making her empathetic when really she's not. She's just able to use what she sees in people's faces and the way they stand to make them think she understands them when she hardly ever does.

"Who lives in those woods, Officer Barrett?"

"Good night, Mrs. Calder. I'm sorry about your kids. And you."

She surprises them both by putting her hand on the door so he can't shut it.

"Look, ma'am…" The officer sighs and rubs at his eyes. "I know you're not from around here—"

She laughs at that, ruefully and with little humor. "I am not from *around* here. I am *from* here."

He blinks at her, slowly. "I thought you were just renting."

"No. This is my house. The others were tenants. The ones you say never stayed long. Tell me why."

Now he's looking at her with something like respect but it could be fear. Something like revulsion and fascination. "Your house? You're not—"

Her chin goes up, her eyes narrow. He doesn't quite cower from her, and why should he? He's got a gun, after all, and outweighs her by a hundred pounds if not more. What could she possibly do to him?

"I haven't been here in a long, long time. Things change," Mari says. "People change, Officer Barrett."

"I see that."

He's no older than she is. He didn't know her then. Whatever he's heard of her has been passed along like the stories he refuses to tell her. So she's become a legend? Or is it more like the sort of story you tell around a campfire to scare yourselves while you eat s'mores?

"My family and I have every right to be in that house. We have every right to be in those woods. Without being attacked," she adds. "If I find out who did it—"

"Like I said," the cop says, and jerks the door from her hand. He speaks to her through the open window of his car. "They're just stories."

She watches him drive away until the red taillights blink like eyes at the end of the lane, and he's gone. Mari turns and stares into the dark, toward the trees and the mountains beyond. At the front porch, she stops to see something tacked into the pillar there. It might've been there forever, faded as it is into the color of the paint, but under the yellow porch light only just now catching her attention. Or it might have been pinned there within the past hour, or the past five minutes between the time she ran out after the cop and her first step back onto the porch.

It's another butterfly, twisted from faded, sun-bleached paper and tied with a bit of equally ragged ribbon. It doesn't fly, this butterfly, though it might if there was a breeze to push its wings. It hangs, limp and dead and almost unseen. Mari plucks it up and crushes it in her palm.

Some stories, she knows, are true.

TWENTY-SEVEN

SOME PIECE OF SHIT HILLBILLY REDNECK HAD thrown rocks at his kids.

Anger still burned in Ryan's gut at the way the cop had handled it. For a moment, unease at his decision to bring them back here did a tumble-turn in his belly, but then he reminded himself that this choice, this book, was going to give them all their lives back. Better than before.

And he was doing it for them, he told himself. To make sure they didn't lose all the things they'd grown accustomed to having. To make sure he could keep providing for them.

But what good did providing do when he couldn't protect them?

Ryan scrubbed at his mouth with the heel of his hand, then took another long pull on his beer. The blinking cursor mocked him. He put his hands on the keyboard, half a page written, and couldn't think of another damn word. He'd organized all the files and reports and made an outline of how he wanted the book to go.

He just couldn't write the damn thing.

It was too hot in here, for one thing. No air-conditioning, and whoever had converted this screened porch into a three-season room hadn't done such a great job with the windows.

Only half of them opened. Besides, there was something disturbing about being this open to the woods outside. During the daytime it was fine. Soothing, even, to watch the leaves shift and flutter. But at night, with the lights inside making it impossible to see out, all he got was the creeps.

He got up and let the ragged, half-broken blinds down. If someone came around again, he vowed, he would beat the shit out of them. If someone messed with his family he would do what he needed to take care of them.

At his desk, he looked at the last folder he'd been organizing. Photos of a filthy child, hair matted, mouth pulled wide in a scream, being carried under the arm of a tall man with a beard. The background was somewhat familiar—the house and the barn, though both were half-obscured by the rampant weeds and bushes of the yard. The drive that was now made of white gravel was nothing but dirt and weeds crushed under the tires of a waiting van. Behind the man was a woman with a grim look, and behind her, half out of frame, a pair of coverall-wearing animal control people using loop hooks to capture what appeared to be several snarling, cowering dogs.

In the girl's hand was an unidentified object. Some sort of toy. Equally as dirty and unkempt as the girl herself, it looked as though it could be some sort of Glow Worm toy—the kids both had them when they were small. Hug the soft worm bodies and the oversize plastic head lit up. This one had material flapping from its sides, something like a cape. Ryan couldn't quite make out what it was, but another picture in the file, this time a close-up of the toy, showed him it was a butterfly. On the back of the picture was scrawled a single word.

Mariposa.

Spanish for butterfly, and the only word the girl would say when they brought her in. It was how they figured out it was her name. Or maybe it was just what they decided to call her and what she answered to. All he knew was that his wife was taken from this house, screaming and clutching a toy butterfly.

Ryan took another drink of beer that had gone too warm and sat back in his chair. The bright light from the laptop screen made his eyes tired. He should pack it in for the night. Get a fresh start tomorrow, when he could surely sit down and pound out a couple chapters. Instead of going upstairs, though, he turned again to the stack of papers he'd organized according to date and content. Flipping through them, he paused to read again the places he'd highlighted or marked with sticky notes.

She was something of a miracle, his wife.

He knew about feral children, of course. You couldn't make it through psych rotations without hearing about some of the most famous cases. Genie, the girl who'd been tied to a potty chair in a dark back room. Louis the dogboy of France. Kaspar Hauser, the German teenager who'd claimed to have been raised in a tiny cell. The common thread among all of these cases was that most of those children—the neglected, the abused, the outright abandoned or tragically lost—were never able to maintain what might be considered a "normal" life.

There was the more recent case of the woman born in the Louisiana bayou and raised by a grandmother who'd been too ill to really take care of her. At five years old, she was sent to live in California with her mother, who'd had many other children but was incapable of really taking care of any of them. She'd been bounced from mother to father to foster care until she was finally adopted. She admitted that though she'd married and had a child, she couldn't really relate to other people. She could live in society, but she'd never really learned to fit in. She preferred to live in isolation, similar to the way she'd been raised.

She'd been raised not unlike his wife.

Upstairs, Mari slept naked in a bed that was just enough

smaller than their usual one that it still felt awkward to him.
Upstairs were their children. Ryan knew without a doubt
his wife loved Kendra and Ethan fiercely, without reserve.
He'd seen her defend them against bullies on the playground
or teachers who were a little too unkind. He had no doubts
about his wife's capabilities for emotion when it came to their
kids. And in their marriage, Ryan had always known she was
a little more distant from him than the wives of his friends,
or the patients who came in complaining about how much
they hated their husbands. Ryan had always loved that about
Mari, that she stepped back and allowed him to be indepen-
dent. That she didn't check up on him.

And look where it had gotten him.

Mari had been fifteen when he met her for the first time,
though he'd been hearing stories about her for years. The Pine
Grove Pixie. His dad's greatest challenge and best success.
The reason Leon Calder spent so many late nights away from
home when Ryan was young, and the reason his parents had
split. At twenty-three and with years of neglectful fatherhood
to numb him, the divorce shouldn't have bothered Ryan as
much as it had, but it had been a long time before he'd gone
to see his father in his new house, and the girl he'd adopted.

The first time he'd seen her, his dad had called out, "Mari!
Come meet Ryan!"

He'd been prepared to hate or at least mildly dislike her,
out of loyalty to his mom if nothing else. After all, this girl
had pretty much ruined not only his dad's marriage but his
career—even though she'd been the subject that had tipped
his dad toward fame, the ethics involved in his adoption of her
had basically guaranteed his dad's forced retirement.

But Ryan hadn't hated her. In fact, the opposite. She'd
been wearing a simple dark pleated skirt and white blouse.
Knee socks. Hair in twin braids. Saddle shoes. Because that
was the uniform his dad had insisted on. She'd been a kid and

should've been way below Ryan's interest—and she had been. At least in that way. At least for a time. She'd come down the stairs in her schoolgirl outfit and fixed him with a look so unwavering and blunt, like nothing he'd ever had from anyone before, that he'd found himself instantly wanting to...protect her. He'd understood then what had so moved his dad.

Later, Ryan wouldn't stop wanting to protect her, but he did start wanting to peel away the layers and get inside her. She wasn't like other women. She was blunt and honest, as though she were incapable of deception, but that didn't mean she *couldn't* lie. It just meant that she didn't.

Annette had come on to him in that same way, her relentlessness erotic and arousing. Who didn't want to be wanted that way? Like you made all the difference in the world to that one person?

And so maybe his marriage had become a little stale and strange and he'd let himself be carried away by an opened set of thighs. He loved his wife and the family they'd made together. That didn't change, not matter what else had.

Ryan rubbed at his eyes until they blurred and the video he'd been letting run without really watching went to static. It was late. The house was dark. The kids had gone to bed early for once, leaving him undistracted by the creaking of the floors above while they wandered back and forth or did whatever the hell they did when they were up late because it was summer.

He clicked off the television and sat in the darkness. Listened for the sound of footsteps and heard none. Then he went upstairs and crawled into bed beside his wife, where he pulled her close to him and breathed the scent of her, that warm familiar scent.

And he wondered if by knowing her better, he was somehow going to lose her.

TWENTY-EIGHT

"SOME KIND OF, WHAT…SASQUATCH?" SAMMY sounded distracted.

Kendra imagined her friend hanging upside down, phone at her ear, while she watched TV. "No. I don't know. I mean… the cop wouldn't say. But it's weird, you know? The old lady from down the lane told me to watch out for stuff in the woods, too."

"Creepy." Sammy's voice crackled and broke up for a few seconds, and Kendra scowled. She held her phone from her ear. Two freaking bars. Now one.

"The service is better up there," she said overtop of whatever Sammy was saying.

"What?"

"I have crap service here!" Kendra lowered her voice, aware that though her dad was holed up in his office doing whatever it was he'd brought them here to do, her mom could be down the hall. "It was better up on the mountain, that's what I was saying."

"So…take a walk. You're probably bored as shit there, right?" Sammy sounded bored herself. "You don't even have internet, right?"

"No. Just basic cable."

"So take a walk."

Kendra rolled over on her bed to look out the window. She could only see a bit of sky, some clouds. The tops of the trees. She shivered. "I'm freaked out."

"By the sasquatch? Girl, please. That is some tired excuse." Sammy snorted laughter.

Not for the first time in their friendship, Kendra wanted to hang up on her friend. Sammy could be such a bitch sometimes. Kendra always thought it was because she was an only child with parents who basically ignored her. She hadn't ever, like, learned how to treat people. But sometimes Kendra thought it was because there was something wrong with *her,* that Sammy thought she could treat her like that and Kendra hardly ever did anything about it.

"Someone took my library book out of the woods by the creek, and I saw footprints there. Big ones. Someone threw rocks at us. And splashed mud all over our house. My dad blamed Ethan, but he said he didn't do it. Maybe he really didn't. It's not a freaking joke."

"Chill, wow. I'm just kidding with you."

"It's not funny, Sammy."

Silence on the other end of the phone, this time not caused by lack of signal strength. Sammy was good at that, too. Making Kendra feel bad for getting upset the few times she did.

"Sorry." Sammy didn't sound anything close to sorry.

Kendra imagined the roll of Sammy's eyes. "It was scary. You'd be freaked out if you were here."

"Bet I wouldn't."

"You would," Kendra said. "You can't even watch scary movies."

The line was silent again, broken every second or so by a piece of Sammy's reply. "...whiny little bitch."

Kendra wasn't sure she really wanted to hear what Sammy had said. "You're breaking up. I can't hear you."

"So take a walk up to that mountaintop or whatever the hell you said it was. Good signal there. I mean, unless you don't want to hear what Logan said about you."

Kendra certainly did want to hear that. She rolled upright, searching for her sneakers. "What did he say?"

But the call was lost in the moment she shifted to pull on a pair of socks. Muttering a curse, she shoved the phone in her shorts pocket and pulled her hair up into a ponytail, then put on a ball cap. Daddy had said something about ticks out in the woods. Gross.

Kendra found her mom in the kitchen. She was mixing the ingredients for bread dough into the machine's pan. A tray of cookies sat on top of the oven. Her mom had flour on one cheek and her hair was a mess, but she looked up with a smile when Kendra came down the stairs.

"Hi, honey. Want a cookie?"

"Sure. Can we go play in the stream? I promise to make sure Ethan's careful." Kendra helped herself to one of the gooey chocolate chip cookies and waited for her mom to forbid her.

Her mom paused. Turned. "You really think that's possible?"

"Well…I can try." Kendra put on her winningest face. "Please? It's hot as balls here…and crazy boring."

Her mom laughed and shook her head. "Kiki. Yuck."

"Please?"

Her mom sighed. Her dad would've said no by now without even listening to Kendra's reasons for wanting to go. But her mom had never been the type to hold them back, even from stuff that might be considered dangerous.

"I want you back by dinnertime. I mean it. Stay close to our yard, don't go anywhere else. And you text me every twenty minutes."

Kendra rolled her eyes, but nodded, not bothering to point out that her mom was surely not going to get the texts, because that was sort of the whole point about why Kendra wanted to hike to the top of the mountain in the first place. "Sure, whatever."

"Here. Take some cookies and some lemonade. Don't drink the water from the stream." Her mom paused, again with that faraway look she'd been having so often lately. "I mean...it could be dangerous. And don't be gone long. And be careful."

It was a long, long list of commands, unusual coming from her mother, but it made Kendra feel all the worse for lying about what she was really going to do. She hugged her mom. Hard. "Love you, Mom."

Her mom looked surprised, then squeezed her in return. "I love you, too, Kiki."

Outside, Kendra found the monkeybrat already fooling around in the piss-trickle of water that was trying to be a creek, even though he wasn't supposed to be. "Hey, dork. I'm going for a walk. Want to come along?"

"In the woods?" Ethan tossed a stone into the water to make a splash, though he was standing far enough away he wouldn't get wet. "Are you crazy?"

"Are you scared?"

He looked stubborn. "No. Well, sure, yeah! Someone threw rocks at us, Kiki. It really hurt."

"Does your face hurt?" she asked. "'Cuz it sure hurts me!"

Ethan jumped at her, fist raised, but she knew he wasn't going to hit her. He settled for kicking out at her, instead, not even coming close. "Jerk."

"Come with me," she said, contrite and not wanting to be alone in the forest, even if it meant hanging with her little brother. "It's not too far, and there's something cool up there I want to show you."

His eyes lit up. "What?"

"You'll see when we get there," Kendra promised. "C'mon."

Halfway up the mountain, on the narrow and not-quite-there trail, Ethan started complaining about being thirsty and hot, though it was a gazillion times cooler in the trees than it would've been down in the yard. Kendra frowned, sweat running in her eyes and bugs swarming around her. She swatted at them and told him to shut up, or she was going to leave him there.

It was a tempting thought.

"It's just a little farther, dummy, and I have lemonade and snacks in my bag."

He did keep whining, but in another five minutes just before she was ready to give up, haul off and smack him, they eased into a clearing she'd never been in before. Ethan stopped short, nearly tripping her. In a second, Kendra saw why.

It was a house. A small house. Crooked, like the one in the nursery rhyme the monkeybrat had loved so much when he was little. He'd made Kendra read it to him over and over. There was a crooked man, and he walked a crooked mile.

"And they all lived together in a little crooked house," she murmured.

Just like the one in front of her, she imagined. Built of gray and faded boards, with a slanting roof and a door hanging half-open. One open window, hung with ragged curtains. They stirred in the same breeze that tossed the leaves on the trees.

"Whoa," Ethan said. "Weird."

Kendra moved toward it but stopped with one foot on the natural stone step leading up to the threshold. It sure didn't look like anyone lived there, but on the other hand, what if this was like something out of the Blair Witch Project? She looked around at the trees ringing the small clearing, then at the house itself. No weird little dolls made of string and sticks. She listened hard but heard only the soft sigh of wind in the trees.

Ethan was already running ahead to kick at the fire ring in front of the house, scuffing his sneakers in the black soot. He bent to pick something from the fire. "Kiki, look! Is this... bones?"

"Gross, dork! Put those down!" Kendra already had her phone out, lifting it to take a picture of the shack, just to prove it was real.

"Let's go in!"

"No! You can't go in there. It's probably not safe. Look at it."

"It looks okay."

"What if someone lives in there?" she asked him, and they both stared at each other solemnly. "You can't just go in someone's house without being invited."

"Do you really think someone *lives* in there?" Ethan asked.

She looked at it. The clearing showed no signs of any life. The fire ring had been used, but there was no telling how long ago. There weren't any beer cans or anything that would show this off as a place where kids snuck out to party behind their parents' backs. Not out here, anyway. No telling what was in the shack.

"Yeah, probably Bigfoot."

"Bigfoot doesn't live in a house," Ethan said in scorn.

Kendra gave him a steady, intimidating stare. "Okay, then. Not Bigfoot. But someone. Some...thing. You better not go in there. I bet there's things like teeth in jars and quilts made out of human skin!"

Ethan's eyes rounded. "Shut up!"

She'd get in trouble for this later when he couldn't sleep or had nightmares, but it was totally worth it at the moment, watching his face. "I'm serious. Someone lives in that house, all right. The boogeyman!"

"No such thing!"

"Oh, yeah?" Kendra jerked her chin toward the house. "Dare you to go in, then."

Ethan crossed his arms. "Shut up."

"Dare you."

She shouldn't have dared him the second time, because the kid was just dumb enough to do it. Before she could stop him, Ethan had leaped up the small stone steps, two at a time, and yanked open the front door. It came open with a creak that was loud enough to make her scream.

"Get back here!" Kendra jumped after him, yanked the back of his shirt to stop him getting inside. "Jesus, Ethan, no!"

Both of them stumbled through the doorway at the same time.

Inside, everything was shadow. One small room lined with floor-to-ceiling shelves. Lots of books, which seemed out of place in a place like this. An old-fashioned hand-pump at a sink, cupboards underneath. A glass mason jar with several drooping peacock feathers stuck inside it.

At least there weren't any jars full of teeth.

Still, it was freaky. The windows were covered with shredded lacy curtains, hammered right into the wood. A small ladder rested against the far wall, leading up to what looked like a sleeping loft not even tall enough for someone to stand upright in. If someone lived there, they weren't there now.

"Nothing in here," Ethan said.

He was right, but Kendra still didn't like the look of it. "Let's get out of here."

For once, her brother didn't argue. He hopped ahead of her, down the stone steps, back out into the grass. In the doorway, Kendra thought she heard something shift in the sleeping loft, something like a sigh, and her heart lurched into her throat as she spun, hands up, expecting to see something looming out of the shadows.

Nothing.

"Shit," she breathed aloud.

Her hands shook, and what had she expected, anyway? To

use her nonexistent karate skills to fend off the boogeyman? She backed up a step, out the door, leaving it ajar.

"Ethan! Let's go!" Five signal bars or not, this place was creepy. "Now!"

"But..."

"Now," Kendra said the way her mom did when she meant business. "Let's get out of here."

At the edge of the clearing she looked back. It might've been the shadows or the fact she needed glasses, but what she saw made her shove her brother along faster.

The door to the shack had closed.

TWENTY-NINE

BARE FEET PRESSED THE SOFT GRASS. CLUCK, cluck, clucking chickens scratched and pecked in the yard beyond. Victor, tail spread wide, showed off for her. She would find his feathers in the grass, take them inside. Long and soft and pretty, they would make her a princess.

In the kitchen, Gran offered a plate of bread and jelly and allowed Mari to sit at the table while she talked and talked. Mari didn't understand what Gran said, her mouth was mushy and mumbly, no teeth and a flapping, slobbery tongue. But Them had come two sleeps ago and so there was food, enough to go around, even with small bits dropped on the floor to satisfy the always begging dogs. After eating, Gran brushed Mari's hair and washed her face and sent her back outside to play with the new kittens in the barn. That was a good day.

Long, long days of sunshine and freedom. Fresh air that tangled her hair and blushed her cheeks. Running, running, spinning in circles, arms out.

That was her childhood.

There were bad times, too, Mari thinks as she scatters a handful of feed for the chickens Rosie from down the lane is supposed to take care of. She bends to let them peck from her hand. There is one red hen called Sally who will sit on her lap and be petted, if Mari lets her, and after a moment or so, she settles onto the ground. Her clothes will get dirty, but she doesn't care.

Her childhood was filled with bad times by anyone's standards. She knows it. Hunger. Fear. Deprivation. Loss.

And yet, back again in the place where she'd been small, Mari only feels content. No carpooling or music lessons or play dates to arrange. No constant blather from the television set. No honking traffic.

Here there is the sound of chuckling water she so longed for. The sigh of breezes in the trees. There is sunshine and the fresh scent of grass and of wildflowers when she goes into the field behind the barn where the weeds have grown high enough to hide her when she crouches.

Here her children don't spend hours in front of their computers or behind a desk or locked inside the shadows. Now they've both gone to wade in the stream, to build a fort from fallen branches. Kendra, who usually clings to her phone like it was going to take her to the prom, left it on the counter this morning. They've both gone brown from the sun, lean from activity. Here they are lovely and wild.

When they come down out of the woods, something in their shifting gazes tells her they were not doing what they said they'd been doing, but to ask them would mean she has to confront them about being untruthful. Then there must be punishment and discipline, and right now Mari wants nothing to do with that sort of thing. Instead, she calls to them, her brightest shining stars. Her delight.

She takes their hands and dances with them in the dirt of the farmyard the way she's done with them all their lives, and even Kendra concedes to dip and sway. Chickens peck and squawk around their feet. The three of them link their fingers. Make a circle.

Never ending.

THIRTY

AT THE KNOCK ON THE DOOR, RYAN TURNED off the TV before saying, "Yeah?"

He'd been watching the same two tapes for the past couple hours, fascinated by the change in the little girl from the beginning of her treatment and the final tape, recorded a few days before Mari left the hospital and went to the halfway house where she'd lived for two years before being adopted by his father. He was even more fascinated in the differences between the girl he met at his father's house, the one who eventually seduced him in front of the living room fireplace, and the one who stood in front of him now with a sandwich and chips on a plate in one hand, a beer in the other.

"Hungry?" Mari asked. "I made you some lunch."

"Thanks, babe." He wasn't hungry. To turn her down would be to earn a puzzled frown, so he took the plate and settled it on the desk. He caught her wrist before she could leave. "Where are the kids?"

"Outside playing."

He pulled her onto his lap for a nuzzle she seemed glad to give him. "You sure they'll be okay?"

"I told them to stay close. We can't keep them locked up, Ryan."

"No. I know that. Just after what happened…"

Mari hesitated, then said, "Sometimes, bad things happen."

He knew that, too. "Are you going out today?"

"No. Do you need something?" His wife made like she was going to get up, but Ryan pulled her close again.

"I thought if you were going to the library I'd tag along. Do some stuff online." There were some secondary research resources he wanted to look into.

"Oh." She shook her head a little. "I wasn't planning on it, today. But I do have to get there this week to return books and pay for the one Kendra lost."

"What do you mean, lost?" Ryan frowned.

Mari kissed him. "Don't worry about it."

"She has to be more responsible—"

She kissed him again, silencing him. "I'll take care of it."

He was only slightly mollified, but let it go.

"How's the writing going?"

It was his turn to hesitate. "Still taking notes. Some stuff doesn't add up. I need to do some research."

"Oh? Like what?" She didn't sound interested, and he was sure it was because she wasn't.

That was a good thing, since Ryan had yet to tell her the subject of his research, his book, was her. It wasn't a lie, he reminded himself, if she didn't ask him outright.

He'd always known how special Mari was, but the more he learned, the more he understood. She'd done more than simply survive, she'd done what hardly any other children who'd gone through what she had had been able to do. She'd thrived.

But there were pieces of the puzzle missing. An entire six months' worth of files were gone, and he thought he knew where they'd be. In storage at his mother's house. Ryan had no desire to ask her for them. It would open up a vitriolic box of venom, at the very least. But he had to find out everything. Like how they'd figured out Mari could speak with words, and how that had changed how they worked with her. Or who was the forest prince she'd spoken of in a few of the early tapes, using her hands to ask for him and eventually stopping when nobody had given her an answer, probably because that early on they'd been unable to interpret her question.

Ryan could, because he'd worn his eyes to blurriness watching those videos over and over again. His dad and Lois had missed so much in the beginning. Mari's simple signs hadn't been able to communicate any kind of complex ideas, yet she'd been very clear about what she wanted. And they'd missed it, time and again, more consumed later with the discovery she'd been able to understand them, and even speak to some degree, all along.

"Oh...need to check a few things, that's all." He didn't want to mention he'd be visiting his mother. "I might have to take a trip sometime soon. Do some more research. Maybe talk to some people."

"What?" She frowned. "Where? When?"

"Just back to Philly, babe. No big deal." He kept his voice light. "I'm going to have to go back, anyway, to meet with Saul and Jack about...stuff. I'll just take an overnight. Maybe," he added quickly when he saw her face. "I haven't decided yet."

Mari bit the inside of her cheek. "Could we all go? The kids would probably like a couple nights in the city. We could go to the museum or something."

He laughed. "That would be silly, wouldn't it? We can take them to the museum anytime. It's not like we don't live close enough. Besides, I'll be working. And..." Ryan sobered. "With our house being rented for the summer, paying for two hotel rooms just isn't in the budget."

His wife nodded, looking away. "Okay."

Ryan reached to pull her close again. "Babe, I promise you. It's all going to work out just fine. Okay?"

He waited. Now she'd ask him what he was writing about. What he needed to research.

"When do you think you might have to go?" she asked instead.

"Next week. Not before then. Listen, Mari," Ryan said quietly, needing to know. "Are you all right? With this? Being back here, I mean."

Her chin lifted. "Why do you ask?"

"No reason. Just…asking."

She got off his lap with a smile. "That sandwich is lame. How about I make you some spaghetti and garlic bread. Salad. I can open a bottle of wine, make it fancy. The kids won't be back for a while."

It was an invitation he was meant to take, and Ryan took it. He let his wife lead him by the hand upstairs to their bedroom, where they made love in the sticky heat of an early summer afternoon, right out in the bright sunshine the way they'd done before the kids came along and lovemaking had become something to in the dark, behind locked doors. And when they'd finished, he kissed her while she giggled and wiggled away from him, leaving him naked in their bed to go downstairs and finish fixing the lunch he'd eat in just a few minutes.

She hadn't asked him about what he was doing, and he supposed he should be glad for that. He'd have told her the truth, had she asked. But he'd asked her a question, and she hadn't given him an answer. It made Ryan realize something important.

In all the years he'd known her, Ryan couldn't think of one time when his wife had ever lied to him. Yet now he wondered about all the times she hadn't told him the truth.

THIRTY-ONE

MARI HAS BEEN COOKING ALL DAY. HOMEMADE corn bread, chili, baked potatoes and toppings. Brownies and cookies for dessert. Blueberry muffins for breakfast tomorrow. She looks at the wealth of this food and knows it's not enough. It can never be enough.

Despite the banquet, she doesn't have much of an appetite. All day she's been trying to absorb herself in work. Cleaning the house that's already clean, caring for the chickens that peck and scratch in the dirt and cluck around her feet and squat in front of her like she's the rooster. She has nothing else to do in the house of her childhood, and too many memories fighting to overwhelm her.

Ryan is leaving her.

For a day, he says. Maybe two. But the fact is, he brought her back here, and now he's going away, and she is afraid of losing everything she holds so close. Terrified of being abandoned. She hasn't felt this way for years.

No mess. Never. No garbage piled high, no dog poop on the floor. She likes coming back to this room, her room, Mari's room, they said. Her things. Today after her session with Dr. Calder, someone had taken away her carefully constructed village of blocks.

Her mouth opened. Wide. Wider. Screaming. Fists punching. Feet kicking. The table, overturned. The bed covers, ripped off. By the time she got to digging her nails into her own skin, tearing lines of red up one arm and down the other, Devonn had come through the door.

"Hey! Here now, stop all that!" Devonn was the biggest man she'd ever seen. Always in white. Big brown eyes. Big white teeth. He smelled always of nosetickle... cinnamon, Dr. Calder said. "What's going on?"

Sobbing, out of breath, disgusted with herself and everything else, Mari kicked at an overturned chair. She tried to tell him about the blocks. How they'd been set up on the floor by the bed, and now they were gone. Not in the box. Not under the bed. Not by the window.

Not. Nowhere. Gone.

She was crouched on the floor with Devonn's arms around her when Dr. Calder came in. "What's the matter with her?"

"I don't know. She started screaming." Devonn pushed hair off Mari's face from where it had stuck from the wet of her tears. "She doesn't seem to be sick."

"I just saw her twenty minutes ago." Dr. Calder got on the floor next to her. "Mari. What's wrong?"

She told him. Or tried to. A low snuffle of loss, a clench and release of fists to show empty palms. She traced a square with one finger in the air, then against the back of his hand, but he didn't understand.

They hardly ever did.

"Do you feel sick?" Dr. Calder put a hand to her head, but Mari jerked away.

Not sick.

But he didn't understand her this time, either. She had

words for so many things, so much to say, but nothing she did could make them hear her. She'd been quiet too long.

Quiet.

Hide.

They were talking over her head, not listening to her. Not paying attention. They wanted to know what was wrong with her, but they wouldn't listen. They talked and talked and talked, but she didn't talk.

"Mine!" Mari stood. Shouted. Her mouth opened. Throat hurt, sore, lips moved. Tongue. "MY BLOCKS GONE!"

Dr. Calder had cupped his face in his hands, telling her what a good girl she was. How proud he was of her. But he was proud of himself, Mari knew that. Because he thought somehow he'd fixed her.

Later, when they discovered she'd been able to talk the whole time, that her choice had been silence instead of speech, there were more tests. More visitors. More being asked to perform for the guests who came with shaking heads, their oohs and aahs...but who most often left without leaving behind any money.

It was the moment everything changed.

By the time Leon took her from the hospital that had been her home since she was eight, she'd learned to read and write, to be unafraid of communicating with spoken words—the limited number of them she knew and had rarely used aloud in her childhood, since Gran discouraged her speaking or making much noise at all—instead of grunts and hand gestures. She could bathe herself, dress herself. She'd grown taller. Filled out. And at thirteen, she was no longer the fascinating case study that had kept so many people interested for so long. Once she was no longer the Pine Grove Pixie, nobody seemed to care.

"This is her?" the woman in the beige dress had said, looking at Leon with perfectly arched brows, a face full of surprise. "I thought she'd be…different."

"Pleased to meet you." Mari had offered her hand the way Leon had told her was polite.

But the woman only shook her head. Other people who came did much the same thing. They expected to see some wild, muttering freak, and when they found out Mari had become something else, they went away and didn't come back.

The money disappeared. Without it, Mari had no place left in the hospital. There was a place for her, of course. They weren't going to just toss her out on the street. The halfway house was going to be the perfect home for her according to the hospital's social worker, an enormous woman with a kind face who didn't know Mari at all.

"They think I'm stupid," Mari had told Leon.

"No, Mariposa. They just think you need some help, that's all. And…maybe you do." He'd patted her shoulder, then her hair, hand resting on top of her head for a long silent moment, before he'd said, "Some of it's my fault. I thought we were doing good for you. I thought we *were* helping you."

Two years in that halfway house, sharing a room with three other girls who'd stolen cars and slept with their mother's boyfriends and set fires. Two years of working in the kitchen and cleaning the bathrooms so that she'd have some kind of skills to support herself with. She'd watched the other girls come and go, some returning, others disappearing forever.

If Leon hadn't taken her in and adopted her against what she knew now must've been every ethical advisory, Mari would probably still be living in the halfway house or one like it. And if Ryan hadn't married her, who knew where she might've gone? What she might've done without her husband? Her children? It's almost not worth imagining.

Yet she imagines it.

In her dreams she's always been wild, but here in this house

the desire calls to her even when she's awake. She wants to
scrounge in the dirt with her fingers, sifting for roots or mushrooms. She wants to strip off her clothes and run naked in the
rain to wash herself clean. She wants to dip water from the
stream to quench her thirst. She wants to run and run and run
from the idea of cleaning toilets and paying bills and attend-
ing parent-teacher conferences where she never knows what
to say because she never went to school the way her children
do. She wants to run away from casual conversation at cocktail parties, where people ask what she does, where she grew
up, where she came from.

Who she is.

True, she doesn't long for the filth and cold and constant
hunger. She doesn't want to live on the floor with dogs, hiding away like some terrible, shameful secret. She doesn't want
to return to the life she had as a child, in which nobody spoke
to her, acknowledged her. Loved her.

She doesn't really want to trade this life for that, but even
in this house, even with the changes time has made in it and
her, she can't help but think about what she might've become
had nobody found her, or if Leon hadn't adopted her. If Ryan
hadn't loved her.

She can't stop thinking about it, so along with the bak-
ing and the cooking and the cleaning, she's been pacing. The
kitchen is the one room she ought to want to avoid, yet she
can't stay out of it. Her hands move in shadow-puppet patterns, signaling her thoughts and emotions to nobody because
there's nobody there to see. Ryan is locked up in his office,
the door closed and locked, the kids are outside exploring.

There is a way to relieve the sting of this anxiety. She bends
down to reach the box she pushed behind the pots and pans.
She slips out a plastic-wrapped treat, her fingers fumbling
so that it flies from her grip and lands on the floor. She's on
her hands and knees again, tearing the plastic with her teeth

to gobble at the sweetness. Licking her fingers to get every crumb. Eating until her stomach clenches in protest and she claps a hand over her mouth to keep herself from vomiting.

There's nobody to see her acting this way. Crazy and wild. And though she doesn't much believe in God, Mari sends up a prayer of gratitude for this chance to be alone. It's harder to act normal when she's with other people, and though her family might accept any number of eccentricities from her, none of them have seen her like this.

She can't let them. If they did, they wouldn't love her any longer. How could they? When she is this unmotherly and unwifely creature? This wild and unlovable thing?

She straightens up, wipes the crumbs from her face just as she hears, "Mama?"

She turns, and there is her boy. Her dear, sweet boy. Mari clutches her fingers tight to her stomach, holding still the language that used to be the only one she used. "Yeah, honey?"

"Is it dinnertime? I'm hungry."

"Oh. Yes. It's dinnertime. Call your sister and Daddy."

Ethan does, but as they're sitting down to the table to eat, something screams from the yard. It's an eerie, cackling scream much the same as what had come out of the woods a few nights before, but this time, it ends in a squawk. Mari freezes with a pot of chili in her hands, halfway between the stove and the table. Kendra screams along. Ryan jumps up, knocking over his chair.

The scream comes again, louder this time, along with the muffled squabbling of the chickens. Mari puts the chili back on the stove. "Something's after the chickens."

They all run. Dirt kicks up under their feet as they run across the gravel driveway and toward the barn.

Blood.

There's so much blood. It paints the earth in splatters of

dark, not even red because it's already soaked into the ground. Here and there, black puddles of it. And in the center...

"Oh, no." This is Ethan, small and sad. "Oh, no, the peacock."

Something might've been after the chickens, but whatever it was has killed the peacock. Its long tail is filthy with mud churned with blood. Its head, the feathery crown also thick with blood, is cocked at an odd angle that clearly shows the bird's neck is broken. Its throat, in fact, is torn apart. Shredded.

Kendra shudders and puts an arm around her brother, turning him away. "Don't look."

Mari can't not look. She has to see. She runs through the dirt of the barnyard and falls to her knees beside the peacock's corpse. She doesn't touch. She looks at it without turning her gaze away, even though the sight is enough to turn her stomach. Not because of the blood or the death, but because of how such a beautiful creature has been made so ugly with it.

"Babe, get up. It's dead. You can't do anything for it."

Ryan's right, of course. He so often is. He's been Mari's guidepost for so many years. Her rudder, steering her through the complicated and confusing seas of social intercourse. Yet when he bends to lift her up, Mari shakes him off.

She remembers this, or something like it.

The chickens ignore their fallen companion, pecking and scratching and clucking, and it's not the chickens Mari remembers because she's never forgotten them. Running behind them to catch them and the way they never squawked until she helped Gran hold them down on the block. How they ran and ran, blood spurting, when their heads were chopped off. Killing the chickens had been necessary to fill her always hungry belly.

But the peacocks had served no use but beauty. They had, in fact, been something of a nuisance, fighting with the chickens for food and making a mess of Gran's garden—when she'd been well enough to plant it, anyway. And the noise had always been scary and strange, never something Mari got used to. Still, she remembers them now, strutting with their feathers fanned out. The little ones in the spring. Another memory sifts to the surface.

She remembers something like this, too, the lolling head and blood-coated feathers. She looks up at Ryan. "Fox."

"Huh? What? You're kidding me." He looks at the field beyond the yard automatically, as though he expects to see the fox there.

Mari stands and gathers Ethan against her. Kendra's backed off a few steps to tap furiously into her phone. "A fox killed the peacock. We'll have to make sure the chickens are locked up at night."

"Shit." Ryan scrubs at his face. "Are you sure?"

She's momentarily surprised by this, that he should turn to her as the expert. "It might've been a dog, but I haven't seen any around here. Raccoons will kill chickens, but I think this was a fox."

"Why didn't it eat it?" Kendra asks suddenly.

Mari looks at her daughter. "I don't know, Kiki. Maybe it got interrupted."

Ethan looks up from where he's pressed his face to Mari's belly. "Are some of the chickens gone? Maybe the fox ate them and wasn't hungry enough to eat the peacock."

"I don't know." The same answer to a different question. Mari pushes her son's hair from his face. "You could count them, but I don't know how many there were before."

"Rosie will know," he says. "I'm sad about the peacock."

Mari nods. "Me, too."

"That's what made those screaming noises," Kendra says, but her face is pale beneath the blush of summer sun.

"I guess we should bury it." Ryan sighs and looks as though this is the last task he's interested in doing.

"After dinner." Mari tugs on Ethan's sleeve. "We can do it after we eat."

"As if we could eat now. Gross," Kendra says in a voice thick with scorn, though her eyes keep darting to the peacock's corpse, and Mari has the idea her daughter's not quite as unmoved as she's trying to pretend.

"Things die," Mari says to all of them. "Sometimes they die naturally and sometimes they get killed. It happens. It's sad, but that's what foxes do. Kill things. And sometimes, it's something pretty that we'd rather have alive. So we'll eat dinner, and then we'll bury the peacock."

Ryan stares. Kendra stares. Only Ethan nods as though what she said makes perfect sense. It's only later, inside over bowls of chili and silence that Mari realizes out in the yard she'd been speaking aloud, yes—but she'd also been using the language of her childhood.

She'd also been signing.

THIRTY-TWO

KENDRA HAD GONE TO THE TOP OF THE MOUN-tain again, searching for a cell signal. She'd waited until Dad and Ethan left for the Humane Society because, after the peacock got killed, she knew her dad would've told her she couldn't leave the yard. Maybe her mom would've, too. But she needed to talk to Sammy, bad.

Except Sammy didn't answer her phone. Kendra got voice mail. Taking a deep breath, biting her lip, Kendra dialed Logan's number. He didn't answer, either. They were probably talking to each other, Kendra thought sullenly and thumbed Sammy a text before slipping the phone back into her pocket.

She'd wait a few minutes to see if either of them answered her, but, restless, she didn't want to sit while she did. She'd avoided the creepy crooked cabin, which meant staying in the trees instead of being in the clearing. Her feet crunched branches and twigs slapped her in the face as she pushed through, waiting without much hope for the vibration of a return call.

The snap of branches behind her didn't bother her the first time she heard it. But the second time, Kendra froze. Heart in her throat, she turned and saw nothing. She heard something, though.

Breathing.

Heavy, harsh. Another snap of twigs and shuffling like feet in the soft bed of leaves covering the ground. A low, muttered voice like a growl.

"Go," it said.

Kendra didn't think twice. She ran. Hard and fast, ducking branches that whipped at her face, scratching. With a quick glance behind her, she saw a figure, impossibly tall. Shadowed. It reached— Oh, shit, was it coming after her?

She jumped a fallen tree and skidded in the dirt, on pebbles, twisting her ankle. She hit the ground with a cry and rolled, getting to her feet as fast as she could. A fingernail broke off against a rock, and pain throbbed throughout her entire body.

The mountainside was steeper here than the path she'd climbed up, and Kendra fell again immediately. She skidded, sometimes on hands and knees, sometimes on her butt. She hit a flatter piece of ground and pushed herself to her feet again.

Sweating, hair in her face, she heard the sound of running water. The creek. She was almost to her backyard, or at the very least close enough to safety that she could turn around and look behind her again.

Nothing. Nobody chasing her. Not even a shadow in the distance.

Panting, Kendra pushed herself harder, anyway. Jumped the creek. She tumbled out of the trees and into a clearing to the far right of her house, on the opposite side of the barn and field.

She was filthy. Her palms scratched. A welt on her cheek stung, and she'd bitten her tongue.

Worst of all, her phone was gone.

It was too much. Kendra burst into tears. She forced herself to put one foot in front of the other until she got into her backyard, where she found her mom hanging sheets and towels on the line.

"Kiki? What's wrong?" Her mom was there at once, holding Kendra's shoulders.

Kendra spit out the story about the cabin and the cell signal and the voice that had told her to "go." The figure of the man, looming. Being chased. And, finally, about her phone.

"Oh, Kiki. Your dad's going to be so angry." Her mom shook her head, but put an arm around her shoulders. "But… you said there was a little house? And…a man?"

Snot bubbled out of Kendra's nose. "Yes. It sounded like a man."

"A real man?"

Kendra frowned. "Well…yeah. I mean, not like a Bigfoot or whatever."

Her mom looked past her, into the woods, her gaze far away. "What did he look like?"

"He was in the trees. And he chased me." Kendra paused. "Not that hard, though, I guess. I mean, if he'd wanted to catch me, he could have."

Her mom gripped her shoulders harder, a strange look on her face. "He didn't touch you?"

"No."

"You didn't see him?"

Kendra shook her head. "Just heard him."

"No more going into the woods, Kendra. Do you hear me?" Mom looked fierce.

As if she would, after this. Not even to look for her phone, which, even if she could find where it had fallen from her pocket, would probably be broken. Kendra drew in a sniffling breath and nodded.

"Do we have to call the police again?" she asked.

Her mom shook her head. "I doubt it would do any good, since he didn't actually do anything to you."

"He scared me," Kendra said.

Mom hugged her close. "Just stay out of the woods, okay?"

"What are we gonna tell Dad about my phone?"

Her mom sighed and rubbed at her eyes. "I'm not sure."

Kendra wiped her face. "I'm sorry, Mom."

"Why?" Her mom looked surprised.

"For going up there after everything else that happened. Being stupid. Losing my phone." Kendra burst into more tears.

Her mom held and shushed her, which made Kendra feel dumb, like a baby, but also better. She rested her head on her mom's shoulder and hugged her, hard. They stood that way for a few minutes.

"They'll be back soon from the Humane Society. Why don't you come inside, take a cool shower. Get cleaned up." Her mom smiled. "We can make tacos for dinner, okay?"

Her favorite. It didn't do much to make her feel better, not yet, but Kendra nodded. She hugged her mom again, and headed for the house. She looked back just before she turned the corner toward the front door.

Her mom was motioning toward the forest. Over and over, the same small set of gestures. She'd seen her mom do something like that a lot over the years, but this was the first time it sent a chill down her spine.

Where are you?

It was a game they played, her and mama. Kendra hiding, mama looking. Kendra giggling, silent. Mama moves her fingers, talking without her mouth.

Where are you?

"I'm here!" Kendra pops out from behind the couch. "I'm here!

She watched a moment or so longer, but her mom had stopped. Now she just stared into the woods like she expected an answer to her silent question, but from who? And Kendra watched, her throat closing, also waiting for an answer, but none came.

Mom turned. "Let's go inside."

THIRTY-THREE

THEY'D NEVER HAD A PET OTHER THAN CARNI-
val goldfish, but Ryan hadn't thought too hard about the decision to get a dog. He'd already half promised Ethan before
they came here, and once the peacock showed up dead in the
barnyard it had seemed like the most natural choice. Christ,
what a mess. And to make things worse, when they'd come
out after dinner to bury the damn thing, all that remained
was a few bloody feathers and a mess in the dirt—whatever
had killed it must've come back and carried it off.

The Lebanon County Humane Society was almost an hour
away and had dogs to spare. Ethan had wanted to take home
every mongrel they saw, but in the end Ryan convinced him
what mattered was that the dog was big and could bark loud
enough to scare off any foxes that came into the yard.

They settled on a mutt with one bent ear and one standing
straight. Something like a German shepherd and collie mix,
with silky black fur, a white bib and a tail that whipped back
and forth so fiercely it created its own breeze. The dog had
looked up at them from its pen, tongue lolling, and given such
a sharp series of barks Ryan had known it was the right one.

He'd never had a dog growing up and honestly had never

much wanted one as an adult, but as soon as he looked at that mutt's face, Ryan knew what to name it. "Chompsky."

Ethan guffawed, eyes bright as he hugged the dog around the neck. For a moment, all Ryan could do was stare at his son, too aware that he'd never had such a moment with his own father. Sure, when he got older he and his dad had been okay with each other, but…never like this. When Ethan left the dog to hug Ryan, small arms going tight around his waist, all he could do was soak it in with gratitude, because he knew his son's affectionate nature had not come from him.

The dog rode nicely in the car and leaped from it as soon as they got home, sticking close to the kids even without a leash. It had some training, at least. Ryan watched, amused, as Chompsky tried with little success to herd them all together. Definitely some border collie, then.

Mari waited for them in the kitchen. She stood quietly at the sink, turning but not startling as Ethan and their new pet scrambled through the doorway in a tumble of laughter and fur. She hadn't protested when Ryan had said they were going to get a dog to protect the house and the chickens. Watching his wife from the doorway, Ryan realized uncomfortably he'd never considered the reasons why she might not want a dog.

"Mom! Look! Isn't he great? His name is Chompsky," Ethan said, one small hand on the dog's collar and his feet skidding along the tile floor as he tried unsuccessfully to keep the mutt from jumping up on Mari.

"Lame name," Kendra put in. "Guess it's better than Zipper, though."

"I liked Zipper, but I like Chompsky better. Chompsky! See, he knows it!" Ethan laughed as the dog left off its pursuit of his mother and jumped to lick at his face.

Through this, Mari stood silent and still.

"Babe," Ryan began, but when she held up one hand, he shushed.

Mari tilted her head, studying the dog that now sat back on its haunches to give her a slobber-tongued, doggy grin. Then slowly, slowly, she got onto one knee, almost like a man proposing marriage. She reached out one hand, not quite close enough to touch the dog's silky fur.

"You want to pet him, Mama?"

The dog whined and went down onto its front paws, rear in the air, tail wagging so fast it became a blur. Mari mirrored the position, adding a small yip that Chompsky echoed. In the next moments, the dog was all over her, slurping and licking at her face while Mari laughed and tried to fend off the attack of affection. Ethan joined in a moment later, the three of them romping until Chompsky rolled onto his back with his legs splayed and gave Mari another yelp.

Ryan froze watching this, a replay of one of the videotapes running through his head. Young Mari had behaved this way in the playroom at the hospital, though there it had been with a large stuffed dog, not a real animal. Now she sat up to give him a small smile that didn't quite reach her eyes. Her fingertips found the dog's belly and she rubbed while Ethan chattered about how they'd chosen the dog, the name, how he was going to teach Chompsky all sorts of tricks.

"He's part border collie," Ryan said.

"That's nice, honey," Mari murmured, never looking away from Ryan's eyes.

Ryan swallowed, the moment passed. There was nothing here but a dog happy in his new home and a family delighted to have a new pet. Even Kendra had consented to crouch on the floor next to her brother in order to rub Chompsky's fur.

"I'm going to get to work on the book." He paused when his wife got off the floor. "You okay with this, babe?"

Mari gave him that head-tilted look, that faint smile. She nodded just slightly. "Like you said, we need a dog. It's good for the kids."

Still, he hesitated in the doorway. "And…you're okay with it?"

"Why wouldn't I be?"

He might've been imagining the faint challenge in her voice, which would've been totally unlike her. "It's supposed to be housebroken. That's what the people at the pound said, anyway."

His wife gave him a steady stare. "And if he's not, it would hardly be the first time I've cleaned up dog shit. Would it?"

All at once he wanted to hold her. Pull her next to him, close his eyes, breathe in the scent of her hair. He wanted to back up time and forget he'd ever thought about bringing her back here. They could find a way to make ends meet without this book. He could put all the files and folders away and take his family away from this place.

But then when she turned and spoke to the dog, making a subtle, barely there set of motions with her hands at the same time, Ryan knew he wasn't going to.

THIRTY-FOUR

MARI'S HAND HURT. PUNCTURED, HOLES SEEP-
ing green goo tinged with blood. When her fingers clenched,
sharp, fierce pain stabbed all through her, making her feel like
she was going to fall down.

The dog had bit her. She'd reached for something in its
bowl, and it had snapped, snarling. Growling. Mari had won
the battle for the hunk of chicken on the bone Gran had put in
there, always the dogs had food though many times Mari was
forgotten. The dogs fought among themselves. Mari fought
the dogs when she had to.

"Be quiet," Gran had said. "Hide."

Them had come, pounding feet on the floor. Loud voices.
Gran fought Them the way Mari and the dogs fight. Gran
won't leave this house. Gran won't take Their medicine,
though she'll eat the food They leave her. Gran won't let
Them help her change her clothes, goddammit, this is her
place, They should get out.

Get out!

Get out!

Mari hid, and later when Them had gone, there was another voice. Another person. Nice hands, washing her face
and cleaning her hands, the sore spots. Wrapping them in ban-

dages. Giving her water, cold water. Mariposa is so hot she is going to fly away.

"Stay with me, little butterfly," the voice says. It is soft, gentle, the voice of her protector.

Her forest prince comes to her from the woods. When Mari opens her eyes, he is there. Making everything better.

THIRTY-FIVE

"SURE, IT COULDA BEEN A FOX." ROSIE LOOKED over the dirt in the yard.

The chickens had scuffed it up, covering the blood, but Kendra couldn't forget that it was there. Ethan had snagged the single raggedy feather from the peacock's tail, but Daddy had told him not to take it in the house. He said it was bad luck.

"What?" Rosie laughed at this when Kendra told her. "Bad luck? Is that what he thinks causes it?"

Kendra shrugged and kicked at the dirt with the toe of her Chucks. "Dunno. He just told him not to take it in the house."

Ethan had hung it up in the barn, instead. Now he walked slowly behind one of the fluffy chickens and waited until it squatted before he picked it up. He held it in one arm while he petted its head. The chicken clucked, and the monkeybrat laughed. Rosie laughed, too, as she scattered some feed for them. Kendra felt for the comforting weight of her phone in her pocket before remembering she'd lost it.

"If it wasn't a fox, what do you think it was?" Kendra asked.

Rosie turned to look at her. "I didn't say it wasn't. Foxes kill chickens. Your dog might kill 'em, too, you're not careful."

"Chompsky won't," Ethan said.

Hearing his name, the dog let out a single, sharp bark. His

tail swept the dirt back and forth. Kendra bent to scratch his head. "Chompsky doesn't even chase chickens."

Rosie snorted. "Dogs'll do what they do. Just like men."

Ethan had already put down the chicken he'd been holding and was now after another one. He hadn't heard what Rosie said, or if he had, didn't care. Kendra did, though.

"What's that supposed to mean?" It wasn't as if she hadn't ever heard women diss on dudes before. Sammy did it all the time. But Kendra was kind of partial to guys even if they could be jerks and not reply to text messages.

"Oh, you could ask your mama that question. She'd know better than me, I guess." Rosie chuckled.

"Don't *you* have a husband?"

Rosie shot Kendra a sideways look. "He died. Cancer."

"I'm sorry." She really didn't care, but it seemed like the polite thing to say.

"I ain't," Rosie said. She straightened as the chickens pecked around her feet. She kicked out, just a little, to shoo them away. She put her hands on the hips of her overalls. She clucked, imitating the chickens.

"Kendra! Ethan!"

Kendra turned to see her mom on the front porch. She waved, catching her mother's eye. Mom shaded her eyes, then came across the driveway and around the side of the barn.

"Hi, Rosie. Kiki, where's Ethan? I told him to clean up his room."

"He's chasing chickens." Kendra had cleaned her room before coming out, not because she was into cleaning but because she hardly had anything here that needed putting away. And without her phone, hardly anything to do.

Her mom sighed. "Hi, Rosie. We're going to be grilling burgers for dinner. Would you like to stay?"

Rosie looked surprised. "For dinner?"

Her mom's smile always made Kendra feel like everything

was okay, no matter what else was going on. Rosie seemed more taken aback than warmed. The old lady shrugged.

Mom gestured. "I made potato salad. Corn on the cob, too. And biscuits. There'll be plenty of food."

"You'll have enough to feed an army."

"You're welcome to join us," Mom said. "Kiki, go tell Ethan he'd better get his butt inside and clean up his room, or I'm going to have to get angry."

"Children need discipline," Rosie said.

Mom looked at her with raised eyebrows. "Of course they do."

Rosie snorted. Kendra didn't need to stick around for more of that conversation—in fact, as much as she might've been interested in hearing the monkeybrat get in trouble any other time, she didn't really want him to get yelled at in front of Rosie. She found him in the barn, looking at the feather he'd hung on the wall.

"Mom said you'd better clean your room, or you're gonna get in trouble."

"I'm sad about the peacock, Kiki. I don't think a fox killed it."

"What else would? Besides, what difference does it make if it was a fox or a raccoon or a coyote? It's dead," Kendra said flatly.

"Maybe that thing in the forest. The one that lives in that little house."

"That's not a thing," Kendra said, feeling proud of herself for believing it. "It's some hillbilly dude. C'mon. You need to clean your room so Mom doesn't get mad."

Ethan sighed and scowled, then stomped off away from her without saying anything else. Outside, around the back of the house, Rosie sat at the splintery picnic table where Mom had already put out paper plates, napkins and cups. Also the bowl of potato salad and a pitcher of lemonade.

"Where's my mom?" Kendra asked.

"Getting the meat, I guess." Rosie pointed toward the house.

"I guess I should help her." But the back door was locked, and when she knocked, her dad took forever to open it.

When he did, he didn't look happy. "Kendra. What?"

She made to push past him. "I have to help mom with the burgers."

"Go around."

She stopped, incredulous. "Huh?"

"This is my office, Kendra, not a highway. Go around. I'm working."

Her mom appeared around the side of the house with a platter of meat patties. "Ryan, relax. Kiki, come help me. Ryan, can you please get the grill started?"

She took the platter from her mom while her dad closed the door without a word. Kendra gave her mom a scowl.

"So we still have to walk all the way around, even though the kitchen is literally right through there?"

Mom sighed. "He's busy, Kiki."

The next minute the door opened again. Her dad came out and shut the door heavily behind him. He did a double take at the sight of Rosie, then gave Mom a squeeze.

"Let's get this started." Her dad rubbed his hands together and bent to look at the tank of gas under the grill. He twisted the knob. He lifted the grill lid and pushed a button.

Nothing happened.

He pushed the button again, then again, muttering curses. Kendra put the platter on the table with a heavy sigh. Rosie snorted softly.

Mom looked over at them both with a small smile. "Honey, maybe you need to use a lighter or something."

"No, no, I'll get it."

This was going to take forever. Kendra scooped some potato salad onto her plate and grabbed a plastic fork. She could starve before her dad got the grill going.

Rosie frowned. "You don't pray before you eat?"

Kendra paused, fork halfway to her mouth. She glanced at her parents, both of them working on the grill. "Huh?"

"No," Rosie said. "I guess you wouldn't."

By the grill, her dad muttered a curse, but Mom burst into laughter. Kendra took a bite of potato salad, her teeth scraping on the plastic fork. Rosie took a biscuit.

Mom turned toward the table, shaking her head. "Well…I guess I could always just make them on the stove. It'll only take a few minutes. C'mon, Ryan. Don't fuss with that anymore."

Her dad kept muttering but followed her mom, along with the platter of meat, into the house. This left Kendra sitting alone across the picnic table from Rosie. The old woman stared at her.

"Your daddy sure does love your mama, ain't?"

"I guess so." She didn't like to think much about her parents' relationship beyond the fact that it worked better than, say, Sammy's parents' did.

"Are you a good child?"

The question surprised her. "Um…"

"Are you a good daughter?" Rosie asked. "You and your brother. You good kids? I already know your brother don't listen good."

Kendra frowned. "He's okay. He's not that bad."

"Children should obey their parents, that's all." Rosie took another biscuit and bit into it, crumbs gathering at the corners of her mouth. "Children who don't obey their parents deserve to be punished."

"I… We obey our parents."

"How sharper than a serpent's tooth it is to have a thankless child," Rosie muttered. "Jesus said that."

Kendra was 100 percent positive that Shakespeare had said it, but she didn't argue. "I'm not thankless."

"Huh." Rosie snorted and looked around the backyard, then gave Kendra a sly sort of grin. "Most people don't stay here long, you know? Rent the place for a week or so, get their hiking and hunting in, then leave. Oh, once we had a family that tried it out, but they didn't last long."

"Did someone throw rocks at them, too?" Kendra asked sourly.

Rosie scowled. "If you were my daughter, I'd wash your mouth with soap for that sass."

Kendra didn't offer an apology, though Rosie was clearly waiting for one.

"I guess your people don't scare easy," Rosie said finally. "But you'll be heading back to the city soon enough."

"I don't think we are leaving," Kendra said, just to be a jerk. "My dad's working on a book, and he's not even close to finishing. And besides, my mom likes it here. A lot. This was her house, you know."

"She picked it?"

"No," Kendra said. "This was her house. I mean her actual house, where she grew up."

Rosie's hand jerked, knocking against the bowl of potato salad. Kendra was quick enough to keep it from spilling off the table, but Rosie looked as shaken as if she'd dumped it all over herself. She got to her feet, one hand on the table to keep herself steady.

"You shut your lying mouth."

Kendra settled the bowl carefully and fixed Rosie with a long stare. "I'm not lying."

"Your mama grew up in this house?"

"That's what I said." Kendra wished she hadn't said any-thing. Based on the look on Rosie's face, the old lady was going to have a heart attack, and there was no way Kendra was going to do CPR.

Rosie began to laugh. Spit flew from her mouth as she bent at the waist, guffawing. She pointed at Kendra, but couldn't manage to speak for a minute or so.

"Oh, wait until he hears this," Rosie crowed at last. "Won't he feel stupid, though?"

"Who?" Kendra asked.

But Rosie only shook her head and backed away, face going sober. She slurped at her teeth. "Tell your mama I'm sorry, I can't stay for dinner."

"But—" Kendra called after her, but Rosie only gave a backward wave as she left.

THIRTY-SIX

THE MASTER BATH RENOVATION WAS DONE well. It has a shower better than the one in the hall bath and a vintage-looking claw-foot tub that's probably a reproduction. Mari fills it and adds a foaming bath cube Ethan bought her from the school's holiday shop last Christmas and which had been packed, forgotten, in her travel bag for months. It doesn't smell very good, too much like chemicals to her sensitive nose, but it gives the water a luxurious and silky feel she's completely enjoying.

She's not much of a bath person, normally. Mari likes showers because they are quick and efficient, allowing her to get clean in the least amount of time possible so she can move on to other things. Like many other memories she's shoved aside and which are now rising inexorably toward the front of her mind, she thinks now of how she used to fight the bathtub. She sinks down in the water now, remembering strong hands holding her as other hands scrubbed her hair and pulled the tangles free. She remembers screaming.

It seems so silly now. Her own children had never fought the tub—they loved it, in fact. They'd play for an hour in the water, dipping it into cups and floating boats. Splashing. They'd never even complained when she got soap in their eyes.

A stack of magazines she found in the living room cupboard sits next to the tub. It's an odd collection. *Doll Collector. Archery Hunter. Civil War Stories.* Whoever lived here before sure had varied tastes.

Mari doesn't collect anything, but the doll magazine fascinates her. Settling into the steaming water, she flips through page after page of dead-eyed dolls. There's another toy on the page. Soft body, hard plastic head like the others, but this doll isn't in the shape of a person. It's a worm with a green body and a nightcap on its head.

She knows this toy. Her children had toys like this, but she's remembering something else. Something like it, not the same...something she had held tight against her to light up the night until one day, it went dark and never shone again. Mari closes her eyes.

Did she have a toy like this? Maybe not exactly the same, but close enough that she can still recall the feel of its soft body, the hard box inside it, the plastic face. Her fingers squeeze the magazine, mindless of how she's crumpling it.

"For you." The forest prince has brought her a present. "For when it's dark. So you don't have to be afraid."

Mari squeezes it close, watching it light up. She strokes the soft body, the hard head. She looks at him. "Butterfly."

"Shh," he reminds her, and forms her fingers into the motions of a butterfly, fluttering. "Remember. Quiet. So they won't hear you."

They'd convinced her it was imagination. That only Gran had been in the house with her. No matter how many times she'd tried to describe or explain him, nobody had believed her.

Mari looks to the bathroom window, to the darkness outside. Then again to the picture in this magazine. She hadn't imagined that glowing butterfly doll. That doll had been real. So then, had the boy who gave it to her been real, too?

For the first time in years, she thinks he was.

She hears the click–click of claws on the tiles. Chompsky sits, head cocked, to look at her. He pants, smiling, and she thinks how much she's come to love this dog even in the short time he's been theirs.

She hadn't loved her gran's dogs. They smelled bad, barked too much. They bit. They stole food from her hands if she wasn't careful. They weren't pets the way Chompsky is, and yet she can't keep herself from thinking about those dogs from the past any more than she can stop the rush and press of all the other memories coming back to her.

The bath holds no more interest for her. She's not sure what prompted her to think she wanted one in the first place, except that it's what women are supposed to do when they want to relax. Now her skin's crawling from the bubbles and her stomach's upset from the heat. She runs the shower, cold, and stands beneath it shivering. Mari tilts her face to the water and opens her mouth to wash away the taste of the past, but it takes a long, long time.

THIRTY-SEVEN

KENDRA HATED GROCERY SHOPPING, BUT WHEN Mom had asked if she and Ethan wanted to come along, Kendra had jumped at the chance, especially when Mom promised lunch. Fast food was always a treat because Mom hated the taste of what she called "fake" burgers. And after Kendra had watched that documentary by the guy who ate at McDonald's every single day she'd been a little scarred herself.

She hadn't counted on the fact that they really were out in BumFuck. No McDonald's, no Burger King, no Wendy's. Kendra groaned as her mom drove slowly along one of the main roads in town.

"How about here?" Her mom pulled into the parking lot of a long, low building with a big red rabbit on the sign. "Look. It says 'make the red rabbit a habit.' Cute, huh? They have ice cream. And onion rings."

Kendra had never wanted greasy fries and a strawberry shake so much in her life. Ethan was already bouncing up and down in the backseat, begging for chicken strips. Inside the place looked like something out of an old movie. Diner booths, a jukebox, old records on the walls. Her mom laughed in delight, looking around. Ethan jumped over to the jukebox. Kendra studied the menu. A buck fifty for a Hollywood Burger? Where were they, the Twilight Zone?

Kendra looked across the room at the counter, the bored teenager working there, and was sort of jealous. At least *that* kid had a job, earned some money, probably had friends to hang out with. When she got back to Philly, Kendra was going to be broke and behind on all the gossip.

She probably *was* the gossip.

"Help you?" asked the guy behind the counter without even glancing at her.

Great. Now she was such a nonperson even pimple-faced fry jockeys didn't bother to check her out. She might as well get the upsized, triple-burger meal with bacon and some fried pie for dessert. So what if her face broke out and she gained, like, fifty pounds just by breathing the smell of it? Clearly she wasn't worth paying attention to.

Her mom was placing the order, one item at a time, carefully, the way she always did. It could be infuriating how she took her time, reading each item off the menu, but when Kendra glanced away from the plaques shellacked with newspaper articles featuring the Red Rabbit, the cashier didn't look annoyed. If anything, he was even slower to ring up the items than her mom was saying them. Kendra sighed. So much for "fast" food.

"Ellie? Ellie Pfautz?" the manager asked from behind the counter.

The manager looked to be about four feet tall, with a stringy gray ponytail sprouting from under her baseball cap and—gross—a mouth full of crooked, jutting teeth. At least the ones that weren't missing. Kendra looked behind her to see if the woman was talking to someone, but there was nobody there.

"No, it can't be." The woman shook her head as she eyed Kendra. "But you look just like her."

"I'm not from around here," Kendra said.

"Kiki, what do you want to drink?" her mom asked, and the manager turned to her.

"Oh, my God," the manager said. "Oh, my God."

The restaurant hadn't been full when they'd come in. Maybe eight or ten people in the booths, another three behind her mom in line. It seemed like every head turned at the sound of the manager's voice. Kendra's mom looked around, then at the woman.

"I'm...sorry?"

The manager looked back and forth from Kendra to her mom, then again. "Oh, my God. It's...you look just like Ellie did," she said to Kendra. "And that's your mom, huh? You're her mom?"

"I'm her mother, yes."

Kendra's stomach was twisting with unease—it was probably never a good thing to be singled out in a backwoods burger joint by the manager who sounded like she'd just accidentally put her fingers in the fryer. But her mom was calm, her voice cool and only a little curious. She'd clutched her purse closer to her side and reached for Ethan's hand to pull him close, too, but that was the only sign she gave that anything might be wrong.

"And you're the one who..." The manager shook her head as if in disbelief. "Your mother, was she Ellie Pfautz?"

Kendra's mom took two steps back from the counter. Now everyone was definitely looking at them. Kendra's mom saw it, too, her gaze sweeping the place, skating over Kendra, before settling back on the manager.

"Yes?" She sounded uncertain.

The manager moved closer, each step shuffling and awkward as she heaved the weight of her body from side to side. "I knew your mother."

Kendra's mom made a small, helpless noise.

"She worked here." The woman had a sort of gleeful and horrified look on her face like she hadn't been the one to fall into the hot oil, but was watching someone else take a dive. "Oh, my God."

If she said "oh, my God" one more time, Kendra thought she might scream. Even Ethan had stopped his bouncing. His hand linked through Mom's fingers as he looked up at her, then at the manager. Kendra moved closer, too. It was crazy, like she and Ethan could somehow protect her. Kendra didn't even know against what. Against something, though.

The manager's face split in a wide smile that tried to be friendly but came off grotesque. "You didn't know?"

"I didn't know my mother," Mom said in the voice that would've made Kendra or even Ethan stop talking. Even Daddy would've changed the subject. Mom didn't get angry often, but when she did…

"You didn't know your mother?" The manager's voice carried.

Nobody was even pretending not to stare now.

"No. I never knew her." Mom gave the cashier a pointed look. "My change?"

"Oh, sure." He fumbled with the drawer.

Mom took the couple dollars in change from the cashier and tucked them into her wallet, then gave Ethan and Kendra each a quarter from the coins before dumping the others loose into her purse. She always did that, and somehow that made all of this all right. It was normal, even if none of the rest of this was. Kendra clutched the coin in her fist, even though a quarter had long ago stopped being exciting. She rubbed the edge of it with her thumb. She didn't want her burger or shake anymore.

The drama hadn't ended. The stupid manager wouldn't quit. She heaved herself forward to lean on the counter. "You back in town? You in that house, huh? Ollie Barrett told us about you but I have to say, nobody believed it."

Mom nodded, her expression giving away nothing. She'd gone blank and far away. Kendra had never seen that face on her mother before. Anger, annoyance, boredom, polite disinterest. But never this blankness.

It scared her.

The manager laughed and looked over Kendra and Ethan. "And these are yours? Wow. Well, I guess you done all right for yourself. All things considered, I guess you were pretty lucky, then. I mean, nobody'd have thought, huh? I mean, Ellie had the baby right over there." The manager pointed to the restroom doors. "Right in that ladies' room! Can you believe it? And here you are, what, thirty-some years later? All growned up. Who'd have thunk it?"

Kendra blinked rapidly. Ethan had been following their mom so closely that when she stopped, he bumped her. Their drinks shifted on the tray she held, slopping over her mom's hands and onto the floor. Kendra pulled up so short her sneakers squeaked on the dirty tile floor.

"Kiki, take this tray to a table, please. And grab some extra...extra..." Her mother drew in a breath, the only sign so far that she was at all upset. Her eyes darted back and forth, her face no longer blank. "Paper cloths. Paper hand wipers."

"Napkins?" Ethan offered.

"Yes," their mom bit out. Her voice sounded stilted and strained. It made Kendra's stomach hurt worse. Ethan had backed up a step, his small face anxious. Kendra's mind twisted the way her stomach had.

Her mom had been born in the bathroom of a fast food restaurant? What kind of fuckery was that?

"Nobody even knew she was pregnant," the manager continued. "I heard she said she didn't even know, but I want to know how anybody could possibly not be able to tell they're pregnant?"

"Maybe she was so fat she couldn't tell," Kendra said so loudly the sound of her voice shocked herself. "I mean, you could be pregnant and nobody would be able to tell by looking at you."

The noise of a dozen pairs of eyes rushing to fix themselves on any place but the manager was also the sound of Kendra's mom's sigh. "Kiki."

Kendra lifted her chin, jaw tight. She'd crossed her arms over her chest at some point, like she was daring that bitch behind the counter to say anything. But the manager, like most bullies, didn't. She looked shocked, then angry and then, finally and much too late, in Kendra's opinion, ashamed. She didn't say anything, though, just turned and waddled to the back of the kitchen.

The cashier let out a short, sharp snicker he quickly silenced when Kendra glared at him. Then he gave her an admiring, up-and-down glance that might've been flattering if he'd been cute—or she hadn't just been a total bitch to a stranger in front of a restaurant full of hillbillies. She didn't even smile at him, just turned to her mom and Ethan.

"Can we take that stuff to go?"

"Sure, honey." Her mom sounded like her normal self again.

In the car, her mom turned the music up loud and they sang along with stupid summer songs by lame fake rocker chicks who thought lyrics about dental hygiene mixed with liquor made them sound badass. Ethan made up some words of his own, most of them rhyming with or talking about poop, which made their mom laugh so Kendra joined in. They ate their food and tossed the trash in the pail out in the yard before they started to unload the groceries instead of leaving the trash in the car the way they usually did—or even taking it in the house the way their mom usually told them to.

"Let's not tell your dad we got fast food," their mom said, too casually. "He'll be mad we didn't get him anything."

"Okay," Ethan said without a question.

Kendra nodded, too. But later, watching her mom in the kitchen as she stocked the cupboards with food they didn't need and probably would never even eat before, please God, they went back to Philly, she wondered if her mom had another reason for not saying anything. Maybe her mom didn't want her dad to know about what the manager had said. Kendra didn't blame her.

She wished she didn't know, either.

THIRTY-EIGHT

MARI KNOWS HER LIFE HAS BEEN STRANGE. OF course she knows. She can't be in the life she has now, remembering the one that came before, and not understand that it wasn't normal. More than not normal, it was freakish. Insane.

Now she knows a little more than she did before, and wonders if she's better off with this image in her brain of a young woman giving birth in a bathroom. Mari's mother had been only nineteen when Mari was born, from what she can remember overhearing from the doctors and social workers who'd spoken around her for a long time before realizing she could understand them. Nineteen is young, only a few years older than Kendra. Mari was seventeen when she started sleeping with Ryan—and if he hadn't been considerate enough to pull out that first time in front of the fireplace, who knows? Maybe Mari might've been pregnant at seventeen.

But she'd have *known* she was pregnant, she thinks with her hands on her belly that's still flat and firm, though crisscrossed with the faint and silvery lines of stretch marks. She'd known almost as soon as she got pregnant each time. Of course they'd been trying; she'd been married; it had been something they both wanted. She'd had no reason to hide it or pretend she didn't know about it, the way Mari's mother had felt she had to do.

There'd never been any mention of a father.

She didn't remember everything she'd heard during those long months in the hospital when *They* talked around and above and behind her, but hardly ever *to* her. But she's sure she'd have remembered if they said anything about her father. Her mother was gone, that was all Mari had ever known. Aside from a few photos on the walls in her grandmother's house she doesn't even know what her mother looked like.

The manager knows. This seems brutally unfair, that a stranger should be able to so vividly recall the details of Mari's life that have been kept a secret from her. That Kendra should look so much like Mari's mother she could be confused for her, when Mari has always felt Kendra looks so much like Ryan and hardly at all like herself.

That woman had spread out the past like shaking a tablecloth to get the crumbs off.

She chokes back a sob that hurts her throat. Her palms sting; she's clenched her fingers so tight she's dented bloody half-moons into her skin. The kids have hidden themselves away in their rooms. Ryan is locked in his den, working. She could go to him and tell him what she learned today, but the truth is she's afraid to tell him she found out that her teenage unwed mother gave birth to her in a bathroom.

Because...what if he already knew?

She wants to run outside and strip out of the loosely wrapped Thai fisherman pants and white tank top she picked out from her closet this morning, when she thought all she'd be doing was taking a trip to a town that had no memories for her. But she doesn't. Mari takes deep breaths instead and uncurls her fingers.

Back in her first days at the hospital, Mari hadn't been able to express her anxiety or her terror to anyone who could understand her. She'd raged in silence, knowing that already it was too late—They had come for her. It didn't matter if she made noise. Yet she'd been unable to cry aloud, or even to hit at things. She doesn't remember how long she was in the hospital before someone realized that not only could she understand everything they were saying, but she could reply. Had been answering. What sounded to them like grunts or growls, what looked to them like random fluttering motions, was how Mari spoke. But once they knew, everything had changed. They'd stopped trying to train her and started teaching her, instead.

Leon had been the one to figure out what she was doing with her repeated hand motions. He'd taught her the words she needed to say when things were becoming particularly traumatic. It was their code for Mari's frustration or for needing a break or for emotions she had forgotten how to name.

"Rough time," she whispers. Then again. "Very rough time."

It had been hard and frustrating. Mari can remember breaking down, kicking and screaming, fighting at the hands that tried to comb her hair, brush her teeth, shove her feet into shoes. She remembers crouching over her plate and bowl, snapping at the hands that tried to take it away before she'd gobbled up every last scrap. And she also remembers the delight of a soft bed, a full belly. She remembers when she no longer had to fight against the language of her hands but could open her mouth and tell the world what she wanted and who she was.

But who *is* she?

This table is not that old table, the cloth not the same, but Mari pulls it from a drawer and drapes it over the top so folds of fabric hang down and make a cave. The dog's sitting at her feet, cocking its head to look at her. This dog might snitch a scrap that falls on the floor, but he doesn't jump up on the counters to get it. He doesn't lift his lip and growl when she takes something from his mouth. This dog is something to love, not to battle. She bends to scratch between his ears, then gets on her knees to let the dog cover her with sloppy, drooling kisses. Mari puts her face to Chompsky's silky fur and smells shampoo, not filth. She would cry into the dog's neck, but no tears come. She strokes it over and over again while the dog pants and flops onto her lap, gazing up at her with adoration.

Mari growls softly.

Chompsky's ears perk. He licks his chops. Tilts his head and offers a low whine. Mari echoes it. Chompsky barks, leaping to his feet, front feet low and back haunches high, tail wagging. Again.

Mari doesn't bark. She doesn't growl. She reaches to rub his fur again and looks up when Ethan skips into the kitchen. Was it only a few short months ago that he'd stepped on broken glass and needed stitches? Now he walks with no sign of a limp. The injury hasn't even made him cautious.

"Hi, Mama."

"Hi, baby."

"What are you doing?"

Mari flicks the hem of the tablecloth. "Making a cave. Want to come inside?"

Her boy grins, face lighting. She has always thought of him as hers, not Ryan's, but again she sees a shadow of the man in him and mourns. She's startled to realize it's not because she doesn't want him to grow up— but because she doesn't want him to grow up to be like his father.

Together they crawl into the space she's made. It's dim there. The tile floor is cool. The dog comes, too, inching beneath the hanging fabric on his belly, then lolling with a doggy grin. Ethan giggles, pulling his knees up.

"This is fun. It's like a fort," he says. "Can we bring some pillows in? And snacks?"

"Not just yet." Pillows for sleeping, snacks…these will make this cave even more like the one she used to know. There's danger here, in giving in to all of this.

But right now, she needs it.

There is danger, but there's comfort, too. Making the known out of the unknown, out of remembering the safe places. The manager at the restaurant had seemed to think Mari was lucky. Mari thinks so, too.

"Mom?" Kendra's bare feet pad softly on the tiles. The tablecloth twitches. "You guys are under here again?"

Mari gestures. "Come in. Sit with us."

Kendra does. Her legs are longer than Ethan's and Mari's, too. She has to hunch to keep her head from hitting the bottom of the table. She scoots closer to Mari. The three of them breathe together and the dog wiggles around until he's lying on all of them.

"Mom, are you okay?" Kendra asks.

Mari shrugs. "I'm a little upset, that's all."

Her children are silent, but both of them take her hands. She wants to cry again, but again does not. Ethan uses her hand to rub the spot between Chompsky's eyes.

"Will you feel better soon?" her boy asks.

"I hope so. I think so."

"That woman was a stupid bitch."

"Kiki," Mari says because she knows she should admonish the girl for using grown-up words, "that's not nice."

"*She* wasn't nice."

"She wasn't," Ethan adds. "She was a poopy buttface."

Mari's laugh chuffs out of her. It feels good. Kendra giggles a moment later.

"A diarrhea poopy buttface," Mari's daughter adds. "With corn in it."

Ethan guffaws. Chompsky barks softly. Now Mari weeps, but it's with laughter. Her stomach aches with the force of it.

She gathers her children to her for a hug. Loving them. Nothing more than that matters.

THIRTY-NINE

RYAN SKIMMED HIS HAND UP MARI'S THIGH, over her hip then around the front to cup her bare breast. She'd pulled only a thin sheet up over her, and the room was warm enough that when he moved over to press his naked body to hers their skin stuck together a little bit. She didn't move, though she made a low murmur.

When he nuzzled at her neck, though, she pulled away. "Don't."

Ryan froze, utterly shocked. "What?"

"I said don't, Ryan." She moved away from him to the very edge of the bed, leaving inches of space between them.

He tried to think if Mari had ever moved away from him like that and couldn't remember. Even after having the kids, when she'd still been recovering and unable to have intercourse, she'd always been willing and in fact, eager, to fool around with other things. He moved against her again. "Babe, what's wrong?"

She shoved him with her elbow hard enough to push him back and sat up, her legs over the side of the bed. In the moonlight, her naked skin gleamed. The fall of her dark hair down her back made her look exotic, foreign. She sighed and rubbed her thighs.

Ryan sat up, too. "What's wrong?"

Her shoulders shook, and he didn't understand what was so damned funny. Annoyed, Ryan tugged her shoulder to pull her around. What he saw stunned him more than her refusal of his advances had.

She was crying.

"Babe, babe," he said and pulled her close to him. This time, she let him. "Are you sick? Is it something with the kids? What?"

She curled against him, her face hot. The sheet tangled between them. She gripped his shoulder hard, her fingers digging into him so hard he winced. Her tears slicked down his bare skin and the hard-on he'd been nursing wilted. Anxiety made him push her away so he could turn on the light. He needed to see her face.

"Mari. What's wrong?"

"Why did you bring me back here?" she cried in a low, strangled voice that raised the hairs on the back of his neck.

"I thought…we needed… It was a place to go to get away," he began, the words clumsy on his tongue. "Because of what happened at work, the book… I'm sorry, babe. I didn't think it would bother you so much."

But that was lie, wasn't it? He'd known she would be affected. How could she be anything else? He hadn't imagined the extent of how she might react, that part was true, but that had been his own stupidity, his blind spot. His greed.

And now she was crying. Something she never did. All because of him.

Mari sat up and swiped at her face. Her uncommon tears had left tracks on her face. She pressed the heels of her hands into her eyes, fingers curling into the hair at her temples. She shook her head, then pulled her hands away to look at him.

"What happened at work? Really, Ryan."

His gut clenched. He reached to the side of the bed for his

boxer shorts and pulled them on. "It was a mistake. That's all. My patient killed herself and her husband's trying to blame me."

"Was it your fault?"

That she would even ask the question stunned him into a sputtering reply. "No! Of course not!"

"Why does her husband feel like it's your fault?"

Ryan's shoulders sagged. He said nothing, but she read it on him. She must've known, he thought, then felt an instant pettiness that she was forcing him to say it aloud. That she was making him admit what they both could've continued to ignore.

"How many times did you fuck her, Ryan?" Mari asked. Tears gone, voice sober. This was the woman he knew. Solid.

"It was a mistake. An accident."

Her low, strained laugh made her unfamiliar again. "Ah. I see. She slipped on a banana peel and landed on your dick?"

"That's not fair."

"What," Mari asked, "is fair?"

"I'm sorry. I'm so sorry, babe. I fucked up. I know it. But it's not my fault she killed herself." Ryan spoke faster when it looked like Mari was going to interrupt. "She had a history of transference, which is when a patient believes herself in love—"

"I was raised by your father, Ryan. I know what it means."

He went silent at that, mind abuzz and throat dry. Suddenly, everything Ryan had ever known was crumbling beneath him.

"She had a history of attempting to seduce her therapists," he said finally, when it became clear his wife wasn't going to speak. "She'd had four before me. I believe she slept with at least two of them, if not all."

"And you wanted to compete? You wanted to be the best, her favorite? What?" Mari's mouth twisted, but her solid and unyielding gaze pinned him.

Ryan made a miserable noise from someplace in his throat. "She just kept coming at me. And finally, I gave in."

Mari was silent again for the span of several breaths. Then her laughter growled up from her belly once more. The sound chilled him. When she got off the bed to pace the narrow strip of floor between him and the dresser, Ryan wanted to reach out and snag her wrist. Get her to stop, look at him. He didn't.

"You gave in," she said finally with her back to him. Her shoulders shook again.

He couldn't tell if she was laughing or crying, but Ryan got out of bed and touched her shoulder tentatively. "Mari. Babe. I am so fucking sorry, you don't even know."

"No," she said. "I guess I don't."

He didn't know what to say after that, but he took his hand away. They'd never fought, not really. She'd annoyed him and he'd irritated her, but their entire marriage had sailed along on smooth waters he'd come to take for granted. Now she had every right to be furious with him and to feel betrayed.

"Today," she continued before he could speak, "I went into town and a woman told me she knew my...my..."

She struggled against sobs. The tears were bad enough, but this ratcheting sound of grief throbbing out of her mouth was enough to make him want to weep himself. It was worse that she was doing that thing with her hands again. He recognized the patterns, the shift of her fingers, the tap of a palm against her heart. He thought he'd mastered the lexicon that his dad and the rest of the team studying her had made so they could understand her. She'd so quickly taken up spoken language, regaining what had been lost in such great leaps that it had become unnecessary for them to use hers to communicate. What Ryan understood from what he'd read and watched so far, once Mari had started to talk with her voice, she'd given up using her hands. Now he didn't know what she was saying.

She obviously hadn't forgotten, though. Just refused to go

back. And that was how he knew his wife. As a woman who looked forward, not back. If he'd ever heard her say she regretted anything, Ryan couldn't remember it.

He was counting on that now.

"Babe…Mari. Honey…I'm so sorry." He reached for her again, and this time she didn't shrink from his touch. She didn't lean into it, either. "I screwed up. I know it. And it was over almost as soon as it started. I promise you."

He thought of Annette, breasts heavy in his hands as she rode him, her mouth slick with her favorite red lipstick. Such a cliché, that lipstick, but then everything about her had been from her bleached and overprocessed hair, her thong peeking from the back of her too-tight jeans, her tiny baby voice. Annette Somers had made a doll of herself. A man's plaything, because that was the only way she'd known how to be. It had been Ryan's job to help her overcome the insecurities and the mess she repeatedly made of her life. He'd failed in that.

"I never loved her," Ryan said. "And it was never because I didn't love you."

Mari let out another rasping, agonized sob and turned to cling to him. Ryan buried his face in her hair. She shook against him, and her tears were scalding.

"Then why?"

"Because she kept at me and I was stupid. Because I was so damned stupid." Ryan shuddered with his own tears. "I ended our professional relationship. But when I broke off the other, she…killed herself. She'd threatened to commit suicide many times before. She'd been hospitalized four times previously with attempted suicide. She had a long history of mental problems and depression. I was stupid and wrong, but I'm not the reason she died."

He believed that, no matter what guilt he felt about any of it.

"But it's going to be okay, babe. I promise you that. The case will be settled. I'll get another job. And there's the book."

She drew in a low, shivering breath. "The woman in the restaurant today knew my mother. She said she knew her. She recognized Kendra, then said she recognized me. She knew who I was, Ryan. And she said…she said my mother had me in the bathroom at the Red Rabbit! How, how… What should I think about that?"

He looked at her, startled. "What?"

"She said she knew my mother because she'd worked there. In that restaurant. She said my mother had a baby in the bathroom, said she didn't know she was pregnant. That nobody knew until she had the baby." Mari drew in another breath, slower this time. Her eyes were bright, and she'd chewed on her lower lip, bringing blood.

Ryan, relieved she wasn't harping on the fact he was an unfaithful prick, wiped the crimson with his thumb. There'd been a file on Mari's mother in the boxes, one of the slimmest. There hadn't been much information on her, and nobody seemed to know how to find out more. Or to care. Mari had been the prize for men and women like his father. Linguistics experts, therapists, graduate students writing their theses. The fact that there was no parent to step forward and claim the "Pine Grove Pixie" had been a good thing, at least until funding ran out and there was nobody to take her. Nobody but his father, anyway. But there had been information in the file, and he had read it.

"Your mother, by all accounts, did have a baby in the bathroom of the Red Rabbit. She was not quite twenty-one at the time, said she hadn't known she was pregnant. Refused to name a father—"

Mari shook her head. "No. She was nineteen."

Ryan held her by the upper arms and gently pushed her inches away so he could look down into her face. "No. She was older than that. She never told anyone she was pregnant. She went into the bathroom and gave birth. No charges were filed against her since she wasn't a minor and didn't try to hurt the baby or anything like that. But it's all documented."

She shook her head until stray dark hairs fell forward over her forehead. "Them. Those Them, those Them with the writing sticks. The writing…" She broke off with a gulping noise, almost a gag. She shook her head furiously. Drew in a longer, deeper breath. She looked up at him with clear eyes shimmering with tears. "I heard the doctors talking. I remember them saying how old she was when she had me."

He shook his head and pulled her closer to stroke her hair from her face. "Your mother did have you when she was nineteen. You're right. But there's no record of your birth. It's believed she had you at home without ever telling anyone she was pregnant. It's why you were able to be…hidden…for so long, honey. Nobody knew about you."

Her tears stopped. Her expression shifted into steadiness. "I don't understand."

He kissed her, tasting salt. "The baby your mom had in the Red Rabbit bathroom wasn't you."

FORTY

MARI STARES AT THE FILE BOXES. THE PILES OF folders. This is the work her husband has been doing. The book he's writing.

About her.

"How long?" She sounds calm, but her fingernails are once more cutting into her flesh. She keeps her voice low because she doesn't want to wake her kids. She doesn't look at Ryan. She can't stand to see his face.

"I've always known parts of it. I mean…you're a textbook case study, Mari." He sounds miserable.

"So you knew. All of this. For how long?"

"Not all of it for that long. When the stuff at work happened, I thought I could take my dad's research and turn it into something. He always talked about it, you know. Writing your story."

"Not to me," Mari says, lip curling but fists unclenching. She turns to him then. "He never asked me! And neither did you!"

Ryan looks contrite, but she knows that look. It's the face of a man sorry he's been caught at what he was doing wrong, not sorry for doing it. And in that moment, she remembers that she loves him but can no longer feel that love.

This is betrayal worse than his infidelity—the truth is, Mari always expected Ryan to cheat on her. There were so many other more beautiful women, smarter women. Women who didn't catalog everything in the cupboards or wander the house naked at night. Who'd been raised by families, not by a pack of dogs and a silent, senile and demented grandmother.

No matter what Ryan did with another woman, or women, he came home to Mari and their children, and that is what matters to her. There is a disconnect here, and she knows it. She should rail and scream, slap his face, sob into her hands at her broken heart, but the fact is she only wishes she could unknow about it so they could move on with their lives.

But this other business of him knowing her whole life, planning to use it for his advantage and worst of all not telling her—as though it wouldn't matter! That gouges her so deeply she isn't even sure what she feels could be called pain.

"It was never a secret," Ryan says hesitantly. "I knew who you were, Mari. It never mattered to me."

"It matters to me." The words come out on a hiss she keeps from becoming a growl. She chews her lower lip and tastes blood, slicks it away with her tongue and rubs the sore spot with one fingertip. "You brought me back here, to this place!"

"I didn't know, I swear to you, how bad it was. Until we got here and I really started looking at all the notes. Until you—" Ryan breaks off.

They stand and stare. Mari wonders if this is how she should've felt about learning he'd been cheating. This feeling of trying to breathe and not finding the air. The feeling that everything in her life was going to slip through her fingers like water through a broken vase.

She taps a pile of the papers. "If I'm not the baby she had in the bathroom, who was it?"

"She gave it up for adoption. It was a girl."

"I have a sister."

Ryan shrugs and scratches his fingers through his hair, making it stand on end. The rumpled look usually suits him. Now it makes him look tired. "Yes. But it was a closed adoption."

"So I can't find her?"

"If she comes looking for your mother, she could find you. But other than that, I don't know where to begin. Do you want to find her?"

Mari isn't sure. That baby would be a woman now. She might have a family. She might not want to discover a sister, and Mari might not want to see what her own life might have been like if their mother hadn't pretended she didn't exist. Still...a sister. Mari has never imagined having a sister. The thought of it is overwhelming. Frightening.

"And my mother? You really have no idea where she is?"

"After she gave up the baby, she was diagnosed and hospitalized for schizophrenia and bipolar disorder. You'd've been about two years old. She was admitted to Harrisburg State Hospital and was there until at least 1989, when she was released."

Mari swallows hard. "What happened to her?"

"No records. Either she was never hospitalized or arrested again, or she changed her name. Or couldn't give anyone her name."

"She could be alive."

"She could, yes." Ryan pauses. "But it's really unlikely. Babe, I am so sorry about all of this. I hope you believe me."

"I believe you. I'm not sure it matters, but I believe you."

She's pleased to see the way that sets his mouth, like he sucked a lemon. She sees so much of his father in him now, with his rumpled hair and the lines around his eyes. Ryan had always been her prince but it seemed she'd been his fool.

He hangs his head but gives her a sideways look. "Your story is inspirational. Really. You're a success story."

"For who? Your father? You?" She manages a bitter laugh.

"What do you think that book would do to us, Ryan? Our family? The kids? Did you think of anything beyond your-self?"

"Of course I did! Everything I've done is for this family!" Ryan shouts so suddenly it sends her back a step. "If I could sell that book, if it was as popular as I think it could be, it would be entirely for this family! We're drowning in debt, Mari, but you wouldn't know a goddamn thing about that, would you? No! Because you don't pay the bills, I do. Because you have no idea of anything beyond your tiny little world. You've spent your whole life being taken care of!"

"Not," Mari says, "my whole life."

"Your whole life with me."

"Why did you marry me, Ryan? Was it because you loved me? Or because I just kept going after you until you couldn't say no?" Mari pauses, the words bitter. "Or was it because I was some sort of prize you could take from your father, get what he didn't."

"I loved you. I still love you. Christ," Ryan says with a swipe of his hand over his face. "What do you want me to do? What *can* I do but say I'm sorry?"

She thinks on this for only a second or two. "Leave."

Clearly, he's not expecting this. "The hell I will!"

She gives him a steady, solid stare until it's his turn to step back. "I want you to leave, Ryan."

"In case you don't remember, sweetheart—" the pet name does not sound kind "—someone's renting our house until September. That's four weeks away. And frankly, we can't af-ford a hotel bill."

"Go stay with your mother." She spits this suggestion. She needs time to herself, to think. "Take the children," she adds. "She'll be thrilled to have you all."

"For how long?" Ryan asks again.

She wants to tell him forever, but knows that's not a practical answer. Because what *will* she do without Ryan? Does she really want to find out? "The weekend, at least. Maybe a week."

"What will I tell the kids?"

"Tell them you're taking them to see Grandma, Ryan. It's not like you've never gone to visit her without me before." In fact, most of the time they visit her without Mari, who has no issue with her mother-in-law but is all too aware of the former Mrs. Doctor Calder's issues with her.

"Fine." He's angry.

She doesn't care. Ryan turns to fuss with a pile of papers on the desk. She stops him when he goes to shove them in his briefcase. "No."

He looks up, still clutching the papers.

"Leave that. I want to look at all of this. I want to see it."

He shakes his head. "I really don't think you do."

"Oh, Ryan, you're so wrong."

He flinches at that, which makes Mari happy and sad at the same time. She knows the flavor of fear. The weight of frustration. Those are longtime friends. But anger? She's worked very hard in her life to keep anger far from her. It's never served her purpose. Now she wonders how she could never have known its power.

"I want to know this. I have memories, Ryan. Of this house. Of what happened here. Of what I was."

"You were a little girl," Ryan says gently, "who had the misfortune to be neglected and abused. None of it was your fault, Mari. And now look at you. You're a strong, beautiful woman. A good mother. A good wife."

"I ate scavenged food I fought the dogs for. I hid from people because my gran had made me so afraid I'd be taken away. I lived in filth, Ryan. I remember those things and yet so much of it is blurry."

"Maybe it's better if it's blurry."

She shakes her head. "How can I stand knowing you know when I don't!"

"Fine." He doesn't say it angrily this time, but in resignation. "I'll leave the files. I'll take the kids to my mom's but only for a few days. And when I come back, we're going to talk about all of this. We'll talk about what happened at work, about the book, whatever you want to talk about. We're going to make this okay, Mari. I promise you."

Ryan has always been her prince. He has promised her so many things in her life and always made them happen. She wants to believe him this time, too.

But she doesn't.

Still, Mari nods. She turns her cheek when he moves to kiss her, but she allows him to hug her. Ryan sighs.

She doesn't follow him to bed. She waits until he leaves and then turns to the stacks and boxes of folders and files. She doesn't look up when he murmurs good-night.

Instead, she starts to read.

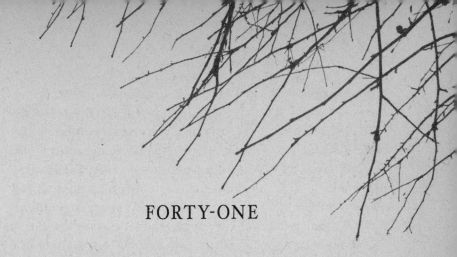

FORTY-ONE

GRANDMA CALDER'S HOUSE SMELLED LIKE THE candles she liked to burn year-round. Vanilla, sugar cookie, apple pie, pumpkin spice. All the sorts of treats she never actually baked. Underneath it, the hanging odor of cigarettes she always said she was quitting but never did. Kendra breathed it in and wanted to pinch her nose closed, but didn't because Grandma was hugging her so close.

"Kendra, sweetie. My God, you've grown. Look at you. You're going to be as tall as your dad. And Ethan, c'mere and give your grandma a kiss." Grandma kissed and hugged them both, then turned to their dad. "Ryan."

"Hi, Ma."

She offered him her cheek. His kiss looked as if it pained both of them. Kendra hoped she never felt that way about her kids—or her parents. Though the truth was, she sort of felt like that about her dad at the moment.

Something had gone down, she didn't know what, just that her parents had been fighting and now her dad had put on this big, fake smile and dragged them here to his mom's house. Grandma liked to call them a lot and send emails, usually stupid forwarded jokes or warnings about urban legends she could've easily disputed by looking them up on Snopes, but they usually only visited her every couple of months. Every once in a while Kendra and Ethan might stay the weekend while their parents went away on a grown-ups-only trip, and there'd been a few times when they were younger that Kendra by herself had gone for a whole week, then Ethan after her. Never at the same time, because Grandma said it would overwhelm her. It wasn't that Kendra didn't love her grandma, she just didn't really like the way Grandma treated her mom.

"I bought cookies. They're in the kitchen—go grab some," Grandma said to Ethan. To Kendra, she said, "I suppose you don't eat cookies anymore?"

"Of course I do, Grandma."

Grandma's brows rose. "I thought all teenage girls were obsessed with diets."

"Only ones with eating disorders."

Grandma snorted. "Please tell me that's not you, Kendra Jean."

As if. "No, Grandma."

"Go on, then."

Ethan had already jumped ahead, and Kendra followed him. She knew an invitation to get lost when she heard it. She slowed her steps when she got to the hall, though, listening.

She didn't hear what her dad said, but her grandma was a little deaf and therefore thought she needed to talk extraloud.

"Well, what do you expect from her, Ryan? I warned you."

"Ma. Not now, okay? Jesus."

"I'm just saying, how can you be surprised?"

Kendra's dad's voice dipped again. She realized she'd totally stopped. If either her grandma or dad shifted a little bit to look down the hall, they'd see her eavesdropping. She took another couple steps.

"Can't you just enjoy this visit, Ma? Do you have to bring up the past over and over again?"

"Watch your tone with me, Ryan. I'm your mother."

"And Mari's my wife," Kendra's dad said. "No matter what happened in the past, no matter where she came from and what she was."

"You're just like your father." It was clear Grandma didn't mean this as a compliment. "Well, I suppose you should come in. Have a cup of coffee. We can go out to that new place for dinner, if you want. That buffet place."

"Sure, Ma. Whatever you want."

At the sound of that, Kendra ducked quickly into the kitchen. "Hey, brat, don't eat all the cookies."

The monkeybrat looked up with crumbs around his mouth. "I miss Chompsky."

"He's staying behind with Mama."

"To protect her?"

"What does she need protection from, doofus?" Kendra snagged a cookie.

"Whatever ate the peacock. That's why Daddy said we needed a dog, remember?" Ethan rolled his eyes, making it obvious who was the real doofus.

"Whatever." Kendra poked him. He poked her. They'd have gone at it, but then their dad and grandma came into the kitchen and both of them pulled their hands back, acting innocent.

"Not too many cookies," their dad said. "Apparently your grandmother's taking us to the Belly Buster Buffet."

That sounded disgusting, but gave Kendra an excuse to escape upstairs with her suitcase to the small sewing room with the daybed that was always hers during visits. She heard the mutter of her dad's voice in the room next door and pressed her ear to the wall to listen.

"Mari. It's me. I wish you'd answer. Anyway, we got here okay. The kids are fine." There was a long, long pause. "I know you have every reason to be pissed off at me. But I want you to know that no matter what, I do love you. I always have.

And not because you were something I had to steal from my dad or a prize or anything like that. I love you for who you are and who you were when I met you. Not whoever you were before that. I love you. Call me, babe. Bye."

Blinking, Kendra sat back, uneasy. That's what happened when you listened to private conversations. You heard things you didn't like. What had her dad done?

And why did everyone keep talking about what had happened in the past? Rosie, the manager at the Red Rabbit, Grandma...now Daddy. It wasn't the best thing in the world to have your mom give birth to you in a bathroom, but it wasn't like women didn't have babies in weird places all time. There was a whole TV series about it on the Discovery Health Channel.

Somehow, Kendra didn't think that's what everyone was going on about. Something worse had gone on in her mother's life. Which was probably why she never talked much about it. But what was it?

What could possibly have been so bad?

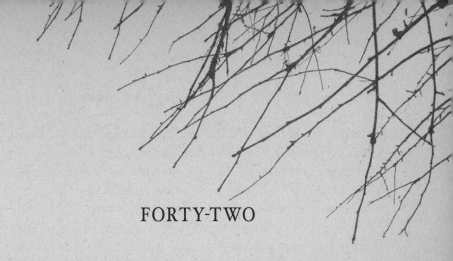

FORTY-TWO

THERE'S TOO MUCH INFORMATION. SOMEONE—
Ryan, she thinks by the familiar handwriting on the labels—
has sorted through all this material to put it in chronological
order. But there's still too much. Boxes and boxes of notes,
written by Dr. Leon Calder. Printouts and handwritten letters back and forth between him and colleagues. Test results.
Scribbled pictures Mari doesn't recognize and yet knows she
must've drawn because her name is on them. Report cards,
height and weight and immunization records. The daily menu
from the hospital, along with notations about her reaction to
the foods and the bowel movements she had after them.

Leon had taken notes on everything but had done little in
the way of correlating what he observed. Apparently this had
directly resulted in the loss of the grant money that had allowed for Mari's care and keeping. She found the letter and
documents stating his application had been turned down, the
grant not renewed, the reason being "insufficient presentation
of results gathered from the scientific observations provided
for by previous distribution of funds."

She also found the file of paperwork in which Leon had
petitioned for her to become his legal ward. This, at least,
makes her smile because she remembers the day the picture

paper-clipped to the front of the folder was taken. She'd worn a pretty pleated skirt and white ankle socks. Saddle shoes. A white blouse with puffed sleeves. A new hair band Leon had given her himself. He'd told her he loved her as much as he could ever love a daughter and asked if she wanted to come home to live with him forever. Mari had said yes.

But now, in another box marked only "Mari, 15–17" she finds many more pictures. Many more pages of notes. And these tell a different story. She reads, scanning with her finger the way Leon taught her so she can keep the words in their places, not wiggling all over the pages the way they tend to do when she doesn't concentrate. In these pages, Mari reads about more tests. Experiments Leon wrote about that she'd never even known he was doing. And all on her.

He'd documented her menstrual cycles and how she'd reacted to criticism and how quickly she picked up new tasks. He'd written at length about his choices in her wardrobe and of his plans to encourage her to continue her education— something Ryan had not done. Leon had written extensively about the subtle psychological profiling he'd done, everything from withholding affection to gain a response to testing her tendency to hoard sweets by purchasing candy for her but telling her she had to finish it all before he would buy her any more. He'd also journaled of his pride in her accomplishments. How much he'd gained by his research. But never once did he mention how he'd felt about Mari herself. Never once had he written that he loved her.

Mari sits back. Her back and knees ache from bending over all of these boxes. Her eyes itch and burn from the dust. Even her fingertips feel swollen from flipping through so many rough-edged papers. She's been at this for two days, since Ryan left with the children, with barely a break.

The notes about her when she was still wild didn't faze her—she barely remembers those times and any information they gathered seemed necessary for them to understand her. It's also mostly boring and says very little about who she really was. The folders of information about her progress are even less important, because she remembers those times better. But what she holds in her hands now is proof that the man who'd said he wanted to be her father viewed her as no more than an experiment, a learning tool, something to study—even up to just a few days before he died! This, like her husband's infidelity, is something else Mari wants to unknow.

Weeping comes easier now, and like the anger she wonders why she waited so long to appreciate what strength can be found in tears. At the very least, releasing the emotion leaves her feeling worn and empty, not coiled spring-tight. At least when she looks at her reflection in the window glass she sees who she is and not who she was.

Still, it's all too much. Maybe Ryan was right. She shouldn't look at this. She shouldn't know that Leon didn't truly love her, at least not in the way she'd wanted him to. That he referred to her as "proof of the Forbidden Experiment" or "a modern living example disproving Avram Noam Chomsky's language theory."

"Chompsky." The dog at her feet looks up with a tilted head and an inquiring whine. She can laugh at the name now. How fitting that Ryan named the dog after the renowned linguist whose theories on language have shaped the treatment of every "wild" child discovered in the United States since the fifties.

From these boxes of files and folders Mari has not only learned a lot about herself, but also about the others like her. Abandoned, lost or isolated children. Raised without love or human social interaction, some horrifically abused and others, like her, simply ignored. She sees now what Ryan meant by "success story." Unlike most of the other children documented in these materials her husband's been hoarding, Mari did learn to talk and interact. She married, had children of her own. She has not spent her life in assisted-living care or mental hospitals.

And if she's felt for most of her life as though she doesn't quite fit in, as though she's not sure how to connect with people in those shallow surface ways that seem to come so naturally to most—well, she's not alone in that even among people who were raised "normal." Yet here, too, she's lucky. She read the story of a woman raised by her grandmother in the swamps until age four, isolated and ignored. That woman, according to her autobiographical essay, many of the passages highlighted in yellow with Ryan's notes scrawled in the margins, has never been able to connect with anyone but her child.

Mari, at least, has loved.

Leon, her only father. Ryan. Kendra and Ethan. This dog, she thinks as Chompsky rests his nose on his front paws, eyebrows twitching as he watches her.

It's all too much, and she gets up from the chair not caring if the papers scatter onto the ground. The dog scrambles out of the way. Mari stretches, easing the kinks in her back and shoulders. She rubs at her eyes, blurring her vision.

She strips off her clothes, not bothering to fold them. Naked, she leaves the three-season room and steps into night-damp grass. Her feet leave marks but no sound as she walks. Her ankles and shins get wet. She doesn't care. Mari lifts her face to the night sky and looks for the moon and the stars.

They, at least, haven't changed.

Stay, she says to the dog with her hands, and the dog understands.

She needs the woods. She needs the sough of breezes in the trees and the smell of earth littered with pine needles. She needs to dig with her hands in the dirt.

Her feet are soft and easily bruised now. Her skin not used to the chill. She shivers, nipples going tight, and she cups her breasts as she remembers the feeling of her babies nursing there.

She is naked in the night. Free. But it's not the way it used to be when she ran from Them into the woods, bare feet hard and crunching on sticks and stones without even a flinch. When she could stand out in the heat or the cold and barely feel it.

Mari climbs the mountain. It's dark but not quiet—there's the shuffle of animals in the undergrowth and the soft coos of birds in the trees. The breeze she craves. The distant sound of an airplane or something overhead reminds her that no matter how much she wants this to feel like the wilderness, society is close enough to grab her if she lets it.

Her feet guide her. Maybe it's memory. Maybe instinct. Maybe just stupid, dumb luck, because when she stumbles into the clearing she feels at once she knows this place and also that she does not. It's not like the meadow with the ringing rocks, which she knew at once from memory.

Golden light spills out from small windows in a strange, small house. The one Kendra told her about. Mari is stand-ing naked in someone's front yard. She's not so wild that she can't be embarrassed by it. Yet when the door opens, Mari doesn't move. When the shadow figure of a man comes out onto the small porch and lifts a hand to his eyes so he can scan the clearing, she stays still. Her skin is tan yet still pale enough that it will stand out if she moves from the cloak of shadows cast by the trees all along the clearing's edge.

She waits for him to call out, but he doesn't. She thinks he'll move into the grass, looking for whatever it was that called him out. It's what she would do, she thinks, if someone came into her yard in the night and made noise. Except she knows she barely made a sound.

She smells a fire and sees a ring of rocks. This is a camp, then. It must be. Who else would live out here in a house she can see is tiny even with only the moon to light it. And if it's a camp, maybe he's a hunter. Maybe he has a gun.

People in rural Pennsylvania own guns they're not afraid

to bring out even when it's not hunting season. Maybe this time, she thinks as she backs up one careful step at a time, it won't be rocks hitting her but bullets, instead. A twig snaps. She can't see the man's face but his body turns in her direction. He still says nothing, but she sees the gleam of his eyes. He can't see her, she knows he can't, but she turns and flees, just in case.

Mari runs down the mountain, bursting with a flurry of giggles she has to bite back, afraid he might hear. No gunshots. No shouts. She's made it back to the safety of her yard without anyone seeing her running naked through the trees. Her feet hurt. Her arms, legs, belly, thighs, all scratched. She has bruises that will throb and ache later but are at this moment only a murmur of pain.

In her yard she gives in to laughter. Tips her face and laughs at the moon and the stars that have watched her. She spins and spins until dizzy, she falls into the grass. She rolls in the softness and gets up with bits and pieces of flowers and weeds clinging to her bare skin, then stumbles to the hammock strung between two trees. Mari folds herself into it, not willing to go back in the house where she might have to remember everything she ran out here to escape.

She's so tired she can't keep her eyes open. She hasn't slept more than a few hours at a time for the past couple days, so her exhaustion is not unexpected. She falls asleep there, naked in the hammock in her backyard, and even that is not a surprise.

What shocks her, though, is that when she wakes she is surrounded by folded paper butterflies. Too many for her to count, as anything beyond what she can tick off on her fingers still becomes the vague "many" unless she concentrates on the numbers. Strung from bits of ribbon the same as the few she's found before, but these are bright and colorful. Not faded. They hang from the trees around her and the morning breeze pushes them into flight.

Mari blinks and blinks to clear her eyes, but the butter-flies don't go away. She lurches to her feet, scanning the yard, but it's empty. She listens and hears nothing but the furious pounding of her heart.

But there in the grass just in front of her, just the size of what might've been two human feet, is a trampled-down spot of grass just now beginning to spring back up. Settled into it are two things. One, a library book. And two, Kendra's cell phone.

FORTY-THREE

RYAN DIDN'T WANT TO LISTEN TO HIS MOTHER'S lectures about the choices he's made as an adult. He understood why she had such bitterness toward his dad, even though she'd been the one to leave him and not the other way around. Even now she couldn't talk about Ryan's dad without curling her lip. So much for not speaking ill of the dead. On the other hand, it was as though she couldn't *stop* talking about him, either.

She was good with the kids, though. No matter what she thought about her son's father or her daughter-in-law, Jean Calder loved her grandkids. She'd taken them shopping, leaving Ryan at home to try and get through to Mari, who still wasn't answering the phone. He'd have been more worried, except he knew she sometimes turned the ringer off on her phone and forgot about it. And that the cell service in the Pine Grove house was terrible.

It *was* possible she was ignoring him on purpose. Ryan thumbed the phone to end the call, then slipped it into his pocket. He rubbed his eyes, pinched the bridge of his nose. He was so freaking tired.

He put in a call to his lawyer, who depressingly went from assuring Ryan that everything was going to work out, to cautiously suggesting he might want to consider making sure his assets were listed in his wife's name. That he might want to think about a different line of work.

That was that, then. He was well and thoroughly screwed. And he'd done it to himself—that was the worst of it. He'd been stupid and not only lost his job, but maybe his wife, too.

Mari had made him leave the files and folders, but Ryan had brought the computer containing his notes and outlines for the chapters he'd begun to draft. He opened the laptop, brought up the file he'd simply titled Book. In school he'd never much liked English classes. He couldn't have said what a gerund was, or how to diagram a sentence. But writing this book, for the first time Ryan had felt like he was managing to do something interesting with what he'd learned in school, instead of simply chasing after his father's legacy.

He scanned the lines of text and made some changes. Took some notes. He called Mari, and again she didn't answer. He didn't leave a voice mail this time. He'd have tried the house phone, but realized they'd never used the landline and he wasn't even sure if one existed or what the number was. So if she'd turned off the ringer on her cell and forgotten to check it, he was pretty much out of touch with her. A thin irritation corkscrewed through him. Why'd she have to be so damned irresponsible? What if this was an emergency?

Except he knew that was unfair. Mari might be a lot of things, but not irresponsible. She didn't take care of the household finances, but she did damn near everything else from the grocery shopping to cleaning to keeping track of everything the kids needed. Ryan couldn't have said where the school absence excuse slips were, or what size shoes Ethan wore or the name of Kendra's English teacher. He knew Mari could answer all those questions without a second's hesitation. She kept the gears of Ryan's life moving smoothly, without snagging.

What was he going to do without her?

FORTY-FOUR

"SURELY YOUR MOTHER WOULDN'T APPROVE of that shirt." Grandma's lip curled as she held it up.

Kendra hadn't really been thinking of buying the black, fitted T-shirt with the picture of a zombified Bettie Page and the neon green lettering that said "F★@% you, I found Jesus" on it, but as soon as Grandma took it from her hands and hung it back on the rack it became the only shirt she wanted. She took another off the rack and held it up. "She wouldn't care."

That was probably true. If Kendra came home with that shirt, her mom would probably look it over, shake her head and simply tell her that she couldn't wear it to school or out in public. Mom wouldn't forbid Kendra from having it, she'd just make sure Kendra understood the consequences of wearing it.

Grandma frowned. "Even *your* mother wouldn't allow you to wear a shirt like that, Kendra Jean."

Kendra hated the way Grandma said "your mother" only a little more than she hated the way she used her full name. She didn't put the shirt back. She hung it over her arm as she moved to the next rack of clothes.

"You're not buying that shirt."

She looked at her grandmother. Ethan had ducked away to look at a glass case full of buttons and bumper stickers, so it was just Kendra and Grandma facing off over a rack of T-shirts with dirty slogans. Kendra's heart pounded, but she gave her grandma a blank look.

"Sure I am. I have my own money."

"It's not a question of money," Grandma said. "You can't buy that shirt, it's filthy. And disrespectful."

"Maybe that's why I like it," Kendra said.

For a moment she thought Grandma was going to burst into a screaming hissy fit right there in the store, but she just shook her head. She closed her eyes and pinched the bridge of her nose as though she had a very bad headache. When she opened her eyes, she bored right into Kendra's skull with a glare.

"Your father will never approve of it. I'm sure about that."

Kendra frowned. That was true. Her dad wouldn't like the shirt at all. And with a price tag of twenty-nine-ninety-five, it was kind of an expensive way to throw a tantrum. "He barely pays attention to anything I wear."

"Well, he should."

"Grandma, can I get this?" Ethan held up a package of gummy candy that looked like a hamburger complete with lettuce, tomato and onion, and fries on the side. "It's gum."

"Sweetie, let Grandma buy you some better gum than that. Come on, this store is nothing but junk." Grandma turned to go as Ethan put on a sad face and prepared to put the gum back.

"I'll buy it for you," Kendra said.

"Kendra." Grandma had a warning tone in her voice.

Kendra ignored it. "Mom doesn't care if we have gum. C'mon, monkeybrat. Let's pay for this stuff."

Behind her, Grandma let out a long, low sigh. Kendra pulled out two twenty-dollar bills from her wallet, all the money she'd saved up from her allowances since before they went to Pine Grove. There'd been no allowance since then, and she'd felt bad asking for it, not that there'd been anything to spend it on, anyway. Now the brand-new bills felt stiff in her fingers. She put it on the counter next to the shirt she didn't really want and the gum her brother really didn't need.

Back out in the mall, the monkeybrat chattered nonstop to Grandma while Kendra held back, the bag holding her purchases clutched so tight her fingers cramped. Grandma was ignoring her, which was cool with Kendra, whose rebellious nature had been totally tapped out. Was the shirt worth it? Probably not, but she'd been unable to stop herself from buying it, anyway. Now it made the bag so super heavy she wanted to dump it in the nearest trashcan.

No, what she wanted was her mom.

Kendra let Grandma and Ethan walk ahead of her as she pulled out the stupid flip phone her dad had given her to replace the one she'd lost, and tapped in a text to her mom.

I want to come home.

Her phone buzzed a moment later. She grabbed at it, but saw it was only a message from Logan. Any other time this would've made her squee, but now she just tucked it back in her pocket without answering.

FORTY-FIVE

THERE WAS A BOOK WITH PRETTY PICTURES
and many words. Mari could sound out a few of them if she
ran her finger along the black letters on the white pages. She
liked the pictures better, though. Colorful ink drawings of
mermaids, a sea-witch. *Puss in Boots.* Mari knew the fairy-tale
stories because the forest prince had read them to her, over
and over again. The forest prince, like the one in the stories.
He looked like the boy in the picture. Golden hair. Golden
skin. The happy prince, the one made of gold.

The forest prince brought her food when there was nothing to eat. He untangled her hair when the knots were too
thick even for the comb. In the snowtime, the forest prince
made sure the stove always had wood to burn.

Gran used to chop the wood, but she didn't anymore. She
used the ax to kill chickens, too. Mari used her fingers to
twist their necks until they stopped squawking. The ax was
too heavy for her to lift, and the forest prince said it was too
sharp for a little fairy girl. She could hurt herself. He cut the
wood and stacked it on the back porch so Mari could put it
in the stove.

The forest prince's name was Andrew. That was what Gran
called him when she used to talk. Gran didn't talk now, not

even when Mari sang to her. Gran didn't do a lot of things she used to. Mostly she just sat and stared at nothing Mari could see.

Mari pushed her fingertips over and over the lines of the pictures, lips moving as she tried her best to figure out the meaning of the words. It was called reading. She wanted to know what these lines and squiggles said, but all she could do was look at the pictures and remember the stories the forest prince told her.

She heard the crunch of sticks in the woods and the book flew from her hands. She was on her feet, ready to run, heart pounding, but then the forest prince stepped out of the trees and crossed the yard to get to her.

"Mariposa." He grinned.

Mari squealed with delight. Giggling as he tickled her, she kicked her feet high in the air. He was so tall. When he lifted her, she flew.

"Just like a butterfly."

The forest prince put her down, her feet bare on the wooden boards of the back porch. They were cold. The snowtime was coming, she could tell by the way her breath blew out in front of her like smoke and by the way Gran shivered and shuddered unless Mari piled her with blankets, but it wasn't here yet. The wind pushed the pages of the book so they fluttered like a butterfly's wings.

Mari rubbed her tummy, put a hand to her mouth. *I'm hungry.*

"I brought you food." Andrew shifted his backpack from his shoulders. Opened it. Inside were good things to eat. Cans of beans, a box of rice. A package of snack cakes, only a little squashed. An open bag of chips.

Mari dove for the chocolate cake and tore open the plastic. It was so good she licked the wrapper while Andrew laughed, watching. His hand passed over her hair. She'd tried to pull it

back in a ponytail this morning, but the rubber band snapped
and she couldn't find another.

Some for you? Mari offered the last few crumbs.

Andrew shook his head. He looked at the sky. At the woods
beyond the flowers in the yard. He'd be leaving soon. Mari
knew this because he always left. Andrew was a prince of the
forest. The wicked queen didn't like it when he visited here.
He could never stay long.

He had taught her lots of things. How to find good things
to eat in the woods. How to build a fire and keep it going—
because even if she was too small to chop the wood, it was
still up to her to keep the stove burning. Andrew was the one
who taught Mari how to keep completely still when They
came and Gran told her to be quiet and hide.

Read to me?

"Come here." Andrew pulled her onto his lap and opened
the book.

She knew all the stories, but she would listen to him read
them to her over and over again. All the days. Sleepy, Mari let
herself sink into his warmth. His breath on her face smelled
of chocolate. He pressed his cheek to hers.

Stay, she said when he got up to go.

"You know I can't." Andrew looked around the porch. "If
I could, I would stay here with you always, Mariposa."

Why not?

Andrew frowned. "They'd come looking for me, and they'd
find you. Take you away. So even though I have to go, it's for
your own good."

No go.

"No." He shook his head. "I don't want you to go. I have
to take care of you. Make sure you're safe. That's my job."

Why?

Andrew looked surprised. "Well…I love you, Mariposa."

She didn't know what that meant. He took her hands and

curled the fingers against the palms, then pressed first one, then the other, to her chest over the beating part. Then he took them and put them on his face as he looked carefully into her eyes.

"When you want to make someone else happy, or keep them safe," he said, "or when just being with them makes you feel like a better person, that's love."

Love. Her fingers curled. Pressed to her chest. *Love?*

Andrew nodded. "I want to take care of you, make sure you're all right."

I love you.

He grinned and ruffled her hair. Then squeezed her. "I have to go check on Gran, but I'll be back later."

Gran had been asleep for a long time. When Andrew came back, his face was full of words even though he only had a few to say. "Mari, what happened to Gran?"

Mari shook her head, not sure what he meant. Gran was always that way now. In her chair. Knitting or mumbling to herself. Sleeping next to the stove. She didn't even wake up long enough to eat, which was okay with Mari because it was messy, trying to feed Gran. She can't chew. Her teeth are gone, the ones in the jar she keeps next to her on the table are never in her mouth.

Andrew shook his head. "Mari, listen to me. How long has Gran been…asleep?"

She shrugged. *I don't know.*

"Think! One sleep? Two? More than that?"

She wasn't used to him shouting, and Mari's lower lip trembled. Hot tears filled her eyes. Andrew became a blur. She took a step back, then another. Her shoulder knocked into the door frame.

She held up her hands, fingers waving. *Many.*

Andrew walked back and forth, fast and faster. "This is bad, Mariposa. I have to go."

Don't go.

But he went, as he always did. He came back again before she'd even had one sleep. He didn't bring food, but he took her hands and squeezed them.

"Mariposa, you have to listen to me." Andrew looked out the window to the front place of grass. "They're coming."

They. Them. The ones in cars. They came to take Gran away. They came to bring her back. They didn't know about Mari because Mari always, always hid.

Mari ran into the kitchen. Beneath the table, her special place. She dove into the pile of blankets she shared with the dogs. It was dark under there, tiny spots of light shining through the holes in the knitted blanket hung over the tabletop.

"Mari, no. You don't understand! This time, you have to come with me."

Mari clutched at the blankets. Andrew's feet slapped on the floor, but from the front door Mari heard voices. Voices of Them. They're shouting, something about Gran.

"I'll come back for you, Mari. I promise. I'll come for you." Then Andrew was gone. The back door didn't slam behind him, it closed as softly as a whisper.

"When was the last time someone was out here? My God," said one of Them. Big shoes made lots of noise on the floor beside the table. "It's filthy. She's been dead a least three or four days, maybe a week. Christ."

The sound of water running in the sink. More feet. More voices. More Them. Mari buried her face in the blankets and waited for them all to go away.

This time, they didn't.

"Jesus Christ."

One of Them had lifted the blanket, making it light under the table. A face, a big face, covered in hair, eyes open wide.

"There's a kid in here!"

Mari wasn't fast enough to run away. They grabbed her. Held her tight. She kicked. Screamed. Bit. They held her. Held her down. They shouted, they whispered.

"Honey, what's your name? Can you tell me your name? Oh, God, Glenn." This was a lady Them, with yellow hair like Andrew's. Big blue eyes. "Look at her. Have you ever seen anything like it?"

"We're not gonna hurt you, sweetheart," said the man Them with the hair on his face.

Mari screamed.

"Shh, shh, honey, it's okay." The lady Them held out a cookie. Mari knew cookies, but she wouldn't take it. Not from this lady Them. "Can you tell me your name? And come out here? I'll give you this cookie."

"How about this?" The man Them held out a snack cake. "Found a couple of them on the counter. Maybe she likes these."

"Can you tell me your name, sweetie? Are you hungry?"

Mari was always hungry. She patted her tummy, put a hand to her mouth. *I'm hungry.*

"Holy shit," said the lady Them. "Glenn. Do you see that?"

"Look at her. She's crazy."

The lady Them and the man Them squatted on the floor in front of Mari. The man Them tossed Mari the snack cake, and she tore the plastic from it to shove it in her mouth, greedy in case they took it away.

"I think we need to call social services," said the man Them.

"I think we need to call more than that," the lady Them said.

This is what Mari remembers when she uncovers the book. It's been tucked down deep in one of the boxes, below a stack of papers it seems nobody thought were very important. The book's smaller than she remembers, but she cradles it against her chest. She presses it to her cheek, her eyes closed, and breathes in the scent of the paper.

She understands now, why she fell in love with Ryan. Why he became her prince. The boy in her long-buried memories had planted that need to be saved within her, and she'd spent the rest of her life thinking that was what she needed.

Who could blame her? She had no memories of her infancy, though someone must've taken care of her before she was old enough to fend for herself. She'd spent the first eight years of her life learning that if she cried there was nobody to listen. If she hurt herself, nobody to offer comfort. Being taken out of this house had been terrifying, yes, and she'd fought it. But even a child who's been taught to fear the touch of strangers can quickly learn how much better it is to be fed and clothed and kept clean—even if that means being poked and prodded and tested.

They'd given her other toys to replace the dirty, battered butterfly that no longer lit up. A doll with blond hair and a soft dress, a stuffed duck, a stack of blocks. Mari had kept none of them. There was very little in her life she'd ever kept for sentiment, though those same parenting magazines that had warned her about the trials of potty training had also shown her it might be important to tuck away keepsakes for the sake of her children, even if she herself felt no special connection to a blanket or a doll. She had a box for each child in her closet at home, and she did try to put things away in it she thought they might like someday.

Suddenly, though, this book in her hands is more than a collection of words and pictures. This book is a tangible, memorable bit of her past that isn't like the pages of notes someone else took about her, or even the videotapes she doesn't remember being recorded.

Like her memory of the stuffed and glow-faced butterfly, she remembers this book.

And she remembers the boy who tried as best he could to save her.

"Andrew," she says aloud just to test it. She looks through the windows to the grass outside. There's no more sign of any footprints, but she remembers those, too.

FORTY-SIX

"I WANT TO GO HOME, DAD." KENDRA MADE sure her grandmother wasn't around to hear this. As much as Grandma annoyed her, Kendra didn't want to hurt her feelings. After the T-shirt incident, Grandma had bought both Kendra and Ethan a shitload of junk, and sure it was nice being given things, but…that was just stuff. Shirts and CDs and bottles of nail polish are just things. They're not her mom.

"I know." Her dad hunched over his computer. He'd been typing for an hour on that book.

"Dad!"

He stopped with a sigh and twisted in his chair. "What, Kendra? Can't you see I'm working?"

"When are we going home?"

"In a few days. You're visiting your grandma now. Enjoy it."

"You don't," she said.

That got his attention. "That's a shitty thing to say."

"I'm sorry, Dad, but it's true. And I don't want to stay here while you go back to Philly. Neither does Ethan." Kendra assumed that was true, anyway—the monkeybrat hadn't exactly said so. "Can't you take us with you?"

"And do what with you? I have to go back for…" Her dad paused, which meant he was thinking of a way to lie to her.

"Work. And you guys can't go back to our house because someone's in it, and you can't stay by yourselves in a hotel room, either. You're staying here with Grandma. That's the way it is."

Kendra groaned and scuffed at the carpet. "I don't want to stay here."

"I thought you liked visiting your grandmother."

Kendra shrugged. "For a day or two, sure. But she's really annoying."

Her dad sighed. "You just have to understand, honey. That's the way your grandma is. She loves you and Ethan."

"Why does she hate Mom so much?" That was the real question that had been bubbling to the tip of Kendra's tongue. Like a burp or puke, it could no longer be held back. "I don't get it."

"I don't want to talk about it," her dad said in that "this is final" tone, but Kendra was tired of that answer.

"Is it because Mom was born in that bathroom at the Red Rabbit?"

He winced. "Who told you that?"

"I was there when the dumb b…rat told everyone who was in there." Kendra scowled and went to the window overlooking Grandma's backyard. Her dad had never lived in this house as a kid, so there was no swing set, no basketball hoop. Just an expanse of green grass perfectly trimmed by the man Grandma hired to come every week.

"Your mom wasn't born in a bathroom. Her mother had another child after your mom was born. That's actually why her mother was hospitalized and why she never…" Her dad stopped again. He looked pained. "Look, Kiki, this is something we should talk about with your mom, okay? And I promise, we'll tell you the story when I get back here from Philly and we go back to Pine Grove. But it's not really for me to tell you."

"Is that why Grandma hates her, though?"

Her dad shook his head. At least he wasn't trying to deny his mom hated his wife. "No. Grandma thinks your grandpa was wrong to adopt your mom, that's all."

"Well…why did he?"

"Because she didn't have anyone else to take care of her." Her dad looked at his computer screen, which dimmed and then went to the screensaver. He looked back at her. "And then when I fell in love with your mom, Grandma didn't like that, either."

"But it's not like you were really brother and sister." Kendra's nose squinched up at saying this, and her heart stepped up its beat. It was gross and seemed private to talk about this with her dad, but she couldn't stand not knowing anymore. The entire summer had been crazy.

"No. Not at all. But you know how people are. It's why we don't tell most people how we met, right?"

She knew that without even being lectured. Not that her mom and dad had ever told her and Ethan to lie about how they'd met or anything, but after the first time a naive Kendra had told her teacher that her mom and dad had the same father, she'd learned her lesson.

"I was already grown and out of the house when your mom came to live with my dad. But your grandma didn't like the idea of it. And listen, honey, it's really easy for your grandma to blame my dad for everything, but I can tell you that marriages don't end over one issue. The reality is that my parents fought a lot. Grandma can be…difficult. And I guess my dad had his problems, too." He sighed again. "But he was doing what he thought was right. Besides, if he hadn't, I'd never have met your mom and fallen in love with her, right? And wouldn't have had you guys."

"What happened to her?" Kendra asked then.

"To Grandma? She divorced my dad."

"No. To Mom. When she was young. What happened to her in that house that you guys don't talk about?"

"I told you, Kendra, I don't want to talk about it without your mom here. It's for her to tell you, if she wants to."

Kendra's frown tightened, hurting. She crossed her arms over her stomach. "Can we go back with Mom, then? If we can't go with you to Philly. Can you take us back to Pine Grove?"

Her dad sighed and looked sad. "Me and your mom have been having sort of a fight."

Everything inside her started to tumble and twist. Kendra bit down on her lower lip, hard, to keep back tears. Her voice shook, though. "Are you going to get divorced?"

"No!" Her dad's voice softened. "No. Remember when I said that marriages don't end over just one thing? Most issues can be worked out. Your mom and I are going to work out those issues. I promise you. Okay? It's all going to be all right."

Kendra nodded solemnly.

"But right now, you need to leave me alone so I can get some work done." Her dad turned back to the computer and tapped a key so the screen lit.

Kendra knew better than to listen at doors and read over someone's shoulder, but she couldn't help seeing, could she? If it was right there. Her mom's name in black and white. She didn't say anything, just backed out of the room and went into her own to throw herself on the bed and bury her face in the too-flat pillow.

She still had too many questions. None of this was okay. And she didn't believe her dad when he said it would all work out.

Most of all…what was her dad writing about her mom?

FORTY-SEVEN

FOR THE SECOND TIME IN AS MANY DAYS, MARI climbs the mountain. It's easier in the daytime. Shorter trip, too. The trees still close in around her and the birds still titter, but in the sunlight it's easier to see how close the clearing really is to her house.

Of course, not being naked probably helps, too.

She shades her eyes when she comes out into the sun. The small house doesn't look any bigger than it did in the dark, but it's not quite as strange. She can see how it's not as ramshackle, that the lean and tilt of it is part of the design to make it look as though it's part of the landscape. Cleverly done, actually. A closer look reveals a propane tank tucked against the bank in the back of the house, camouflaged with a fence sort of like the box they put their garbage cans in back in Philly, though there the box is made of vinyl to match the house and this one's made of bark.

It's still a sort of fairy-tale cottage, with uneven stone steps and windows hung with what looks like shredded curtains but turns out to be mosquito netting. She steps closer. She thinks she should call out, but what can she say? She can't go around calling out a man's name. Somehow that feels like more a violation than showing up bare naked in someone's yard. At least then it had been dark and she could pretend he hadn't seen her. If she shouts and he replies, there will be no more pretending.

She's saved by a sound. She closes her eyes for a moment, remembering the blade hitting wood; she knows this noise. Someone's chopping with an ax. Mari picks her way across the clearing toward the sound, passes through another set of trees and up a little higher to another clearing. This one offers a lovely view out across the mountain. She can pick out the singing rock meadow and the line of what she thinks is her rooftop, and beyond that, the smudges of what must be the town.

And she sees him.

He's different now, but of course, so is she. They've both grown older. But when he turns at the sound of her feet on the snapping twigs and smiles, Mari knows him as though no time has passed at all.

"Andrew."

He's not wearing a shirt and his jeans hang low on his hips so the bones jut out. Sweat gleams on his tanned skin, broad shoulders, tight belly. His blond hair is rumpled with sweat, too, standing up from his head in jutting spikes.

"Mariposa."

Her knees go weak at the sound of the name nobody's called her in so many years. Nobody until she came back here. She sinks to the ground in slow motion, and he's there to take her by the elbow and lead her to a boulder where she can sit. She can smell him, the scent of hard work that isn't at all like Ryan has ever smelled. His fingers are hotter on her skin even than the sun.

Without a word, he passes her a drink from a metal canteen that looks like army surplus. The water inside is warm, but she gulps it gratefully. Some sloshes onto her hand. The sun is so bright it gives him a halo when he steps back to look down, making a shadow so she doesn't have to squint.

"It *is* you, isn't it?" He tilts his head and a shaft of sun stabs at her from over his left ear. "It has to be."

"Yes. And you…oh…it's you." She shudders with warm water drying quickly on the back of her hand and gives him back the canteen. "I'm sorry. I don't know what to say. Or do."

It's okay.

His hands move; he speaks but not with words.

Mari has never wept more than she has over the past few days, but now more tears come surging up and out of her. She gasps. The sobs rip out of her and she buries her face in her hands, overtaken and overwhelmed.

She is aware that Andrew is pulling her elbows so she stands. Below the smell of dirt and wood and sweat, she breathes the smell of *him*—a scent she'd forgotten she ever knew. It's more than a smell, it's a flavor; it fills her nose and mouth, into her lungs. She shakes against him, her cheek and then her lips pressed to his skin.

At first he's just holding her while she weeps, but then he's kissing her. Forehead, cheeks, her closed and tear-swollen eyes. His hands stroke over her hair, soothing.

It's Mari who kisses his mouth; she finds his lips with hers and opens them with her tongue. Her arms go around his neck. The kiss is desperate and longing. Lunging. She has never kissed any man other than Ryan, and never like this. This is what kisses are when the world is coming to an end and all that's left is heat and hunger.

This kiss is wild.

And it breaks the way wild things do, fierce and sharp and hard. His fingers grip her upper arms, holding her at a distance. His teeth have grazed her lip, and Mari touches the tip of her tongue to the sore spot.

Andrew links their fingers tight and takes her back to

the tiny cabin, where he sits her at the minuscule table with matching seats that fold up so cleverly into the wall. He pours her a drink, cool this time, from a pitcher he pulls from a tiny fridge hidden in a cupboard. The only light is sunshine through the net-covered windows, so there are lots of shadows.

She needs them.

"This...house. Your house?" She looks around at the small loft where he must sleep. The cupboards, the tiny camp stove, the bookshelves. "This is where you live?"

He stares until she has to duck her head and laugh. "What?"

"It's just...hearing your voice," Andrew says. "It's not what I was expecting."

"What were you expecting?"

He shakes his head, his smile rueful and sort of embarrassed. "I don't know."

"Did you live here back then?"

Andrew laughs, shakes his head. Gives her a curious look. "Oh, no. I lived close by with my parents. Don't you remember?"

"No." She pauses, thinking. "There was someone who didn't like you to spend time with me. Your...mother?"

"Yes."

"You snuck off to take care of me," she says in a small, wondering voice, bits and pieces coming back to her, but not the whole. "Even though you'd be punished for it."

Andrew clears his throat. "Yeah."

"Why?"

For that he seems to have no answer, at least not one that comes easily. She knows enough to sense his discomfort. To change the subject. Perhaps for now it's simply enough to know that he did, even if she doesn't understand his reasons. "And you built this house later?"

"Yes."

"All by yourself?"

"It's very small," he says.

Mari holds the cup in her two hands and sips the cool water. The water in Philadelphia doesn't have the same flavor, somehow crisp and fresh. She rolls it on her tongue before swallowing.

Andrew looks around. "It's a green house."

She thinks at first he says greenhouse, the kind you plant tomatoes in for the winter, but then she understands. "Really? Like from recycled materials?"

"Mostly, yes. Solar panels." He points upward. "Spring water. Compost toilet. Minimalism."

"What do you…do?" It sounds so much like all the stupid cocktail party conversations she's always hated because she never has anything to say, and Mari bites her lower lip in protest at her own words.

Andrew doesn't seem to mind. He looks at her carefully, his eyes moving over her until she flushes with heat that has nothing to do with the sunshine outside. It's not quite shame, though she should be ashamed at what she's done with him. When he touches her hair, she closes her eyes and leans into his touch the way Chompsky pushes his head against a palm to beg for a scratch.

"I work for a publishing company that puts out several different magazines about minimalist and green living. I write and edit articles. That sort of thing."

"So, you're a writer."

He smiles. "Sort of. Mostly I'm just a guy."

"And you live here." Mari looks around at this small house, this tiny, incredible house.

Andrew nods. "Yes. I rent land to a company that put up a cell phone tower. It lets me do pretty much whatever I want."

They share a smile.

"But enough about me. You've changed so much. What do

you do?" he asks softly. "What have you done? Tell me, Mariposa, what have you done for your whole life since you left?"

It seems like too much to say, but she manages to say it. Some of it's with words. Much of it is in other ways. Sometimes she fumbles with a gesture, but he knows what she means. She tells him of her life. Of Ryan. Their children.

"It sounds like a good life," Andrew says.

She'd thought so.

"But you." Mari takes his hands. "What about you? All these long years? What else have you been doing?"

His smile reminds her of the times he came and brought her food or helped her chop the wood that would keep her warm. His hands move.

Waiting for you.

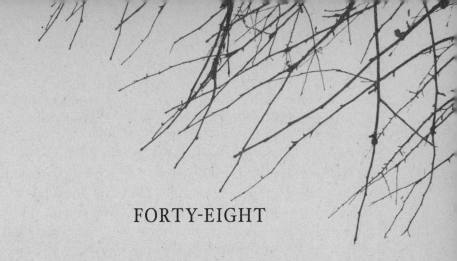

FORTY-EIGHT

ETHAN HAD BEEN WATCHING CARTOONS FOR two hours straight while Grandma went out to get her hair done. Kendra didn't like babysitting at the best of times, but at least when her parents went out they paid her for the hassle of being in charge of her brother. Now all she got was a headache from the constant jangle of the stupid cartoons that were way lamer than anything she'd watched when she was a kid.

She was bored with her non-smartphone, had exhausted all the movies on her iPad and read all the magazines her grandmother kept in a series of various-sized Longaberger baskets displayed around the living room. She wasn't hungry, not that there was anything really good to eat here, and she wasn't interested in playing any of the ancient board games even if she could wrestle the monkeybrat away from the moron box.

In the dining room, away from the drone of animated characters, she looked at the wall of bookcases. In their house, the shelves would've been filled with…well, duh, books. Her mom read everything, mostly nonfiction like biographies and books about history, but she liked novels, too. Grandma didn't seem to like books very much. Her shelves were filled with things like plates and teacups that were meant for looking at, not eating and drinking from. She had weird porcelain figurines and a truly gross collection of glass ballerinas that looked as if they might come alive at night and suck your eyeballs out. But no books.

Photo albums, though. At least twenty. All labeled in the same handwriting that signed birthday and Christmas cards. They had dates on them, too. Kendra picked one from when her dad was just a little boy. She settled into a chair at the dining room table and flipped through the pages, laughing at the clothes and hairstyles. There were pictures of her grandparents, Grandma looking much the same though in the pictures her hair was blond and not gray, and the lines around her eyes and mouth were deeper.

Ethan wandered into the dining room. "When's Grandma coming back? I'm hungry."

"Make yourself a peanut butter sandwich."

"I don't want a peanut butter sandwich. Grandma only has soynut butter, anyway, and I don't like it." He kicked at the carpet. "When can we go home?"

"Not until the end of the summer, monkeybrat. Dad said."

"I mean back home to Mama."

"I don't know." Kendra put away the album and pulled out another. Unlike the others, this one didn't have a label or a date on it. She flipped it open about halfway through.

Her grandfather had died before she was born, but she'd seen enough pictures of him to recognize his face. She didn't know the little girl in the pictures with him. The little girl wore a baggy dress, her hair in two messy pigtails. She wasn't looking at the camera, but at something far off in the distance. She clutched a book of fairy tales.

"What's Mama doing in that picture with Grandpa?" Ethan hung over Kendra's shoulder.

She shook him off. "Get off, dork. That's not Mom."

"Sure it is. Doesn't it look like her?" Ethan pointed at another picture of the same little girl, brow furrowed in concentration, hunched over a tray of food on what looked like a cafeteria table. "That's how she looks when she's hungry."

Kendra took another look. Then another. The little girl in the picture did have dark hair like their mom. And the same dark eyes. But…

"Grandpa didn't adopt Mom until she was fifteen. Before that she lived with her grandma in the Pine Grove house."

Ethan pulled up a chair next to hers and propped his elbows on the table to study the album. "It looks like Mama to me. C'mon, Kiki, look at her."

They didn't have pictures of their mother from when she was a child. Kendra had never thought to ask why. It was just one more of those weird things in their family that they didn't really talk about. She flipped a page. Looked closer. The other album she'd looked at, the one with her dad as a kid, had not only been labeled but also captioned.

"Ryan's First Birthday!"

"Ryan's First Bike!"

Lots of firsts for Ryan, Kendra thought. But this album had only photo after photo, neatly placed in the plastic sleeves but without any notations at all. She slid one of the pictures, this time of the same girl in front of a chalkboard scribbled with a bunch of different markings that didn't make sense to Kendra at all. Written on the back of the picture in faded, smudged pencil, was a single word.

Mariposa.

"See?" Ethan said with a shrug. "Mama."

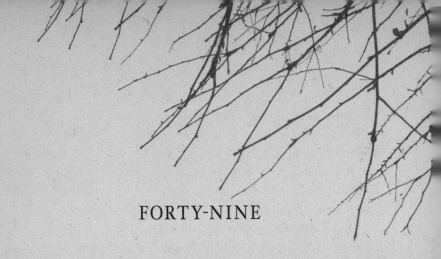

FORTY-NINE

ONCE MARI COULD'VE SAID ANYTHING WITH her fingers and a grunt or two, but back then she never had as much to say. She can't quite manage now. This question seems too impertinent to ask aloud, but she has to find the words.

"How did you know I'd be back?"

Andrew shrugs. "I didn't."

"But...you were waiting?"

His smile quirks. "I thought you'd be back. I hoped. I wanted to know what happened to you."

"You could've looked me up."

His brows rise. "How? They took you away."

There's no point in false modesty. "Apparently, I'm a case study. You could've looked me up online."

"And done what?" He gestures at his tiny room. "Called you up? Dropped by to visit? What could I have said or done? Would you have been glad to see me, Mariposa?"

"Yes. Yes, yes and yes." She reaches for his hands, but Andrew steps back.

There's only enough room for him to take one step before he bumps against the row of cupboards. This feels like a rejection, and Mari stops with her hands still outstretched. He turns his face, not looking at her.

"Yes," she whispers. "Because…you saved me, Andrew. I might've died without you."

"But you didn't." He sounds a little angry, and now he looks at her. "You moved away. You grew up."

"Of course I grew up. So did you. It's what happens."

"You got married," he says accusingly. "You have children. A family. A house in Philadelphia. You have a life."

"*You* have a life," she points out. "You built this house."

He doesn't really need to point out that it's not the same. The life she's made came to her from circumstance and fate, not necessarily by choice, but it did come to her and she's made it her own. Mari looks around this small dwelling, this tiny space, then into Andrew's face. He has kind eyes, lines around them. If she looked in the mirror, she might see lines around her own. It's what happens when time passes.

"When I was a little girl, you seemed so much older than me. But you're not, are you?"

"Not so much. No. Six years."

"My husband is eight years older than I am." She laughs softly.

"Your husband." Andrew sounds disgusted.

Mari can't quite blame him. She's somewhat disgusted with Ryan herself. But she's not sure if Andrew's curled lip is meant for Ryan…or for her.

"You were there for me, Andrew. You were the prince from a fairy story. And later, when I met Ryan—" Mari shrugs, making no excuses but somehow understanding more about her life than she ever has before "—he became my prince, too."

"And you forgot me." Andrew's accusation is gentle but an accusation just the same.

"I was a child. They took me away. I'd spent so long hiding from anyone who came—" She pauses, her turn to accuse. "*You* told me to hide. *You* told me they'd hurt me. I spent the first eight years of my life living in squalor when, at any time, any of those people could've—"

"Taken you away. Which is what they did."

She stands suddenly, like being shot from a gun. There's no room for her to advance on him, not without getting right up in his face, but after what they did together in the field, is it any more intimate to be nose to nose with him now?

Her voice is too loud. Startling. "And would that have been a bad thing? Would it have been so awful, Andrew, for someone to have taken me away?"

"Yes!" His cry echoes. He grips her arms so tight he will leave bruises. He shakes her and bares his teeth like a dog. "It was my job to take care of you. Protect you. It was my job to make sure you were all right."

"Why?" she cries. "Why?"

"Because," Andrew says, "I loved you."

Tears well in his blue eyes. She cannot stand to see him cry. Somehow, she is cradling him against her and they have sunk onto the cramped floor of his kitchen so she can rock him. When her children were small, scraped knees or bumped heads brought them running to her, and she cradled them this way. It wasn't something she was taught how to do from experience.

Motherhood, despite her fears, had come to her as naturally as it had been difficult for her to return to speaking with her voice. She's never had to do anything else. Being a wife and mother has been her career. Comforting Andrew this way is not like mothering, and nor is it quite like comforting a lover, but just like all of this has been, something else entirely.

His eyes open and stare. "Stay with me."

The idea is simultaneously so ludicrous and desirable she's not sure whether to laugh or cry. "Here?"

"Here?" he echoes. "There. In your house. It is yours, now. Isn't it?"

"It was always mine, even when other people were living in it."

He finds a smile. "So. Is there room for me there?"

Mari smiles, too, thinking he must be joking. "With me and my family? My husband? He wouldn't be a fan of that."

"Do you care?" Andrew shifts to sit up, no longer cradled but sitting across from her, knees folded because there's no room for him to sit any other way. "I thought you told him to go."

Her head tilts, eyes narrowing. Did she tell him about that, or did he somehow assume? She says nothing at first.

You told him.

Andrew's fingers trace patterns in the air.

To go.

"I did tell him to go," she says. "I was angry. I needed time. It doesn't mean he's not coming back."

"You could tell him not to come back."

Mari gets to her feet. Looks down at him. Her stomach churns. She can still taste him. The smell of him still surrounds her.

What has she done?

"You don't even know me," Mari says. "Not really. I'm not a little girl anymore. And you're not my prince."

Andrew stands. In this small kitchen he looks impossibly tall. Broader than Ryan. Stronger.

"I could be," he says.

FIFTY

THE HOUSE IS QUIET WHEN SHE'S ALONE, BUT Mari's always enjoyed that. When her children were small, she would sometimes creep away from the constant sounds of their chatter. Hide away in the pantry with the door closed, breathing in the scents of the spices, in the dark, and count the seconds until they noticed she was gone and came looking to find her. They still did that. The moment she went missing, one or the other of them, if not Ryan, was calling out her name.

Nobody calls her name now.

Mari stands in the kitchen of this house and breathes. And breathes. It smells of cleanser and fabric softener from the counters she just scoured and the loads of laundry she's been doing. It doesn't smell like dog shit and mold. It doesn't smell like fear.

With her eyes closed, Mari can imagine herself anywhere. She could be on a tropical island with blue ocean waters surrounding her. A snowy mountain peak. Inside the depths of a cool dark cave with blind white fish swimming in dark and silent pools of mineral-rich water.

But she knows where she is.

And she remembers.

★ ★ ★

"Mariposa. Butterfly." The words sounded different, but Andrew was pointing back and forth from the fluttering bug on the flowering bush to the girl and back again. "Mariposa."

Butterfly.

She got it. She was a butterfly. What she didn't understand was what that meant. But the sun was shining and the birds were flying overhead. The dogs were sleeping in the shade while the chickens took their dust baths. They rolled and coated their feathers, squatting, then got up and shook themselves. Over and over, until Mari laughed and rolled in the dirt, too.

Andrew hadn't brought food today, but that was okay. Gran was having a good day. She cooked something on the box that got hot when you turned the knobs. She left most of it in the pot, and Mari had eaten her fill. Only the biggest dog, Peppy, can reach it and only then if she stands on her hind legs, so Mari didn't even have to fight anyone for it.

Get up. You shouldn't. Dirty.

Mari didn't care about dirty. Why should she? In the heat of summer there was splashing in the creek to cool off. There were shady patches in the grass to lie in. There were these puddles of dust she shared with squawking chickens that scattered if she moved too fast but that would sit quietly beside her if she moved slow.

Andrew was making that face, though. The madface. His eyes scanned the yard, the fields beyond. The trees. He wanted to get back into the trees, Mari thought, but she patted the dirt beside her. Andrew should roll in the dirt. Maybe he'd feel better.

He shook his head, instead. "No. I have to go. They'll be wondering where I am."

Mari liked it better when Andrew didn't sound so loud. His voice reminded her of when They came, when she must be silent, silent, quiet, quiet. No sound. No noise. Not even a breath. She didn't like when Andrew spoke aloud because he didn't sound like Gran, who only ever mumbled, toothless mouth smacking. Or the dogs, who growled or barked or whined when they wanted to speak.

No, when Andrew used his voice to talk to her, he sounded like a Them, and since he was the one always telling her to hide from Them, it made Mari feel tight and tangled inside like the long pieces of yarn that came out of Gran's basket when she was using the clacking sticks to make blankets.

Stay.

He shook his head. *Can't stay.*

Mari stood and shook off the dirt the way a chicken did, scattering the hens that had been sitting beside her. She slapped at her bare skin. The sweat on her palms left marks. She dodged past him and ran to the creek. She squatted in it, splashing. She gestured.

Andrew. Come.

He followed but didn't go in. Andrew wore long pants, shoes, a shirt with buttons. His hair was shorter than it had been the last time he came there. He shifted from foot to foot and looked at the thing wrapped around his arm just above his hand. This thing told Andrew when it was time for him to leave. Mari hated it.

Up, fast, quick like a dog snatching a bone away from another, she grabbed him. Fingers moved, undid the clasp. She took it, dodging his grasp. She threw it in the water and laughed at the splash.

She didn't laugh when he grabbed her. Shook her. Her arms would turn black-and-blue. Andrew shook Mari so hard she fell into the grass, against a rock. It cut her leg. There was blood, not as much as the time the dog bit her, but enough.

"She bought me that watch for my birthday, Mari! It'll be ruined, and she'll want to know what happened to it! And what am I supposed to tell her? I'm not even," Andrew said through short, panting breaths, "supposed to be here. If she knew—"

From her place in the grass, her blood painting red on the green, Mari made the question with her hands. *What would she do?*

Andrew's *she* is different from the Them he warned Mari against. She must be. Why else would he go back to *she,* when he made Mari promise to hide and never ever show herself when the other Them came?

"She'll punish me. That's all." He shoved his hands in his pockets.

Mari didn't know what that meant. Punish. Her lips formed the same shapes, but her tongue tripped on the sounds. Andrew scowled again.

"Shut up. Don't talk. Don't speak, Mariposa. I told you. If you talk like that, you'll be tempted to talk to Them when they come."

She didn't know what *tempted* meant, but she knew the sound of his madvoice. The ditch between his eyes meant angry. She didn't like when Andrew was mad, because she was afraid that meant he wouldn't be back.

And what would she do if Andrew didn't come back?
Stay. Please. Stay.

"I can't, Mariposa! I can't stay!" Andrew shouted, sending her back. "Don't you get it? I'll get in trouble! She'll punish me. You don't get it. You just don't understand."

His scary voice, madvoice, softened. "Of course you don't. I know you don't. C'mere."

She didn't want to go to him. He was still making the madface only now it was like the sadface, too. She wanted to be sad, too, when he looked that way, but she was still a little scared.

"Mariposa. Come here. Don't you know I'm just trying to

protect you? I just want to make sure you're all right. That They don't come for you. You should be safe, and you're safe here. Where They can't get you."

She understood almost none of this. The jumbled sound of his words made a mush in her head. She saw his face, his mouth moving, she heard the tone of his voice. But she wasn't quite sure what he meant.

Stay.

"I'll come back, Mariposa. I promise. I will come back for you. I will take care of you."

But Andrew didn't come back for a long, long time.

There's a knock on the back door, and she knows before she opens it who it is. Who it has to be. He doesn't look angry now or sad. Mari has words now for the expression on Andrew's face.

Contrite.

"I'm sorry," Andrew says.

It's okay.

He smiles at the flutter of her fingers. "You don't need to talk like that anymore. You have a voice now."

She steps aside so he can come in. They stand awkwardly in the den, surrounded by Ryan's boxes of files and folders. Andrew looks around, taking in all of it, then looks at her with raised brows, proving again they really don't need words to understand each other.

"Come in," she offers. "Let me make you something to eat."

FIFTY-ONE

KENDRA HAD FLIPPED THROUGH EVERY SINGLE album at least three times, even the ones without pictures of her mother in them. Looking for clues. Trying to figure out what the hell had happened to her family.

Sammy's parents had been on the verge of divorce forever. Her mother threatened to leave her dad every few months, and her dad spent the night away from home at least as often as that. Both of them usually ignored Sammy when they were fighting and got on her case when they weren't, so honestly Sammy preferred it when her parents were mad at each other. Sammy spoke of divorce as something inevitable and meaningless. Something to look forward to, maybe. Two sets of holidays and presents, two allowances. Two parents guilty enough to overindulge instead of ignore her.

Kendra knew lots of kids whose parents were divorced. Most of her friends had more than one set of parents, and some had more than two. Stepsiblings all over the place. She thought about her father with another wife, of having to share her house with a stranger. Of Ethan not being her only brother.

She wanted to puke. Ethan was a brat sometimes, but he was her brother and she didn't want another one. She didn't want her life to change.

Her door creaked open, and she turned, expecting to see
Grandma or possibly her dad. It was Ethan. His pajama bottoms were a couple inches too short, showing his ankles. His
shirt was inside out, and she was pretty sure he'd worn it for
the whole week. Gross.

"Kiki, can I sleep in here tonight?"

"Sure." She moved over and shoved the album to the side.

Ethan ran across the floor as if something was chasing him
and took a flying leap into the bed. When he was a lot smaller,
he'd curl up against Kendra just like this, and she'd read him
a story. Now instead of Pooh and Tigger or the hungry cat-
erpillar, all they had was this album full of old pictures. She
reached for it. Flipped the pages.

"What do you think she was doing there?" Ethan looked
at a series of Polaroid photos, yellowed with age.

In them, Mom was sitting at a table, her hair in pigtails. She
was grinning, missing her two front teeth. Her hands were
above her head and blurred, as though they were moving. In
the last picture, Grandpa was sitting with his arm around her.
Mom was laughing into the camera. In most of the earlier pictures, she looked unhappy, but not in these.

"I don't know, monkey. But she looks happy, doesn't she?"

"Yeah. She does. I like it better when she looks like that."

"Me, too." Kendra flipped the page. More pictures. They
weren't labeled, so they could only guess at what's going on.

"She was in the hospital," Ethan said. "Do you think she
was sick?"

Kendra shrugged. "I don't know. If she was sick, I guess
Grandpa was taking care of her. But…what kind of little kid
is sick like that?"

"Whattaya mean?" Ethan rolled to look at her. "She hardly
ever gets sick."

"Grandpa was a psychiatrist like Daddy. Which means that
if Mama was sick, it was in her head."

Ethan looked at Kendra with a frown. "You mean like crazy?"

She looked again at the pictures.

"What kind of little kid is...crazy?" Ethan asked.

"I don't think she was crazy." But even as Kendra said it, she thought of all the strange things her mother did, the stuff other mothers didn't. "I think she was just...different."

"I don't care. I miss her. I want to go back home. To where Mama is," he added, even though Kendra hadn't reminded him again that they couldn't go back to the house in Philly until the end of the summer. "Make Daddy let us go back, Kiki. Please?"

"I can't, brat—he already said no."

"We should run away, then." Ethan said this so matter-of-factly it was clear he meant it.

"Right." She nudged him with her elbow.

"Can you at least call her?"

"Her phone must be turned off. She isn't answering or can't get a signal. Or maybe she just doesn't want to talk to us," Kendra said.

Ethan's face screwed up into a frown. "No way. Mama would never not want to talk to us."

Kendra wanted to believe that was true. "She'll call us when she remembers she turned off her phone. Then we can tell her we want to come home. Okay? But until then, we just have to hang in there."

"I don't like it here," Ethan said like a confession.

Kendra pulled him closer. "No. Me, neither."

FIFTY-TWO

MARI REMEMBERS CRACKING OPEN EGGS AND letting the yolks drip raw into her mouth, but she scrambles them now with butter and some crumbled bits of bacon. She makes toast, too, thick slices of it she spreads with more butter and strawberry jam. The food's so simple it's almost not a meal, yet when she sets it on the table and sits across from Andrew to eat it, he looks at her as if she's set the table with gold.

"I'm an adult, Andrew." She's annoyed at his look of wonder. "I'm married. I have children. I can drive a car. I'm not that grotty, silent child who hid under the table."

"I know you're not." Andrew lifts his fork and tilts it from side to side like he's trying to catch the light with it, but then he pokes it into the fluffy mess of eggs and bacon on his plate. "It's just nice to have someone cook for me, that's all."

Mari thinks of that tiny house high up on the mountain. A doll's house, but this man in front of her is no doll. Time has dug lines around his eyes and streaked his hair with just a strand or two of silver. She sits across from him with her own plate, though she's not hungry. Instead, she sips from a mug of tea she really only wants to warm her hands with.

"So. What now?" she says.

Andrew pauses, mouth full. He chews and swallows. He

looks into her eyes. "Did you think about me while you were away? Ever?"

"Honestly, I…forgot about you." Until she came back here.

Andrew's mouth thins and his eyes narrow. "Thanks."

"I was eight years old when they took me out of here. They put me in a psych ward with children who were so disturbed it wasn't that they didn't know how to speak, it was that they simply couldn't. I spent months being poked, prodded and tested every single day for hours at a time." Mari paused to swallow the bitter taste of those memories. "I think I repressed a lot of what happened here. You included."

"They were cruel to you."

"No." She shakes her head. "No, Andrew. They weren't. But they were doctors, and they were determined to fix me."

"You weren't broken," Andrew says.

Mari laughs at this. "So says you, with your eco-friendly house and your wireless internet connection and your work-from-home job. You grew up in a house. Went to school. You had parents who took care of you."

Andrew tilts his head to look at her; he gives her a slow, knowing blink. "You think it was so easy for me?"

"I think you didn't go hungry or cold. I think you had a normal family."

It's his turn to laugh. "Normal. Right. That's what you think?"

"Wasn't it?" Mari takes a piece of toast and chews it, the jelly rich and sweet but doing nothing to push back the ache in her gut.

"If you call being raised by a pair of fundamentalists who thought the devil'd already taken my soul and it was their duty to save it *normal*." Andrew puts an emphasis on the word that shows what he thinks of it. "If you call being made to kneel on grains of rice while I recited bible verses by rote normal. They never beat me, but they didn't really have to. When you hear every single day how your soul belongs to Satan, you begin to believe it."

Mari had grown up without religion. In their house, they celebrate Christmas with Santa and presents, Easter with candy, because it's what Ryan had grown up with as a child. She doesn't believe in Satan any more than she believes in God. Still, hearing the loathing in Andrew's voice, she can understand some of what he felt.

"I'm sorry." She reaches for him. Their fingers link tight. This feels so familiar it's like holding her own hand.

"They never took any part of the blame for my sinful state." His face twists. "By the time I figured out why, exactly, I was so doomed to burn in the everlasting fires of hell, my old man was dying of cancer. It might've been the perfect time for him to say he was sorry, to at least explain to me that none of it was really my fault, but nope. To his dying breath he blamed the world, he blamed my mother, he blamed me for looking like her. I was with him when he died, and the only thing I regret was that he didn't hold on longer so he could suffer more."

Mari's glad she didn't eat much, because at Andrew's flat, solid tone her stomach twists so much she'd probably be sick. "I'm sorry."

His laugh is as twisted as her guts. "So don't talk to me about normal, Mari. Normal is what I tried so hard to save you from. From the first moment I saw you, I knew there had to be a better life for you. I was only six years old, and I knew it."

She means to ask him how that had happened—how he'd seen her when she was just a baby. Her memory of childhood is patchy and she only remembers meeting him in the woods when she was older, but she's curious now how long he knew her before she was taken away. How he came to be her protecting prince. Before she can ask, Andrew's pulling his hand from hers and standing. He paces along the kitchen floor, his bare feet scuffing it.

He goes to the sink and draws some water into his cupped hands and drinks, then splashes his face. He turns to her, dripping, mouth working on words he can't seem to force from off his tongue.

"You are so beautiful," Andrew whispers over and over. "I knew you would be lovely. I didn't know you'd break my heart with it."

This is the sort of prayer she understands. She studies his face and thinks hard about what this is. What it was.

What it might become.

She's never entertained even the thought of being unfaithful to Ryan. Now she sees again how the stage was set for her to love Ryan by loving this man in front of her. And she wonders, did she ever have a choice in loving Ryan at all, or was she destined to marry him because of something that had set itself in her childish brain?

Their current issues aside, how will she know if she would have chosen her husband if she's never had any other options to choose from?

She brings Andrew's fingertips to her lips. She kisses each one until he cups her cheek with his hot palm and draws her closer. She feels his heart beat beneath her cheek and the soft sigh of his breath against her hair.

"Come upstairs with me," Mari offers.

FIFTY-THREE

RYAN GOT BACK TO WEST CHESTER FROM PHILLY later than he'd planned, but hell. After those depressing-as-shit meetings with his lawyer, he'd needed a few drinks. The bright spot of it all was that it turned out he wasn't the only one being named in the suit by Annette's husband, and that he hadn't been the only one previously sued by the guy, either. The malpractice insurance company apparently had a thick file on Mr. Somers and they were inclined to settle out of court just to get rid of him.

It didn't get Ryan his job back. Kastabian and Goldman had never liked him, anyway, and were just looking for a reason to get rid of him from the practice. But he wasn't going to lose his license, and they weren't going to go after him for breach of contract or anything ridiculous like that, so even though he'd have to look for a new place to work, at least he *could* work.

Which was a good thing, he thought as he pushed open the door to his mother's house, because the book was going to shit.

He'd emailed query letters to twenty different literary agents, promising them the book was a guaranteed hit, perfect for Oprah to tout on her show and Dr. Phil to base an episode on. He'd listed his credentials, which were pretty damned impressive, and made sure to let them know the project was based entirely on his dad's work. He'd even sent along the first fifteen pages he'd managed to get down so far—who knew writing could be so much freaking work?—with the explanation that they weren't completely polished, but that's what editors were for. Right?

So far, not a single one had wanted it. Several of them had sent form rejections, a bunch hadn't answered and one rude bitch had even replied with a letter suggesting he take a few writing classes to improve his "skills."

"Eff that noise," Ryan muttered, digging in his mother's fridge for something to eat.

It wasn't as if he was going to be a *writer,* for Chrissake. He pulled out a plastic container full of what looked like chili and lifted the lid to sniff it. At the sound of the voice behind him, he let out a shout and whirled, sending the chili spattering all over the floor.

"Oh, Ryan!" his mother cried in a voice thick with disgust. "Are you drunk?"

"Jesus, Ma. No. You just scared me." Ryan blinked in the bright light from overhead, then at the mess on the floor.

She was already bustling to the closet to pull out a mop. "You smell like a liquor store."

Liquor stores, in Ryan's experience, hardly smelled like anything. But compared to the time in college when she'd said he smelled like a bum someone had rolled in an alley, he guessed this was better.

"I had a couple drinks. Not a big deal."

She sniffed loudly to show what she thought of that, and to Ryan's surprise, handed him the mop instead of setting to the task herself. "Here."

He took the mop and looked again at the mess. His stomach growled. "You have more chili?"

"No. Your son ate most of it, then was up until long past bedtime with a stomachache."

Ryan looked up at her. "Is he okay?"

"Nothing a little Pepto-Bismol couldn't fix. What?" his mother added, affronted. "You think I can't take care of a little bellyache?"

Ryan leaned the mop against the counter and stepped over the splatter to grab the paper towels from the holder. He tore off a few and used them to scoop up most of the muck, including the plastic container that had split and chipped. He tossed it all in the trash, then looked again at his mother, who watched from the doorway with her arms crossed.

"What?" he said.

"Has she called you yet?"

He didn't have to ask who she meant by "she."

"No. I'm sure she misplaced her phone or something."

He didn't mention to his mother that Mari had been righteously pissed off with him. That maybe she was ignoring him on purpose—that even though he could easily imagine her doing that to him, he was getting a little concerned that she wasn't at least calling to talk to the kids. He wasn't going to give his mother any more ammo against his wife. Hell, even if this all ended up with Mari being his ex-wife, he wasn't going to give his mother the satisfaction of having one more thing to snark about.

"Your children are missing their mother."

Ryan straightened with another handful of messy paper towels. "Ma, don't."

"What?" she cried, all wide eyes and innocence.

"She's my wife. She is their mother. Of course they miss her. I miss her, too." He dumped the paper towels in the trash and washed his hands. He paused, recognizing how this all could go and not wanting to get into it with her. "Are they okay? The kids, I mean. Have they been saying stuff?"

"Your daughter barely says a damned word, and your son just keeps saying he's bored," his mother said, and Ryan knew this was more than her usual irritation with anything related to Mari. She was pissed off. She'd never have referred to her beloved grandchildren by anything but their names, otherwise. It was the same as when she said "your father" instead of Leon or even "your dad."

"Bored!" she continued. "Despite the hundred dollars I dropped like it was change from the bottom of my purse at that video game store. Despite the trips I've taken them on! Bored, Ryan. And I have to tell you, as a child, you were never bored."

Ryan, in fact, could remember long and horrid stretches of boredom on the endless car trips his mother had insisted on taking instead of a fun vacation, like a trip to the beach. He'd never understood how a woman who spent so much time getting ready in the morning could claim she loved camping and cross-country road trips so much. She'd spent a huge portion of the time in the car either haranguing his dad about his driving, complaining about the poor service they got at hotels and in restaurants or demanding her husband and son "appreciate the natural beauty" they were passing on their way to some touristy spot.

"What are you saying, Ma? That my kids aren't perfect angels?" The mop was going to be worthless without a bucket and cleanser. Ryan didn't have to be a housekeeper to see that. He yanked open the cupboard under the sink and looked in vain for a bottle of spray cleaner and some dishcloths. Mari kept them under the sink, but it seemed his mother had some complicated system of where she put her cleaning products. Irritated, he turned to her. "Where's your cleaning spray?"

"I'm saying, Ryan, that they could use a little talking-to from their father about gratitude. You've spoiled them dreadfully."

"Spoiled?" Hands still empty, Ryan went to the closet from where she'd pulled the mop and yanked it open so hard the fuzzy kitten calendar hanging from a nail on the door swung wildly. "You think my kids are spoiled?"

"I think they've been indulged. Yes. I think they've been let to run—" she paused until Ryan half closed the door to look around it at her "—wild."

"Oh, for—" He couldn't quite bring himself to drop the f-bomb in front of his mother, no matter how much she might've deserved it. "Enough, okay? Would you just stop, Ma? I know all about Mari. I know you hate her because you think she stole Dad away from you, but the fact is you probably had more to do with it than anything else, you just don't want to admit it."

Shit. Too far.

Ryan's mother gasped, one hand to her heart. He felt immediately guilty and closed the closet door.

"How dare you?" she managed to say through quivering lips. "How. Dare. You."

"You think I don't remember, Ma, but I do," Ryan said as gently as he could. "I was away at college, but I remember when he started talking about bringing her home. You didn't support the idea at all from the start. He was talking about giving a lost soul a home…."

His mother's bitter laugh stopped him. "Is that what you think of her as? A lost soul?"

Truthfully, he didn't. Mari was one of the least lost people Ryan had ever met. If anything, he'd thought of her as a curiosity at first, before seeing her as a woman he could love. He shook his head now. "No. But Dad did."

Another bitter laugh. "Well, that was your father, wasn't it? Trying to fix things that couldn't be repaired? Everything except our marriage."

Ryan had spent countless hours listening to the litany of complaints of spouses toward each other. He'd spent a good portion of his career counseling people on how to deal with the problems in their marriages, often by first helping them to turn toward their personal issues and solve them. He'd learned to tune out his mother's complaints about his dad because he didn't really want to either counsel his mother or be privy to the endless sniping she seemed helpless or at least unwilling to stop. He wasn't any more interested now than he'd ever been.

"All I'm saying is that it takes more than one small thing to end a marriage."

"One small thing? You think the hours he spent with her, away from me…away from you, for God's sake, Ryan! The hours and hours of time he gave to her instead of spending them with his family. You think that was one small thing? Or how he used to talk about her endlessly, as though she were some magical creature, some fairy-tale princess. My God, it was disgusting. And ridiculous," she added. "And then to have him say he wanted to bring her home, into our house, that wild, uncultured, uncivilized…thing? She was an animal, Ryan! And he wanted to bring her to live in my house!"

To his mother, who'd never even allowed Ryan a pet fish because of the "mess and the stink" they made, it must've seemed like an awful imposition. Still, his throat burned with anger at the way she'd described his wife.

"You act like she was wearing rabbit skins and throwing her own crap. By the time Dad decided to adopt her, she wasn't like that anymore. She'd spent years being rehabilitated."

"He spent years trying to fix her, when we both knew she would never, ever be right."

"What's that supposed to mean?" Head starting to pound, Ryan closed the closet door with a thud.

His mother gave him a steel-eyed glare. "She had something about her that ensorcelled him. You, too. I know what it was. I saw the way she looked at him, then at you. The way she moved her body."

"If you're suggesting Dad had a sexual interest in Mari,

you're wrong. And more than that, Ma, you're disgusting."
Ryan spat the words like bullets and watched her flinch from
each one.

"He chose her over me!" she shouted, fists clenched and
waving in fury. "You both did!"

There it was. Something he'd always known was at the root
of his mother's behavior but had never been brought into the
light. "You're jealous of her."

"Of course I'm jealous of her," his mother said as though
the words were razors slitting her tongue with each syllable.

He could've pointed out that maybe one of the reasons his
father had spent so much time at work was to escape his constantly nagging wife. Or that Mari had never been a threat
to her. Or even that it was inevitable that Ryan would fall in
love with someone other than, thank God, his mother, and
that she'd have disliked his wife no matter who he'd chosen.
He could've pointed out that his mother had spent so much
of her life disgruntled and dissatisfied with everything she'd
been given that she could never be satisfied with what she had.

Instead, Ryan hugged his mother.

"I love you, Ma." He couldn't remember the last time he'd
hugged her like this—maybe at his wedding, just before walking down the aisle. Maybe longer ago than that, as a little boy.
Hell. Maybe never.

"You just don't know about her," his mother said. "Not
everything. If you knew everything…"

He pushed her gently from him. "If I knew everything,
what? Do you think there's anything I could know about my
wife that would ever make me not love her? We have two
beautiful kids, Ma. We have a good life. We have a good
marriage."

Had a good marriage, he thought. Before he'd gone and
screwed it up. Before he'd taken it for granted.

Maybe Ryan had his own lessons to learn about being satisfied with what he had.

"Your father told me everything he'd learned about that girl. You think the fact she spoke with her hands was romantic, like something from a story. You think that the fact she lived in filth and poverty was somehow something to be worn like a badge of honor."

"It wasn't her fault."

"Well, neither were all those years of care she got, all those years of therapy, anything she can claim as her own effort. Do you know," his mother said, "your dad did most of that work for free? Because the grants wouldn't cover the costs?"

"I knew that. Yeah. It's one of the reasons I thought it would be important to do volunteer work myself. Helping people who needed it but couldn't afford it."

His mother pushed him away. "And how's that been working for you, lately?"

Ryan backed up until he hit the counter and ran a hand through his hair. He hadn't given his mother any details about his reasons for taking his family to Pine Grove, or about his job or the case. Not about the book. He hadn't gotten around to asking her for the lost files, yet. All she knew was that a patient of his had died, and her husband was suing him. "I've had to quit that for a while. I'll get back into it."

"Uh-huh."

"Maybe," Ryan said, "you'd just like it if we left."

That hit her where it hurt, but Ryan took no pride in it. She was his mother, after all, and even if she could be the most annoying woman on the planet, he knew that most of the time she acted out of love. Her own twisted version of love, but even so, sometimes that was the only kind there was.

"I didn't say that. You know I love having you here."

Sure, because it meant they weren't with Mari. "We can't stay forever. My business is going to be over soon in Philly.

Another couple days. And in another few weeks it'll be time for the kids to go back to school and back home."

"So...stay until then. You know I never get enough of my grandchildren."

"I thought you said they were spoiled and indulged," Ryan said.

His mother sniffed. "That doesn't mean I don't love them."

"I know you do, Ma. And I'm glad for the help." Ryan hesitated, deciding to come at least a little bit clean. "Mari and I have been having a few problems. We needed some distance."

His mother's gaze flared. "I knew it."

"Don't start." He held up a hand, but his mother was already off and running.

"I told you, Ryan, if you only knew—"

"Enough!" Both of them looked reflexively at the ceiling, but if they'd woken the kids there was no sound of them from upstairs. He fixed his mother with another hard glare. "I know you hate her. I know you always will hate her. But I've told you before and I'm going to say it again, just so we're clear—I love Mari. All marriages have rough spots, and this one isn't because of her."

His mother looked shocked. "What is that supposed to mean?"

"It's not supposed to mean anything. It means that I screwed up. It's my fault. I..." Ryan ran his hand through his hair again.

"You look like your father when you do that."

He stopped. "I had an affair with a patient. The one who killed herself. I lost my job because of it—"

"Oh, Ryan!"

"And I was facing charges," he continued, cutting her off before she could go into full-on wailing. "But they're being settled out of court. I'm not going to lose my license. They couldn't prove it."

His mother looked stricken. "But you did it. It's true."

He nodded. "I needed to get away for a while."

"So you went…there?" His mother's lip curled. "Why on earth? You could've—"

"Come here?" He laughed harshly. "Right. She knows you can't stand her, Ma. She'd never have come here."

His mother's back stiffened. "I have never treated your wife with anything but politeness."

He found a laugh at that. "Yeah, well, having you over for the kids' birthdays and holidays when you ignore her like she's a stranger is a lot different than asking you to put her up in your guest bedroom."

"I'm sorry," his mother said.

It was the last thing Ryan ever expected his mother to say. "She's a good person, Ma. I wish you could understand that. Hate Dad if you have to. He's dead now, and anyway, he was the adult who made the decisions, not her. You have to stop blaming her for what she couldn't help."

"Oh, Ryan, you don't understand. I know she can't help where she came from or what she is. But what you don't understand is that she will never be…"

"What?" he challenged. "She won't ever be what? Normal? High-class, like you? I hate to say it, Ma, but if class is determined by how you treat other people, Mari's got a lot more than most people I know."

FIFTY-FOUR

MARI'S OFFER HANGS BETWEEN THEM FOR A long moment before Andrew answers.

"No," he says.

It breaks her heart. Mari sits at the table, her face in her hands. "You don't love me. You said you did, but you don't."

"Mariposa, that's not the only way to love someone. I mean, it's not right."

She knows it's wrong. She presses the heels of her hands to her eyes to hold back tears. "Go away, then."

"I don't want to go away. You don't understand…"

She doesn't want to know. Doesn't want to hear.

"I need to try calling my kids again. I can't seem to get a good signal out here." She's changing the subject, she knows, even if what she says is true.

She doesn't care about reaching Ryan, who hasn't called her once since she'd asked him to leave. Probably pouting. But Kendra hasn't answered any of Mari's dozen texts, and that's more worrisome. Kendra's attached to her phone at all times, even the cheap replacement. Either the messages aren't getting through—not so much of a surprise, considering the poor service out here—or she's ignoring the texts. Mari hopes it isn't the latter, though she supposes, depending on what Ryan told the kids, it would be understandable if they ignored her.

"You had my daughter's phone," she says suddenly. "And the library book."

Andrew looks uncomfortable. "I didn't know they belonged to your daughter."

"Why did you take them in the first place?"

For that he seems to have no answer.

Mari turns her back on him. She thumbs in Kendra's number with a simple message. Call me, honey. Love you, Mama.

After a moment, Mari thumbs Ryan's number. Her message to him is even shorter and simpler.

Call me.

She's not really sure she wants to talk to him, but she supposes at some point, she must. She can't ignore the situation forever. At some point, Ryan will tire of his mother's hovering and snide remarks the way he always does. He'll want to come back. He has to soon, anyway, because the summer will be ending and even though she's the one who told him to leave, she can't imagine he'd go back to Philly without her.

He won't abandon her.

Suddenly, so fast she loses her breath, Mari's world spins until she staggers.

She falls to her knees on the nubbled rag rug, the knots digging into her flesh so that she thinks of Andrew saying how his parents had forced him to kneel on grains of rice. Only seconds have passed and already her knees hurt. She can't imagine what it must've been like for him to do it for hours.

"Mariposa. Don't."

"Don't you tell me what to do!"

She forces herself to her feet. Forces herself to breathe. But it's not working. Panic sweeps her and she flings open first the fridge, gasping aloud in relief at the sight of every shelf and drawer filled. Milk, eggs, butter, yogurt, ketchup, mayo, mustard. She catalogs everything with her hands as though only by touching can she make it all real.

Then the cupboards. Everything is there. She could live on this bounty for months, especially if she's sparing. Even if Ryan never comes back, even if Mari is cut off from everything, she can survive.

At the sink she runs cold water and gulps it until her stomach sloshes and then she leans over, mouth open and throat convulsing, convinced she's going to vomit. Slowly, breathing deeply, she forces away the nausea. She's going to be fine. She will be fine.

"Rough time," she mutters. "Rough time. Rough. Time."

Breathing in. Breathing out. She grips the sink and sips at the air as she murmurs. She blinks. The world no longer spins.

To her surprise, Andrew pulls her close. He kisses her forehead, not her mouth. Mari closes her eyes, comforted. She remembers something like this from before, though she was much smaller.

"I may have forgotten you," she says, squeezed up tight and close against him in a way different than Ryan has ever held her. "But right now I can't remember a time when I didn't know you."

His hands stroke once, twice, over her hair. "I've never forgotten you."

She tips her face up to his. "Tell me how you met me. Tell me about the first time you saw me."

She wants to know what it was about her that made him fight so hard to keep her safe. Mari wants a fairy story. But Andrew only strokes her hair back from her face and gives his head the tiniest of shakes.

"Can you remember the first time you met me?" he says.

She thinks and thinks again, then harder. She looks into

his eyes. They're kind eyes, blue ringed with a darker edge and white flecks in the irises.

"No. But I told you before, a lot of what happened when I was younger is hard to remember."

"Maybe," Andrew says, his hands making a ponytail of her hair at the base of her neck, "it's because I was always part of your life."

"Were you?" She lets him tug her hair to tip her face further.

He's smiling, but a little sadly. "Feels like it. Doesn't it?"

There are more questions to be asked, but there always will be. Mari looks at Andrew. She looks toward the window, the blue sky and the hint of green that indicates the tops of the trees. She doesn't need to ask him anything else right now.

FIFTY-FIVE

"HERE." GRANDMA SLAPPED DOWN A THICK folder in front of Kendra, who had her feet up on the coffee table. "You should read this."

Ethan was staring with blank eyes at the television, more mindless cartoons, but he looked around now. He reached for the folder, but Grandma slapped his fingers. Actually slapped them, so the monkeybrat pulled them back with a cry. He looked stunned, which is how Kendra felt.

Grandma might be annoying, but she'd never been mean to either of her grandchildren. She'd certainly never hit them. Now Ethan stuck his fingers in his mouth and stared at her, wide-eyed. He looked as if he might cry.

Kendra frowned. She might tease her brother, she might call him names, she might even poke him herself when he got really annoying. But that was her job and her right as his sister. Nobody else was allowed to treat him that way.

Not even Grandma.

"What is it?" Kendra said, sullen, not even making a motion to reach for it.

"It's the truth about your mother," Grandma said in a stiff, formal voice that cracked. She cleared her throat. "The real, whole truth that nobody seems to care to know."

Kendra didn't trust her grandmother's opinion about her mother any farther than she could toss her cell phone without breaking it—which wasn't far at all. And if Kendra's dad didn't want to know what was in that file, it must be something he thought was so awful he didn't want to know. "What's that mean? The real, whole truth?"

"You don't know anything about your mother. And I've kept silent all these years because I love your father. And I love you. And Ethan." Grandma's voice broke, then. Hard. Tears brimmed up and fell down her cheeks.

Kendra had seen her grandmother cry before, but this was the first time she believed the tears were real.

"I didn't want to hurt you. So I kept the story to myself. All of it. But I knew. Oh, yes, I knew all along." Grandma shuddered and her mouth looked as if she'd sucked on a lemon. "But now, it's time."

"Why now?" Kendra asked, not even caring if she sounded like a little bitch. "What's so important about now? I mean, it's not like we ever thought you loved our mom. We know you can't stand her."

Grandma looked as though she'd stepped in something that smelled bad, but the tears still tracked down her cheeks and made stripes in her makeup. She'd hate it if she knew how she looked, Kendra thought. Old and wrinkled and smeared.

"When you're a mother, you'll understand what it's like to want to protect your children and do what's best for them. Someday, Kendra, I hope you'll understand what it's like to be a real mother. One who doesn't leave her children—"

"Our mother didn't leave us!" Kendra shouted. "She would never!"

"Of course she did!" Grandma shouted, just as loud. Spit flew from her red lipsticked mouth. "She could hardly do anything else, could she? How else could she behave, given what she came from? What she was?"

Kendra had heard her grandmother say such a thing before. "What do you mean, what she was?"

Ethan had begun to sniffle, his eyes darting back and forth, big as saucers. Usually even the tiniest hint of tears would have Grandma woo-wooing over him, but not this time. Now she barely looked at him. Her eyes bore into Kendra's.

"Read that file. Then you'll know. And make sure your father reads it, too."

"If he reads it, will he take us back h-home?" Ethan cried. Snot bubbled out from his nose.

Kendra grimaced. Gross. She looked at her grandmother, who just shook her head and pointed at the folder.

"No," Grandma said, "I'm sure that once he reads that, he won't take you back to her. Ever."

With that, she made a grand exit, leaving Kendra to stare after her with her jaw gaping in amazement and fury. Ethan burst into full-on sobbing. Kendra cringed away from the glistening snot sliding all over his face but did pull him closer. There were tissues handy on every end table, but she handed him one of the doilies from Grandma's couch instead. He scrubbed at his face.

"Don't read it," Ethan begged her. "And don't show it to Daddy! Don't, Kiki!"

Curiosity killed the cat. How many times had Kendra heard that? And what had she ever learned from listening at doors but half stories and mysteries that didn't get explained? Here was her chance, once and for all, to learn whatever was "the truth."

"Whatever it is, Grandma thinks it's going to make us not love Mom. Or make Daddy not love her. Which is just stupid," Kendra said in a low, hard voice meant to drive the tears right out of her brother's eyes. She felt like crying herself, but forced it back. She wasn't going to let Grandma get to her like that.

"I don't think you should read it, Kiki. Throw it away."

But she couldn't.

FIFTY-SIX

THIS DAY HAS NO SOUNDTRACK, BUT IT'S AS idyllic as any movie. Andrew takes Mari up the mountain and through the woods to explore old places and show her some new ones, too. By the time evening starts to fall, Mari's cheeks are sunburned from their picnic at the top of the mountain, and her feet and calves ache from the hours of hiking. She's bone-tired but refreshed. She takes Andrew's hand as he helps her over a fallen wooden fence at the edge of the field. By the time they cross it, the sun's started dipping below the edges of the trees and the chickens have all gone inside the hen house. Mari hears their muttered complaints, but doesn't expect to see Rosie stepping out holding a hen by the neck in one hand.

"Oh. Shit," Andrew mutters and drops Mari's hand.

"Rosie? What are you doing?"

Rosie holds out the hen, whose feet swim in the air. "This one's not laying anymore. She'll make a nice pot of soup."

Mari isn't sure she can be affronted—technically the chickens are hers, or at least they belong to her property, but since Rosie's been the one taking care of them all these years it seems she has some sort of right to them, too. Still it would've been nice if the woman had asked her first.

"Oh. I didn't know you just…took them."

Rosie's smile slips over her face like the growing shadows in the field. She looks at Andrew, her gaze hard and somehow hot. "Chickens that don't lay aren't of any use but in the soup pot. Hello, Andrew."

"You…know each other?" Mari supposes she shouldn't be any more surprised by this than she was about the chickens. Rosie, after all, lives in the only other house on this lane and would be Andrew's only other neighbor.

"Of course we do. He hasn't told you?"

Mari looks at Andrew, whose shoulders have hunched. He's looking at the ground where the toe of his boot digs into the dirt. "Why would he? You never mentioned him, either, Rosie."

The words come out with a faintly accusatory air, and Mari realizes that's exactly how she meant them to sound. Rosie had known of the tiny cabin in the woods and the man who lived there but hadn't mentioned it. It was strange, at the least. Slightly sinister, if Mari thought harder about it. As though Rosie knew, but hadn't wanted her to know.

Andrew says nothing, not even when Rosie sidles closer and shakes the hen at him. The poor bird is dangling from Rosie's fist like she's already killed it. Mari doesn't want to watch it suffer, slowly suffocating.

"Kill it, if you mean to," she says. "But don't choke it like that."

Rosie looks at the chicken, surprised, as if she's forgotten she held it. She tosses it to the dirt where it lands on its side and scrambles in the dust before getting to its feet and shaking its wings.

"I wondered how long it would be before you found her," Rosie says to Andrew. "Like calls to like. Sin to sin. No matter what we try to do. You always were full of sin."

Mari tastes sourness, bright and sharp. "Andrew? What's she talking about?"

Rosie laughs. Here in the darkening yard it has a slightly maniacal sound to it. "Oh, Mari. Pretty Mariposa. Pretty like a butterfly and just as stupid."

"Don't you call her that." Andrew's eyes flash.

"What's that? Mariposa? Or stupid." Rosie's gaze pierces Mari. "You don't know about him, do you?"

"I know all about him," Mari says stubbornly, though by looking back and forth between Andrew and Rosie, it's clear she's clueless. Her chin lifts, though. Her fists clench. She stands her ground. She might not be sure what's going on, but she certainly won't stand for being called stupid.

"Do you? I don't think you do. Because he didn't tell you, did he? Of course he didn't," Rosie says bitterly. "He wouldn't. Because if you knew… Well, I thought better of you, Mari. That's all. You with your nice family and those children. That handsome husband who gives you so much trouble."

Mari shakes her head. Earlier the world had threatened to spin out from under her. It tips again now. She digs her heels into the dirt, wishing she was barefoot so she could curl her toes into the earth, too. The solar lights lining the driveway have started to come on, and a light inside the barn she didn't notice before has now become bright enough in the dusk to make a square of light. All of this means she can clearly see Rosie's face, twisted in disgust, and Andrew's look of shame.

"You don't know anything about my husband."

Rosie laughs again. The sound curdles in Mari's ears. "Sure I do. How he got into trouble at work. Even an old woman like me can look stuff up on the internet. I know all about how he lost his job, how he slept with that patient of his. How he killed her."

"Ryan," Mari says, "did not kill that woman."

Rosie shrugs, unconcerned. "She took her own life, but he was her doctor. Wasn't he supposed to be helping her? Not driving her to jump in front of a train."

"Disturbed people aren't rational. It's not anyone's fault. And certainly not Ryan's."

"Disturbed people. You'd know about that, wouldn't you? And you," she says to Andrew, "I guess you'd know a thing or two about it, too. Huh?"

"Shut up," Andrew says firmly. "You can just shut up."

"That's a nice way to speak to your mother," Rosie says, and Mari gasps aloud. Rosie turns. "That's right. He didn't tell you, did he?"

Andrew makes a low noise in his throat. "You're not my mother."

Mari can't keep up. There are too many words. Emotions. All of this is swirling around her, a tornado of anxiety, but though she's in the center of it, there's no calm place to keep her safe.

"No, I'm only the one who raised you like my own when she wouldn't. I'm only the one who took care of you when you were sick, made sure you had clothes and food and a roof over your head!" Rosie shakes her fists at him. "I'm only the one who made sure you got your schooling, made sure you learned your Bible! No, I ain't your mother, praise Jesus, and I thank the good Lord I'm not!"

Mari steps back. Back again. She's never liked the sound of raised voices. They make her cringe.

"Tell her," Rosie says and spits to the side. "You disgusting, devil-ridden piece of hell-bound filth."

"This is the woman who gave you the watch," Mari says, then louder, "the one who punished you for getting your clothes dirty? Rosie is the one who made you kneel on the rice to pray?"

He nods once, twice. "She did raise me. She did all of those things. Yes."

"And yet you'd run away, like you always did! Always running off into the woods." Rosie spits to the side, a great glob that glistens in the light from the barn. "And I never knew, did I? Why you were so hell-bent on getting back here, no matter how many times I warned you off. That was your filthy secret, yours and your father's. Well, then I learned why and I prayed for your soul, Andrew. I prayed the sins of the father had not been visited upon the son, but my prayers went unanswered. Didn't they?"

Rosie heaves a great sigh and for the first time sounds more sad than angry. "I tried with you, son, I truly did. But there was too much of your daddy in you, wasn't there? And too much of your mama, too, I guess. No matter what I did, it was always going to come to this."

"Andrew," Mari says with as much dignity as she can maintain considering she feels as though she might vomit into the dirt from all the stress. "Please. Tell me what's going on."

He turns to her. He takes her hands, an action that makes Rosie spit again. Andrew ignores her. "You want to know about the first time I met you?"

Mari nods, uncertain of why it's important to tell her now. Not sure she wants to know, if the look on Andrew's face is any indication of how he feels about the story. But his fingers squeeze hers, and Mari remembers how Andrew always did his best to keep her safe.

Andrew draws a long, slow breath. "I was six when you were born. My father had promised me a ride into town with him to go to the hardware store. That's where he told *her*—" he jerks his chin at Rosie "—we were going."

Mari thinks Rosie will interrupt to complain again, but she says nothing. She's listening, too. Maybe she doesn't know the whole story, either.

"But we didn't go to town. We came here, to his mother's house. We came here a lot. Rosie wasn't supposed to know when we visited, and my dad always made sure I knew not to tell her. But she knew, anyway, I think."

"I knew," Rosie mutters with a shake of her head that sends her gossamer hair floating all around her face. "Oh, yes. I knew about it."

The hen has abandoned them and gone back to her sisters, too dumb to be happy she's survived another day. The three of them stand in the harsh, white light from the barn that makes the shadows so much deeper as Mari tries to wrap her mind around what Andrew has said. His mother's house? Whose mother?

"We came into the kitchen. The dogs were barking and jumping. You know how they were." Andrew's thumbs stroke over the back of her hand. His smile is meant to reassure her but only sends another swirling vortex of anxiety around her. "They were barking so loud it should've been impossible to hear anything else. But I heard screams."

Screams are never good.

"My father told me to stay in the kitchen with Gran, who was sitting at the table pretending she didn't hear anything, but he wasn't paying attention when I followed him upstairs and down the hall. The bedroom door was open. I could see directly into it. I could see her there, sitting on the bed, her legs spread. I was embarrassed, I thought she was, you know. Peeing."

"But you kept looking, didn't you?" Rosie says with another bitter laugh. "Just like your father."

Andrew looks into Rosie's eyes, and his look is dark. Black. Nothing blue about those eyes now. For the first time since meeting Andrew again, probably for the first time in her life, Mari is scared of him.

"There was a lot of blood. I'd never seen so much blood. And she was screaming, cursing. When she saw my dad, she called him every bad name I'd ever heard and a lot of ones I never had. She put her hands down between her legs, where this tiny head with dark, dark hair was pushing out. And my father turned around, saw me. 'Get some blankets, Andy,' he said. So I ran into the other bedroom and pulled the quilt off the bed, and I dragged it down the hall to give them. And there was the baby in her arms. Covered in blood and screaming. I'd never seen a baby so small like that. I didn't know they came out so bloody."

Even at eight, Ethan knows where babies come from, how they're made and how they're born. Still, knowing and seeing are two different things. Mari can't imagine what the boy Andrew must've thought about seeing a woman give birth.

Andrew shivers and takes in a long, deep breath. "And my father said, 'you can't tell anyone, Andy. Nobody. Don't. Tell. Anyone.'"

Rosie gives a low groan but says nothing.

"And Ellie said, 'Andy, isn't she beautiful? I'm going to name her Mariposa, because she's so beautiful, just like a butterfly. And it will be your job to protect her, Andy. You'll have to help me protect her. You will help me, won't you?' And I said…I said yes."

Mari doesn't want to be holding Andrew's hands any longer. His grip is too tight. It's no longer a comfort, but a set of shackles. He's not stopping the world from spinning, but instead has put his finger upon it like a globe, turning it fast and faster.

"So I did what she asked. I protected you. And like my father had said, I didn't tell anyone. Especially not *her*." He throws the word again at Rosie.

"All I knew was you had some fascination with running back there through the woods to that house! No matter what I did, I couldn't keep you from it! The same as him," Rosie adds bitterly and spits again, then again as though she's sick from the words. "No matter how I punished you, you still ran back there. If I'd known there was another child—"

"What would you have done?" Andrew challenges, letting

go at last of Mari's hands and confronting Rosie. "Would you have taken her, too? Raised her up to kneel on rice until her knees bled? Locked her in the closet for hours at a time just because she said she was scared there was a monster in there, and you wanted to prove that Jesus didn't allow monsters in children's closets? What would you have done if you'd known?"

"I wouldn't have left her there alone with nobody to take care of her!" Rosie screams. "You can hate me all you want to, Andrew, but the sin is not mine! It's your father's and his sister's, the pair of them, sick as sin. I tried, oh, how I tried, to keep you from it. You call me cruel, but everything I did was to help you. And in the end, you didn't go so far away did you? You could've gone anywhere in the world, but you stayed right here. Right within spitting distance of this house. And why? So you could make sure it would be here for her when she came back? So you could keep it safe for her, make sure nobody else lived in it, right? Did you tell her about what you did to make sure it would be here for her? Did you?"

"Shut up!" Andrew screams, and advances on Rosie so fast the woman can't back away and Mari can't reach to stop him, even if she could move, which she can't.

She's still reeling from everything Andrew has said, trying to make sense of it. How the pieces tied together. How they'd made her who she was.

Andrew's fingers close around Rosie's shoulders and he shakes her the way she shook the chicken earlier. Rosie fights him. For an old lady, she's strong. Or maybe Andrew, despite his rage, isn't willing to really hurt her. She kicks at him, missing his nuts but bending him over, anyway.

Panting, she turns to Mari who's stood in stunned silence during the whole violent episode. "Ask him what he did to keep people from that house."

Andrew stands, hands out. "Mari. I didn't know it was you.

All I knew was someone new had moved into the house. And I never meant to hurt anyone, especially not you...."

Mari hears the sound of ringing rocks. She feels the thud of the stone on her leg. She gasps and gags, acid burning in her throat, but swallows down hard to keep her gut in its place. "You were the one throwing the stones?"

Andrew says nothing. He doesn't have to. He looks ashamed, and that's enough of an admission.

"You asshole! You hurt my kids!" Mari flies at him.

Andrew doesn't even try to get out of the way when she smacks him across the face first in one direction, then the other. The second blow sends him again to his knees. She thinks about kicking him in the face but steps back instead, chest heaving yet unable to get enough air.

"The police said it was kids," she says miserably.

"Oh, the police know about us back here in the woods," Rosie says. "They know to leave us alone—that's what they know."

"The mud. The noises. The peacock?" Mari cries, beyond sickened.

Andrew nods without looking up at her. "I thought...I knew one day you'd have to come back here. You'd have to come home. So I kept the house empty as I could. I didn't know it was you this time. Once I knew..."

"I don't understand." Her voice is thick like syrup. The words drip. She wants to speak clearly but stringing the syllables together is too much effort. "Why, Andrew? Why would you do any of this? Why would either of you do any of this? Are you crazy, out of your mind? You...you were supposed to protect me, take care of me, not mess with my head. Not ruin my life!"

"Is your life ruined?" Andrew shouts, getting to his feet. "You got out, you got away, you got help, didn't you?"

"Not from you!" She wants to hit him again but punches

her fists against her own thighs, instead. She looks at Rosie. "You're sick, both of you. You're sick and crazy. And I can't believe..."

She trails off into tears. The fairy story's happily ever after ending has been destroyed, which is no surprise because she's old enough to know better. She doesn't want to hate her prince, Andrew, the boy who did his best to keep her safe the only way he thought he could. She doesn't want to hate him for throwing rocks at her children in some misguided attempt at keeping her home ready for her. Mari wants to remember where she came from and know that she's become something better, that whatever happened to her in the past shaped her into who she became and, therefore, she should regret nothing.

She has one simple question for him, the boy who became the man in front of her. "Why did my mother ask you to take care of me?"

Andrew's mouth has closed up tight, and his blue eyes still look black. Rosie is the one who shuffles her feet in the dirt of the chicken yard and lets out a long, aggrieved sigh. "Oh, Mariposa. You want to know why?"

"Yes."

Another sigh, and the answer as complicated as the question had been simple.

"He's your brother."

FIFTY-SEVEN

ACCORDING TO LEON CALDER'S FILES, ELLIE Pfautz had lived with her disabled mother, Eleanor Pfautz. Her father had died when Ellie was a child. Her brother, Ronald, older by twelve years, lived in the house down the lane with his wife. Ronald provided financial support, making it possible for Ellie and her mother to live with only a little help from the state.

At age thirteen, Ellie Pfautz dropped out of school when it became apparent to everyone involved that she'd become pregnant. Father unnamed, but certainly not unknown, at least not to Ellie…or her brother. She gave birth to a son at the local hospital. Ronald and his wife had adopted the child, naming him Andrew.

Ellie continued to live with her mother, and six years later she gave birth again. This time at home, to a daughter she called Mariposa. Ronald and his wife didn't take this child, for whom there was no record of birth. By this time, Eleanor's increasing disability had made it impossible for her to work and Ronald's monetary support had become inadequate as he struggled with the cancer that would eventually kill him, so Ellie entered the workforce. She held a series of jobs, being fired from a number of them and quitting others.

Finally, two years later, Ellie became pregnant a third time, again hiding the pregnancy. But this time, she had the baby in the bathroom of the fast-food restaurant where she worked. Unable to hide this child, Ellie gave the baby up for adoption at the hospital where they'd taken her. While there, she behaved so erratically, she was admitted to the psych ward at Philhaven for evaluation, where a diagnosis of schizophrenia was made.

Mari's mother was institutionalized and never returned home. She died from a drug overdose shortly after being released a year later. The death was ruled accidental. Eleanor continued living in the house, allegedly alone and cared for by her son until his death three years later.

In monthly and then weekly home visits to care for the elderly and eventually senile but still mobile woman, not one person had ever noticed there was someone else living in the house. There were reports about the woman's medical condition, her mental health and the fact she often chased off the home health nurses before they could even get in the front door by brandishing a cleaver. But not a word about a child.

Only after Eleanor's death, some five years after her daughter's, did authorities arrive to find a terrified, speechless child huddled among the dogs under a kitchen table. She'd been living with what turned out to be eleven dogs and an uncountable number of cats, a couple dozen chickens and a pair of goats. And the peacocks.

They'd taken her away.

They'd fixed her.

And she'd become Kendra's mother.

Kendra closed the file carefully and thought about burning it. But no, it contained the answers to a lot of unasked questions. Made a lot of sense.

But mostly, it just made her love her mom all that much more.

With the folder in her hand, she knocked on her dad's door. When he turned to her, she held out the file to him. "Take this," she said. "I think you should read it."

FIFTY-EIGHT

RYAN DROVE.

He'd been angry with his mother in the past—she'd done her share of shit-talking about his dad and her daughter-in-law, but she'd always been good to his children. That she'd used them in such a way was inexcusable.

The file sat beside him on the front seat. Kendra had chosen to sit in the back with Ethan, a distinct snub toward Ryan that he couldn't find it within himself to blame her for. Ethan was quiet, a quick glance in the rearview mirror showing him to be asleep while Kendra tapped away on her phone. The bluish light highlighted her stony face. She looked up once, her eyes meeting Ryan's in the rearview. He'd been the one to look away.

"Take this," she'd said when she handed him the file. "But if I find you put this fucked-up *Flowers in the Attic* stuff into any book about our mother, I will never speak to you again for the rest of our lives. I will hate you forever, Dad. And I'll make sure Ethan hates you, too."

He'd known she meant it. Hadn't even been able to scold her for swearing at him. Ryan had seen the end of his relationship with his daughter in her eyes and had thought only of doing whatever it took to salvage it.

So, now he drove. His mother had begged him to stay at least until the morning. She'd shown remorse, at least, he'd give her that. She'd been acting out of love, she said, but Ryan was done with that sort of love.

"You think that just because of this—" he'd held out the file "—I could ever stop loving my wife? You think this changes anything?"

"You deserve to know. Your father did. He should've told you long ago. Hell—" his mother had sniffed "—he should've told *her*."

Maybe she was right, Ryan thought, hands gripped so tight on the wheel his fingers had begun to ache. It might've changed everything and nothing, had they both known the truth about Mari's history. But he didn't want that.

"All of this, everything that's happened to her or was done to her, and yet all you can do is blame her for it. Or see the bad. You know what, Mom? Mari is a wonderful wife. And she's a good mother. She's an excellent mother. She's a better mother than you ever were or could be, and that's what really bugs you the most, isn't it? That's what really sets your hair on fire. That she came from all 'that' and yet still managed to become a better person than you." He'd said all this to her under his breath so he wouldn't scream. The kids had already gone out to the car, their bags half-packed. On the run like refugees. Yet Ryan had kept his voice down because he was afraid if he shouted at his mother the way he wanted to, he might never stop. He might scream on and on, and there'd be no going back from that.

Shit, there was no going back, anyway.

"You'll be sorry you said those things to me, Ryan. Maybe not tonight or tomorrow or next week. But someday, you'll be sorry you talked to me this way. And when you are," his mother had said with wounded dignity, that familiar martyr-

dom he'd always looked past because it was part of her, "I will
be here, ready to forgive you."

"Plan on waiting a long, long time," Ryan had said and
left her.

He'd felt there was something missing from his father's research, some piece to the story left untold. It turned out it was
all in the file his mother had somehow absconded with—either
because his dad had left it behind when he'd moved out, or
because she'd stolen it for some sick reason of her own. She
hadn't admitted to that, but she hadn't said anything else, either, which led Ryan to believe she'd kept it on purpose. It
would've been like her, to take the thing that would have the
worst effect and hold on to it until she thought giving it up
would get her something she wanted.

When had she first read the file? When Mari was a child,
long before Ryan's dad had even considered bringing home
the wild child to live as his daughter? Or had his mother only
discovered it when her husband decided to go ahead and foster Mari without his wife's consent or participation? Or was
it even later, after Ryan's dad had moved out, taking most everything with him but that one file. It didn't matter. Ryan's
mother had known for a long time about Mari's parentage,
and that was enough.

Now Ryan knew, too, and so did Kendra. And Ethan because, though he was too young to grasp all of it, Kendra had
insisted he not be kept in the dark. The time for secrets was
finished, Kendra had said.

"I just wanted to protect you," Ryan had told her.

Kendra had given him a solid, unyielding stare. "I know.
Ethan should know, too. We love our mom, it doesn't matter
about any of that, but if he grows up someday and finds out by
accident, it'll be much worse than if you just let him know."

So Ryan had given his son a condensed but not sanitized
version of the story he'd only known pieces of before. Now

Ryan navigated the increasingly rural roads, away from West Chester and heading toward Pine Grove. It had been a mistake to take them there, but he could fix it. He'd get Mari, take her and the kids back to Philly. Sell that piece-of-shit house that should've been sold years ago. He'd get a new job.

Ryan would make all of this right, no matter what it took. It was his job, to love and protect his wife and family. He'd messed it up, but he could fix it.

He'd have to.

FIFTY-NINE

MARI WANTS TO RUN AND RUN AND RUN, INTO darkness and the shelter of trees. She wants to give up and be wild again, streaking along the paths of pine needles and seeking solace in the splash of the cold springwater creek. She wants to unknow all of this, forget what has happened, erase the memories of Andrew. All of them.

Instead, she runs to the house. Throws open the back door onto the screen porch. Boxes and folders and videocassettes and notebooks stare at her. She hisses, the sound too loud, and claps a hand over her mouth.

Mari shudders.

Chompsky whines from his place in the doorway. The small sound catches her attention, and Mari gets to her knees to reach for him. He comes reluctantly, shaking until she smoothes his fur over and over again in the soft spots over his eyes. She can't say she ever wanted this mutt, but he's hers now.

She straightens her shoulders. She takes her hand from her mouth. She breathes in, breathes out. She finds the voice she's worked so hard to learn. The voice she's earned, damn it.

"No more."

All of this is part of a past she doesn't want to remember. Her surrogate father had collected the data, viewing her as a curiosity, a freak, something to learn from. There'd been fondness, if not love. Her husband had taken advantage of her trust to be unfaithful to her, then intended to exploit his father's work and her history for his own benefit. These files represent years of betrayal—whatever truth was inside them is better forgotten. Destroyed.

In the kitchen, she finds matches, but they won't do. Not strong enough for what she has in mind. They will start a flame but not an inferno. Only a pyre will be big enough to get rid of all this.

This is crazy, but she comes from crazy, doesn't she? Mari still doesn't believe in sin, but she damn sure came from *something,* and none of it good. She bends over the sink, heaving at last, though all that comes up is air and slick sour spittle. She rinses her mouth and closes her eyes against the waves of red haze threatening to send her plummeting into the sort of darkness that is without comfort.

All she finds in the cupboard is a bottle of olive oil…but it will burn.

Matches elude her, though she tosses the drawers where she'd have kept them at home. Whoever set up this kitchen last loved half-used pencils, the ends gnawed. Twist-ties from garbage bags. Miscellaneous detritus she has no use for, but no matches.

With a cry, Mari dumps the final drawer. The contents spill. She kicks at the mess on the floor. The dog doesn't care who's making the storm, all he knows is that he wants to get away. With a yelp, Chompsky flees, probably upstairs to the spot under the bed he prefers when it thunders.

She remembers the ancient grill outside. What had Ryan said? The ignition was bad, something like that. He'd used one of those small lighters. He'd probably left it out there.

She's calmer now. More focused. This only makes Mari more determined to finish. From the porch she takes one box,

overflowing with papers, out the back door to the small con-
crete pad immediately against the house. The grill is there and
sure enough, the utensils are still hanging off it. The lighter's
there, too.

Mari flips the lid open. Turns the knobs. She expects to
hear the hissing of gas, perhaps smell it, but it's silent and without any odor beyond the leftover stink of charcoaled burgers. Next to the grill is the big metal garbage can. She dumps
the box inside, save for a handful of the papers from the top.

It takes a few tries before the lighter works. The flame is
blue and small, but when she touches it to the grill's rack it
ignites with a whoosh and a burst of flame higher than she'd
expected. The heat is immediate and intense, and she shields
her eyes just briefly before holding the handful of papers to
the flame.

A second later, fire.

She gives it a few seconds before tossing the burning paper
into the garbage can. Doesn't wait to see if it catches—there's
plenty more to use if this fire goes out. She bangs through
the back door, grabs up another box, another tower of papers
and folders. Back outside, those go in the now-smoldering
can, and she holds another pile of notes to the grill's flame to
add to the blaze.

She is going to burn all of this. Every last piece. Not so she
will forget the life that came before. She can never do that. But
so that nobody, ever again, can use it without her permission.

Back and forth, Mari runs empty-handed into the porch
and comes out again with more papers. The boxes of videotapes are heavier, and she takes the time to unspool some of
them. The long black tape catches fire faster than the paper,
but the plastic cases melt and stink, making black smoke she
has to back away from with her eyes stinging.

She thinks there should be more satisfaction in all of this,

but all she feels is tired. Her eyes burn. Her throat closes
against the sting of the smoke.

"What are you doing?"

She whirls at the voice, though she can't be surprised. Of
course he didn't leave just because she ran away. "Go away,
Andrew. I can't see you now."

The light shining through the screened porch windows
is pale yellow. The flames from the garbage can, orange. In
between them are the shadows, black and shifting. Andrew's
hands dance in them.

I'm sorry.

"Don't!"

I'm sorry, Mariposa.

If he touches her, she will punch him in the face. She
will light him on fire. Mari thinks this but knows she won't.
"Just...please, go."

"I never meant to hurt you."

She thinks of how he held her in the field. The taste of
his mouth. Sickness rushes upward through her again, leaving her cold, though by now the flames have started shooting out of the garbage can and the heat is strong enough to
make her eyes water.

"You knew," she says. "All along, you knew!"

"I wanted to tell you, but...you were... I was..." He struggles with his voice as his hands make old patterns she used to
know and can remember but not decipher. "I'm sorry about
what happened. I didn't want to hurt you."

"But you did!"

"I'm sorry," he says and looks as though he means to say
more, but falls silent.

She can't listen to him any longer. Can't see him. Can't
know him.

Pushing Andrew away, Mari runs into the house.

SIXTY

"MAMA!" ETHAN SHOUTED. HE WAS OUT OF THE car before anyone else. His sneakers crunched in the gravel, and he ran toward the house, leaving the car door open.

Kendra hung back for a minute longer. Her dad did, too. She didn't want to get out of the car and watch her parents dance around each other the way Sammy's parents did. If her mom didn't kiss her dad and hug him the way she always did, even if she was annoyed with him…Kendra didn't want to see it.

She'd survive if her parents got divorced. Everyone did. But she didn't want them to get divorced, Kendra thought. She didn't want everything to die.

Her dad had twisted to look at her. He looked old and tired. And sad.

"I'm sorry, Kiki. You know that."

She nodded, unable to answer him.

"Your grandma was wrong to show you that file."

"I'm not sorry—" Kendra began, when the low, heavy *whump* reached them.

"What the hell?" Her dad got out of the car.

Like Ethan, he left the door hanging open. With the keys still in the ignition, the warning ding-ding chime kept bleating, but he was already running toward the back of the house. Kendra leaned through the two front seats and twisted the key. The noise stopped. The headlights stayed on, but that's not what was lighting up the backyard. That was a shifting, orange light.

Kendra got out of the car. The smell of smoke hit her at once, and she pulled the sleeve of her hoodie over her hand to cup her nose and mouth. Something was burning. A lot.

By the time she rounded the corner, she could see it was the back of the house. The screens of the porch had blackened, the wooden frames licked with flame. A few had already fallen. The interior of the three-season room was hazy with smoke. Flames hurtled several feet into the air from a big metal garbage can, and the stinky old grill her dad hadn't been able to get working right was entirely consumed in fire. There was another explosion as she watched.

Ethan wasn't crying, but their dad was holding him by the back of his collar while he struggled, arms out toward the house. Kendra threw up her other hand to block the glare. Her eyes watered, but she looked as hard as she could through the smoke and shadows, looking for her mother.

She saw a man, instead. Tall, dressed in darkness, more a silhouette than anything else. The mountain man. She knew it without a doubt. As she watched, he disappeared through the back door and into the house.

Her dad turned, his fingers still gripped tight in Ethan's shirt. "Kendra, stay back! Get back!"

He grabbed her by the back of the collar, too, and was pulling her toward the barn. Away from the flames, yeah, but away from their mom, too. Kendra kicked and twisted, trying to get him to let go.

"Oh, sweet Jesus." This came from Rosie, who appeared from the barn. "Oh, God! Oh, Jesus!"

Kendra was pretty sure neither God nor Jesus was paying

much attention at the moment. Her dad let go of her. She rubbed her throat where the zipper had stung her.

Ethan was still struggling in their dad's grip. "Mama's in the house, Daddy. You have to go after her!"

"Oh, Jesus, no! Andrew!" Rosie screamed.

Kendra's dad looked at her. "Kiki. Call 911. Now."

She fumbled to pull her phone from her pocket and thumbed in the numbers, but the signal bars went from five to none seconds after she hit Send.

"No signal, Dad!"

"Try again." Her dad, grim-faced, started toward the house. "Keep trying."

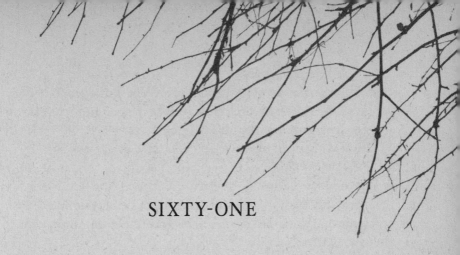

SIXTY-ONE

MARI HADN'T KNOWN A FIRE COULD BE SO loud. Not just the crackling, like cellophane being crinkled in a fist, but the creaking and screaming of the house as it's consumed. This house is old wood and no challenge for the fire.

Each of her children had come home from kindergarten with "stop, drop and roll" instructions, coloring books featuring a friendly-looking dog in a fireman's uniform. Several times they'd gone to demonstrations at fairs of what to do in a smoke-filled house. Touch the doors to see if they're hot, cover your mouth with a wet cloth. Most important, stay low to the ground.

All of this information races through Mari's mind even as it seems useless. Chompsky is surely upstairs in the bedroom, hiding under the bed, and so far the fire has forced its way into the kitchen and living room, but not up the stairs. It won't be long, of course, but for now she can run along the hall ducking into the bedroom to get on her knees and lift the dust ruffle.

Chompsky's not there. There's a chew toy and several stolen socks to prove he'd been there, but now only dust bunnies swirl gently in the breeze she created. The overhead light suddenly flickers and goes out. Maybe the fire's cut the electricity.

Mari gets to her feet. She can't scream, her throat hurts too bad for that, so she claps her hands. Over and over. No dog comes. She runs into the hallway, where the smoke has now started billowing up the stairs.

Andrew appears at the top. "You have to get out of here!"

Not without the dog.

He doesn't see her or doesn't understand. Or doesn't care. Andrew lunges for her, but Mari ducks his grip and leaps through the doorway into Ethan's room. No dog under that bed, either.

The dog, she signs. The overhead light is still on in here. Andrew can see her. Now he gets it.

"Dog! Here, dog!"

"Chompsky!" Mari calls.

No dog in Kendra's room, either.

A long, low creaking groan rips up the stairs, followed immediately after by the roar of them collapsing. More smoke. More heat. Coughing, eyes stinging, Mari covers her mouth and nose though it doesn't help.

"We have to get out, Mari. Listen to me!"

And there, at the end of the hall, Mari glimpses a hint of something furry in the shadows of the bathroom. Six running steps get her there. She skids on the tiles—Chompsky in his fear has peed on the floor. Her knees connect with the toilet. Arms pinwheeling, Mari grabs the shower curtain, which tears off its hooks and sends her tumbling into the tub. Right on top of the terrified dog, as it turns out. He snaps, teeth bared and flashing white in the dimness, but Mari was long used to biting dogs and deflects him with her arm. He doesn't mean it, anyway. She grabs him by the collar and pulls him and herself out of the tub.

Chompsky will not move. She lifts him, staggering. She will not die here.

She will not.

The window in the master bedroom opens directly onto the

flat roof over the front porch. There's a small railing around it, like it was meant as some poor excuse for a balcony, but that just means when Andrew opens the window for her, the dog doesn't slide off when she throws him out. Mari follows him, but Chompsky runs to the edge of the roof, decides jumping is not for him, and leaps over her and back through the window, into the house, past Andrew who's got one leg over the sill.

Mari sees her husband's car. She sees Ryan and the kids. Rosie is there, too. The four of them stare up at her with wide eyes and wider mouths. It's a short enough drop from here to the ground that she knows she can risk it—better a broken leg than being burned alive.

Yet even as she sees herself rolling herself over the edge, holding on with her hands to lower herself at least a few feet closer, Mari moves instead toward the window. She shouldn't—she knows she shouldn't. Her kids are below and she needs to think of them. But something about that dog, his helplessness in a situation far beyond his ability to cope with, drives her need to save him.

Andrew blocks her way. "I'll get him."

"No," Mari rasps.

It's too dangerous for Andrew to go back inside, just as it would be for her, and as conflicted as she feels about him right now, she can't allow her brother to put himself in that position. He's already sacrificed so much for her—she can't ask him to make the ultimate sacrifice, too. But he's already pushing her back and closing the window behind him.

"Mari! Jump down!" Ryan's voice calls her.

Mari looks over the edge to the ground, then over her shoulder to the house. She hears breaking glass and more creaking wood, along with the growing roar of the flames. She sees her kids staring up at her in fear and horror. She knows what she has to do.

She climbs over the railing and grips the rotted wood tight as she rolls off the edge, her belly digging into the edge.

The wood gives way.

She's braced for a fall, but the ground is still hard. Her ankles twist, both of them, maybe not broken but definitely sprained. Mari rolls into the gravel on her hands and knees, then onto her back with the breath knocked out of her.

Ryan leans over her. "Babe, are you okay? Holy shit."

She's still not sure what to think about Ryan, but everything that happened seems diminished with the sight of the house burning down in front of them. They reach for each other at the same time. Then her children are there, too, and while there will always be many things about this whole summer Mari regrets, the fact her children had to see her escaping a burning house and falling off a roof is one of the worst.

She clutches them all to her. Ethan's soft, sweet cheek. Kendra's long hair. Even Ryan's strong arms, holding her. It's a dream mingled with a nightmare.

The front door opens. Andrew, Chompsky in his arms, staggers out in clouds of smoke. Through the door Mari sees the front staircase, shimmering with fire but not collapsed. The dog writhes free and, yelping, runs toward the barn. Ethan shouts after him and twists from her grasp to follow.

Andrew collapses in the gravel, facedown.

Mari struggles free of her husband's embrace, her daughter's clutching fingers. Pain flares in her ankles when she moves. Her hands, too, are stung and scraped raw. So are her knees, her pants shredded.

"Who the hell is that?" Ryan shouts.

Above them, the windows blow out. Glass scatters. Mari has covered Kendra with her arm, but splinters of glass sparkle in her daughter's hair and some has cut her cheek. Ryan looks unscathed, but he's dragging both of them away from the house, leaving Andrew behind.

"You have to help him," Mari says as her husband dumps her and their daughter onto the bit of grass where someone long ago unsuccessfully tried to plant flowers.

"Help him," Mari insists, pointing toward the still-not-moving Andrew.

She hears Rosie screaming, but the noise is vague and in the background. She ignores it. She would get up and run to Andrew if she could do it herself, but her legs are in so much pain she can't move. Worse, she must've inhaled too much smoke because the world is tipping toward gray. She's going to pass out.

"You have to," she manages to say. "He's my brother."

AFTER

MARI STOOD IN HER KITCHEN SURVEYING THE mountains of potato salad, the platters of deviled eggs, the baskets overflowing with rolls. Desserts lined the counter—brownies, cookies, cakes, Jell-O layered with whipped cream and fruit. She looked out the window over the sink to the yard outside.

There her boy ran with Chompsky chasing him. Some neighbor kids followed. The screams were shrill and plentiful. The sounds of summer.

The murmur of Kendra's voice passed by in the hall. Instead of texting or even talking on her phone, she had a flock of girlfriends with her today. Mari thought she caught the name of the new boy Kiki liked, but the giggles overtook any other bits of the conversation. They crossed through the dining room and through the French doors to the deck outside.

There was music out there, muffled by the windows and doors, but as the girls went out, the music came in. Some boys from the high school, including the one who has her daughter pink-cheeked and flustered, are playing in their rockabilly band. It was supposed to be a block party, but most of the action centered at Mari's house because of the long, sloping yard that made the best set-up for the boys' band.

There was so much food nobody could possibly eat it all. Everyone had brought dishes to share. Mari snagged a deviled egg and ate it without a plate, licked her fingers, pulled more lemonade from the fridge to set on the table.

"Hey, Mari, where's your powder room?" Evelyn asked. "Great party, by the way."

"Thanks." Mari pointed. "Down the hall. You'll have to jiggle the handle."

"Got it."

Evelyn had hired Mari to work in her coffee shop three months ago. Mari had never had a job before, but now she worked. And she liked it—the sense of independence it gave her.

Left alone again, Mari made sure nothing else needed to be set out. The sliding glass door onto the deck slid open, allowing Ethan, the dog and the gang of kids to spill inside. They attacked the food, swarming it. Her son paused with a plateful of brownies in one hand to give her a one-armed hug but didn't linger long enough for her to squeeze him back. He was out with his friends before she could do more than touch his hair.

Through the glass doors she could see Ryan reigning over the grill with a beer in one hand, tongs in the other. They'd been talking about him moving back in. The counselor who'd been seeing them both had said it was the next logical step in reconstructing their marriage. Mari had not yet made her decision but she thought of what choice she would make every night when she went to bed by herself.

A lot had changed in the past year.

With a platter of cupcakes in her hand, she used the other to slide open the glass door. A neighbor from down the street helped her, closing it after. She was greeted with cheers. The platter was taken. She was handed a bottle of something cold and sweet but with the bite of liquor underneath it.

"Burgers will be done soon," Ryan said.

"Sounds good," she said.

The music from the band got suddenly louder. There was cheering, and when she looked across the lawn, she could see groups of teens dancing on the grass. The younger kids were still playing tag. Some older folks pulled up lawn chairs. Only the teenagers were rocking out.

There was another person in a lawn chair, set a small distance from the others. Ethan ran past, swiveled, darted close enough to say something to the man sitting there while the dog offered up what was surely a slimy, slobber-covered tennis ball.

"Be back in a few minutes," Mari said to Ryan, whose attention had already been recaptured by the importance of cooking meat.

She crossed the line, being called out to or calling out to party guests. She paused by the man in the lawn chair, who turned to look up at her. Andrew's hair had grown back. He had a few marks on his face, though she knew beneath the long-sleeved shirt and long pants he wore even in the heat, he was covered with scars. Andrew walked with a cane but was grateful to be able to walk at all.

"Yeah. I'll tell her. Talk to you soon." He disconnected the call as Mari walked up. "Beth says hi."

Beth. The sister neither of them had yet met in person, though they were planning a reunion for later this summer. Mari handed him a bottle from the same cooler hers had come from. "I brought you a drink."

"Thanks. Great party." Andrew lifted the bottle to his lips and sipped. Sometimes he could look her in the eye. He was getting better at it. "Thanks for inviting me."

They still had to dance around what had happened between them. Mari supposed it was something they would never forget but would never talk about. She hadn't told Ryan. Not even the counselor. For Andrew, she knew it was shame. For herself, it was a matter of forgiveness.

"Food's ready, if you want some." She didn't offer him help in getting up. He was sensitive about feeling helpless, a matter she respected. She did hold the chair steady for him, though, when he pushed himself up and made sure he was sure-footed before he set off toward the house. She watched her brother greet her husband, both of them friendly enough though she doubted they would ever be really close.

Sometimes the past snuck up on her with creeping, quiet feet. She couldn't put the life that came before completely from her mind and wasn't sure she wanted to. But here, watching friends, family, coworkers, seeing how much had changed in just one short year, Mari felt completely centered in the life that had come after.

After betrayal. After shame. After everything, including the truth. None of it had broken her, and she didn't pretend she wasn't proud of that.

She let her feet glide through grass that was just a little too long and enjoyed the brush of it on her toes. Down the sloping hill, past the band, the swing set, beyond the garden shed. The battered lawn chair was gone, tossed in the trash. The trees that had marked the line between her yard and the field beyond still stand, but the field itself has been torn up and replaced with a new development of big houses on tiny plots of land. She didn't particularly like it, but that was part of living in the suburbs. Neighbors and houses and people around.

She looked up toward the house, but nobody paid attention to her way down here. Mari closed her eyes. She breathed.

The music allowed no quiet, nor did the sound of voices and screams of running children. Mari opened her eyes and then opened the shed door to pull out the marshmallow sticks. Later, they'd have a fire in the pit and make s'mores. That's what people liked to do at parties. Well, she liked it, too.

Mari looked for one more moment back toward the trees, then, sticks in hand, she climbed the hill toward the deck, back to the party.

★ ★ ★ ★ ★

LOVELY

WILD

MEGAN HART

Reader's Guide

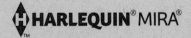

1. Despite her "wild" upbringing, Mari has managed to create a solid life for herself, mostly through her children. How do you think she's able to be a good mother without having had any examples in her own life?

2. Mari isn't like "other" mothers, and her daughter is particularly aware of it. How important is it for teenagers to fit in, even through their parents?

3. Ryan fell in love with Mari for complicated reasons, but hers were very simple. Why do you think Mari fell in love with her husband?

4. How would Mari's life have been different without Ryan's influence?

5. Not all of Mari's childhood memories are bad. What were some positive aspects of her upbringing?

6. How did the forest prince affect the rest of Mari's choices, even into adulthood?

7. Ryan's selfishness impacts his family in an enormous way.

Are his actions forgivable? Are the changes his actions created for the better or ultimately damaging?

8. Mrs. Calder's resentment of her daughter-in-law creates tension throughout the novel. How did Mari's upbringing and history affect Mrs. Calder's feelings about her, and was that fair?

9. Mari eventually learns the truth about her history. Would it have been better for her to never know?

10. Andrew and Mari have a complicated relationship. Will they be able to make it work somehow, or will it always be skewed?

LISTENING GUIDE

NOTE FROM THE AUTHOR:

I could write without music, but I'm so glad I don't have to. Included is a partial playlist of what I listened to while writing *Lovely Wild*. Please support the musicians by purchasing their music!

"Didn't Leave Nobody but the Baby" —Alison Krauss, Emmylou Harris & Gillian Welch
"Strange & Beautiful (I'll Put a Spell On You)" —Aqualung
"Ghosts" —Christopher Dallman
"Lux Aeterna" —Clint Mansell
"Glasgow Love Theme" —Craig Armstrong
"The Blower's Daughter" —Damien Rice
"Here Is the House" — Depeche Mode
"Mad World" —Michael Andrews, featuring Gary Jules
"Calling All Angels" —Jane Siberry with k.d. lang
"Hallelujah" —Jason Manns
"You've Been Loved" —Joseph Arthur
"Beeswing" —LJ Booth